THE CURIOUS AFFAIR OF THE SOMNAMBULIST AND THE PSYCHIC THIEF

LISA TUTTLE

ISIS
LARGE
PRINT

First published in Great Britain 2016
by
Jo Fletcher Books
an imprint of Quercus Editions Ltd.

First Isis Edition
published 2018
by arrangement with
Quercus Editions Ltd.
An Hachette UK Company

A catalogue record for this book is available from the British Library.

ISBN 978–1–78541–512–8 (hb)
ISBN 978–1–78541–518–0 (pb)

Published by
F. A. Thorpe (Publishing)
Anstey, Leicestershire

Set by Words & Graphics Ltd.
Anstey, Leicestershire
Printed and bound in Great Britain by
T. J. International Ltd., Padstow, Cornwall

This book is printed on acid-free paper

To Michelle with thanks for the eyepatch
and, of course,
to Colin.

CHAPTER ONE

On a Train Going South

I admit I did not plan my escape very well, but the fact is that I had not planned it at all.

It was the end of June, 1893, and I had been in Scotland for barely two weeks, a guest in a grand — if somewhat ominous, chilly and under-populated — country house, where I had intended to remain for at least another month along with my friend Miss Gabrielle Fox. Or, rather, my erstwhile friend. The thought of Gabrielle, who must have discovered my defection by now, made my stomach plunge. I felt sick with nerves and unhappiness as I sat, shut in alone in my sleeping compartment while the night express rocked and swayed and rattled through the border country. I could ill afford the extra five shillings for a private compartment, but I had paid because that is what a lady must do. Even though I did not expect to be able to sleep, I lacked the energy to remain as alert and vigilant as one must be in a third-class carriage against importunate strangers.

Gabrielle Fox, known to readers who follow the reports published by the Society for Psychical Research as Miss X, had been my closest companion for nearly four years. Although she had originally been my employer, by the time economic difficulties forced an end to that arrangement, a sympathetic understanding had developed, and our relationship became a partnership in which we shared work and its rewards equally. When she was hired by the SPR to conduct investigations into various types of supernatural phenomena, or to test the claims made by mediums and spiritualists of all kinds, I went as her assistant, and wrote up our findings for publication.

Then Miss Fox was put in charge of an official SPR investigation into a haunted house in Perthshire. Instead of being part of a larger team, she had absolute authority to decide how to conduct the affair, when or if to bring in experts — and of what sort — and told expense was no obstacle. The house was turned over to us as the owner had gone abroad, leaving only a small staff to manage the upkeep at our direction, and a coach and horses, also at our disposal.

Throughout the first week, although we were both aware of certain *atmospheres* — a cold spot in the hall, a room in which neither of us could bear to stay for more than a few minutes — and heard noises to which we could assign no source, there was nothing so definite as an apparition, nothing that might not be explained away as the product of imagination.

For the second week, Gabrielle had invited others, including a well-respected psychic medium, to join us, and planned a séance.

I never doubted her honesty; I had not the slightest reason to suspect she was planning any trickery. So I

2

cannot explain why, on the morning of the day that our guests were to arrive, I felt driven to enter the drawing room, go to the heavy round table made of dark wood that we intended to use for our séance, crouch down on the carpet, look up at the underside of the table and run my fingertips across it.

Thus I discovered the thin wires with the hooked ends — so useful for making objects appear to move through the air — tucked away out of sight, attached to the wood with bits of wax, as well as other hidden things: long strips of the finest, lightest gauze, a piece of charcoal, a stick of chalk, a small rubber ball, a baby's rattle.

These were not random objects, such as might have been secreted there by a visiting child. I knew their meaning and their purpose, for had I not seen these things and others like them used by the pretenders we had revealed to be fake mediums?

We.

From the moment of this discovery, I understood that I could no longer use the word "we" with reference to Miss Fox, for no one else could have hidden such things in this place. Whether she had done so in collusion with the medium who would be arriving later that day, or with the intention of using them herself to create illusions of a ghostly haunting, I did not stay to learn.

While Gabrielle still slept in her room — she was for preference ever late in rising — I hurried up to mine and swiftly packed my bag. I knew that the carriage was

3

to be sent to the station to meet the 11:15 train, and if I was quick enough, I could catch a lift.

I was, and I did, and from the local station I took the next train bound for Edinburgh, and from there boarded the night express to London.

Shut in for the long hours of the night on a train speeding south, I had plenty of time to reflect and regret my impulsive actions, to reconsider and know I had done the right thing, and to make resolutions for the future. There was nothing else I could do.

Eventually, I fell into a restless sleep until the knocking of the porter woke me, as he announced: "Next stop, King's Cross Station."

I was back in London, which I still thought of as home, although I had nowhere to go. My sister was, at present, out of the country, and I knew that the furnished rooms I had shared with Miss Fox, in a street near the British Museum, were now let to someone else. There were a few old friends who might have taken me in, but I did not wish to impose — certainly not by turning up on their doorstep unannounced. Most of the people that I knew in this city I knew in connection with Miss Fox, and naturally I did not wish to approach *them*.

After paying the train fare I had little more than twelve shillings left in my purse. I had no bank account, no property and nothing of any value that I might easily pawn or sell. My most urgent need was for gainful employment. Until I knew what my income would be, there was no point seeking lodgings.

I set off from King's Cross Station for the ladies' employment bureau in Oxford Street. It was a fine, dry, warm morning, so I went on foot rather than spend any more of my limited funds on cab or omnibus fares.

The bag that had been light enough when I took it down from the train grew heavier with every step, until I was obliged to stop and set it down for a few moments. As I caught my breath and rubbed my aching arm just outside a newsagent's shop in Gower Street, I casually read the notices on display in the window. Amidst the descriptions of lost pets and offers of rooms to let, one gave me pause:

Consulting Detective Requires Assistant
Must be literate, brave, congenial, with a good
memory & willing to work all hours.
Apply in person to:
Mr J. Jesperson, 203A Gower St

Why not? I thought. I had always enjoyed solving mysteries, and had nothing to apologise for where brains, observation and memory were concerned. The advertisement said nothing about the use of weapons or physical strength. After all, he was not looking for a bodyguard, but an assistant.

I looked from the number on the card to the two doors immediately right of the window where it was displayed. One door, marked 203, led into the shop. The other, painted glistening black, bore a brass plate inscribed *Jesperson*.

My knock was answered by a lady in early middle age, too genteel in dress and appearance to be mistaken for a servant.

"Mrs Jesperson?"

"Yes?"

I told her I had come in response to the advertisement, gesturing towards the shop window as I spoke, and she let me in. There was a lingering smell of fried bacon and toasted bread that reminded me I'd had nothing to eat since the previous day.

"Jasper," said she, opening another door and beckoning me on. "A lady has come to apply already, a Miss . . .?"

"I am Miss Lane," I said, and walked into a room where I immediately felt at home.

The general atmosphere of a pleasantly crowded, comfortable, cheerful place, rich with the familiar scents of old books, paper and ink and tobacco, toast and tea, is just what I like, in a home or an office, and this room appeared to be office and living room in one. The floor-to-ceiling bookshelves, crammed with volumes and adorned with small trinkets, oddities, photographs and postcards, gave it the look of a slightly eccentric scholar's study, as did the very large cluttered desk, piled high with papers and journals, but there were also armchairs near the fireplace and a table bearing the remains of breakfast for two. This quick impression was all I had time to absorb before Mr Jasper Jesperson, springing up from his seat at the table, commanded all my attention.

He was excessively tall and very young in appearance — the smooth, pale, lightly freckled face beneath a crown of tumbled, red-gold curls was that of an angelic child. But his blue eyes were sharp and penetrating, and when he spoke his voice was deep and well-modulated.

"How do you do, Miss Lane? You fancy yourself a detective, do you?"

"I do not say so. But you advertised for an assistant, someone literate, brave, with a good memory and willing to work all hours. I am all those things, and I hope you will find me congenial."

His eyes met mine and something sparked between us. It was not that romantic passion that poets and sentimental novelists consider the only connection worth writing about between a man and a woman. But there was curiosity in that look, on both sides, and a tentative recognition — or at least the hope — that here there might be a congeniality of mind and spirit.

Mr Jesperson nodded his head and rubbed his hands together. "You have worked before, of course, in some capacity requiring sharp perceptions, careful observation and a bold spirit, yet now you are suddenly cut adrift, in need of employment —"

"Jasper, please," Mrs Jesperson interrupted. "Show the lady some common courtesy!" Laying one hand gently on my arm, she invited me to sit down and offered me a cup of tea.

"That would be lovely, thank you."

She lifted the fine white china teapot, assessing the weight of the contents with a practiced turn of her wrist. "I will fetch more. Would you like a plate of bread and butter, or anything else to eat?"

A lady always refuses food when she hasn't been invited to a meal — but I was too hungry for good manners. "Bread and butter would be most welcome, thank you."

"I'd like more as well, please, Mother — and don't forget the jam."

She raised her eyes heavenward and sighed as she went away. Her son did not notice, his attention focused upon me. "You have been in the Highlands, in the country house of a wealthy family. You expected to stay there for the whole of the summer, all your needs taken care of, until something unpleasant happened, or — no, you made a shocking discovery, as a result of which you terminated your visit and left at once. You travelled down by the night express train, but once arrived you were at a loss as to where to go in this big city, for you have no family here, and insufficient funds for what might be an extended stay in a good hotel. Thinking of the good and inexpensive lodgings for women students at University College London where, I venture to guess, you may have been a student yourself —"

I interrupted him. "Now you have gone too far."

"Self-educated? I do beg your pardon. I, too, am happily unmoulded by any conventional school or university. But I remain fixed in my belief that you were in search of lodgings when you turned onto Gower Street."

"I was *not*," I said firmly. "My first priority was to find employment, and to that end I was headed to Oxford Street, where there is a well-known ladies' employment bureau."

He stared at me, crestfallen. "Was I wrong about everything else?"

"Well, no," I admitted. "But anyone with eyes might guess I'd come from a well-to-do country house in Scotland considering the time of day, my state of dress and that there are no foreign stickers decorating my portmanteau."

"And the abrupt departure? I was right about the shocking discovery, was I not?" He had recovered some of his confidence.

But I remained resolutely unimpressed by his deductions, as I explained: "I was on foot, alone, there not having been time to send a letter to inform my friends of my impending arrival, and I have no family here at present. I think almost anyone might have made the same assumption." I sighed. "Though I do not deny that a discovery did shock me — I found I had been wrong to ascribe honesty and strict professionalism to someone I counted as a friend. Perhaps I should not have run away, but stayed to confront her with the evidence . . . but there is no need for me to go into the details now."

"Of course not," he said warmly. And then: "It's yours. Do not worry about references — you are your own best reference. The job is yours, if you want it."

Although pleased, I could not help feeling he was being a bit rash in offering to hire someone he had known for barely five minutes as his assistant. Or was it my own lack of caution that I queried? I was in desperate need of security, but it was surely foolish to expect it to be supplied by a man I had just met, simply because I felt comfortable in his room?

"I should like to know a little more about this job, first," I said cautiously. "What would my duties be?"

"Duties is the wrong word. Your role, if you like, would be that of an assistant-detective, helping me to gather clues, deduce motives and solve crimes by doing whatever that might require. You've read the Sherlock Holmes stories?"

"Of course. I should point out that, unlike Dr Watson, I'd be no good in a fight. I have a few basic nursing skills, but —"

"Don't worry. My mother's the nurse. I'm a crack shot and have mastered certain skills practised in the Orient, which give me an advantage in unarmed combat. I cannot promise to keep you out of danger entirely, but if that does not frighten you . . .?" He took the answer from my face and broke into a broad smile. "We're agreed?"

How I longed to return that smile and take the hand he offered to shake upon it. But without a home and only twelve shillings to my name, I must have more. "This is awkward," I said. "But again unlike Dr Watson, I have no medical practice to provide me with an income . . ."

"Oh, money!" he exclaimed, with that careless intonation possible only for people who have never worried about the lack of it. "Of course, you should receive a percentage — depending upon the extent of your contribution, it might be twenty or even fifty per cent of whatever the client pays. And if you wished to write up the more interesting cases and sell them to the magazines, you'd keep whatever you made from that."

Mrs Jesperson came back into the room with a laden tea tray as her son was speaking.

"I cannot pay you a salary," he went on. "The best I can offer is an equal share in whatever comes our way."

My heart was sinking fast. "I wish I could afford to agree," I said sadly. "But my financial circumstances are too precarious — I cannot even afford a week's rent on a furnished room in Bloomsbury; not if I wish to eat, too."

"But you can stay here!" exclaimed Mrs Jesperson. She looked up from pouring the tea to frown at her son. "Didn't you explain?"

He took a teacup from his mother and handed it to me. "I thought you might have deduced as much from the wording of my advertisement," he said to me calmly. "The part about working all hours — my assistant must be close by, ready for any eventuality. It's no good if I must write you a letter every time I want your help, or send someone to fetch you."

"There's a room upstairs, furnished and waiting for an occupant," said Mrs Jesperson, handing me a plate of white bread, thinly sliced and thickly buttered, and then a little glass bowl heaped full of raspberry jam. "And I provide three meals a day." My worries vanquished, I gave Mr Jesperson my hand and thus began a new chapter of my life.

CHAPTER
TWO

Porridge in Gower Street

Before my fortuitous sighting of Mr Jesperson's advertisement, my new occupation had never occurred to me as a possibility. And yet, why not? A detective solves mysteries. The fact that they were not the sort of mysteries that had drawn me to join the SPR was a positive attraction to me after the disillusion that accompanied my hasty retreat from Scotland. Now, forced to wonder if *any* of the supernatural events I had investigated with Miss Fox were anything more than frauds or fantasies, I found it a relief to turn my attention to mysteries of a material, worldly nature.

In my new career, I imagined stolen objects would be recovered, missing persons found, villains outwitted and evil plans foiled. Mr Jesperson and I would solve straightforward crimes, and present clear and satisfying solutions to problems without any connection to the troubling, ambiguous world of spirits and spiritualism.

That is what I thought — but the reality of the cases we were asked to investigate was quite different.

Over the next few months there was nothing to make me regret my decision. Life on Gower Street was comfortable, and if our fame did not grow as rapidly as

Mr Jesperson had so confidently expected, there were yet clients enough to keep us busy throughout that summer. We solved a number of strange and puzzling cases, but our reward was largely in the work itself, for our first clients were not wealthy, and some of them begrudged paying for unwelcome information.

Lack of income did not worry me as much as perhaps it should, or as it had in the past. For once I was comfortably situated, living rent-free and with all meals provided. The household was run so smoothly and competently by Mrs Jesperson that I never stopped to wonder what it cost. The truth is, I did not wish to question it for fear of disturbing my new-found happiness.

Mrs Jesperson was the sort of unappreciated marvel who works behind the scenes of many fine establishments. She kept things going by clever contrivances and sheer hard work. There were no servants — she claimed she did not need them — and because our surroundings were always clean and comfortable, and she was such a good cook, I believed her. Of course, there was a charwoman who came regularly to help with the heavier tasks, but I rarely saw her, and did not notice when she ceased to appear.

It was only on the first day of November, a day that began, inauspiciously, with porridge, that I understood how wilfully blind I had been.

Porridge is, of course, a healthful, nourishing breakfast, no doubt greeted with smiles of pleasure in many households throughout the land, but familiar as I was by now with Mr Jesperson's fondness for bacon and eggs, and with his mother's natural wish to please her only son, the sight of the lumpy beige mass in three bowls on the table struck me as an augury of doom.

There was no cream. Mr Jesperson anointed his liberally with milk and sugar, but I refrained, sprinkling mine with salt in the Scottish way.

No one remarked on the absence of toast. We had, after all, dined together the previous night upon boiled eggs — one each — and toast of remarkable thinness. There was only one conclusion to be drawn: we were now so hard up that even the cleverest, most economical housekeeper — as was Mrs Jesperson — could not keep up a pretence of plenty.

After breakfast, I helped clear away and do the washing up, and took the opportunity to peek inside the larder. Milk was delivered daily and there was still a bit of butter, but apart from a sorry-looking cabbage and canisters for flour, oats, rice, sugar and tea — I did not enquire within — the cupboard was as bare as Old Mother Hubbard's.

Although I tried to be discreet, Mrs Jesperson saw me snooping and said calmly, "I'll pick up something for dinner when I go out."

But when she came downstairs again a little later, she did not have the appearance of a woman bent on begging the greengrocer or the butcher to let her have a little more on tick. She wore what looked like an entirely new hat, having managed to achieve a most pleasing and fashionable effect with a few cleverly placed trimmings, and from her ears depended a beautiful pair of blue faïence and gold Egyptian earrings.

I was impressed, if surprised, but the same sight caused Mr Jesperson to throw down his newspaper and leap to his feet. "Mother — no."

"There's nothing else for it," she replied, her manner serene.

"I forbid it."

A touch of exasperation tightened her lips. "Jasper."

"Please, don't."

"What, then, would you have me do?"

"Give me a little more time — that's all — just a little more time."

The earrings swung as she shook her head. "I told you last week — there is no more time. We could all be out on the street tomorrow morning, starving, unless —"

"I'll move," I said quickly, turning to Mrs Jesperson. "I'll stay with friends; you can let my room."

She smiled at me sadly. "Thank you, Miss Lane, for the offer, but unless we were to let out every room and sleep in the cupboards ourselves, I'm afraid it would not suffice. Last month, although our lease was renewed for another year and the landlord was kind enough to agree to monthly payments, I was unable to make the first instalment. And not only is the rent outstanding, I owe the butcher, the baker, the greengrocer, the . . . but no, the coal man doesn't give credit." Her gaze softened when she looked at her son, standing still and silent, his shoulders slightly bowed. "I'm sorry, my dear," she said. "But life in London is too costly. I've done what I can to economise, but there are limits. In the country, we could have a garden, and keep chickens —"

"You want me to give up my life to dig potatoes and tend poultry?" The bitterness startled me; I had never heard him speak less than kindly to his mother.

She felt it, too. "No, Jasper. I meant that I would do those things for you. I want you to be happy. You are very gifted and I have always felt it best to allow you to pursue your own course. I know it is what your father would have wished. You must have your chance. But in the meantime, we must have a roof over our heads."

"I'm sorry, Mother. I'm a beast." He went to embrace her and I looked away, giving my nose a sharp rub against a rush of useless sentiment. What must it be, to have a mother like that? My own mother had blamed me for not being the beautiful little fool she had expected to console her for the lack of a son — she could never see me for who I was.

Mrs Jesperson pulled away from her son with a regretful sigh and straightened her hat. I asked her what she meant to do.

"Jasper doesn't like it, but I mean to go to his uncle to ask him for a loan."

"*Another* loan," Mr Jesperson corrected. He looked at me, his usually bright blue eyes darker, smouldering with unhappiness. "He made a condition: if there were a 'next time' I would dance to his tune. He thinks it disgraceful that the mother of a grown man should have to go begging . . . and of course he is right! Only I won't — I can't — accept his condition. He'd put me

16

in a solicitor's office and have me copying documents night and day . . . or he'd article me to an accountant, or make me a clerk — something well below my abilities, and deadly dull — no, Mother, don't object; I know what he intends and I know why: hasn't he told me often enough I'm too clever by half and need to be taken down a few pegs? And *if* I suffer in silence, if I'm a good boy for six months or so, I'll be allowed to climb the ladder, to gain a little more responsibility and more pay, year by year, until I'm *nearly* as well-paid and respectable as himself, with a good position in Her Majesty's Civil Service."

"Would that be so bad?" Mrs Jesperson asked softly. "To have your talents recognised and use them for good? Isn't that what you want? Would it be so hard to take a more usual route, like everyone else, to put up with restrictions and being told what to do by people who aren't as clever as you only for a year or two —"

He cut her off. "It *would* be too hard. If I didn't die of boredom after the first month, I'd slit my throat during the second."

Perhaps Mrs Jesperson had heard it before; she only shook her head again. "He may take pity on me . . . but if he sends me away with nothing, what do you propose we do about the rent?"

They stared at each other for a moment, in a highly-charged silence, while I twisted my hands together helplessly.

Then he spoke. "Let me deal with it. Don't go to Uncle today, Mother. I'll visit the landlord. Perhaps I can reason with him, man to man. It may be we can effect a trade — the barter system may work for us here as it once did abroad."

I did not understand until he said, "A man with many properties and many tenants is likely to have one or two mysteries he wants solved."

She bit her lip. "Do you really think he'd *pay* to find someone who had run out because they were as poor as us — and if he is so vengeful, how —"

"I wasn't thinking of that. There have been three cases of burglary — expensive jewellery taken — reported in the papers this past month."

"From properties managed by Mr Sims?" She looked as surprised as I was by this striking coincidence.

"No," he said impatiently. "That's not the point. When stories like that are published, people of property become nervous about their own safety. They are more likely to notice suspicious behaviour and might want a detective."

"I think it more likely they'd want a nightwatchman. Oh, very well, Jasper. If you can get Mr Sims to allow us another month, *however* you do it, I'll manage the other bills myself."

"Thank you, O most wonderful, glorious of mothers. I shall make certain you do not regret giving me another chance." He kissed her soundly on the cheek.

Outside it was damp, chill, and heavily overcast — typical of London at the beginning of November. There was an acrid flavour to the murky air that made me anticipate fogs, and despite the relative dryness of the morning, everyone hurried past, as if anxious to get indoors.

Mr Jesperson, too, seemed driven, setting off at such a rapid walk that I nearly had to run to keep up with him. I think he sometimes forgot how much longer his legs were than mine.

However, as soon as I gasped out a protest, he drew up sharply. "Forgive me! I am such a brute."

"I should hardly say that."

He took no notice. "I can see my faults, just as I can perceive the weaknesses in others. I know I am self-absorbed, devilishly proud, often unfriendly — only consider how I spoke to mother — my dear mother, who has done so much for me and never complains. She deserves better, and so do you. Please take my arm, Miss Lane. *You* shall set the pace."

Pleased yet embarrassed by his consideration, I could think of nothing to say, which was just as well, for he still had much to tell me.

"I am sure you will agree if I say that men often like to keep females innocent and dependent, never letting them grow up for fear it will somehow spoil their nature, but perhaps you may not have noticed how women can do something very similar to men? I have been thinking how a woman may look after a man — her husband or her son — so *well* that he may become a sort of monster . . . like a gigantic baby who takes and takes, never questioning how these good things come to him, at what price they have been purchased. He has only to want and his needs are met. Small wonder if he believes the world revolves around him."

"But that is not *you*."

He went on as if I had not spoken. "I had to grow up very quickly after my father died. Under other circumstances, if I had been sent away to school, things could have turned out very differently, but my mother decided to take me abroad — in part, to get away from interfering relations, but mainly because it was cheaper. She thought travel might provide a better education for me than staying here — and she was right!" He let out a short laugh.

"Abroad, especially in the more remote places, I had to be my mother's protector. I was not treated as a child, as I had been in England. Suddenly, I was the man, and it was up to me to look after my mother, not the other way round. I learned how to work, how to bargain, how to barter, how to trick people and how to steal. It was that or starve. I learned many things that were useful in those distant lands — but then we came home."

I gave him a sidelong look. He had rarely spoken to me so personally, and I wondered if he would have said these things to me face to face. Walking along side by side, he might almost have been thinking aloud.

"I feel completely British," he continued. "I couldn't be more so; this is my home, and yet England is a foreign land to me. There are so many things I don't know — simple things, important things, like how to behave. My mother takes care of me now and I let her. Our roles have been reversed. For my part, I thought I should be able to earn enough to pay the bills, one way or another, by doing what pleased me. But that has proved more difficult than I expected."

He fell silent, yet I found it easy to follow his unspoken thoughts, travelling on the path well-known to us both, of our adventures over the past several months. There had been successes enough to confirm our initial decision to set up in practice together, but although we could be proud of our work, pride did not pay the rent.

He sighed. "I have found the work I want to do. I think I am good at it. We are *both* good at it — you agree?"

"I do."

"There is a need for good detectives, especially in this city, teeming as it is with rogues and rascals." We had reached New Oxford Street, its pavements crowded with jostling, noisy crowds, and as he spoke, without a stumble or hesitation, he steered me adroitly out of the way of a red-faced, puffing man barrelling towards us unseeing behind his armful of parcels.

I agreed; one had only to read a newspaper to become aware of the many sudden deaths, unsolved crimes and mysteries in the city. "Perhaps we should take out another advertisement — try a different newspaper this time?"

His answering sigh sounded more like a groan.

Of course. Advertisements cost money. *Everything* costs money in our modern world.

"My uncle thinks I am spoilt, a dilettante. He knows I have a brain. Unfortunately, he lacks imagination and doesn't approve of that capacity in others. He decided I would do well to study law; I had always found it easy to memorise laws and cases, and with my memory well-stocked, could construct glib arguments to impress my tutors. But they did not impress *me*. I had never realised, until I looked into it, how *artificial* and *absurd* our legal system is. And once I had seen the truth I could not bear to continue — I would have had to play a part, to pretend I believed in things I did not, to act as if they *mattered* — and to do so, I would have been untrue to myself. Even if I did not slit my throat, it would have been another type of self-murder. Do you understand?"

I frowned. "I understand your *feelings*, but I can't agree with your assessment of our legal system. Is it not widely agreed to be one of the best in the world, one of the great benefits of the British Empire? And how could a society exist without laws and courts, and barristers and judges to impose justice? It is no mean thing to be a good lawyer — why, if women were allowed to practise law, I have often thought —" Just in time, I stopped myself from mounting that particular hobby horse, which would certainly have carried me far away from *his* concerns.

He said, "I agree entirely. Society *must* have a legal system, just as it must have a financial system — and ours may well be the best in the world — my point is merely that it is highly artificial. Just as the value of paper money is imaginary — a commonly accepted fantasy — so it is with the law. It is a game. A great game, and important, but not one I wish to play. Having seen behind the curtain, I know it is only make-believe. I might *pretend* to take it seriously, but I should only be acting a part, and sooner or later, if I was not found out first and disbarred, the weight of that pretence would crush my soul."

We had reached Holborn, where Mr Sims had his office, and suddenly the futility of our mission struck me and I stopped walking. I had let myself be swept along by my partner's enthusiasm, but now, anticipating an awkward encounter with a man to whom we owed money, I had to ask:

"Do you have any reason for thinking Mr Sims needs our services?"

He looked down at me with his most guileless blue gaze, and I could not help thinking what a mystery he was to me still. Sometimes he seemed one of the cleverest and most multitalented of men; at others, a mere play-actor. "Only what I said before: that a man in possession of several properties and as many tenants must have at least *one* problem preying on his mind."

"So you do not, in fact, know anything about his personal circumstances?"

A slight smile hovered about his lips as he shook his head.

"Oh, I don't believe it," I muttered. I had not realised until the moment my hope was deflated, that I had been hoping for anything at all.

"You *must* believe," he said, holding my gaze. "It is our task to make *him* believe that whatever problem is preying on his mind — and trust me, there will be something — is one we can solve."

I began to get angry. "What has belief to do with it?"

"Everything. If you can believe in our ability to solve Mr Sims' problem as thoroughly as you believe in *money* — as unquestioningly as you accept that those grubby bits of paper called bank notes possess an intrinsic value that makes them worth collecting and protecting — *he* will believe it, too."

We were standing in front of a shoe shop, and the people going past buffeted us like waves, pressuring us to move on, but I held my ground, determined to have it out with him rather than let him sweep me along once more. "How can you say that when you don't even know if he has a problem?"

"Of course he does! Who doesn't have problems?" The provoking man stared at me as if *I* was the one being absurd.

As levelly as I could I said, "Not problems that require hiring investigators."

He shrugged. "That is the gamble. Perhaps Mr Sims — unmarried, prosperous bachelor that he is — has no troubles in his life; perhaps it runs entirely smoothly in its well-worn channel. But if there is something preying on his mind — well, then, the purpose of our visit will be to remind him of it and convince him that we can help."

"And if we cannot?"

He made an impatient noise. "My dear Miss Lane, do you not realise that your negativity will ensure the very failure that you fear? You must have a positive outlook! In my experience, people make their own luck. Especially when dealing with others — confidence is all. If our man is worried about something, we must

24

seize the moment and convince him *we* will solve it for him. And we can do that only if we believe in ourselves."

All at once I lost my appetite for argument. He had trust in himself, and so did others. His confidence was justified. But what did I have to offer? I felt myself drooping, and looked down at my feet as I said, "Perhaps it would be better if you went to meet Mr Sims on your own."

"No, why?" Before I could reply, he had seized my hand and given it a shake, making me look up at him. "Miss Lane, we are partners. I trust your judgement. If you think this is wrong — "

"No, of course it's not wrong," I said quickly. "Only . . . unusual. I have never heard of any detective, in fact or fiction, touting for custom in this way. What next? Go from door to door to advertise our services? Why should our landlord have a mystery for us, any more than our coal man, or the shopkeeper next door?"

"He has more property than either of those individuals."

"It is . . ." I had meant to say "absurd", but stopped, not wishing to be insulting, and instead said, "It is a gamble."

"Yes, but we have nothing to lose, and will lose nothing by this *absurd* venture." His eyes flashed as he spoke the word, and not for the first time, I wondered if he could read my thoughts.

Then, lightly, he shrugged and said, "Our visit will not be wasted. If he has no reason to consult a detective, perhaps this happy, untroubled man may take pity and agree to give us more time to pay. Or he may find some other sort of work for me to do, even, as my mother suggested, be his nightwatchman. I would turn my hand to almost anything to put off the evil day when I'm a slave in an office."

With that, our conflict was dissolved, and we continued along the busy street to our destination.

Mr Sims' office was above a stationer's shop. Climbing the stairs, we could hear a man's voice, one half of a conversation:

"Please, dearest, try not to worry. I'll call tomorrow and we can — No, no, it might be better if Arthur was not at home." A pause. "No, of course I don't mean you to keep secrets from your —" Another pause. "Don't apologise, there's no need, you know you can always — I'll see you tomorrow. About four? Good-day, my dear."

Mr Jesperson rapped firmly upon the office door.

"Come!" called the same voice.

We looked in on a tidy office furnished with a few chairs, two substantial wooden filing cabinets and a large desk, on the surface of which I noticed little more than a pen-set and blotter, a silver-framed photograph of a couple — possibly a wedding portrait — and an unfamiliar, complicated object made of dark wood, black metal and wire, the purpose of which I could not divine.

Behind the desk sat a dapper, dark-haired gentleman in his mid-thirties. He looked surprised to see us, but his surprise was nothing to mine upon realising that he was alone in the room. Had we overheard him talking to an imaginary visitor, perhaps rehearsing an expected encounter?

"Jasper Jesperson, at your service," said my friend, removing his hat as he bowed.

"Ah, Mr Jesperson." The puzzlement cleared away. "I beg your pardon; I was not expecting . . . I did not recognise you." He rose. "Please, come in and take a seat."

Mr Jesperson stepped aside so that I could enter. "Allow me to introduce my partner, Miss Lane."

The man gave a start of surprise, but came around his desk to greet me more formally, then pulled out a chair. "Please sit down, Miss Lane." He looked over my head. "Partner?"

"I thought my mother had made you aware of my new line of business. We have formed an agency to conduct private investigations under the name of Jesperson and Lane."

"Oh! Ah! Yes, I *see* — or, rather, to be perfectly honest, I don't. That is, Mrs Jesperson quite naturally discussed your new line of work with me — it sounds *most* intriguing — but I don't think, no, I am quite certain she never mentioned that your partner was, er, a lady detective. Surely that is most, ah, unusual? Not that I have any objections, of course, why should I? But a woman investigator . . . well . . ." He shrugged and gave up the struggle to define his problem as he rounded the desk to resume his usual seat.

"I suppose you have come to pay . . . I usually do business with your mother."

"I hope we may do business together," said Mr Jesperson firmly. "You expressed your astonishment at the idea of a lady detective, yet surely you can imagine situations in which the fairer sex excel, and some in which a man would struggle against obstacles that a woman's presence would banish. A lady, for example, might find it easier to confide her most private concerns to *another* lady. Miss Lane would probably get a clearer picture of your sister's worries and how to solve them than even you might manage."

Mr Sims' eyebrows shot up. "What the devil! I beg your pardon, Miss Lane. But, see here, Jesperson, what do you know of my sister's concerns? *How* can you know?"

Mr Jesperson waved an airy hand. "I only guessed. Am I right in thinking that your brother-in-law's behaviour is causing her some . . . disquiet?"

"See here, you can't possibly have *guessed*! Was it the maid? If she's been gossiping . . ." His hands on the desk clenched into fists.

"Calm yourself, Sims. There is no gossip. I have never met your sister, or her maid. It was purely a matter of deduction. After all, I am a detective."

"But —" Mr Sims looked bewildered. "How . . . what evidence could possibly have led you to the conclusion that my sister is worried about her husband?"

Sitting back in his chair, Mr Jesperson wove a tale. "My mother is an intuitive soul, as you may have noticed. She told me that she had the impression that you were struggling with a problem not your own, but on behalf of someone else, perhaps your sister."

"I never said anything about my sister to your mother."

"You said nothing; she merely mentioned to me that she had intuited it, and just now, as we came up the stairs, we inadvertently overheard your side of a telephonic conversation."

At this phrase, the strange object on the desk revealed its nature. I had, of course, seen telephones before — I had even used one once, telephoning from a central exchange — but never one so compact and elegant as the contraption on Mr Sims' desk.

"You addressed this person as 'dearest' and advised her not to worry, and I know you to be unmarried. You suggested meeting when her husband was not present, but there was no hint of anything improper. Do you remember, the first time we met in this office, I asked you about the people in this photograph? You said it had been taken on the occasion of your sister's marriage, little more than a year previous."

"It will be two years in December," said Mr Sims. He looked more friendly now. "Well, what a memory you have! You make it sound so simple, but I am sure most people would not make anything from those few overheard words."

"Most people are not detectives. You are trying to solve your sister's problem yourself, Mr Sims, and you cannot. There is no shame in that; if there is a mystery to it — and I think there is — it will take a good detective to unravel."

"Or possibly two," said Mr Sims with a look at me.

"Two for the price of one," Mr Jesperson cheerily replied.

From the faint cloud that appeared on the landlord's face, I feared my friend had rushed the jump. "Your services are very expensive, I suppose?"

"That depends on the case, and how long it takes us to solve. And since we already owe you a month's rent . . ."

Understanding cleared away the cloud, and after a few more words it was agreed: we were no longer considered to be in arrears, and we would have a roof safely over our heads for another month, at least.

Of course, the agreement of his sister, Mrs Arthur Creevey, must be obtained first, so Mr Sims telephoned to her whilst we waited, and a meeting was arranged for half-past four that very day.

CHAPTER
THREE

A Cat and a Snake

Satisfaction put an extra spring in his step as we left Mr
Sims' office and took the stairs back down to the street,
but Mr Jesperson was not one to say "I told you so". I
stifled my impulse to apologise for not having trusted
him, for the successful outcome did not take away from
the absurdity of seeking work in such a manner.

And *was* this the sort of job we wanted? Until we
spoke to Mrs Creevey we could not guess what worried
her about her husband, but if she set us to spy upon
him and we discovered something she would rather not
have known — a second family, a problem with drink,
or some worse vice — I could too easily imagine the
outcome. How often the messenger is punished for the
bad news he brings. What if Mr Sims, embarrassed by
what we had discovered about his brother-in-law,
decided to evict us?

Preoccupied by such worrying thoughts, I followed
my partner's lead through several turnings away from
the bustle of Holborn and into a maze of quieter streets
without taking heed of where we were going, and it was
only when he suddenly stopped that I realised we were
in a neighbourhood unfamiliar to me.

"Where are we going?" I asked.

He stared with narrowed eyes at a row of shops across the road, then shook his head. "Not here," he said, and moved on.

"This isn't the way home."

"Ah, you are beginning to learn your way around London, at last."

It was true that despite having lived here, off and on, for some few years, I still found the great city baffling, and was easily led astray or lost in its warren-like streets, so I made no reply. When he stopped a second time, I noticed that once again he had chosen a position with a good view of a row of shops. It was the same thing the third time, and now I recognised that he was making some sort of assessment of the butchers' shops. I could not imagine why. Even if he had a few coins on him I doubted they would be enough to purchase a single chop in the cheapest place, and no shopkeeper would extend a line of credit to a total stranger.

As we watched in silence, a small, scruffy mongrel went into the butcher shop. A few moments later it came trotting out again, clutching a marrowbone in its jaws.

"That's our man," murmured Mr Jesperson. He pulled a cloth bag from his coat pocket, took off his hat, stuffed it into the bag and handed it to me. "Your shopping, I think . . . Sister."

I stared at him, uncomprehending, as he ran both hands through his hair until his curls stood out in a bright, untidy mass. He blinked at me, a shy, tremulous smile widening his mouth, and in a flash I saw a stranger — a hulking, half-witted boy — before he turned to cross the road.

Suddenly, horrified, I understood what he meant to do and I seized his arm. "No! You mustn't!"

He turned back. The stranger was gone as his familiar eyes met mine. He said softly, "A kind man who gives bones to stray dogs would take pleasure in giving a few scraps to a penniless, starving lad when I show him the hole in my pocket. He'll feel the warm glow that comes from being charitable, and we'll be well fed for once."

"You're not a lad," I said sharply. "You're a grown man, pleased to think you're cleverer than the average butcher. Would he feel that warm glow you speak of if he knew he'd been tricked? Honest people don't beg — at least, not from strangers. Not here in England. And we're not in such desperate circumstances yet. Even if we were . . . do you really think tricking a kindly butcher out of a bit of meat is preferable to going cap in hand to your uncle?"

By the time I ran out of breath, Mr Jesperson was as still and blank-faced as a statue, and I felt a bleak despair overwhelm me. It was over. I had done it again. For the second time in half a year I had alienated the only friend I had in the world. But at least this time I had not run away. I had spoken my mind. I might wish I could take them back, but I knew my words were true.

And so did he. After a moment, the life came back to his face as he drew a breath.

"Thank you," he said quietly. "Miss Lane. To my mother I may always be a boy, but *you* don't see me that way, thank heaven. I fear sometimes I let the pleasures of plotting — of an *idea* — carry me away. This is London, not Benares. I am not who I was there."

He put out his hand to me and for a moment I stared, wondering what he meant by it — were we to shake hands in agreement? — before remembering I had his hat.

I gave it back to him and he put it on, then offered me his arm, and we walked on. Again, I was so preoccupied that I scarcely noticed the direction we walked in.

"My mother cooks vegetables wonderfully well, yet I still want meat," he said. "I know it is only a fleshly desire — for flesh! If I were more evolved spiritually, I would be a vegetarian. In Benares, I spent a year refusing to let the flesh of any animal, fish or fowl pass my lips. It was a requirement of the spiritual instruction I had decided to undergo. I was nineteen, then, and believed I had attained my full growth, but the following year when I resumed my life as a meat-eater — lapsed into sin, I suppose my teacher would have said — I grew another inch. So even if meat is bad for the soul, it must be good for the body. Unless, of course, there is something *bad* about being as tall as I am."

I couldn't help laughing. He bent his head down to give me an inquiring look. "Friends again?"

"Of course!" I felt myself blush. "Please forgive my scolding."

"Sometimes I deserve a scolding. I am grateful I have you to keep me right."

We left the poorer streets for more prosperous-looking ones, where the houses stood proudly three and four storeys high. I had found it to be true of London that almost every street was another world, each with its distinctive atmosphere. This one, with its noble ranks of houses built of brick and stone, came with the sound of weeping and a buzz of conversation where a crowd had gathered.

As we drew nearer, it was obvious that the crying came from a well-dressed little girl, who could not be consoled by the white-whiskered gentleman in a shiny top hat who was crouched beside her.

Perhaps a dozen people stood around, craning their necks, looking up towards the rooftops.

"Send for the fire department," said a man.

"Naw, they'll never come," said another.

"Leave it alone, it will come down by itself," said a young woman in a smart, dark blue coat and hat. "Trust me, if it got up there by itself, it can get back down. Cats are wonderful like that."

I looked up, following the gaze of others, and at last made out the small black form of a cat perched on a narrow pediment above the top storey window. The pediment — if that was the right name for it — was a sort of inverted triangle jutting out from the wall, and must have been purely decorative. In some other position it might have provided a surface on which to display a potted plant, or to hold a lamp, but in that place, unattached to anything else and so far out of reach, it had no obvious purpose. It was difficult to imagine how the animal had reached it, unless it had jumped down from the roof. But it would surely be unable to jump *up* so far, and I could see no way for it to get down. Just looking at the tiny, living creature on that isolated spot so high above the ground made my stomach clench in sympathetic fear.

By asking a few questions, Mr Jesperson quickly established the facts: the cat belonged to the little girl and it had run away from her while she was visiting her grandfather — the prosperous-looking, white-whiskered gentleman — who lived at the far end of the street. No one knew how it had managed to achieve its present, lofty position, but there it was, and there it seemed it would stay, unless — as a short man in a brown suit repeated — the fire department were alerted and would agree to bring one of their especially long ladders with which to rescue it.

"It might be reached from the window below," Mr Jesperson said. "Have you tried speaking to someone in the house? They'd only need to open the window, let someone out onto the ledge —"

"There's no one home," said the lady in blue. "They've gone away and the house is shut up until Christmas."

"Someone must have the keys. Perhaps next door?" Mr Jesperson looked up, his eyes measuring the distance between the windows on the two adjoining houses. "If I could get onto the roof, from either side, then perhaps . . ." He began to walk closer, staring hard at the building as he went, and I trailed after him.

I heard the lady say, "We might tempt it with a bit of fish?"

Tempt it where? I wondered. A leap from that ledge would be disastrous. Nor could I imagine how Mr Jesperson could possibly reach the cat from the roof, not even with his long arms. The man insisting on the need for the fire department seemed to me to have the best idea, and when I heard him instructing one of the little boys who'd been attracted by the excitement to run and fetch them, I thought we might leave them to it.

But I suddenly saw that Mr Jesperson had taken off his shoes and socks, and before I could ask what he meant to do he was in motion, trotting away from me. When he reached the house, he immediately pulled himself up onto the lower window ledge, and then began to climb the brick wall.

I held my breath. Of course, the wall was *brick*, rather than stucco or smoothly plastered, but the spaces between the bricks were not deep enough to offer purchase. Yet somewhere, somehow, he *must* have found hand- and footholds, for he continued, steadily, to pull himself up a sheer wall. It would have been no challenge to a lizard, perhaps, but for anything larger, it should have been impossible; I wondered if even a monkey could have done it.

The other people around me began to gasp and call out in surprise as they noticed this redheaded stranger in a black suit steadily inching up the wall. Reaching the first-storey window ledge, he scarcely paused, but used that ledge as a launch pad to get to the window above, and then the next, like a swimmer on a sea of brick. And then he was standing on the ledge of the top window and — the stretch might have been too great for a shorter man, but looking up, with his bare feet flat on the window ledge, his eyes were almost level with the cat's.

Time dragged in silence; then Mr Jesperson said something I did not understand. Perhaps a nonsense syllable, a name, or only the sort of gentle noise people make to attract a pet, but whatever it was, the cat responded with a slightly surprised-sounding mew.

When Mr Jesperson raised his hand, the little creature — it was no more than a kitten — stepped confidently into it, and allowed itself to be lowered to his chest and placed inside his shirt.

How it was for my friend I cannot say, but for me, watching him, the descent took far longer and was more tense and nerve-wracking than the climb upwards. Perhaps it was simply that I had been too surprised by his unexpected ascent to realise how dangerous it was, whereas on the way down, every fractional split-second pause as his fingers and toes sought out holds was a moment when he might fall to his doom — and we all knew and feared it.

Finally though, he pushed himself away from the house and landed, surprisingly lightly, on the ground.

There was a moment of awed silence from the watchers as he walked the short distance to the pavement where the white-whiskered gentleman and the little girl were waiting. Then, as he scooped the kitten out of his shirt and put it into the eager, trembling hands of its mistress, a round of cheering, applause and whistles rose from the crowd.

I had to close my eyes for a moment. When I opened them, there he was, standing before me, a bemused smile on his face. "Are you all right?"

"I should ask you!" I exclaimed. "What you did . . . it looked impossible."

"You should have looked more closely at the house. The original occupants must have dreamed of a flower-bedecked cottage. See those iron hooks above each window, and there by the door? They're for hanging plants. The remains of the old trellis is harder to make out, but when I saw how high and wide it was, I knew it would enable me to make the ascent. Unless it was so ancient and rotten that it would fall apart at my touch — but that seemed unlikely."

I bent down to rescue his hat, which he had left on the ground beside me on top of his boots and socks.

He was still being cheered when I handed it to him. He put it on, then took it off to the crowd first on one side, and then the other, then bowed to them. After that, he did something I'd seen street performers do at the end of their act: he bowed again and rolled his hat down his arm once, twice, three times. The final, flourishing bow left the bowl of the hat presented to the audience, and this crowd, like any that might gather on a street corner to hear a song or see a magic trick performed, showed their appreciation in the traditional way.

Coins — silver and copper both — clinked merrily against one another as they landed in the hat. Mr Jesperson looked startled, then pleased, then abashed, and turned his head quickly to see what I thought of it.

But he had not begged; he'd risked his life with no thought of reward and he deserved it. I smiled at him and held up my hands, lightly clapping them together to show my approval.

It had started to rain, although only lightly, which was dispersing the casual crowd. The show was over. Mr Jesperson, hat at his feet, hastily resumed his socks and boots. Only the little girl and her grandfather remained. She was too pleased with the return of her kitten — kissing and petting it extravagantly — to pay attention to the man who had rescued it, but the elderly gentleman with white whiskers and a distinctly military bearing approached and introduced himself as Colonel Robert Mallett.

"I won't insult you by offering you money, sir, but I should like to thank you. You have my deepest gratitude for what you have done today, having restored the smile to my granddaughter's face. And you have piqued my curiosity. Rarely have I seen anyone climb like that — and never in this city! Am I right in thinking you were born on St Kilda?"

"No, sir," replied Mr Jesperson with a puzzled smile. "I am a native of London."

"Then your father, or your mother perhaps?"

He shook his head. "I am not familiar with St Kilda."

"It is a remote Scottish island. The people — quite inbred, of course — have developed peculiarly prehensile

40

toes as the result of climbing the rocky cliffs to supplement their meagre diets with eggs from the nesting fulmars."

Mr Jesperson smiled. "I do have Scottish relations, but not from the islands. My toes are quite flexible, but I do not think extraordinarily so. As a boy, I was often compared to a monkey, and I have perhaps spent more time honing my climbing skills abroad than most people would consider normal."

"Hmmph! Well, whatever your reason, I am glad of it. Perhaps, on some later occasion you will permit me to invite you to dine?"

"You are most kind."

"Let me give you my card," said the Colonel, reaching into an inside pocket. His words reminded me of the cards we'd had printed — a necessary investment Mr Jesperson had insisted upon, although we had scarcely made a dent in the box of 200. As my friend made no answering gesture towards his own pockets, I guessed that he had forgotten to carry a supply.

Fortunately, I had a few with me, and I quickly retrieved one from my purse — worn chatelaine-style from my belt; my sister had made me a present of it on my last birthday, assuring me it was *à la mode* in Paris, and it did add a touch of style to my sadly worn, workaday dress — and slipped it into the Colonel's still-outstretched hand.

"Jesperson and Lane," he read aloud, and then his eyes moved to my face. "You are . . . Miss Lane?"

"Yes, sir."

"A lady detective! Well, well."

"If you ever have need of our services . . ." I quickly began.

"I hope I shan't, but I shall remember," he said, closing his fist gently around the card. "If I should hear of anyone who requires the aid of a detective agency, I shall send him to you."

"We would appreciate it," said Mr Jesperson. "It is rather more difficult to make one's name in London than I had anticipated."

"You have lived abroad a long time?"

At Mr Jesperson's nod of assent the old gentleman said, "We shall have stories to trade when we dine. *Au revoir.*"

After they had gone, Mr Jesperson picked up his hat and inspected the treasure within. "Would you mind putting this in your purse? I'm afraid I really *do* have a hole in my pocket."

The coins clinked richly and weighed the little purse down most satisfyingly. I decided it looked and felt much better plumply filled than it had when hanging limply flat. By now it had started to rain in earnest, and I regretted that lack of forethought that had sent us out of the house without an umbrella.

Mr Jesperson recalled a tea shop not far away: "We might spend a little of our cash and reward ourselves for a successful morning's work. It will be quicker, I think, if we go this way." He steered me down a narrow passage out of the wide street. Scarcely had we entered it when I felt something tug at my waist; a moment later I felt my purse pulled away, and I whirled around with a cry, trying to seize it and failing.

A rough-looking young man stood there, blocking the exit, my purse clutched fast in one fist and a wicked-looking knife in the other.

"Mine, now," he said in a low, threatening voice. "And anything else you've got, hand it over. Don't think of trying to fight — my knife is sharp and thirsty for blood."

My blood ran cold. I could not have moved for anything.

"You're quite right," Mr Jesperson said in a relaxed and conversational tone. "It is very sharp, your knife, and you should not try to fight. You would not want to cut yourself, would you? But your knife is thirsty. Better not move. It's very slippery, in this rain. Your hand might slip; your hand might easily slip. Your hand is wet, the knife is wet, you might slip and cut yourself."

The young man frowned and shook his head. He took a step towards us and then stumbled, slipping on the wet ground, and although he did not fall, he jerked his arm to save himself. The blade flashed; he sucked in a sharp breath, and a thin bright line of red bloomed on the back of his other hand — the one in which he held my purse.

"Oh, dear," said Mr Jesperson. "You've cut yourself. I thought that might happen. How unfortunate. But I have a clean handkerchief with which to bind your wound. May I?" He stepped forward and spoke again, his voice cracking out like a whip. "Put that down or you will do yourself a worse injury. Drop it, now."

Astonishingly, the young villain dropped the knife. After a moment of confusion, he looked at Mr

Jesperson, approaching with a white cotton square, and meekly held out his wounded hand for dressing.

"Now, how can I work when you're holding something? Give me that, and I will make it better."

My purse was released into Mr Jesperson's grasp without a murmur, and without looking around, he handed it back to me. I clutched it close as I clenched my teeth and wondered if I should run away. But I was afraid in case any movement would break the spell, so I stayed stock still and watched as Mr Jesperson wrapped his handkerchief around the man's hand and tied it, saying emphatically, "Now you are better, and you have my handkerchief. It's a good one; fair exchange, you agree?"

The robber nodded mechanically, staring at his bound hand. Mr Jesperson clapped him firmly on the shoulder, twice. "Now go home. Go home. You'll be well after you've rested. Go home and go to sleep and forget all about it."

Sheep-like in his obedience, the rough young man turned and ambled away.

In a flash, Mr Jesperson was at my side. He took my arm in his firm grasp and propelled me along, down the alley and out into a more populous thoroughfare. I felt as if I had woken from a horrid dream. He slowed to a more decorous pace and asked me if I wanted to rest for a while in a tea shop.

Feeling a bit dazed, I shook my head. "I'd rather go home." The shower of rain had passed; we were wet, but would get no wetter.

44

"Are you sure? I hope I haven't hypnotised *you*, as well."

I stopped short and stared up into his face. "Is that what you did? You hypnotised him?"

"Something like that. I made *suggestions* — and he turned out to be a very suggestible fellow. Which is fortunate for us. It wouldn't have worked on everyone. We were lucky."

"Luck! Luck has nothing to do with it — you *did* something — and I don't understand how."

"Oh, I don't really know *how* it works, myself." He had started walking again as he spoke and I hurried to keep up with him.

"But how did you learn it?"

"In the first place, by watching snake charmers in India. I watched them very closely. I observed, and I practised."

This made no sense to me. "Snake-charming? But that's —"

His eyes narrowed as he smiled down at me. "Quite. Of course, I had to adapt the traditional methods and put them into words, for the better understanding of snakes of the two-legged variety."

CHAPTER
FOUR

Back in Gower Street

By the time I had changed into dry clothes and gone back downstairs, Mrs Jesperson had returned. The first thing I saw was that she had her shopping basket and it was full. The second thing I noticed was that she was not wearing her Egyptian earrings.

We chatted for a few moments in the hall and then I followed her into the kitchen, where Jasper had put the kettle on.

"Oh, well done, Mother!" he exclaimed at the sight of the basket filled with a loaf of bread, apples, cheese, butter and potatoes. Then he frowned. "But where on earth did you get the money? You haven't been to see —"

"Your uncle? No, of course not, Jasper dear. I agreed you should have it your way, and I'm very pleased to hear from Miss Lane that that you were lucky with Mr Sims." Gently but firmly she took over the business of making tea.

"So now you have ensured that we needn't worry about the rent for at least another month. I am relieved. But there are still our meals to get —"

"Did Miss Lane tell you I also managed to earn almost nine shillings by the dramatic rescue of a kitten?"

"That's very nice, dear — will you slice the bread? — it will make a dent in the money I owe the butcher. But how was I to know? Since I was not allowed to approach *your* uncle, I decided to pay a call on mine."

Jasper frowned. "Great Uncle August?"

"Don't be silly. I could hardly get to Edinburgh and back this morning."

"I didn't know you had any other uncles."

She turned from him to set out cups and saucers as she said, "I don't, really. It's only a manner of speaking."

I knew exactly what she meant, but, judging by his face, Jasper was not familiar with the common phrase "getting money from uncle". Or perhaps he was, but did not want his mother to know he knew she'd pawned her earrings.

"Well, whoever he is, he must be jolly generous — or jolly fond of you, Mother dear, and that's easy to understand, because I know *I* am." He grabbed her about the waist and gave her a smacking kiss.

"And so say all of us," I offered, hoping it didn't sound too stiff or mechanical a tribute, because I was, truly, very grateful to have been allowed to become a part of their household.

While we sipped our tea in front of the fire — built up with coal we were no longer obliged to hoard quite so parsimoniously — Mr Jesperson quizzed his mother on what she knew about Mr Sims' sister.

"She is his only near relative, I believe, and he seems to have had the duty of care for her after the death of their parents some years ago."

"But she is married," I pointed out.

"Yes, she is now. I recall that Mr Sims originally did not approve — he considered Mr Creevey was not . . ." she hesitated, frowning a little as she searched for the most accurate phrase, "Not quite *right*."

Mr Jesperson looked up. "He's a criminal?"

"Good heavens, Jasper! Certainly not. His background was poor but honest — at least, Mr Sims never said anything to hint otherwise."

"So she married a poor man?" I said, wondering how they came to have a telephone.

"No." Mrs Jesperson gave a very genteel little sniff. "Poor once, but now a successful tradesman. By the time he met Miss Sims he was still under forty and well established, with his own business and enough money to think of marriage. Mr Sims should have been grateful considering his sister's age — I'm sure she's quite thirty and not what anyone would describe as a beauty. She was lucky to get a husband at all . . . not that thirty is so terribly old, and it was a good match for them both, by all accounts."

I was agonisingly conscious that Mrs Jesperson had remembered that she was speaking to another spinster who might have been described in the same way — I had no illusions about my appearance, and I would not see twenty-seven again. Mrs Jesperson was embarrassed now, uncomfortable because she had meant no offence and an apology would only compound it.

Mr Jesperson stretched his long legs out towards the hearth and asked his mother about Mr Creevey's business.

"He offers a removals service. Mr Sims told me his brother-in-law has more than one van now and several men who work for him, and could take an easier role in the business, but apparently Mr Creevey prefers lifting and carrying to directing other men to do so whilst he lounges at his ease." She stood up. "Speaking of lounging, I must get busy, or you won't get a proper meal today."

I offered her my help in the kitchen, but she gestured for me to keep my seat. "I'm sure you have your own business to be getting on with, thank you all the same."

My business, I decided, must be to write letters I had put off for too long. Our little job for Mr Sims and his sister had secured the rent for the next month, but it was as urgent as ever to find more work.

Ever since I had left the investigation in Scotland, I'd had nothing more to do with the Society for Psychical Research. Mr Jesperson took a keen interest in psychical research — as in so many other, diverse matters — and subscribed to various journals to keep abreast of the latest developments; therefore, I knew that the investigation had continued in my absence, and that a full report was expected to be published in due course. There had been no scandal, neither had there been any great revelations, and Miss X — otherwise known as Gabrielle Fox — remained in charge.

I knew she had powerful friends and supporters in the Society, and I had seen how convincingly she could play the innocent. If I tried to tarnish her reputation I had no doubt she would retaliate and utterly blacken mine. For that reason, and because of my past close association with her, I had decided to say nothing.

Gradually, as I came to feel settled in Gower Street, I had written to a few friends to let them know where I was, but a fearful caution had kept me from contacting anyone too closely involved with the SPR; I had not written a single word to Gabrielle, or to any of her particular friends, in or out of the Society. I did not know how she had explained my abrupt defection to others, whether she had hinted at "nerves" — or something worse; whether she had claimed she'd dismissed me for fabricating evidence of ghostly phenomena. Or even if she had kindly explained my disappearance with some invention involving illness or aged relations.

The truth is that I was afraid she would seek me out. Ever since I'd left I'd imagined her on my trail. I'd kept expecting her to turn up, to resume the argument I had run away from. She liked to have the last word, and given enough time she would wear me down; convince me I had misunderstood, that she had done nothing wrong, or — and this was worse — that it didn't matter. Perhaps she would say that the ends justified the means; there was no benefit to us in proving a house was *not* haunted, but a story about a haunted house was something we could *sell*, and we needed that.

But that had ended. I wanted never to see her again, never to feel the buffeting force of her personality against mine, when my certainties would be forced to weaken and yield.

I counted the weeks since our parting and realised it had been more than four months. Was that long enough for her to have lost interest, to decide I no longer mattered, even if one of her friends were to tell her where I was? Knowing Gabrielle as well as I had, I thought she might still feel driven to seek me out in order to explain herself, to persist until she had won me over again. On the other hand, she was such a restless soul that she had surely moved on to other projects by now, missions far more deserving and demanding of her time than an old friend who had fallen by the wayside.

I had no wish to return to the fold, but it was absurd not to use my few contacts with the sort of wealthy and intellectually adventurous people who just might find themselves in need of a private detective agency.

Mr Jesperson had done his bit towards finding work for us, and now it was my turn. Leaving him absorbed in his reading, I went upstairs for my address book.

Writing that first letter was like walking blindfolded into a room full of people not knowing if they were friends or foes. Because I did not wish to contradict anything Gabrielle might have said to excuse my absence, I could only apologise in the vaguest terms for my long silence and pray that Lord Bennington, Lady Florence, Mrs McWhortle, Mr and Mrs Traill, would forgive my bad manners in not writing before now.

I went on to inform each of my former colleagues of my new circumstances, to enclose a business card and express the wish that if they, or anyone in their circle of friends, should ever find themselves in need of the services of someone who could provide a discreet and successful investigation into *any* sort of mystery, crime or puzzling circumstances, could they please think of Jesperson and Lane, 203A Gower Street, London.

I wondered as I sealed the last envelope and set it, with a sigh, on the pile to be posted, if there had been any point to the exercise. I could imagine Lord Bennington reading through to the end with a puzzled frown, only to throw the page onto the fire. Detectives? What would he, what would *any* of the well-bred, well-behaved gentlefolk of his acquaintance ever want to do with such snooping, spying, vulgar creatures as that?

CHAPTER
FIVE

Cake in Kensington

The Creeveys lived in a fine house on a quiet street in Kensington. When we arrived, the glossy white front door was opened to us by a rosy-cheeked girl who looked so pleased with herself as she took our names and ushered us within that I fancied she was only playing at being a maid. She walked with a bounce and paused to smooth down her skirt and apron before she opened the inner door to announce in a high, strangulated voice:

"Mr Jesperson and Miss Lane to see you, ma'am."

Mrs Creevey had a homely face with a prominent, square jaw and a nose with a bump in it, but her brown eyes were meltingly lovely, and she looked so honest and sympathetic that it was impossible not to like her.

She was quite taken with the idea of a *lady* detective, exclaiming that if she had known such a career was possible before her marriage, she might have considered it for herself: "For I do love to read about crimes in the newspaper, especially when they are unsolved, and I try to work out the answer. Only there is seldom enough information to go on — they don't give you all the clues, unlike in a novel."

"True," said Mr Jesperson. "The newspaper reporters don't know what's important — and nor do the police. What unsolved crime has your attention at the present, may I ask?"

"The jewel thefts," she said promptly. "I don't know if you noticed, but there were three burglaries in private homes in October, and the second was only a few streets from here."

"Yes, I have read the reports, but it has not been suggested that there is a definite connection between them. You think the same hand is behind them all?"

"Don't you? It seems likely to me. Surely the police must think so."

He smiled. "You are thinking like a detective, Mrs Creevey! I'm sure that with your help we'll manage to solve your *own* mystery quite quickly."

She blushed and put a hand to her cheek. As she turned away, flustered, she seemed to realise that she had overlooked the formalities in her eagerness. We were all three still standing in a little semi-circle on the slate-coloured carpet near the sitting room door, never having made it as far as the sofa and chairs grouped near the fire. She quickly invited us to sit down and hardly had we done so before the door opened and the maid came in, almost staggering under the weight of a large silver tea tray.

Mr Jesperson leaped to his feet and relieved the girl of her burden, to be rewarded with much giggling and eyelash fluttering.

"Thank you, Sukie, you may leave us now," said Mrs Creevey. "We're not to be disturbed until Mr Creevey returns, is that understood?"

"Yes, ma'am. You want me to show Mr Creevey in?"

Eyebrows raised, she replied, "I imagine Mr Creevey will find his own way in his own house. You are not to *announce* him."

"No, ma'am. Yes, ma'am." She backed away. "What should I do now?"

"Ask Mrs Moyle. I'm sure she'll find something for you."

When the maid had gone out, Mrs Creevey explained: "This is her first position."

As she poured out the tea, I took the opportunity to look around the spacious sitting room, decorated in shades of grey with striking touches of white and black. It was simply, even rather sparsely furnished, without any clutter. There was a sofa, on which I sat beside Mr Jesperson, and several armchairs, as well as a few small tables. There were no pictures hanging on the walls, which were covered in dove-grey silk. The floor-length curtains, of a silvery-grey fabric with a pattern of linked rings in black and white, had been drawn against the early dusk. The whole effect might have been chilly and unwelcoming, but I found it attractive, calming and elegant, and the fire blazing so cheerfully in the hearth kept us warm enough.

There were two cakes — cherry and lemon drizzle. Mr Jesperson took a slice of each; I declined and sipped my tea as we waited for Mrs Creevey to begin.

"I don't know what my brother has told you —"

"Nothing at all," replied Mr Jesperson. "We thought it would be best to hear all the details directly from you."

"I see. Of course." Our hostess took a deep breath. "My husband suffers from recurrent bouts of somnambulism. It began in his childhood. It happened less often when he grew older, but never stopped — not entirely. Even after he was a grown man, Mr Creevey would wake to discover evidence that he'd been abroad in the night. On occasion, someone else would see him and he would learn about it that way. His eyes were wide open, you see, and he moved with such confidence that no one would suspect he was not in a perfectly normal waking state, unless you attempted to engage him in conversation. He came close to being arrested once for not responding to a policeman's questions, but fortunately the constable had seen a play featuring a sleepwalker, and he knew not to risk waking him too abruptly, and instead followed him for the next hour, making sure he came to no harm, until he saw him return safely to his own rooms.

"But by the time I met him, Mr Creevey had not walked in his sleep, to the best of his knowledge, for almost three years. He was thirty-five years old, and it was natural to think that somnambulism had been a problem of his youth. He had moved up in the world, established his own business and had his own home. By his own efforts, he had risen out of poverty and become a man of substance. He was able to think of marriage." She looked down shyly, her plain face pinker than ever. "He proposed to me."

"Did he warn you about his problem?" I asked.

"It was not a problem. Not then. Our only problem was my brother Henry. We have always been close, especially so since the death of our parents. Henry did not approve of my association with Arthur and could not countenance the idea of a marriage between us. He said hurtful things." She stared at the grey carpet for a moment before raising her dark shining eyes. "But my brother has changed his mind. He has come to see what a good man Arthur is and admits he was unfair, and that he spoke too hastily out of fear for me. And, to some extent, I think, from the fear of losing me. I did not need his permission to marry, but I did not like to go against his wishes — since the death of our parents, he is my only family . . ."

"I understand," I said quickly, as she struggled for words.

She gave me a grateful smile. "That is why, when Arthur proposed, I asked him to give me time to think. I already knew my mind, of course, and I didn't like to tell him the real reason I was hesitating — that my brother disapproved and I was hoping to change his mind. But it was very hard on poor Arthur, who did not know he'd already won my heart.

"One night, I awoke suddenly in the certain knowledge that I was not alone.

"It was a warm night and I had gone to bed with my window open — my room was at the back of the house overlooking an enclosed garden. There was a full moon that night, so my room was well lit, and the moment I opened my eyes and turned my head, I saw Arthur Creevey sitting in a chair in the corner."

"You were certain it was he?"

She smiled. "I knew him too well to mistake him. But what was I to think? He made no response when I spoke to him. I got up and found that although he was sitting upright, his relaxed posture and slow, steady breathing made me think he slept.

"After some time, he stood up, went to the window and without pausing, even when I spoke his name, swung one leg over the sill and then the other and — vanished.

"How I kept from screaming I shall never know. I raced to the window and looked out, and there he was on the ground, moving away from the house. As I watched, he scaled the fence at the bottom of the garden and was lost to my sight.

"Next morning, I sent a telegram asking Arthur to meet me. When he heard what had happened he explained about his somnambulism — a trouble he had believed past. Now that he knew he still suffered from it, he told me that of course he could not expect to marry.

"But something had changed in me. I knew, then, that I could never be happy without him. Henry would have to accept it. Together, we would find the answer to his problem."

Mr Creevey had consulted a doctor, an alienist called Dr Linton, who had studied under Charcot in Paris. His advice was to marry without delay. He claimed that the sleepwalker went in search of something he was denied in his waking life. And what had Mr Creevey sought but the woman that he loved — in her bedroom! The answer was obvious. His nocturnal wanderings would cease when he had made Miss Sims, Mrs Creevey.

"And he was right," she told us simply. "Marriage *was* the answer. At least, it was until a month ago, when his old affliction returned."

She turned her head and gazed into the fire.

"Pardon me for asking," said Mr Jesperson, his voice very gentle, "but was there anything —"

She cut him off. "Nothing. We are still as happy together as on our honeymoon — I should say happier, except for this problem."

"Trouble at work?" I hazarded.

She shook her head. "Nothing that preys upon his mind."

"What does the alienist think?" asked Mr Jesperson.

Her expression changed to a scowl, although she tried to smooth it away, and she moved as if her position in the well-upholstered chair had become uncomfortable. "Dr Linton is no use. Arthur has given up on him."

Although he scarcely moved, my friend became more intent. "Indeed? And yet he was right about your marriage."

"He is not right about our marriage *now*," she responded fiercely. "When Arthur told him how happy we were together, he smirked and asked the most intrusive and intimate questions — and then refused to accept Arthur's replies as truth. The man has a bee in his bonnet about . . . about *conjugal relations*. He believes that something about me, or our marriage, makes Arthur so unhappy that he is driven to roam the streets of London in search of . . . of something else." As she spoke her face suffused with blood and she pressed her hands to her bright red cheeks either to hide or to cool them.

"Thank you for being so frank with us," said Mr Jesperson gently. "I am sure you are quite right to disregard the alienist's conclusion. But he had one good idea — if we can find out where your husband goes at night, the answer to what drives him may reveal itself."

He then asked if she could recall anything that stood out about the days before her husband walked in his sleep. Had anything unusual happened? Did his mood change?

She shook her head helplessly. "Not to my knowledge. But you had better ask him." With a glance at the pyramid-shaped clock on the otherwise bare mantelpiece, she said, "He will be here any minute now. He always telephones to me to say if he will be late."

Mr Jesperson's gaze swept the room and I guessed he was looking for the telephone, having been much taken with the compact, elegant model on the desk of Mr Sims.

"Mr Creevey has a telephone at his work? Was that your brother's idea?"

"My brother?" She smiled. "Oh, no, he would never have thought of it. That was down to my husband. It was not long after our marriage that he became enamoured of the idea. He said that we must have one in the house and he must have one at work — he soon convinced Henry that *he* had better get one for his office, or risk being old-fashioned. Now Henry has joined my husband in his evangelistic fervour. In the future, they like to declare, *everyone* will conduct business in this way. Telegrams and letters will fall out of favour."

I could not repress a smile. Mrs Creevey caught my eye and I saw we shared a common understanding. Just then the door opened and a most striking vision of manhood entered the room.

Tall — even taller than Mr Jesperson — and built on a massive scale with broad shoulders and powerfully muscular limbs, he wore his blonde hair long and sported an impressive beard. He was handsome in a rugged, Nordic fashion that seemed somewhat at odds with his modern clothes, and out of place in this London drawing room. He would have looked more at home in a Viking longboat, or on the battlefield clad in a suit of armour. He was like a hero out of an old-fashioned storybook.

When I saw the look — ardent yet protective — that he turned on the homely, unprepossessing figure of his wife, I liked him even more, and could not imagine how Mr Sims had dared to object to their marriage. She basked in his love and it gave her an unexpected radiance. I felt certain, even before he began to speak, that there could be no truth in Dr Linton's notion regarding any marital unhappiness.

As was usual with somnambulists, Mr Creevey had no memory of where he went or anything else that happened while he slept. In the past, he said, his somnambulism had been caused by stressful events: the death of his younger brother, the death of his mother, hard times at school, money problems, the fear that the woman he loved would reject his suit . . .

"But I have nothing that troubles me now. I am entirely comfortable," he concluded.

Mr Jesperson said, "Your wife has told us that the first incident took place on the night of the third of October. Then the thirteenth, the twenty-fifth and finally the twenty-ninth. In all, you went out on four separate occasions."

"That is correct."

"Can you think of anything — however seemingly insignificant — that links those four days — or nights?" Before he could answer, Mr Jesperson said sharply, "Give it careful thought. There will be something — of that, I feel certain — but it may seem so trivial as to be unworthy of consideration. But even if it is as small a thing as what you ate for breakfast on those days, or a recurring dream, I want to know about it. Do you keep a diary?"

"For appointments — I keep it in my office."

"Nevertheless, take a look, see if it jogs your memory. I'd like you to think about those particular dates and write down everything you remember of what happened on the day before. Every detail that comes to mind, no matter how seemingly insignificant."

Mr Creevey agreed to try.

"Another thing — I want you to keep a personal diary, recording your experiences and impressions each day."

The big man shifted in his seat. "I'm not much for writing."

"Writing is not the issue — pictures would do as well. Record the facts as you like, as an *aide memoire*. It may help us to see why you sleepwalk on one night but not another."

"I could help, my love," said Mrs Creevey. "You know how we sit and talk over the events of the day of an evening . . . I could take notes, and afterwards write it up. After a little while, we may notice a pattern."

"That's it exactly," said Mr Jesperson.

"And if there is no pattern?"

"There will be," he said confidently. "But we will not rely solely on your memory to solve this case. I suspect that when we know *where* you are going, we should be able to deduce *why*."

Mr Creevey looked him in the eye. "You intend to follow me?"

"With your permission."

He sighed, his shoulders slumping, and then nodded. "You must do whatever you think necessary."

"I shall feel better knowing someone is keeping an eye on you," said his wife. She stood up. "I'll see to it that the guest room is made up. Will you stay for dinner, Mr Jesperson?"

"No, thank you; I don't wish to intrude any more than is necessary. I'll go now, with Miss Lane, and return later . . . What time do you go to bed?"

It was agreed that he should come back at eleven o'clock, and we departed — with several slices of cake.

CHAPTER
SIX

An Invitation and a Visitor

Over the next few days we made no significant progress with the case of the somnambulist — who was completely non-ambulatory on the nights that Mr Jesperson spent in his house. Mr Creevey did his best, and searched his memory and his wife's for more details, but nothing he related regarding meals, moods or moving furniture was remotely helpful.

I spoke with the alienist, Dr Linton, and interviewed the household servants about their recollections of those particular days and nights, and Mr Jesperson spoke to Mr Creevey's employees, observed him at work and scoured the shelves of the London Library for works relating to somnambulism, but despite our best efforts we were as much in the dark as ever.

Perhaps this was a case for an alienist or a priest, rather than detectives? It could be that something from the past had stirred in Arthur Creevey's mind, sending him out to grieve before his childhood home, or beside the grave in which his mother, who had died in the month of October, was buried. The month having ended, Creevey might rest in peace for another year.

The brief period of optimism about our future faded as quickly as the coins vanished from my purse. Letters arrived from those old acquaintances I had written to; friendly enough, but not one so much as hinted at any prospect of employment, and only the envelope from Lord Bennington contained anything I could share.

"We are invited to a séance," I informed Mr Jesperson, as we three sat beside the fire. "On Wednesday evening at Lord Bennington's house in Belgrave Square."

This piece of news startled his mother into looking up from her sewing and asking how I came to be acquainted with that noble gentleman.

Mr Jesperson explained: "Lord Bennington is a patron and supporter of the Society for Psychical Research. He financed the last investigation that Miss Lane was involved in."

Turning his attention back to me he asked, in an elaborately casual way, "Any good? Or two hours of hymn-singing interspersed with saccharine remarks from an Indian spirit guide regarding life beyond the veil?"

"I don't think it will be that. The medium is described by Lord B as 'the most amazing psychic and material medium I have ever encountered'. He is called Christopher Clement Chase."

"You don't say! C. C. Chase? What a coup!" Mr Jesperson beamed. "Miss Lane, you *are* a dark horse. From what you've said, I imagined you scarcely knew Lord Bennington, when in truth you are a member of his inner circle."

"No, no, I am not — truly," I hurried to correct him. "Indeed, when I ventured to write to Lord Bennington, I was not at all certain that he would remember me."

"You are too modest," he replied. "*Of course* you would have made an indelible impression. Quite naturally, he wishes for a person of such intelligence and insight to be present when he introduces C. C. Chase to the *crème de la crème* of London spiritualists and psychic investigators. I am honoured that he is willing to include me — I am certain this will be a most exclusive gathering."

"Who is this Mr Chase?" asked his mother.

"If what I have read about him is true, he commands powers the like of which have not been seen since the heyday of Daniel Home. He is an American, but has been in Europe for several years, and it was in France that his powers first came to public attention. Unlike most mediums, he welcomes examination by sceptics and scientists, does not insist on darkness, and makes solid objects move about, appear and disappear. The man has been seen to *levitate*." He shook his head slowly. "I have read a great deal about the ways in which fraudulent mediums create their effects. I have a good idea what to look for. Most of them are very simple tricks. Whatever Mr Chase does must be on a higher level to fool as many scientists and other intelligent observers as he has done in France."

I frowned uneasily. "You think he has fooled them all — Lord Bennington, too?"

"No," he said quickly. "I have no evidence, and therefore no opinion on that subject. I did not mean to imply that he is a fraud — indeed, I admit that I very much hope that he is not. I have always regretted being too young to have witnessed Mr Home in action. And Mr Chase sounds like a medium of more dazzling talents than even Mr Home." Sighing blissfully, his eyes unfocused and he stared into space.

I gazed into the fire with a less happy sigh as I wondered how Lord Bennington would react if my friend exposed his impressive new *protégé* as yet another one of the many frauds that infested the ranks of spiritualists. The Society for Psychical Research had been founded to do proper, unbiased research into the unexplained, but hope was often stronger than reason. Lord Bennington, as I well knew, was eager for scientific proof of the existence of a spirit world and the reality of life beyond death. And even if he had been truly open-minded, no one liked it made public knowledge that they had been deceived.

"Do you need a rest?" Mr Jesperson asked.

I looked around in surprise. "I beg your pardon?"

"Are you tired? Do you need to recover your strength to go on?"

Still puzzled, I shook my head. "I haven't anything particular I need to do just now."

His eyebrows went up in surprise. "*Don't* you? What about replying to Lord Bennington's *extremely* thoughtful and most gratefully received invitation? You must write to him and accept for both of us. What are you waiting for?"

"Jasper!" his mother said reproachfully.

I laughed. I liked it that he didn't stand on ceremony, that he felt comfortable enough to treat me as though I was his sister, and he the brother I'd always wanted. "There's no hurry."

"But if you write it now, I can post it when I go out this evening."

I was in no hurry to go downstairs the next morning, and decided to wait to break my fast until Mr Jesperson had returned. He usually ate breakfast at the Creeveys' house, where the cook had made it her mission to fatten him up, but he did not forget us at home, bringing back small treats including pastries, rolls, muffins or cake.

I enjoyed those treats, but looked forward even more to his company. I admired his mother and was grateful to her, but we were not the most comfortable companions. It was entirely my fault, I knew. She had asked me, several times, to call her Edith, but as I did not extend the same invitation to her, nor explain why, our friendship had foundered.

I had tidied my room and had just started a game of Patience when I heard Mr Jesperson arrive, and the sound of voices in the hall before they moved into the front room made me hesitate. Although I was more than ready for a cup of tea, it occurred to me that although she never made me feel unwelcome, his mother must miss the days when she'd had her son all to herself, so I finished my game and found other reasons to delay before I went downstairs.

Entering the front room, I saw at once that the female seated near the fire with Mr Jesperson was not his mother. Her back was to me, but even before she turned I knew who it was, and my stomach clenched in sick surprise as I recognised the blue silk dress and the springy black curls escaping from a jaunty new tri-cornered hat.

Miss Gabrielle Fox turned and gave me the mocking, triumphant smile I knew so well; one eye was narrowed and gleaming, the other was hidden, as usual, by a patch. Today, the patch was of violet silk, a hue that complemented her hat. I felt myself tense defensively, and spoke before she could.

"What are you doing here?" Realising how rude that must sound, I quickly apologised. "Forgive me. I wasn't expecting a visitor." Unsettled, I turned my accusing gaze on my partner.

"Why didn't you let me know?"

He gave an unconcerned shrug. "Would you have me ring a bell? I had no idea where you might be. I met Miss Fox on the doorstep; intercepted her before she could knock."

I looked around the room, wanting to escape her sharp gaze — and his. I must be cool with her, but perfectly calm.

"Have you offered Miss Fox any refreshment?" I asked, seeing no sign of the tea tray. "I haven't had a cup of tea yet myself," I added.

"Forgive me. I was so interested in your story, I forgot the social niceties," he said to Gabrielle.

My heart nearly stopped as I wondered what *story* she had told him.

"Tea would be lovely." She twinkled at him before turning back to me. "You may remember how I like it. China, if you have it, a little sugar, but no milk."

"I'll get it," said Mr Jesperson before I could make a move.

My heart sank. To be left alone with the clever Miss Fox was exactly what I'd feared. Well, I must move past that. Steeling myself, I sat down beside her on the seat Mr Jesperson had abandoned. "So, what is this *story* you have been telling Mr Jesperson?"

"My, you are businesslike. Well, I shouldn't be surprised. You must have a great many clients and it would never do to relax, and simply *chat* with them as if you were old friends . . . even if they *are* old friends." She pouted reproachfully.

Although I wanted to take exception to her claim of friendship, I tightened my lips and said nothing.

"I expect you will be very good at solving crimes," she said. "That's what I said to Mrs Traill when she told me of your new venture. And that is why I came here today."

"To ask us to solve a crime?"

She widened her eye. "I hope it is not a crime, but it is certainly a mystery. Did you ever encounter the De Beauvoir sisters?"

The name was familiar, bearing a hazy impression of two identical and rather insipidly pretty faces. "Twins, and very young," I said, frowning as I pursued the memory. "I think they do a sort of mind-reading act."

71

"No act. They are quite prodigiously talented, with a genuine gift of clairvoyance."

"And what have they to do with your mystery?"

"They *are* the mystery; at least, they are part of it." She moistened her lips and leaned a little closer to me. "They disappeared almost three weeks ago. Vanished. They went up to bed at the usual time, with no hint of anything wrong, but in the morning their beds were empty and the girls have not been seen nor heard from since."

"How old are they?"

"Just sixteen."

"Did the family go to the police?"

She shook her head gravely, and I guessed they had reason to fear a scandal. Her next words confirmed my thought.

"A certain young man has also gone missing. I don't know how closely you follow events in spiritualist circles these days, but he is quite a star, recently arrived from Paris, expecting to take London by storm —"

"Christopher Clement Chase?"

She looked at me, astonished, her eye blinking rapidly. "Certainly not! No — I had heard rumours that Mr Chase is now in London, but — why do you say that?"

Interesting, I thought. Was it possible *she* was not invited to the séance; that she had fallen out of favour with Lord Bennington and his set? "I suppose I have heard the same rumours as you, so when you mentioned 'a star, recently arrived from Paris' his name came to mind."

"Mr Chase has not disappeared, too?"

"I have no reason to think so. Before you arrived here today, I had heard nothing of *any* disappearances. Please, go on."

She wriggled a little more deeply into her chair as she composed herself. "The man I speak of is French: Monsieur Ribaud. He is a materialising medium, reported to have great powers. I have never seen him myself. I understand he is about four-and-twenty, attractive and charming, and only a week before the De Beauvoir sisters vanished they were witnessed in conversation with him. I don't mean to imply there was anything improper — it was at a social gathering in a respectable private house and they were well-chaperoned — but one or the other of the young ladies kept close beside him for almost the whole evening, and the general impression received by anyone who noticed was that there was a strong, mutual attraction."

"To and from *one* of the sisters?"

"Ah, well." She gave me an amused, conspiratorial look. "The De Beauvoir family certainly hoped they might return from Gretna Green — or Paris, or wherever people elope to these days — with one sister now legally Madame Ribaud, the other happy to have acted as her chaperone. They couldn't even mind that the fellow was French, not when they bear the name of De Beauvoir."

"But if they were *both* in love with him, and he married neither . . ." I raised my eyebrow suggestively.

Gabrielle smirked. "The more days that went by without a word, the more it seemed the girls were lost to respectability, living under assumed names somewhere with their dastardly seducer.

"And yet, *no one* has heard anything more of Monsieur Ribaud. What of his plans to impress English spiritualist circles with his ability to materialise objects from thin air? Never having seen him perform, I am unable to judge, but his reputation is good. He'd done a few private sittings — I had expected to attend one before he so suddenly disappeared — and he was booked for a week in the Egyptian Hall, with the possibility of another show at the London Pavilion. Would he really throw all that away — the chance of money and fame — to run away with two young misses?"

"I don't suppose he has a private fortune?"

"Far from it! And the girls have taken nothing — literally, not even a bag between them. Like most people who must try to live by such talents, he relies on wealthier friends, and as I understand it, none of them, not in France, nor in England, has heard from him in weeks. It's as if the three young people simply vanished into thin air."

"Perhaps they went to America under assumed names and are now astonishing audiences in New York or Baltimore," I suggested.

"Leave a sure thing here to begin all over again as strangers in a strange land?"

I could imagine many situations ranging from the prosaic to the gothic that might make any sixteen-year-old girl determined to run away, especially with a gallant protector.

"That's what *I* thought," said Gabrielle, as if she'd read my mind. "I thought: depend upon it, he thinks he's rescued them from the family prison, and they're making a new life in another country. Soon enough we'll be getting reports from Boston or Montreal about this astonishing psychic trio. But when I learned that Hilda Jessop was missing, too, I knew I was wrong and the De Beauvoir family was wrong. They had no evidence for a romance — the girls had only met their supposed seducer once before they disappeared. They assumed a connection because they vanished the same week that he did."

"Wait — you're saying there is no connection? That's —"

She narrowed her eye impatiently. "Of course there's a connection. Pay attention! But they made the *wrong* connection — as did I, before I knew. You see — it wasn't only one young man and two young ladies who went missing. There were *four* who vanished. In one month, four psychic mediums have disappeared without trace."

CHAPTER
SEVEN

A Missing Medium

Mr Jesperson entered with the tea tray as I tried to recall what I knew of Miss Hilda Jessop.

She had hovered on the edges of spiritualist circles for years, her age now in that indeterminate region between forty and sixty. At one time, it was said, she had been considered a most compelling soothsayer, credited with predicting events which subsequently came to pass, but then she had been caught cheating — paying servants for information, even bribing one to steal a letter — and that was the end of her promising career. Yet she had clung to those who would shun her; perhaps she simply had nowhere else to go. Which naturally raised the question: if she had nowhere to go, where had she gone?

"Who reported Miss Jessop as missing?"

Miss Fox replied promptly. "I did. But the police took no more interest once they learned she had not paid her rent for several months. It's true, the midnight flit is not unknown to her. But the family with whom she is — was — boarding are fond of her, and generous; they never would have pressed her for money. There was no reason for her to leave."

Unobtrusively, Mr Jesperson set down a cup of black tea on the occasional table nearest to Miss Fox. He raised his eyebrows at me and indicated the teapot.

I shook my head and leaned in closer to Miss Fox. "When did you learn she was missing?"

She sat back with a sigh, noticed the tea and sent a smile in Mr Jesperson's direction before she replied. "Oh . . . There was a gathering last Tuesday night — All Hallows Eve, you know. The Traills were the hosts and Hilda was expected, but never arrived. Thinking she might be unwell, I called on her the next day — at least, I tried. The children in the house told me she had not been seen since Sunday, when she had been observed setting off for church. Chapel, I should say. No one could say when, or if, she had returned. Fearing the worst, I begged the landlady — Mrs Bicker or Beaker, something like that — to unlock her door." She paused for a sip of tea, and a faint, pained expression flitted across her face. I understood: the tea was Indian, not Chinese.

Sighing, she set the cup down and continued her tale. "Hilda was not there, but all her possessions were. Her clothes, her books, all her pathetic trinkets, the silver-backed brush and mirror set on the dressing table — and her cards."

I felt a chill. No one, running away from debt, would leave behind anything that could be pawned. And her cards, a special deck that had come all the way from Egypt, she would surely have kept. "You think something happened on her way to — or from — church?"

"No. As soon as I saw her room I knew — Di, the bed was unmade. Could you imagine Hilda leaving for chapel without first making her bed?" She reached for my hand, and I did not resist. "You will help me find her?"

"Of course." No other answer was possible. I knew this was not the sort of case we should be accepting, with our need for paying work as desperate as it was. Miss Jessop was one of the forgotten souls of this world, without family or wealthy friends to pay for her return. But I knew I must do my best to ensure she was not lost without a trace.

"Thank you," Gabrielle murmured, pressing my hand. Then, to my great surprise, she released it to dip into her bag, bringing out a beaded purse. "Is there a daily rate, or do you charge by the hour?"

I was ready to say we'd discuss payment later — a "later" that might never come — but fortunately Mr Jesperson spoke first. "We charge a standard daily fee for our services, and because there is no way to predict how long an investigation may last, it is usual to ask for a small retainer in advance . . . if you've no objection?"

"Your hand," said Gabrielle to me, and — when I held it out, uncertain what she intended — shook a pile of coins into my palm. When I had to close my fingers to stop them spilling over, she snapped the purse shut. "I hope that will be enough for now, but do ask if you require more."

I was startled, not by her generosity but by the fact that she had so much money on her. "Thank you," I murmured. "This is much more than —"

"You needn't worry — there will be more to come."

"I wasn't worried," I said, holding fast to the silver. "Only surprised. When we last met —"

"My fortunes have improved," she said swiftly. "A haunted house is nothing to this. I have found a prodigy — someone with such talents — a psychic genius! I should love you to meet her. But perhaps you've lost interest in psychical research."

"*I* am certainly most interested in that subject," said Mr Jesperson, eyes alight, reclaiming her attention with his burst of natural enthusiasm.

Gabrielle looked from him to me with her little cat smile. "Then may I invite you both to a demonstration of the most remarkable talents of a newcomer to London — my *protégée*, Signora Fiorella Gallo — tomorrow evening in the West London Methodist Mission Hall." Reaching into her bag again, she flourished two bits of pasteboard. "Complimentary tickets. I do hope you will help me spread the word. There are still some seats available for purchase at the door, sixpence a head."

Miss Jessop's last address was in Longridge Road, a very short walk from the Earl's Court underground station. When I got there, I was surprised to find that it was not the shabby boarding house I had expected, with rates listed in the front window, but a terrace of yellow brick and white stucco, built so recently or maintained so well that the air had not yet turned the facade to the smudgy grey so typical of London.

Still half-expecting to learn that Gabrielle had given me the wrong address, I stepped up to the door. I was alone, having agreed with Mr Jesperson that the most efficient use of our time was for me to question other residents of the boarding house about Miss Jessop whilst he went in pursuit of more information about Monsieur Ribaud.

My knock was answered by a severe-looking person wearing a starched white apron over a plain dark dress. Her face softened when I identified myself as a friend of Miss Jessop's.

"Oh! Is she — is there some news?"

"I'm afraid not. A mutual friend commissioned me to investigate."

"Would that be Miss Fox?"

"Yes."

When she still only stared, her expression most tragic, I was forced to ask: "May I come in? I'd like to speak to the other residents, to everyone who knew Miss Jessop."

She gave a start. "Oh, goodness, what must you think of me, keeping you standing outside in the cold and damp? Please, if you'll wait in the hall, I'll see if Mrs Ballantyne is available."

I looked around the entrance hall and saw no sign that this was anything but a private family home. There were perhaps an unusual number of umbrellas in the stand behind the door. Otherwise, the boots, shoes and coats on display suggested there might be as many as half a dozen children.

Before long the servant returned to admit me to a parlour and the presence of Mrs Ballantyne, a motherly-looking woman built on ample lines. She was surprised, yet clearly relieved to discover my professional interest in the affair.

"Thank goodness someone is taking this seriously. The police will do nothing — they say there is no evidence that Miss Jessop did not leave of her own free will. But why should she do that? This is her *home*."

"Miss Fox told me the police thought she might have left to avoid paying rent."

"That's absurd!" She looked on the verge of jumping out of her chair and rushing down to the local police station to give them a piece of her mind.

"Did she owe you money?"

"Yes." She sank back and made a graceful, regretful gesture. "But I had told her often enough that she would *always* have a home here, because of our lasting debt of gratitude — we owe her more than she could ever owe us."

She told me the story. Jumbled and not always easy to follow, it included a careless nursemaid, an ember from the nursery fire and a baby just beginning to crawl who saw the pretty flame . . .

Miss Jessop, laying out her customary, solitary card game in her room, had a vision and rushed pell-mell down the stairs and into the nursery, arriving in time to snatch up the infant, still unharmed. In Mrs Ballantyne's dramatic imagination, Miss Jessop had prevented the house from burning down and saved them all; at the very least, her action had saved the baby from a nasty burn, so her gratitude was understandable.

"How long has Miss Jessop been living with you?"

"A year in September. She'd had to leave her other place . . . in fact, she left under a cloud, owing several months' rent."

I remembered the dismal lodging house in a back street close by Paddington station where I had met Hilda Jessop — it was a far cry from these pleasant surroundings, and it was far from usual — in my experience — for people fleeing debts to move up in the world.

"How did she come here?"

"It was Mr Thwaite — the Reverend Thwaite — who suggested her."

"Mr Thwaite is the minister of your church?"

She looked amused. "Not *mine*, dear. We're C of E. Miss Jessop is Methodist, a member of Mr Thwaite's little flock."

"And how did you come to know Mr Thwaite, if you don't mind my asking?"

"He's another of our boarding lodgers."

"How many do you have?"

"Three on full board — that's Mr Thwaite and Miss Arnold, and poor, dear Miss Jessop — and then there's the lodger, Mr William Wallace, who dines at his club, or with relatives, and is often away on business as he is just now."

"I would like to speak to them all, if I may."

"Of course. I think you'll find both Mr Thwaite and Miss Arnold are in. As for Mr Wallace, well, I don't know when he'll return, but he won't be able to tell you anything about Miss Jessop. He's hardly ever here, and when he is he keeps to himself."

"Was he here when she disappeared?"

She frowned in thought. "I'm not certain . . . no, he was away from Friday morning until sometime on Tuesday, that's right."

"I understand one of your children saw her last?"

With a look of distress she launched into an explanation of why, although the children had seen her heading off for her usual Sunday morning worship, no one had been there to witness when — or if — Miss Jessop returned. The Ballantynes had gone to visit relatives for the day, so instead of the usual hot meal, Mrs Ballantyne had left a selection of cold meats, cheese, bread and salad for her boarders, but returned to find it untouched. Miss Arnold had gone out to eat with her aunt and uncle, and Mr Thwaite — who could confirm that Miss Jessop had attended the morning service — had been royally entertained by some of his parishioners, and thus was too full to want anything more when he returned to Longridge Road at about eight o'clock.

"Perhaps Miss Jessop was invited out to dine?"

Mrs Ballantyne had never known such a thing. And the fact that Miss Jessop had not touched the cold collation proved nothing, for she had a small appetite, and could be forgetful when it came to meal times — in fact, it was not unusual for her to lose all track of time as she read, dozed, or laid out her special deck of cards. Sometimes, Mrs Ballantyne would send up one of the children to knock on her door if she did not appear at the table.

"Did you do that on Monday?"

"I don't recall . . . I've been so busy . . . although I do remember I went up myself on Tuesday. The door was locked and I supposed she had gone out. It was only when her friend called the next day that I realised there was anything wrong."

"May I see her room?" I asked.

"Of course. I have left everything as it was."

Miss Jessop's room was at the top of the house with two others, one the residence of the aforementioned boarder, Miss Arnold, and the third shared between the cook and the woman who had opened the door to me: the general servant Mrs Ballantyne referred to as Bicker.

As Mrs Ballantyne was about to open the door I asked, "Was the door locked from within or without?"

She looked blank. "How should I know?"

"Well . . . if the key was not left in the keyhole —"

"No, it certainly was not."

"Did you find it in the room?"

"I never thought to look for it."

"Do you mind if I search the room?"

"I'm certain poor, dear Miss Jessop would have no objection."

The room, at the front of the house, was of a reasonable size and comfortably furnished. The bed was still unmade and I felt chilled at the sight of it. Could there be a plainer indication of sudden flight, or even abduction, than this single bed, covers thrown back, pillow still showing the hollow where a head had lain?

Apart from the bed, the room was tidy. I saw the items Gabrielle had mentioned: the brush and mirror, a shelf of books. Her cards — that famous pack of cards — were wrapped in a dark purple silk scarf on the same shelf, but something was missing.

"Her Bible."

"She would have taken it to church," said Mrs Ballantyne. "I'm sure she always did."

So we were back to the original question: did she return on Sunday afternoon, or not? Had she set out for church, Bible in hand, without making her bed?

I looked inside the wardrobe and saw that Miss Jessop's selection of garments was nearly as slender as my own, and more aged. Rusty blacks predominated. I saw no coat, but one pair of shoes: a pair of sensible, lace-up leather ankle boots, soles well-worn. Beside them there was a collapsed, empty carpet bag and a hat box.

I asked Mrs Ballantyne if she could enumerate and describe what was missing. "I presume Miss Jessop had two hats . . . and another pair of shoes? Do you remember what she was wearing the last time you saw her?"

My questions flustered the lady. "Oh, dear . . . I don't think so . . . I'm afraid I never took much notice of what she wore — she always looked the same, respectably dressed, of course, if rather shabby." She brightened, seeing a chance to be useful. "Her coat is missing! She had a dark brown overcoat. And she would probably have worn her brown hat — a different shade of brown from the coat; it had a wide brim. Oh, and there was a green scarf . . ."

I picked up the pillow, but there was nothing beneath it, and nothing but the rumpled sheet beneath the blankets. I looked under the bed where two down-at-heel slippers lay. I looked inside the drawers where she kept her gloves and other small items of apparel. There was a pile of envelopes and a pad of writing paper, a pen and ink, no diary, but an address book. I looked through it, hoping for a note suggestive of some suspicious relationship with one of the names, but it was unhelpful. I searched every corner of the room and every inch of the floor in fruitless pursuit of a clue. But if Miss Jessop had been taken from her bed, her abductors had not been so obliging as to drop an initialled handkerchief or a foreign cigarette to help us with our deductions, and at last I had to give it up.

I kept — with Mrs Ballantyne's permission — Hilda Jessop's address book. Possibly someone listed in its pages might have information that would be of more help than the vague smile and apologies offered by Miss Arnold, the lodger across the hall, who had seen and heard nothing from her neighbour's room on the days and nights in question. "She was always quiet and kept to herself. She never had callers."

The Reverend Mr Thwaite confirmed that Miss Jessop had attended his morning service, and that she had not arrived late, nor seemed rushed or flustered — I asked this, thinking of the unmade bed — and said she had been "at peace" when she departed. This struck me as an infelicitous turn of phrase, but I did not consider the spindly, enthusiastic young vicar deserved anyone's suspicion. William Wallace — despite his noble name — seemed the only potential villain in this household, but probably he would clear himself as soon as I met him. I left a note for him and asked to speak to the maid.

She gave me a suspicious look. "My maid?"

"The servant who answered the door?"

"Bicker. But why speak to her?"

I didn't know if she suspected me of trying to steal her servant, or implicate her. "I couldn't help noticing Miss Arnold is a trifle deaf . . . and as you told me Bicker sleeps on the same floor —"

"I'm sure Bicker would have told me if she heard anything unusual."

"Maybe it was not unusual. *If* you don't mind?"

She sighed, giving in. "Very well. But don't keep her too long — and please, try not to upset her. Bicker is the best general we've ever had. We couldn't run the house without her. But if she thinks she's been insulted —"

"I certainly won't insult her. As for upset, I should think Miss Jessop's unexplained disappearance is the *most* upsetting thing." I did not add my opinion that Bicker was more likely to take offence if I went away *without* questioning her.

Mrs Ballantyne rang for her general servant and then, after explaining what I wanted, left us alone together in the parlour.

I sat, but then, as Bicker wouldn't, stood up again. "I'll try not to keep you long," I said. "I just have a few questions: did you see Miss Jessop on Sunday at all?"

"No, Miss. Sunday is my day off. I go to the early service, so I'm usually out of the house before anyone else is stirring."

"What time do you come back?"

"That Sunday I was back in my room before eight o'clock. Between seven and eight."

"And you did not see Miss Jessop when you returned?"

"No, but she was in her room."

When I raised my eyebrows she explained: "I saw the light under her door."

I felt a rush of excitement at this, the first evidence that Hilda Jessop had returned to this house after she left it on Sunday morning. "And did you hear anything? Any sounds from her room, or anything at all in the night?"

She shook her head. "Nothing. I'm a sound sleeper; not much disturbs me, and just as well because Cook snores like the . . . like I don't know what. It seemed like any other night — to me."

She gave me a significant look; I did not know why, but it seemed to call for a response, so I said, "But it was not just any other night for Miss Jessop."

Bicker nodded as if we understood each other, and said, "She expected it."

"What?"

"To be taken. She thought it would be a *good* thing — she wasn't afraid. She told me I shouldn't be unhappy for her because she would be in a better place."

I frowned, trying to make sense of this. "When did she tell you that?"

"A week before she went, nearly. That horrid child had just —" She snapped her mouth shut. "Never mind. Suffice to say, I was not pleased by the way the children were allowed to run riot. The eldest boy was especially disrespectful, although they all — "

"You were upset . . ." I said, to get her back on course.

"Yes! And I had made up my mind to give notice when Miss Jessop — ever so kind to me she was, the dear lady — offered to read the cards. You know she did that every now and again?"

I indicated that I did.

"She said she'd had an idea I was considering changing my circumstances, and the cards might help me to know if I was making the right choice. She wouldn't charge me for it, neither. It was an act of pure charity, so it was."

Wary though I was of upsetting the easily overturned Bicker, I decided to take a risk and interrupt.

"She *is* a very kind woman," I said warmly. "But I thought she had said something about her *own* fate?"

"Oh, that was after the reading. I was ever so grateful — she stopped me from making a great mistake, because something very good is going to happen to me here, in this very house, I'll meet someone —" She turned quite pink and must have remembered I was a virtual stranger and not someone to be entrusted with the details of her romantic fancies, for she dropped the subject and said hastily, "I wondered if she always knew what to do, and asked her if she read the cards for herself. She said no, she didn't like to do that, but sometimes she had visions — they came without asking. Then she told me she'd had one very recently of an angel gathering her into his arms and bearing her off to heaven. She said it was so lovely that she wasn't frightened at all, though it must mean her time was near. I nearly wept, but she told me I mustn't mind because *she* didn't, as the vision meant she would be going to her reward and there was nothing to fear at the end. That's why, when I saw you at the door, and you said you had come about her, I thought they must have found her body, because her soul is sure to be in heaven with the angels, just as she saw it in her vision."

CHAPTER
EIGHT

The Other Missing Mediums

"No one took her. She left suddenly of her own will, quietly and as quickly as if she were fleeing a fire — although she did pause long enough to lock the door behind her. The bed was unmade but her nightdress was missing, which suggests she only paused long enough to put on shoes and her coat and hat before she left. Apart from her Bible, she seems to have left everything — not that she had much to leave." I concluded my explanation, back in Gower Street again.

"She walked out of her life because she had an angelic visitation? But then where did she go? It is not so easy to get to Heaven." Mr Jesperson sighed thoughtfully and leaned back in his chair, tilting it on to its back legs. "I think you are right, there is no evidence of *abduction*. Not in any violent manner. Yet someone may have helped her on her way. And surely *someone* in this big, wicked city knows where she is now."

He returned his feet and the chair's front legs to the floor. "Our Frenchman also appears to have gone away of his own accord." He told me what he had learned.

Monsieur Ribaud had been staying at the Albemarle Hotel. Early in the evening of October 5th, he had walked out of the hotel and had not been seen by anyone since. The chambermaid could attest that his bed had not been slept in when she entered the room the following morning. His luggage and clothes were all there — everything except the clothes he had been wearing and whatever he carried in his pockets.

His friends became concerned when he failed to attend a dinner party on the 6th, and a report to the police was made on the 7th. However, as there was no evidence of foul play, the police were not inclined to expend any effort looking for an adult French citizen who'd simply left without paying his hotel bill. The fact that he'd left without his luggage, and abandoned a theatrical venture described as a "sure-fire money-maker" cut no ice with them: maybe he'd had an attack of stage fright, or common sense, and decided to cut and run before he could be unmasked as the fraud he undoubtedly was.

"Materialists all, those police detectives," said Mr Jesperson with a whimsical smile. "By all accounts, Ribaud was anticipating a thorough conquest of London. He had letters of introduction to Lord Bennington, who had invited him to a little soiree in Belgrave Square. It was there on the first of October that Ribaud was introduced to the Misses De Beauvoir and many of the big names in London's spiritualist community — and I hear that all were quite dazzled by the psychic talents he displayed."

"The first of October?" I took him up on the date, remembering Gabrielle's mention of a social gathering in early October. "I wonder if that was the *only* meeting between him and the young ladies. If he went missing on the fifth . . ."

He looked at once more alert, like a dog catching a scent. "We must ask Miss Fox."

"*She* doesn't know," I snapped. "Miss Fox is rarely precise about details — 'early October', she says, and then it was 'about a week' later that the girls went missing. It is a weakness in her. She forgets or confuses names, too," I added, recalling how she'd mistaken the name of the servant for that of the lady of the house.

Mr Jesperson gave me a mischievous look. "But she didn't forget *your* name, did she, Miss Lane? You must have been quite close, to have shared the deep, dark secret of your Christian name with her. Although it's not quite right to call it a Christian name, is it? Not pagan, but Classical. I don't know why you are not proud of it, and even your old friend abbreviates it to a single, dusty syllable. Don't you miss hearing it said in full —"

"No." I wished I could take his chaffing lightly, but this was my weakness: the name my father the Classical scholar had chosen to bestow remained a sore point with me.

" 'Foam born'. A lovely name."

"But utterly inappropriate."

"I don't agree. Although Athene perhaps would be better."

"Athene is the name of my sister, who is neither grey-eyed nor wise." I stared down at my notes. "Shall we get back to business? As Miss Fox is unable to

93

supply any accurate details about when the two young ladies went missing, we must approach the family. Whether they know it or not, they need our help."

A brief discussion followed about how best to win them over. If they were unwilling to inform the police, why would they talk to us? Lies could get us into trouble. But what was the truth?

"We'll make it up as we go along," said Mr Jesperson. Leaping up from his chair, he added, "I think better on my feet, don't you? Come along, get your coat; we should be able to fit in a bit more investigating before I must resume my duties guarding a non-ambulating somnambulist."

The De Beauvoir family resided in St John's Wood, in a handsome Italianate villa. The maid who answered the door stared with frank curiosity before announcing, "Madam is not receiving."

"Perhaps you would tell your master —"

She refused to take Mr Jesperson's card, putting her hands behind her back and shaking her head. "If it's *Mr* De Beauvoir you want, you'll find him at his club."

"And that would be —?"

But, clearly, anyone who had to ask was not to be trusted. Without another word, she took a step backwards and shut the door on us.

Mr Jesperson and I exchanged a look. He seized the shiny brass knocker and gave several hard raps.

The same young woman opened it, scowling. "Clear off, or I'll —"

"See here, you had better run along and tell *someone* in the household that we are friends of Lord Bennington. And we have news."

She still frowned, but the name of Lord Bennington had touched a chord. "What's it about, then? The young ladies?"

"Yes."

"Wait here."

We stood a good five minutes in the chilly air — at least it felt cleaner on this suburban avenue than it did in the closer streets of the city — before the door opened again to reveal a rather haughty-looking young man of nineteen or twenty years.

"Who are you? Why have you come bothering my mother? What's this about?"

"Mr De Beauvoir, I presume? Allow me to introduce myself. I am Jasper Jesperson, and this is my partner, Miss Lane. We are private investigators."

A look of alarm flickered across his features. "What! Who hired you?"

"If you'll let me explain . . . perhaps inside?"

"And have you 'investigate' our house? I think not!"

"We've been hired by the friends of Monsieur Ribaud, who has not been seen since he left his hotel in Piccadilly on the fifth of October."

"I have never met anyone by that name, I promise you." I thought he was being careful not to say he'd never *heard* of him.

Mr Jesperson dipped his head slightly. "I understand your sisters attended a gathering in the home of Lord Bennington at which —"

Nostrils flaring, the young man burst out, "What do you mean? Can't girls go to a party? It was highly respectable. What are you trying to imply?"

"Four days after that party, Ribaud disappeared. His friends fear he was kidnapped. Some little while afterwards, your sisters, too, went missing."

The young Mr De Beauvoir threw his head back and glared, so that he looked, with his flared nostrils, like a frightened horse. "No! That's a damned lie. Take it back, you contemptible —"

"Do you mean to say the Misses De Beauvoir are *not* missing?"

"They did not run off with that little frog."

"I never meant to suggest they did. But his friends are concerned about Monsieur Ribaud's disappearance, and when we heard two others who had been at the same gathering were also missing —"

"Well, they're not." He settled down, still glaring, but in a sulky, smouldering way.

"We were misinformed?"

"You were."

"Delighted to hear it. It makes our task easier." Mr Jesperson smiled. "Perhaps *they* will be able to shed some light on events as witnesses. They may have noticed something at the party. If we might have a word with one or both of the young ladies now . . .?"

"They're not here."

"But —"

"They're in Somerset. Went to visit our old aunt. Nursing her. Poorly. Our aunt, not the girls, of course. May not be back 'til Christmas. Or New Year. Sorry I can't help." Less smoothly but with more finality than the maid, the young man backed into his house and swung the door shut in our baffled faces.

There was clearly no point in knocking again; this family was too frightened of scandal to admit the girls might be in danger.

"This was a wasted journey," I grumbled, as we turned and walked back the way we had come. "We still don't know the date they went missing, or even their names."

"Wait." Taking off his hat, Mr Jesperson handed it to me, then dug into his coat pocket for what looked like an old rag. After he had shaken and stretched it and popped it on top of his head, it was revealed as a shabby flat cap. "You'd better look after my coat as well — far too nice for a butcher's boy."

"What are you doing?"

"Off to chat up the cook. I hope she likes to gossip. You can't stand around freezing on a street corner, but I noticed a tea room by the station . . . here." He gave me a coin. "You've got your return ticket. If I'm delayed, go home without me."

"But your coat!"

"Oh, don't worry about me; I've my own internal combustion engine, keeps me warm when I'm on the scent. And you may see me sooner than you think, sent off by the cook with a flea in my ear." He grinned, and I could see he did not believe for an instant that he might fail.

I envied his self-confidence and wondered, as I trudged off on my own, what it would be like to have such utter confidence in your ability to charm perfect strangers that you *expected* other people to like you — what it would feel like to believe that whatever good things befell you, they were no more than you deserved.

Yet I had been loved, once upon a time, when I was a child, before I was Miss Lane. It had been out of love, not a reflection of grandiose expectations, that my father had named us Athene and Aphrodite. She was always Athene — "Theeny" from my childish lips — but no one ever called me Aphrodite, or anything like it — with the exception of my mother when she was in a temper. When I was a baby, my sister called me Lamb or Lambie. Then I was Lamb Pie, soon shortened to Pie — and Pie is how I was known to all, until I was nearly eleven years old. Until, with my father's death, everything changed.

Afterwards, only my sister called me Pie, and I became Aphrodite — a bad joke of a name to be sneered and snickered at, and mispronounced. I was grateful when I could be simply "Miss Lane".

It had been Gabrielle's notion to call me Di. Di was so close to Pie, I liked it; I felt known again.

The tea room Mr Jesperson had noticed turned out to be part of the A.B.C. chain, so it was clean and welcoming, and I knew the girls who worked there would not object if I fingered over my one cup of tea for hours. The smell of fresh bread was so tempting that I had a struggle not to order a bun, but I was determined to be economical; I would suffer pangs of guilt far worse than hunger if I indulged myself.

People came and went. An old lady at a table near mine ordered a plate of eggs with ham, and the smell, accompanied by her obvious pleasure in the meal, added to my feelings of martyrdom.

A man dashed in. He was dressed in a striking blue coat with a wide black fur collar, but a floppy grey hat — the sort of thing an artist might wear for shade when painting in the open air — made it impossible to see his face. From his movements, I thought him young rather than old. He did not sit down at a table, nor did he make any attempt to attract the attention of a waitress, but went swiftly to the glazed wooden cabinet in the far corner of the room and shut himself in to make a telephone call.

Not for nothing do they call them "silence cabinets" — not a sound reached me. His back was turned to me, so I was unable to practice lip reading — another skill my partner had been eager to teach me — but still I continued to gaze at the cabinet as I swirled the last dregs of tea in my cup, and tried to think if there was anyone I could call on the telephone, apart from our landlord and Arthur Creevey. By the time — about two minutes later — that the caller emerged, giving me a good look at a bearded, handsome yet rather dissolute and heavily-tanned face, I had not been able to add another name to that short list. I could only imagine using the telephone in an emergency, and I could not think of any emergency in which my first instinct should be to run to the nearest A.B.C.

Nevertheless, I was just thinking about stepping inside the cabinet and pretending to use the telephone

— it might put off the need to return to Gower Street alone by another five minutes — when, at last, I caught sight of my partner's tall, lanky figure, the red-gold of his hair glowing like fire beneath the street lamps in the thickening dusk. I made haste to pay for my tea and met him at the door.

Waiting on the platform for our train, once more wrapped in his coat, his curls crushed under the brim of his hat, Mr Jesperson told me what he had learned.

"The young ladies answer to the names of Amelia and Bedelia. Bedelia is the bold one, Amelia does what her sister commands. They were still in the bosom of their family for the evening meal on Friday 13th of October. *Friday 13th*," he repeated in dramatic, hollow tones. "The servants are all sufficiently superstitious that there can be no mistake about it. It was either that night, or the morning of Saturday 14th that the girls left the house unnoticed. They did not appear for breakfast on Saturday morning, but no one thought anything of it. It was only after midday, when the maid was unable to get into their locked bedroom that anyone was alarmed."

"Another locked door. Was the key missing?"

"The key was in the lock — on the inside. Their bedroom is at the back of the house, overlooking the garden. A set of French doors opens on to a balcony and it would be an easy matter for any reasonably athletic person to climb up or down. Perhaps it was the thought of the balcony scene in Shakespeare's play about star-crossed lovers that led to the idea of an elopement? Yet neither of the girls had an acknowledged lover, and until very recently they had led such sheltered lives that it was hard to imagine any contenders for the part. Still, they had met Monsieur Ribaud . . . and he was no longer around to protest his innocence."

Our train pulled into the station amidst much noise and a gritty swirl of smoke, and as it arrived, I made the connection that had been hovering at the edges of my thoughts.

"The dates," I said urgently. "Not the 5th, but the 13th and the 29th."

He was already there. "Nights when Arthur Creevey went sleepwalking."

But although we discussed it for the rest of our journey, we could make no more sense of it. Could these events be connected? But if they were, then why was it only two out of the three dates? Had any *other* medium gone missing on October 25th, the one other night when Mr Creevey walked in his sleep? Or was it all meaningless coincidence?

CHAPTER
NINE

Magnetic Demonstration

A Methodist Mission Hall might seem an unlikely venue for a demonstration of spiritualism and psychic powers, but Methodism, from its beginnings, has a strong affinity with ghosts — John Wesley's own family had lived in a haunted house.

Or so Miss Fox, herself a member of the Methodist community, had told me.

Other members of the congregation might object to the use of their hall for a demonstration that had more to do with entertainment than with salvation, but if she'd been able to get it at a reduced rate, or free, Gabrielle would have thought it worth the risk. Like Jasper Jesperson, my old friend had a great deal of faith in her ability to talk herself out of trouble and win supporters by sheer force of personality.

My partner and I took the omnibus most of the way, as it was not a pleasant evening for a stroll. A greasy, choking, brown fog had been gathering all day and now came swirling round corners, sneaking out of alleyways to briefly blind the unwary pedestrian, stinging the eyes, catching at the throat, confusing and disorienting, following and clinging like an evil, reeking ghost.

I hoped Gabrielle had sold most of her tickets in advance, for I did not think there would be much demand at the door from people attracted by the hand-lettered poster I saw drooping limply from a lamp post. Anyone sitting comfortably by their own fireside would take one look at the smoky pall of the street and decide to stay home, no matter how interesting the "magnetic" talents of Signora Fiorella Gallo promised to be.

We arrived neither early nor late, and presented our tickets to the dragon guarding the door: an elderly lady in a rusty black dress and an antique bonnet. I recognised her — or at least the bonnet — from similar situations in the past, but when I wished her good evening she stared past me quite deliberately. In her day, I think they called it "the cut direct", and it was both unexpected and painful. I wondered what she had heard about me, what rumours had spread since I'd last had any formal connection with the SPR. It was even more painful to think that my one-time friend and companion might have been the source of some falsehood about me.

The thought was still in my mind when Gabrielle herself appeared before us in a dress I had not seen before: a full-skirted swirl of lustrous dark green silk. Her eye-patch matched her skirt, and her thick black hair had been confined in a net of ribbons studded with tiny bits of mirror-glass that flashed and winked as they caught the light.

"My friends!" she cried, with as much emotion as if months had passed since our last meeting. "I'm so glad you came! I wish I could stop and talk with you, but —"

"You have too many other things on your mind," I said, as Mr Jesperson murmured, "Of course."

"Sit anywhere. I'm sorry the seats are not more comfortable, and the surroundings more elegant, but . . . needs must." She nodded at the rows of hard wooden chairs and benches facing a raised platform at the far end of the big, bare and rather chilly hall. "It seemed important to launch La Fiorella as soon as possible. When people have seen what she can do her fame will quickly spread; we'll fill the finest theatres in the West End." She seized my hand. "A favour?"

As I looked, she unpinned a small brooch from the high collar of her dress. It was a black Egyptian scarab in a gold setting. I did not think it an attractive ornament, but knew it had an occult significance and was one of her most treasured possessions, so I was unprepared when she asked me to wear it for the evening.

I searched my memory for what she had told me and remembered one of the stories. "You think I need my telepathic powers sharpened?"

"It's nothing to do with that. But I know you, Di; you assume that Fiorella is a fraud and will be looking for the trick of it. But she is the genuine article. There is no deception. She has the gift — several gifts, in fact. She can use the power of mind to draw objects to her from a distance — teleportation. Then she can read their histories and that of their owner."

"And wearing your scarab will convince me of all that?"

"If you'll allow me?"

I patted the lapel of my coat. "I won't take it off."

"All the more reason, then, for me to pin it underneath."

Seeing she was determined, I unbuttoned my overcoat and allowed Gabrielle to fasten the scarab to the left side of my fitted woollen jacket.

Mr Jesperson leaned in. "What about me?"

She flashed her teasing smile. "Jealous?"

"Curious."

She made a brisk motion with her hands. "Go on, find seats before all the good ones are taken."

With a movement of her head she indicated the front row, but I preferred that we should seat ourselves in some less conspicuous place. As I looked, my eye was caught by Mrs Traill gesturing vigorously towards the empty seats on her right, three rows back from the stage.

"Mrs Traill, how nice to see you again."

"Viola, *please*; I hope we have not become strangers in the few months since our last encounter, and that I may still call you Di?"

"Of course," I said, awkwardly. "Please allow me to introduce my colleague, Mr Jasper Jesperson." In the nick of time I made out her small retiring husband, nearly invisible in his grey suit against her much more substantial grey side; not for the first time, the image of a mother elephant and her baby came to mind. "Mr Jesperson, my friends Mr and Mrs Basil Traill."

"*So pleased*," she trilled, offering her gloved hand. "A detective, I believe? Miss Lane has written to us about your *interesting* partnership. But I hope it is not your detecting business which has brought you here this evening?"

Mr Jesperson shook his head, smiling, "I also take an interest in psychic phenomena. Miss Fox was kind enough to invite us . . ."

The next few minutes passed in inconsequential chat as more people came in and seated themselves, but by the time the outside doors were closed and Gabrielle Fox stood at the front as the focus of our attention, the hall was barely half full. Not a bad turnout for a complete unknown on a raw, damp and foggy evening, but I could see from the way she stood and raised her chin before she spoke that my old friend was putting on a brave face to hide her disappointment.

"Welcome, everyone." She stood upon a raised platform furnished with two cushioned armchairs and a small spindle-leg table, upon which there was a pitcher of water and two drinking glasses.

"It is my great privilege to introduce this evening a person of remarkable and unusual powers. Many of you here know me, and will understand that I do not lightly give my imprimatur. I have been too frequently disappointed to allow hope to triumph over reason. I do not ask you to *believe* — only to observe. If you suspect any trickery, or can explain in purely materialist terms how Signora Gallo achieves her results, please make yourself known to me, after the show.

"I have observed Signora Gallo very closely since my first encounter with her on a street in Glasgow nearly a month past, and I am convinced she does not rely on trickery or deception. Now, rather than attempt to describe her powers, I will let you see them for yourselves.

"Ladies and gentlemen, I give you Signora Fiorella Gallo."

A door opened on the left side of the hall and a small woman in a red dress bustled out.

Her olive-complexioned face bore a lively, humorous expression; she had none of the solemnity of so many of the mediums I had encountered, and her generous mouth frequently stretched open to reveal gleaming white teeth when she laughed. Beside me, Mr Jesperson turned to catch my eye and we shared a moment of pleasant anticipation.

"Because Signora Gallo's English is fragmentary and rather crude, I will remain by her side to offer translations," Gabrielle said. She waited until the star of the evening had seated herself — an action which, due to her short stature, the lady accomplished by dint of a swift backwards hop — before she took the second chair. Her relaxed, upright posture and serene expression communicated the silent attentiveness she expected from the audience.

I had not been aware that Gabrielle had any fluency in Italian, yet I was unsurprised that she did, for throughout my connection with her, she had revealed many unsuspected talents and much arcane knowledge.

107

In this, if nothing else, she resembled the man seated beside me.

Signora Gallo closed her eyes. Her stillness had an active quality very different from Gabrielle's. Although her body remained motionless, she was not at rest. I imagined that the shutting of her eyes had been like the throwing of a switch, and now a sort of psychic electricity was invisibly flowing.

Barely a minute had passed before her eyes popped open and she held up a clenched fist. Slowly she opened her fingers to reveal something that gleamed in the gaslight: a stream of gold tumbled from her hand, and then Signora Gallo held the object up to reveal an oval locket on a golden chain.

There was a small, ladylike shriek from several rows behind us. "Oh! That's mine! That's —"

Signora Gallo scowled and shook the first finger on her other hand reprovingly. "No! You-a not-a say. *I* a-say who she belong-a to.

"Is-a picture onna innaside. Pretty girl. That lady her mother. She sad for her . . ." Her speech became more halting until, impatient with the struggle to say it in English, she reverted to her native tongue.

In the first pause, Gabrielle interpreted: "The locket holds the picture of a little girl, about five years old. Her name is the name of a flower. This child died last year, just before Christmas. The one who wears the locket is her mother — perhaps you'd like to confirm that?" She looked searchingly into the hall.

Standing, the woman cried eagerly, "Yes! That's our Daisy — so we always call her, although her proper

108

name is Edith — can you speak to her? Can you tell her how much we love and miss her? Could we . . . could we speak to her?"

I stared down into my lap, clenching my fists. I recognised the voice behind me as that of Mrs Rose Cleatherall. She had turned to spiritualism after the death of her youngest child; I had attended at least two séances where she was present. She always asked for the same thing, but having her request granted could not satisfy her for long — how could vague words and promises make up for the irreplaceable and permanent loss of a beloved daughter? Whether the medium who claimed to be channelling the spirit of the child was genuine or a fraud, it made no difference. The only thing that mattered was the belief held by the bereaved; whether she could take comfort in the words she heard, which were always the same: *I love you, I am happy, do not mourn, for I have gone to a better place.*

Inside me, anger bubbled painfully. Why had I let myself believe Gabrielle? There was nothing new about this; Signora Gallo was no different from all the rest. She was a purveyor of hope to the hopeless, bringing anodyne messages from beyond the veil that separated the living and the dead.

Sure enough, within moments the eyes of the little Italian medium were shut fast, her shoulders slumped and she listed to one side, entranced.

"Who is there?" asked Gabrielle. "Can you hear me? Will you speak? The mother of little Daisy longs for a word from her lost child."

That longing was satisfied very soon as a soft, high, lisping voice came from the lips of Fiorella Gallo — an English voice, without a trace of a foreign accent. The voice told Daisy's mama that she lived now on the spiritual plane, embraced by love and light, far from care or pain. No one should weep for her; she was happy, and in time, they would be reunited in the afterlife.

Anyone who has ever attended or even read about a meeting of spiritualists will be familiar with the content, tone and tenor of the message. Does it seem strange that I, who believes there must be more to human existence than is bounded by our solid, fleshly bodies, who has seen things many would call impossible, should call this "communication with the spirits" offensive nonsense? Why is it that I won't believe certain people have a direct line to the spirit realm, and function as human telephones, allowing the dead to speak directly to the living people who mourn them?

There is no actual evidence for it. It is nothing but wishful thinking, the triumph of hope over reason. Spiritualists emphasise the importance of *belief* — and, it is true; sceptics are rarely, if ever, rewarded with proof of the impossible. But since when did believing in something make it true? Who would expect "belief" to have an effect on the weather, on the force of gravity, on the existence of animals or plants, or indeed *anything* we know about the physical world? If the ability to channel spirits, and for the dead to speak to

110

us, are dependent upon *belief*, they are *not* natural forces.

As Fiorella's entranced fluency gave way to broken English once more, and as I listened to the standard, clichéd words of comfort, my brief flash of anger settled into disappointment: cold and dreary and all too familiar.

Like — I supposed — everyone else present in the hall, I had hoped for proof of the survival of the human spirit after bodily death, but this was not it. Gabrielle's desire had led her to see more in the cunning little Italian than was reasonable.

Emerging from her trance, the medium plucked another piece of jewellery from the air and identified its owner. As she related a sentimental, yet inconsequential tale of how it had come into the lady's possession, a sudden suspicion made me unbutton my coat and check the lapel of my jacket, but the scarab brooch was still firmly pinned in place. I stroked the beetle, which was only a little larger than the pad of my thumb, relieved to know there had been no sleight-of-hand by which my friend had only *pretended* to fix her special badge to my lapel.

A gleaming, silver, flat object appeared in the hand of Signora Gallo, and once again, although I had kept my eyes fixed upon her hands, I was not able to see where it had come from, or how the trick that made it seem to materialise out of nothing was done.

Once again, the medium closed her eyes in concentration. But this time, instead of displaying signs of entrancement, she gasped and her eyes popped open.

111

"Signor! Meester Ball — *Bald* — Baldwin?"

"Yes." The response came from a tall, well-built man in the second row. Smiling and relaxed, he patted his breast pocket. In a drawling, amused tone he said, "Why, I do believe that is my cigarette case. Initials W.H.B.?" At her nod he went on: "*Please* spare me your yarns about dead relations. Mine are nearly all still living, and the dead ones never gave a fig for me. As for *this* shiny object —"

"Signor! You must go to Brighton — at once, *tonight*, do not delay!"

The young man laughed scornfully. "Brighton! At this time of year?"

She moved the cigarette case back and forth in her fingers and it flared where it caught the light. "The friend who give you dis, he is dere. He need you help. *Malattia.* You unnerstan me?"

The gentleman's face creased with anger, all amusement fled. "No, I do not."

"Hotel Metropole. Bad mans take alla his money. Do-a this." She beat with her knuckles against the silver case. "Onna his head. V'y bad. Nobody help him, 'less you go. You go Brighton now."

Goaded, he rose reluctantly, scowling and unconvinced, yet — as anyone hearing news of a friend who might be in trouble would be — concerned. "Can you tell me the *name* of this friend?"

She closed her eyes a moment, then nodded. "Guy. *You* call him Guy. Other people say Enry. Meester Enry."

112

Expression and colour drained from the young man's face. "Guy," he murmured. "In Brighton?" He began to move, and there was a general rustling and scraping of chair legs as people on his aisle shifted to make way for Mr Baldwin.

"Wait. Your cigarette case." Gabrielle stepped down from the dais and held it out to him.

"I must go . . ." He looked dazed and fumbled as she handed it to him, nearly dropping the small silver object.

"Of course," she said, her voice warmly sympathetic. "You have a train to catch. I do hope everything will be all right with your friend."

A low, excited murmuring broke out in the hall as people discussed what had just taken place. Mr Jesperson and I looked at each other, but said nothing. I thought that I should like to examine the cigarette case — was it, perhaps, inscribed with something more than the owner's initials? Although the names of W. H. Baldwin and Guy Henry meant nothing to me, I could not assume the same was true for Gabrielle, or Signora Gallo. Perhaps a late edition newspaper had carried news of a man set upon and attacked by thieves in Brighton? Or the entire episode might have been a bit of play-acting from a hired accomplice. Mr Jesperson and I understood each other. When investigating the truth of a medium's powers, it is never advisable to take *anything* for granted — especially not the things she or he wants you to believe.

Gabrielle regained the attention of the audience and waited for the murmur of conversation to die down before she allowed the show to continue. "If you are not too tired, Signora Gallo, I wonder if you would honour us with another demonstration?"

With a good-humoured shrug, the little medium cocked her head as if listening, and a moment later threw up her arm and caught something small enough to be entirely concealed in her closed fist. Pulling her hand down to chest-level she opened her fingers to inspect her catch. And then, surprisingly, she laughed deeply.

Chuckling, she said, "Thees I see before. I know the owner of this leetle bug. Miss Fox! You have 'nother question for me?"

With a start, I pulled back my coat. The scarab was gone.

How was it possible? Although there had been a small disturbance caused by the departure of Mr Baldwin, he had not been seated in our row, and no one had so much as touched me, of that I was certain. I could not have failed to be aware of any attempt to remove the brooch that had been pinned to my inner lapel. Perplexed, I brushed the wool with my fingertips — there were the tiny holes that had been made by the pin, but nothing more, not the damage I would expect if it had been pulled free by a tug at an attached line.

Impossible, and yet there it was: Gabrielle's scarab brooch held between the stubby fingers of Signora Gallo.

Across the hall, Gabrielle shot me a look of triumph. "Yes, that is my brooch, but I pinned it upon the bosom of my friend earlier this evening as a way of

114

demonstrating your powers beyond even *her* ability to doubt. But I realise it is no good asking you to tell us anything about my friend by reading a piece belonging to me — although I am certain you must read in my little jewel the depth and sincerity of my friendship —"

I stood up. "If you don't mind, Signora, I could give you something *else* to read. I would take it as a very great favour if you would be willing to do that."

Signora Gallo sat up alertly, her dark eyes snapping with interest. "Something of you own," she said. "Yes! Much better. This here" — she waved Gabrielle's precious Egyptian relic — "This, no good. No good for tell me about *you*. Only tell story about owner. Story 'bout Gabrielle, story 'bout Doctor who make it a gift to her, stories 'bout —"

"Yes, yes, we get the picture," said Gabrielle, all but snatching the scarab away from her. "That *is* a good idea, Miss Lane. How lucky you brought something more suitable . . . what is it? Please, come forward."

She sounded friendly enough, but I sensed her suspicion, and guessed she would be thinking of my poverty of ornament, trying to recall a single piece of jewellery I might have had about my person. Yet, I thought, if Fiorella Gallo truly had psychometric talents as claimed, she should be able to read the history of *any* object.

Mr Jesperson nudged my knee very slightly. Glancing down, I saw he was offering me his pocket-watch — a precious item, and one with an interesting history, I knew. But I did not take it, because I wished not merely to test her power, but to make use of it — if I could.

115

So I went up to the front of the hall and when I stood before the two of them, pulled an object from the depths of my coat pocket.

"I wonder what you can tell me about the person who owns this?" I pressed the little address book I had taken from Miss Jessop's room into the medium's open hand.

Signora Gallo gave a grunt, disappointed that I had not given her anything of obvious value, but she did not refuse the challenge, closing her eyes in concentration. After a moment she spoke:

"It is lady. English lady. She sad because she have many friends once, but now, not so many. They turn against her, because . . . Ah, because of what she say. She have power, too!" Her eyes opened suddenly, dark and flashing with surprise. "Heeelda?"

I heard Gabrielle's sharp intake of breath.

"Heelda Jess . . . Jess-*op*. She has power, like me, but not same. She has — *visione?*"

"Sight," said Gabrielle."

"Not of the eyes. She see future in here." With her free hand, she touched her head. "She is *clairvoyant*. She see, sometime, what will happen."

"What happened to *her*? Is she all right?" The questions burst out of me.

Clutching the address book to her chest, the medium closed her eyes and screwed up her face. "I see . . . I see . . . ah, I see she is gone away. Weeth a man. Ah! Weeth her lover!" She smiled dreamily, and there was some tittering from the audience and a few guffaws.

This unlikely answer left me speechless.

"Are you quite certain about that, Fiorella?" Gabrielle spoke gently. "Hilda has gone away, yes. But Hilda is an elderly spinster. She had no lover."

"Oh, yes, a fine, beeg, handsome man. He love her. She in his arms. They go away together. Thees leetle *libro* tell me so — I read it here. Not mistake."

The notion of shy, innocent, middle-aged Miss Jessop in a big man's arms should have been nonsensical, but I found it terrifying. The question had to be asked. "Signora — was he a bad man? Did a bad man take her?"

"Oh, no, not bad man. *Good.* She happy go with him. So happy!"

Tears pricked the back of my eyes as I recalled Hilda confiding in the servant at her lodging house, telling her not to weep but to be happy . . . poor, dear Hilda Jessop. She'd had a vision of her own death and accepted it as true believers were meant to, not as something to fear and struggle against, but as a promise of eternal joy in the afterlife. No more worries about money or lonely old age . . . she trusted in her vision of Heaven.

"Where is she now?" I asked.

Gabrielle pressed. "Does Hilda say that she's happy?"

The medium frowned at us. "How I know what Hilda say? I no talk to *Hilda;* I ask her leetle book, this tell me what it know. And it no know where she go."

"Won't you let Hilda speak through you, dear?" Gabrielle asked gently. "We are her friends; we'd love to hear from her, and I'm sure she'd be happy —"

117

Signora Gallo's eyes widened. "She not dead!"

I felt a rush of hope — absurd, yet there it was. I believed that she knew.

"You say Hilda Jessop is alive?"

"*Certo.*"

"Then ask the book where she is."

"Pah!" Abruptly she flung the address book in my direction; I just managed to catch it. Then, in a confusing torrent that mingled half-comprehensible English with her own rapid tongue, she explained why.

She could read the object, picking up fragments about Miss Jessop, because she had carried it around with her and used it, and her handwriting gave the mass-produced notebook an element of her personality. But precious stones and metals, especially gold, vibrated on a higher frequency than other materials, and were thus able to store more lasting impressions for the gifted reader, and when an object was a valued gift, something of the giver was stored in its memory as well. Mr Baldwin probably thought of the friend who had given it to him every time he used his silver cigarette case, which was why Signora Gallo had picked up the details of Guy's predicament. If she could hold a much-loved piece of jewellery — a wedding ring, or something that had been passed down in the family — something that Miss Jessop had handled or worn regularly, and would remember when parted from it — *then* the medium might be able to give us a more detailed and precise picture of what had become of our missing friend.

Alas, if Hilda Jessop had owned anything like that, it must have vanished with her, for there was nothing of value left behind in her room. I somehow doubted she would give a second thought to the items on her dressing table, even if — as seemed unlikely — they were of real silver.

After all that, Signora Gallo announced she was through for the night.

Gabrielle gave her a hard look and received a theatrical yawn in response.

"Try again. Surely there is another object — or two — waiting for your attention."

"No, no, nothing more," she muttered, avoiding her interlocutor's gaze.

"Are you *quite* certain? We don't want any complaints."

But nothing more could be had from the signora. Gabrielle shrugged and addressed the hall.

"Ladies and gentlemen, we thank you for your attention and your patience. Before you go, would you make sure that you have all your valuables about you? Please take time to check any items of jewellery that you came with are still on your person. Occasionally —"

She was interrupted by a sudden shriek. "My ring! My diamond ring is gone!"

Miss Fox shot a sideways glance at the medium, who was gazing into the distance. "Thank you, madam, there is no need to scream. We will recover it for you. As I was about to explain, Signora Gallo has a magnetic attraction to certain objects, which operates without any intention on her part. Objects made of gold, or set with precious stones are drawn to her presence, even when she is too tired to notice. Your ring will soon complete its transition back into the material state. Signora, if you please . . .?"

While others in the audience were gripped by the mystery of the missing diamond, anxiously checking their own wrists, hands, necks and pockets, or attending to Miss Fox's explanation, I kept my eyes firmly upon the little woman in red, and this time I was able to see the almost unnoticeable movements by which Signora Gallo conveyed an object from her sleeve into her fingers.

"*Ecco!*" she cried, holding up the ring as if she had just plucked it from the air, to be rewarded with enthusiastic applause.

And it *was* a wonder, for although I had seen her take the object from her sleeve, it was still a mystery as to how it had come to be there. Remembering what had happened to me — my certainty that the scarab had been securely fastened to my lapel and could not have been removed by any normal means — I found I was baffled. I turned the puzzle over in my mind whilst the medium related various facts concerning the owner of the diamond ring: how her lover had presented it to her with a proposal of marriage, the overwhelming joy she had felt, their continuing happiness together, etc. Any competent confidence trickster could have cobbled together a similar tale, but it satisfied the audience, and when the ring was returned to the hand of its blushing owner, the applause that filled the hall might have been

120

as much for the romantic heroine as for the psychic talents displayed by Signora Gallo.

Before we left, I was determined to have another word with Miss Fox, so while Mr Jesperson moved amongst the crowd, chatting casually and yet with purpose — for he was trying to find anyone who might have more information regarding the missing mediums — I waited patiently until some of the admiring crowd clustered around Signora Gallo and her protector had thinned, and I was able to speak to her privately. It did not take much to get her to agree to visit us again; she promised to bring Signora Gallo to Gower Street the next afternoon. I said I would borrow some more of Miss Jessop's possessions in the hope that they might carry more information that the medium could read.

"If she can help us find Miss Jessop," I said, "I promise you, Signora Gallo will have no more ardent promoter than I!"

Gabrielle positively sparkled with possessive pride as she assured me: "Fiorella will be better than any bloodhound for tracking her. Until tomorrow then — two o'clock?"

Outside, the fog had grown even thicker and more choking. Mr Jesperson and I did not indulge in conversation, but adjusted our scarves to cover our noses as we made our way cautiously through the muffled streets. When we reached Oxford Street, Mr Jesperson stepped into the road to hail a cab.

"What's wrong with the bus?" I demanded.

"Nothing, save I need to go to Kensington and you in the opposite direction."

"Then we'll go our separate ways." Before he could stop me, I waved off the approaching hansom cab.

He gave a martyred sigh. "I don't have time to go to Gower Street."

Nettled, I scowled. "I'm not asking you to come with me."

"You can't go by yourself."

"I am quite accustomed to travelling alone about the city."

"But not at night. You may be standing, waiting, for some time — *I* should worry, even if you don't. Look, there's another cab — let me —"

"No, it's a waste of money."

"I'll pay."

His thoughtless remark made me lash out. "*You?* It's hardly *yours*."

"It is no waste when the money saves us time."

"I am in no hurry."

"I am."

"Then go."

There we stalled. I caught sight of an approaching omnibus and was about to hail it when I realised it was on the wrong route. The silence grew between us. Another omnibus approached.

"Look, a Number 6 — won't that take you —" I began.

"I won't leave you here alone." He spoke over my objection. "You do not ask me to, but I must. It is common courtesy *and* common sense."

Unfortunately, he was right. Although I hated to feel that I was in need of protection, this was a big, bad city, and not all the men who roamed the night-time streets were as gallant as Mr Jesperson. I had no weapon but my wit, which might not suffice if I persisted in putting myself in the way of danger.

So I made no further protest; although I would not get down from my economic high horse and allow the hire of a cab, he could wait with me, and then accompany me back to Gower Street before he set off again, with his rapid long-legged stride, for Kensington.

CHAPTER
TEN

A Nocturnal Perambulation

An unexpected noise, followed by light footsteps on the stairs, startled me awake in the dark reaches of the night. From outside my door, a low voice said, "Go back to sleep; it's only three o'clock."

It may be he spoke to his mother rather than to me, but I went obediently back to dreamland, not even pausing to wonder why Mr Jesperson had not spent the night in Kensington.

When I rose at my usual hour, he was sleeping, and I found I had time to go to the house in Longridge Road and return before he got up.

Upon my return, I sat in the front room, while Mrs Jesperson made a fresh pot of tea and joined us. As her son munched his way through a plate of buttered toast he told us of his nocturnal adventure.

After he had left me, it was so late that few buses were still running, and there were no cabs to be had, so he had simply walked and arrived to find the Creeveys' house dark and still.

He had just been debating with himself over the question of rousing someone to let him in, or keeping watch from without, when the front door opened and the somnambulist emerged.

"I followed him . . . and where do you suppose he went?"

I could not imagine, and motioned for him to go on.

He smiled. "He took up position beneath a street lamp, facing a house on the north side of Belgrave Square."

I stared at him in disbelief. "You don't say . . . Lord Bennington's house?"

"The very same."

"And then?"

"And then, unfortunately, a policeman happened upon our sleepwalker."

A London bobby, patrolling his beat, had noticed the hulking figure standing in the pool of light beneath a lamp, eyes fixed on one of the grand houses that surrounded the square, and quite naturally demanded to know his business. The large man made no reply, and as the policeman became more insistent, had walked away.

"The bobby pursued him and was reaching for his truncheon when I managed to intercede."

"You are lucky he didn't whack *you* with his truncheon. Or haul you both in for questioning." I felt bitterly disappointed that we hadn't discovered Mr Creevey's purpose. "But I suppose you managed to spin some story —"

"I am lucky to have been born with an honest face," he replied, eyes twinkling. "And a fertile imagination. However, the story I told was true. The gentleman suffers from fits of sleepwalking and his wife hired me to keep him out of trouble. The copper was intrigued by the notion of a sleepwalker —"

"I suppose he had seen a play featuring the subject?"

"Something of the sort. I was advised to keep Mr Creevey on a closer rein in future, and he let us go."

"Go where?"

"Creevey went home. I waited a little while to be sure he would not come out again, and then so did I. I'm surprised the soles of my shoes have not worn through."

"You are certain it was Lord Bennington's house he was watching?"

He gave me a reproachful look. "I saw where he went. I should not say he was 'watching' — for what does the sleeper see? — but he certainly faced that house. Who can say what might have happened if the policeman hadn't come by." He crunched up the last bit of toast and licked buttery crumbs from his fingers. "Perhaps Mrs Creevey will be able to shed some light on the matter."

Mrs Jesperson objected when he stood up. "You are not going to Kensington *now*?"

"Why not?"

"You were rambling through London nearly all night in the cold and fog."

Smiling, he shrugged off her concern. "You know how walking *revives* me, Mother. It's a source of power. Even when it tires me physically, my brain is stimulated."

126

With a glance at me, he laughed suddenly. "Don't look so worried, Miss Lane. Of course we can take the underground — or catch a bus, if you prefer."

"I am always happy to walk," I said, feeling rather cross — after all, hadn't I just been tramping the streets this morning while he slept? "I wasn't thinking of saving my legs, but of the time. You have not forgotten, I hope, that we are expecting a visit from Miss Fox and her pet medium?"

"At two o'clock. All the more reason to leave at once."

Our reception by Mrs Creevey was not as welcoming as before. She was cordial, yet I felt a reproach in the way she gazed at Mr Jesperson.

"Mrs Creevey, we won't disturb you long, but we have a few questions. First, did anything unexpected or out-of-the-ordinary occur yesterday?"

"Apart from you not turning up as expected?"

He smiled. "Apart from that."

"Well, there was just one little thing. The telephone. It rang on two separate occasions — yet there was no one at the other end."

"An open line?"

The phrase meant nothing to me, but she agreed. "It seemed someone was there, saying nothing, only listening."

"You answered the phone yourself?"

"I always pick it up if my husband isn't here, and this was sometime after five o'clock, shortly before he arrived home."

"And the second call?"

"Arthur was at home then, it was perhaps half an hour later, and he picked it up, said his name as he always does, and then some moments passed without him saying anything more until he put down the handset."

"What did he say to you about it?"

"That it was a mistake, a crossed line or a wrong number. It happens."

"Has it happened before?"

"Yes . . . I remember one time last month."

"You answered?"

"No — I was puzzled, because he said his name and then nothing else for at least a minute. I asked him about it when he had ended the call, and he said that there was no one on the line and it was probably a fault." She gazed thoughtfully into the middle distance as she remembered. "It seemed strange to me — both times — that he said nothing more to elicit a response. For myself, I said 'hello?' and 'do you hear me?' so many times I must have sounded like a parrot."

"I'm sure most people would do the same," I said. "But perhaps your husband did not feel, as you did, that there was someone listening at the other end."

"Then why remain on the line?"

Mr Jesperson said, "Do you recall the date of that first wordless call — was it just before a night he went sleep walking?"

She blinked. "Why . . . I do believe it may have been. Yes. And he walked last night."

"I know. I followed him."

Emotions chased across her face: surprise, indignation, comprehension, worry. "You knew? And waited outside? Did you think it was perhaps your presence that kept him in bed? That he would not walk until the coast was clear? But . . . I thought he didn't *know* what he did while he slept; that it was outside his control."

"His waking self has no idea what he does, where he goes, or why, I am certain," Mr Jesperson assured her. "When he sleeps, another part takes over. Yet that unconscious part *must* be able to call upon the knowledge and memories of his conscious self. Last night was the first night since we took the case that your husband went to bed in the knowledge — that is, the belief — that *if* he rose in the night, only *you* would know, and as he had forbidden you to follow him yourself, there would be no one to see where he went. If it wished the secret kept, his sleeping self would feel secure."

Mrs Creevey's homely face glowed with admiration. "My, you are clever."

I felt a childish urge to kick his ankle, and if I'd had the concealment of a table I might have done so, especially as he smiled smugly and basked in her praise, when he really should have told her his late arrival was not planned — it was down to *me* — and my stubborn refusal to be put into a cab.

"Would you care for a cup of coffee? I often have one about now, and I think Cook was making ginger biscuits — so nice with coffee."

After she had rung for the maid and given her order, Mrs Creevey asked, "Where did he go? Have you solved the mystery? Will there be an end to it now?"

"The mystery is far from ended, Mrs Creevey. Does Belgrave Square have any special meaning to you — in connection with your husband?"

She blinked and stared. "*Belgrave Square?* Is that where Arthur went? We walked there together once, although for no particular reason, and I can't recall anything that would mark it out as memorable enough to call him back."

"What about Lord Bennington?"

She looked even more baffled. "What about him?"

"Does the name mean anything to you — or to your husband?"

"What should we have to do with aristocracy? I have heard of him, of course, but I couldn't tell you where from. A name from the newspapers, perhaps. Oh — his wife died a few years ago, I remember how sad it was, especially with all those little children."

"Is there no connection between you and anyone in his lordship's household?"

She paused to think carefully. "One or two of Arthur's relations are in service, but none in Lord Bennington's employ. At least, he has never mentioned it. You could ask him."

I looked at the pyramid-shaped clock on the mantelpiece and thought that we would be hard pressed to fit in a visit to Mr Creevey's workplace and get home again before two o'clock.

"Let me go and see if he is awake," she said, just as the door opened to reveal the maid bearing a tray with the coffee service. "I will tell him you are here."

Seeing our looks of surprise, she explained, "My husband awoke with a cough. I'm sure it was caused by wandering around on such a horrible, foggy night. I insisted he stay at home, keep warm and try to recover. That office of his is very draughty, and if anything happens that he needs to know about one of his men can telephone him.

"Please, help yourselves to coffee," she urged as she stood up. "I'll be back very soon, but if you want anything, don't hesitate to ring the bell."

"Well, that changes things," said Mr Jesperson as soon as we were alone together. He stretched out one long arm for the silver coffee pot and carefully poured the steaming dark liquid into two delicate white china cups. "Cream?"

"Yes, please. But what has changed?"

"Our understanding."

"*Our* understanding? It is kind of you to include me, but I haven't the faintest idea — you mean you have solved the mystery?" I looked at him in amazement as he handed me the cup and saucer full of fragrant hot coffee.

"Certainly I have not solved it; but now we have a clue. We know for certain that this is not a case for an alienist to solve. Creevey is being directed by someone. Whoever made those mysterious phone calls is the hidden hand who controls the somnambulist, sending him out into the night for reasons we can only guess at." He picked up a ginger biscuit and chewed it thoughtfully.

"How could a wordless telephone call direct him to do anything?"

"The caller did not speak to Mrs Creevey. It does not follow that he remained silent after hearing *Mr* Creevey's voice. I suspect the caller uttered a word or phrase that would set off a command implanted earlier, under hypnosis, then gave some brief instruction as to where Mr Creevey was to go and what he must do when he got there."

"But he did nothing."

"I know. It is likely that he was primed to walk away if apprehended. He may attempt to carry out his instructions again tonight."

I thought of our first visit to this house, how Mr Jesperson had emphasised the importance of noting anything that was different on the days before every instance of somnambulism, and I said, "You expected something like this."

Swallowing the remains of another biscuit, he shook his head. "No . . . I only hoped to find a pattern in what appeared to be random behaviour. If he walked after rich, heavy food, or an evening spent listening to sentimental songs . . . but instead we have found it has nothing to do with his own life. He is under the control of a person unknown. At some time in the past, Mr Creevey has been hypnotised and instructed to await his commands from a voice on the telephone."

Bizarre as it sounded, the theory made sense. "Will you tell him?"

"Not just yet. We will say nothing to him or his wife. The idea is a disturbing one, and until we have some idea of who is behind it, I don't think it would do any good to cause alarm, as it surely would."

Mrs Creevey soon returned with an invitation for Mr Jesperson to attend upon the invalid. As a female unrelated to the family, I did not expect to be welcomed to her husband's bedside; I hoped I might learn something useful by talking with her.

I had been too caught up in our conversation about the mysterious person behind Arthur Creevey's somnambulism to drink my coffee, or to taste one of the biscuits. I was glad that my partner had left a few.

"They are good, aren't they?" Mrs Creevey poured herself a cup of coffee, with a nod towards the depleted pile of biscuits. "We are so lucky with our cook. She is a pearl above price."

Small talk is not one of my gifts, so with a speed that I hope she did not find brutal, I plunged right in and asked if her husband had ever been hypnotised.

She gave a startled laugh. "Heavens, no! Did I not tell you how forcefully he rejected that very suggestion from Dr Linton?"

"Oh, yes," I said, although I did not remember it. "But considering Dr Linton's ideas about your marriage, Mr Creevey was not likely to trust him sufficiently to make an attempt at hypnosis successful. Perhaps earlier, under different circumstances . . .?"

"Certainly not," she said firmly as she stirred a spoonful of sugar into her coffee. "My husband would never agree to such a thing."

"Why is that?"

"Goodness, I should think a better question should be: Why ever should he *wish* to be hypnotised?"

"Considering that your husband suffers from somnambulism — has done since he was a child — someone along the way might have suggested it, for there is in fact a close connection between the somnambulistic state and the trance state induced by hypnosis." I felt confident in this knowledge, thanks to my recent reading on the subject.

"You don't say. Well, that is very interesting," she said politely. She shook her head. "But so far as I know, no one ever tried to hypnotise Arthur out of his sleepwalking in the years before I met him, and it would be of no use to try to talk him into trying that now."

"You are very certain."

She smiled over her coffee cup at me. "I do know my husband. And for as long as I have known him he could never bear the notion of someone taking control of him; making him act the fool, prance about on stage under the impression that he was in a ballroom, or allow himself to be pricked with burning needles while the audience roared."

I restrained a smile. "But that is stage hypnotism. Hypnotism used for a serious purpose, performed by someone who knows what he is doing, is *very* different." I sensed I was losing her and switched tracks. "But I suppose you have seen some sort of show like that?"

"Yes, as a matter of fact: in Paris, on our honeymoon. The show had been recommended to us

— we didn't really know what we were in for." Her silk dress rustled as she leaned forward. "It was a very high-toned affair, all the best people went to it — variety acts, you know, some very elegant. There was a comic song that may not have been so . . . but we couldn't understand it, anyway. There were some wonderful singers, lovely music, some dancers, and then the hypnotist-magician. He had a rather sinister aspect and wore a long black evening cloak, lined with red silk. He did a few conjuring tricks and then he said he would need a volunteer for the next part of his act. We had seats near the stage, and the man noticed us — noticed Arthur, I should say, and no wonder, for he does stand out, being so big and tall and manly.

"I suppose the performer thought it would be amusing to make such a powerful-looking gentleman dance to his tune . . . but Arthur would not be tempted onto the stage — thank goodness. We had no idea, really, what the act would involve, and when we saw what the magician did to his victim . . ." she frowned sympathetically. "I couldn't bear to laugh for thinking how easily it could have been my Arthur acting the fool."

"On stage, hypnotism may seem a joke," I said. "But when used properly, it can be a powerful force for good. It can be used to ease suffering, take away pain, and may in the future be seen as better than drugs for at least some types of surgery."

"Really?"

Recalling a book published fifty years earlier — John Elliotson's *Numerous Cases of Surgical Operations*

Without Pain in the Mesmeric State — I invented a story about a dentist who was able to put his patients into such a state of relaxation by means of hypnosis that they were no longer frightened to visit him, and many said tooth extraction was utterly painless. Seeing a change in her expression, I stopped. "You've remembered something."

She stared into her lap and smoothed the folds of her skirt. "Yes . . . your dentist reminded me . . . How strange . . . but the morning after we saw that variety show, very early in the morning, dear Arthur woke with a raging toothache." Her eyes flashed up to meet mine. "It was odd because that stage hypnotist had made his poor fool of a volunteer believe he was suffering with toothache, and then pretended to pull about half his teeth. When I heard my Arthur moaning in his sleep I thought he was dreaming about that — for I'd had a similar bad dream myself. But when he woke, his face was swollen and he was in dreadful pain. There was nothing for it; he went off in search of a chemist's shop."

She paused. "When he returned, he was a changed man. No — that's wrong. The pain was gone, and Arthur was *himself* again. The toothache did not return, and by the time our honeymoon was over, he'd forgotten all about it."

"The chemist must have given him some very powerful medicine."

"There was no medicine. It was too early, the first shop he had come to was not yet open, so he went to wait in a cafe nearby and ordered a brandy. A man at

136

the next table asked if he was unwell. He spoke in English. Pain makes one so vulnerable . . . my husband thanked him for his concern, explained he had toothache, and said he thought the brandy he'd ordered was probably the best remedy available, unless he could direct him to a dentist.

"The man said he could do better than that. He claimed to be a healer, said that by the power of God he could take away pain by simply touching the afflicted person. All Arthur had to do was give him permission.

"As he told me later, my husband did not *really* believe; he thought the man probably only wanted an excuse to pray over him and try to convert him to his church, but in pain we reach for any possibility of succour, so he told the gentleman he was welcome to try."

"What did he do?"

Mrs Creevey screwed up her face with the effort of remembering, then slowly shook her head. "I cannot recall. Some words were spoken, I suppose prayers, and when he told Arthur the pain was gone — it was."

My heart pounded with excitement. "What was the man's name?"

She smiled and shook her head. "I'm sure he never mentioned it. Arthur described him as a 'small man', but to my husband, most men are."

"English?"

"I'm not certain. He spoke in English, but . . . I have the idea it was with some faint accent." She shrugged. "Arthur said very little about him. It was selfish, perhaps, but once the pain was gone neither of us gave it much thought." She brightened then, recalling a redeeming fact. "Of course, Arthur was most grateful, and gave the man his business card with the promise that if he ever needed anything moved in the London area, he would supply his services free of charge."

"But you never heard from or saw him again?"

"I never saw him at all. And so far as I know, Arthur has not either — I'm sure he would have told me."

She could not remember the name of the hypnotist they had seen perform — just one act among many. After so long, it would have been surprising if she had. The venue had been the Variétés on the Boulevard Montmartre, and she was able to give me a rough idea of the date.

By the time Mr Jesperson rejoined us I was feeling well-satisfied and eager to get back for our meeting with Signora Gallo, so we did not linger.

As we marched briskly through the fog-shrouded streets to South Kensington Station, Mr Jesperson told me he had learned nothing useful from Arthur Creevey. He knew nothing about Lord Bennington, Belgrave Square had no emotional or autobiographical significance, and he could not recall ever visiting any of the houses or offices there.

"As for the phone calls — he could not remember them. Which is indicative in itself: hypnotic suggestions are often masked with the command to forget all about the surrounding circumstances," he told me.

"Did you ask if he'd ever been hypnotised?"

"He was most vehemently opposed to the very idea. When I tentatively suggested that a qualified, trusted hypnotist — I did not admit I was speaking of myself — might be able to uncover the roots of his somnambulism, I thought he might get up and throw me out."

I smiled to myself. "Did he mention the show he saw on his honeymoon, at the Variétés in Paris?"

"Oh, I gathered he must have seen some such performance at some time. It hardly matters where or when."

"Oh, I think it does. What about the mysterious toothache?"

He looked down at me at his side, matching his pace, and smiled. "What have you learned from his wife?"

I gave him all the details, finishing just as we reached the station.

There was a pause to purchase tickets and descend to the platform. Then, as we waited for the arrival of the train, he asked if I thought the man in the cafe was the same person as the stage hypnotist.

"I do. If Mr Creevey was sufficiently suggestible to believe he would wake with a dreadful toothache, he may also have received a subliminal suggestion about which cafe to take his brandy in. Or the man may have followed him. It was no chance meeting. I suppose he picked Mr Creevey because he wanted someone to do his bidding in London. It's too bad Mrs Creevey couldn't remember the hypnotist's name."

"We'd be no wiser if she had. Odds are, he called himself Mister Mysterioso."

I objected. "*Monsieur* Mysterioso, surely, in Paris?"

139

"In Paris, he'd be a romantic *Mister* — the exotic foreigner from Birmingham."

Giddy with the feeling that we'd had a glimpse of our villain at last, we began to laugh, and were smiling still when our train drew in.

CHAPTER
ELEVEN

Preparations

Returning to the house on Gower Street, we were met by the delicious scent of baking pies and, less happily, a letter addressed to both of us in Gabrielle's familiar hand.

"Oh, no," I said, knowing at once she must be writing to cancel our meeting.

In her note, Gabrielle said Fiorella was too exhausted by the mental and spiritual exertions of the night before to do anything today. Her "reading" of Miss Jessop's belongings would have to wait until she was rested.

"Oh, it is too bad of her!" I exclaimed, thrusting the page at Mr Jesperson.

"You do not believe her?"

"She is up to something," I said darkly.

"Feminine intuition?" He grinned teasingly.

"Deductive reasoning," I responded crisply. I folded my arms and gave him a look. "Go on, see if you can work it out."

He glanced again at the brief letter. "Psychic powers may need rest and renewal just like physical strength. Yet Signora Gallo did not appear worn out at the end of her performance last night; despite her claim, I should have said she stopped out of boredom, not weariness. Nor did Miss Fox voice any concerns before agreeing to come, which might suggest that something happened this morning to drain the Signora's powers — but *you* find it more likely that your old friend is not being honest . . . interesting." He cocked his head.

"I have known her a long time," I replied. "If something had happened this morning, why not say so? It's the tone of her letter that suggests to me that she is hiding something."

"Another missing medium?"

"You mean Signora Gallo?" I shook my head. "There is no sense of strain in her writing. She is keeping a secret, but only a small one. She worries I might find it out before she is ready, if they came here today."

He gazed at me with frank interest, a slight smile on his lips. "How long, do you think, before we learn what secret lies behind the letter?"

"Not long," I said, with perfect confidence.

"Intuition?"

"Everything I have said is based on my knowledge of her character. Miss Fox is impulsive. She learned something no earlier than last night and no later than this morning. Deciding to act upon it, she cancelled our meeting, aware that I might try to dissuade her if I knew her intent. Whatever it is will take place very soon."

Mrs Jesperson came into the hall. "I thought I heard you come in. Why are you still standing out here? The pie is ready; come and have your dinner."

Afterwards, with a French–English dictionary close by, I wrote a letter in my most careful hand and best schoolgirl French to the management of the Variétés, Boulevard Montmartre 7, Paris — I had confirmed the address in a recent edition of Baedeker's *Paris*.

I represented myself as a partner in a theatrical agency who had heard good reports of a stage magician and hypnotist who had once appeared at their theatre. Alas, the man's name was unknown to me, but I provided the dates of his engagement and hoped they might oblige with details of the hypnotist's manager, agent or address. Then I walked down to the post office and sent the letter on its way.

The letter and short walk had not quenched my need to be active. There were still some hours to fill before we could leave for Belgrave Square, and I paced the room and tried to think of something to do while Mrs Jesperson did some mending before the fire, and Mr Jesperson sat absorbed in his newspapers. He was always on the lookout for some interesting crime, but most criminal events that were reported had no real mystery about them, being acts of violence performed by young toughs, thugs and petty villains who went after what they thought of as easy prey and were soon caught.

My train of thought led me back to our recent encounter with the knife-wielding young thug, whom Mr Jesperson had disarmed by use of what he liked to call his "snake charming technique". Hypnotism, mesmerism, mind control, call it what you will, it was a most remarkable power — and more terrifying than any

143

weapon one could see. Much as I trusted him and believed him to be a good person, I still found it disturbing to realise that my partner was capable of exercising that same dark art with which an unknown villain had ensnared Mr Arthur Creevey.

And yet Mr Jesperson's practical knowledge of the subject would give us a better chance than most of solving the mystery behind Mr Creevey's somnambulism.

"Miss Lane, forgive me, but is it truly necessary for you to pace up and down like that?" I stopped, surprised, and turned to face Mrs Jesperson, who immediately tempered her complaint with a forced smile. "I fear you will wear through the carpet, which we cannot afford to replace."

"Forgive me." I dropped down in the empty chair beside her, but once there, I fidgeted uneasily. "I'm full of restless energy. I should go out for a walk if not for the fog. I don't like doing nothing. I hate being useless."

Mr Jesperson looked up from his papers and said pedantically: "Do not confuse *motion* with utility. After all, there are times when inaction is the correct response — when the wisest and most *useful* thing one can do is nothing."

I rolled my eyes. "Is that a bit of Eastern wisdom you picked up on your travels?"

He laughed. "Well — do you know — it *is*. Those are the words — in my own rough translation, of course — of the oriental master who taught me how to fight in the way of the unarmed warrior."

"Not to be confused with snake charming?"

"Oh, not at all. I speak of a method of self-defence practised in China. Come now, have you forgotten? You saw me use it when we were under attack, during the curious affair of the deodand, and perhaps at other times as well — and you must have seen me practising the basic movements."

"Yes, of course," I said. "I had not forgotten, only . . ." only the method he had chosen to use against the man who snatched my purse had been sufficiently dramatic to make me forget that he could as easily have kicked the knife out of that thug's hand and sent him sprawling with a few fluid motions. Mr Jesperson had told me, after the first time I saw him fight in this way, that it had been designed to work to the advantage of anyone confronted by a larger, more physically imposing attacker.

I suddenly found myself on my feet again, remembering he had told me that even women, children and the elderly could protect themselves very well if schooled in this discipline. "Could I learn it?"

"I have no doubt that you could, if you wished."

"Will you teach me?"

We stared at each other in silence across the room for a moment before he said apologetically, "I am not a master. I have never taught anyone. You should find a proper teacher."

"No doubt. But until I find a wise, oriental master and the money to pay him, will you not share your knowledge? At least show me enough so that I can defend myself."

145

His look became defensive. "Why should you need to? Have I ever let you down?"

"Of course not, but what if I were alone?" I sensed we might be circling back to an earlier argument, and before he could vow that he would never let me go anywhere by myself, quickly added, "It might be unavoidable. Or consider this: what if we were set upon by a gang, five against one, say? No one would see me as a threat — they might send *one* to grab me, and if I had skill enough to elude him that would be better, surely, than if you were forced to give in. I might even be able to help you."

Common sense won out over manly pride, and he agreed that it would be a distinct advantage for a female investigator to be able to defend herself, and allowed that he might be able to start me on the right path.

I jumped up. "Shall we begin?"

"Now?" Putting aside his paper, he gazed about the large, cluttered room, judging its fitness as a training ground. "We'll need to clear a bit of space."

I helped to push smaller pieces of furniture into the corners, out of the way. He looked me up and down, then glanced at his mother. "Could you make her a pair of trousers?"

"Mine will probably serve."

Trousers? I stared at the conservatively dressed older woman in surprise. "They're nothing improper," she said quickly. "Loose, like pyjamas. Really, they're more modest and certainly more useful than standard female clothing."

Seeing that I was not completely convinced, she explained: "Jasper must have someone to practise with, otherwise I should not have thought of it. Once I became his sparring partner, I had to learn quickly, or risk coming to harm." She smiled. "I think you are wise to want to learn to defend yourself, Miss Lane. Of course, one hopes never to be obliged to use it, but there have been occasions when I was very glad to have that ability. Not all men are particularly clever nor especially powerful, and yet nearly all of them expect that any woman will be an easy victim to any man."

Mr Jesperson cleared his throat, and his mother stepped aside, leaving me to face him in the empty centre of the room.

"I propose we begin with yielding."

I looked at him uncertainly. He smiled. "What I said before, about inaction?"

"I am to do nothing?"

"Not exactly. The tree that bends before the wind does not break. Let us pretend you are walking along a quiet road. Suddenly, a man appears, running towards you, intent on knocking you down and seizing your —"

His mother handed me the first volume of a triple-decker from her lending library.

"I am a mad bibliomaniac; the sight of the book in your possession has incited me to steal it, encouraged by your size and stature to believe I can take it by simple force," he said swiftly. "Ready?"

"No." I had not expected a game of make-believe. "What should I do?"

"Don't ask me, I'm the thief. Ask yourself. How will you stop the brute who intends to steal your precious volume? Don't be afraid of hurting me; strike, if you must, as hard as you can —"

"I don't . . . I've never —"

"Miss Lane. Are you serious about learning to defend yourself?"

"Yes." In truth, I hated the very idea of fighting and had no wish to perpetrate violence in any form, yet I had even less desire to become a victim.

"Then you must take it seriously. Respond as to a genuine threat. Begin."

I thought I was prepared — I planned to hold fast to the book — but it happened so quickly and I was so shocked by the force with which he bumped against me, that I was lucky to keep my feet. I found my hands were empty.

From the other side of the room, Mr Jesperson waved the purloined volume in the air.

"Can we try again?"

The second time was not much different, nor the third. Even expecting what was about to happen, I was unable to stop it.

"Shall I show you another way?"

I set my jaw and nodded.

"Let Mother demonstrate. Observe."

Moving aside, I gave Mrs Jesperson her book. She looked even less of a threat than I, and I could not imagine her putting up any effective defence.

He came galloping towards her, head lowered, hands ready to grab. The sight made me tense, but not Mrs J.

She neither froze, like me, nor tried to fend him off. She merely turned her body slightly and took a step back. There was no collision, and with nothing to halt his forward motion, her would-be attacker simply kept going. At the last minute she lightly pushed his shoulder and he stumbled slightly before he recovered, turned, and made another attempt.

Again she deflected him, so subtly I could not see how, but her son lay sprawling on the floor.

He jumped up smiling and looked at me. I frowned. "Very theatrical, but I am not convinced. You colluded in your own defeat. It's no good, sir. I have *seen* you fight."

"You are a harsh critic, Miss Lane." He sighed. "I admit, I could beat this little woman if I chose. But the object was not to show off my skills, but to demonstrate how a small, seemingly defenceless woman might deflect a forceful physical attack. A common criminal wishing to seize something from an unprotected woman is unlikely to try anything more sophisticated than to grab and run. When she eludes his grasp, he thinks it was by chance, or that he did not strike hard enough, so he uses more force the second time. He expects *resistance* — feeble against his own greater strength. What he does not expect is to have his own size, speed and weight turned against him. I did not *pretend* to stumble; what you observed was the natural and inevitable consequence of using brute force against someone who has learned to deflect that force, and turn it against the attacker."

"Perhaps *you* should try to take my book, Miss Lane," said Mrs Jesperson. "Experience teaches better than words."

I agreed, and rushed at her — and past her, much as her son had done; I scarcely felt her tap on my shoulder. Coming around, I ran at her again, and was shocked to find myself immediately caught, held captive by one arm, which she had twisted up behind me. I knew, from childhood battles, than any attempt to break free would be unbearably painful, so I kept still and cried, "Pax!"

She laughed, and let me go. "You weren't taking it seriously the first time," she chided. "Try again, and *mean* it this time. Try to knock me flat."

I tried again, and then again, but my efforts did not satisfy her.

"You're running past me — you're *expecting* my evasion; you're anticipating."

Well, of course. She didn't *really* want me to knock her down.

She insisted that she wanted me to try. "If you won't use force against me, how am I to turn it against you? Don't worry about hurting me. Don't think of this as a game. Or, if you must, then let it be a game that *matters*. Get the book — or no supper for you tonight!"

I smiled, but she looked back at me sternly. I squared my shoulders and took a deep breath.

"Ready?"

This time, when I ran at her, I meant it. But she sidestepped me easily.

"Better, much better," she said, as I stumbled and nearly fell.

The lesson continued for nearly an hour. I never did get the book, but when we changed places I had a better understanding of what she had done, and was able to evade her, and keep possession at least once out of four or five tries. I was exhausted when she called an end at last.

"Come up to my room and we'll see if my costume would do for you."

I had nearly forgotten her offer of trousers, but after a session in which I'd found myself sprawled on the floor at least twice, I thought I might move more nimbly and feel less inhibited in different attire.

Mrs Jesperson's trousers were of dark blue cotton flannel, the wide legs so generously cut that they looked like an ankle-length skirt. There was a drawstring waist which I tightened to my satisfaction.

"Are you comfortable? I think they'll do without any adjustments. You're a bit slimmer than me, smaller in the chest, but otherwise we're not so very different in size."

"Thank you, it's very kind; I'm sure I'll find them useful."

"There is another thing . . ." She hesitated. "I hope you won't consider this an imposition, or take offence. Naturally, you will have your own idea about what to wear to Lord Bennington's this evening, and I would not dream of taking the liberty

Her diffidence was worrying. I hoped I wasn't to find myself in the awkward situation of refusing some

151

antique piece of hideous outdated fashion requiring a crinoline cage.

"My clothes may not be in the latest mode, but I hope I shall be entirely respectable, and look well enough in my usual attire," I said brightly. "After all, no one will be looking at *me*."

While I was speaking, she had gone to her big oak wardrobe and now emerged carrying a shimmering, flowing gown of golden silk, sleek and simple, with nothing dated about it.

"From Shanghai," she explained. "I was thinner then, but even so, I recall it was a tight fit. I'm sure I could not manage to squeeze into it now. Would you like to try it?"

As in a fairy tale, I allowed her to help me into the dress. It was like nothing I had ever worn, or imagined wearing. It was beautifully light and the caress of the fabric against my skin felt like a glass of champagne. I remembered how my sister had once said acting was so much easier in the perfect costume. Inhabiting this dress, I could imagine myself another woman: beautiful, rich, mysterious and confident in her powers.

"Look in the glass."

But, afraid of having my dream shattered, I turned away instead, and plucked at the folds of silk hanging loosely at my hips, sagging slightly across the bodice. "It is a beautiful dress, but too large for me."

"A few stitches and it will fit perfectly. I can take it in now and have it ready for you to wear tonight."

"You are too kind. But — it's your dress. I can't ask you to alter it for me."

152

"I've told you, *I* can't wear it, and it's not doing anyone any good at the back of my wardrobe. Unless you dislike it —"

"I love it."

I spoke without emphasis, but she heard my emotion. Taking hold of my shoulders, she turned me round and steered me towards the looking glass. "And it loves *you*. Look! That colour never did me any favours, but with your complexion, it's a wonder."

I hardly recognised the woman in the shimmering golden gown. Where was plain, mousy Miss Lane? My unassertive brown hair looked richer and more lustrous, my skin glowed and there were roses in my cheeks. Beside me, the owner of the dress smiled warmly, sharing my pleasure, and I felt a rush of gratitude.

It was a moment when I should have turned and hugged her, or kissed her, but although I could imagine someone else, someone who was not me, doing just that in a spontaneous expression of happiness, I could not. The costume might change my outward appearance, but that was all.

"Thank you," I said, hating how flat and unemotional my voice and words both were, and I turned away from the reflection. "It is a beautiful dress. You are too kind."

I heard her sniff. "Kind? Call it practical. *I* can't wear it, and as you're to be at Jasper's side this evening, *he* will appreciate it."

She stopped me before I could take it off. "Let me mark where I must take it in."

153

I stood stock-still and let her measure and make adjustments. Before the silence could grow too cold I said, "I don't think your son takes much notice of what I wear."

"For someone who advertises as a detective, you can be remarkably unobservant."

I could feel the heat rising in my neck and face.

"Jasper notices everything. You should endeavour to do the same. There. That will do for now." Careful of the pins, she helped me out of the dress, and I made haste to put my own clothes back on.

"I'll make the adjustments and bring it to your room when I'm finished so you can try it on again," she said. "In the meantime, get some rest."

Retreating to the blessed calm of my own room, I stretched out on the bed. I thought I would just close my eyes for a few minutes — I did not think I could sleep — until I was startled awake by a gentle tapping at the door.

The room was in darkness. The better part of two hours had passed and Mrs Jesperson had come to tell me she had run me a bath. She had also brought me a most welcome cup of tea.

I felt humbled by her kindness. I did not deserve it. How could I reciprocate? My words of thanks were common coin, debased by overuse. I brooded on this in the comfortable solitude of the bath.

Afterwards, I found her waiting in my room, made warm and cheerful by lamplight and the fire crackling in the hearth. She helped me into the dress. This time it fitted perfectly, but as I looked down my front I felt uneasy. There was a high collar, but it was open at the neck, and that opening plunged quite deeply, too deeply for my liking.

"I wonder if another stitch or two . . .?"

"Oh, no," she said firmly. "A brooch would be much better. Perhaps you have something?"

"Just a silver —"

"Wait." Off she went in her brisk, purposeful way, and soon returned. "It's only a trinket, but it will add a clever touch to your *ensemble* as well as providing a practical solution to the problem of your *décolletage*."

The brooch was a little piece of bone or ivory carved into the likeness of a cat's winking face. One eye was shut, the other, a bit of green glass that glittered when it caught the light. It made me think of Gabrielle, and it made me smile.

"Oh, good, you like it. Allow me?"

I let her pin it to the dress, drawing together the bottom quarter-inch of the V.

"Problem solved," I said. "Mrs J, you're a wonder and a marvel. If you're on my side, I know I have nothing to worry about."

"I *am* on your side. I hope you know that, Miss Lane."

This time, I did not shy from the jump. "Won't you call me Di?"

"Die?"

"Di. It's my nickname."

"I see. I've never been one for nicknames — and Diana is such a lovely name —"

155

I stopped her. "It's not short for Diana. I wish it were." I took a deep breath. "My father was a classicist. He unfortunately named me Aphrodite. It's too much."

She did not laugh. "I agree — four syllables is rather a difficult mouthful for anyone who's neither queen nor goddess."

I laughed, relieved to have my hateful secret out in the open, stripped of its power. "What a diplomat you are, Edith!"

CHAPTER
TWELVE

A Strange Meeting in
Belgrave Square

Lord Bennington was one of the most prominent and generous supporters of the Society for Psychical Research, a large, hearty Englishman who cut an unmistakeable figure; but as our previous meetings had been in darkened rooms in the company of our mutual, more flamboyant friend, I did not expect he would remember me particularly.

So it was unexpectedly gratifying that, as soon as the footman announced our names and ushered Mr Jesperson and myself into one of the spacious reception rooms on the ground floor of the house in Belgrave Square, our host broke away from the cluster of guests with whom he had been engaged to stride towards us, hand outstretched and ruddy face beaming.

"Miss Lane. Marvellous to see you again! How good of you to come. And this must be Mr Jesperson. A pleasure, sir, a very great pleasure to meet you."

If Mr Jesperson was startled by such an enthusiastic reception, he did not let on as he returned the hearty handshake. "The pleasure is all mine, Lord Bennington.

157

I'm honoured to have been included in Miss Lane's invitation."

"Included? But of course! I must say, I was surprised, Miss Lane, to hear of your new occupation, but I have no doubt you will make a most excellent sleuthess. You have, of course, attended many a séance — how about you, Mr Jesperson?"

"One or two."

"Ever uncovered any frauds?"

My friend shook his head, smiling a little. "That is not my occupation."

"But do you reckon you could spot a fake? Or tell us how a fellow might make a table fly across a room, or strum a tune on a banjo that's hanging in the air five feet away?"

He shrugged. "I dare say both of us have a good idea when we are being tricked. But we're not here to spoil your party, Lord Bennington."

Our host's shaggy eyebrows rose. "But I insist! If you spot any trickery you're to say so at once — bring the proceedings to a halt, sir! If you can prove it, you *must*."

Eyes gleaming with interest, Mr Jesperson lowered his voice. "You suspect fraud?"

The stocky, red-faced lord snorted. "Ha! No, sir. Quite the contrary. You'll find no trickery — I'd lay money on it. The man is a miracle, a wonder. Never seen anything like it. When I told C.C. I thought of inviting along a detective to watch him work, he thought I meant Conan Doyle. Ha! Said he'd already impressed the creator of Sherlock Holmes — what do

158

you think of that? But I said no, I meant a real, crime-solving detective —" He stopped, frowning. "Er, you *have* solved *some* crimes, I take it? Because when I told him your name he'd never heard of you, and I must admit, nor had I before Miss Lane —"

Painfully aware of how few successes we could boast, I said quietly, "Our clients have no wish to see their affairs emblazoned in the newspapers — I am sure you understand."

This seemed to satisfy him, as he nodded. "Of course." He rubbed his hands together. "However, if you are convinced Mr Chase is the real thing I hope you will say so in public. He's quite happy to see his name in the papers."

"You might have done better to invite a journalist."

His laugh boomed out again. "I have! I have indeed! Look around — do your detective work — see if you can spot him."

Behind us, at the door, the footman pronounced the name of Mr Frank Podmore, and as our host went to greet this distinguished, open-minded member of the SPR, we moved further into the large room.

There were already close upon two dozen people in the room, a far bigger crowd than at any séance I'd ever attended. Certainly too many to be seated comfortably around anything but a knights-of-Camelot-sized round table. Yet there was no platform, and chairs had not been set out in rows as they had been at Signora Gallo's demonstration in the Methodist Mission Hall. There were a variety of couches, chairs, sofas and ottomans, and a few of the guests — the older ones —

had availed themselves of these, but most stood about in pairs or small groups as they chatted and looked about. I imagined that many of them were wondering, as was I, when the guest of honour would make his appearance.

I recognised faces from my SPR days, exchanged greetings with those I knew and introduced them to Mr Jesperson. He was soon drawn into an intense discussion on the subject of thought-reading and I was listening with interest, when I felt myself embraced by the slender, fragrant form of Lady Florence.

"My dear!" she exclaimed. "How lovely — it has been an age. I am so glad you have not forgotten your old friends and interests since taking up a new career as a lady detective."

Although I had never felt we were close friends, this sort of effusion was customary from her, and as usual, her manner was soothing to the nerves and soul. This lady was sister-in-law to Lord Bennington, and her knowledge about his household and the comings and goings in Belgrave Square might, I thought, be useful in connection with our investigations in the case of the somnambulist. That is, if I could ever insert a question of my own into her torrent of conversation.

Lady Florence is a charming woman, warm and friendly, but she fears silence as nature abhors a vacuum, and in her determination to keep it at bay she will talk about everything and anything, with scarcely a pause for breath.

After she had exclaimed over my beautiful dress and how well it made me look, quizzed me briefly about my new career as a detective, and touched lightly on topics ranging from the difficulty of engaging a good governess to instances of premonition in dreams, she suddenly asked me if I should like a chance to "freshen up". Although I was feeling fresh enough, I perceived that she wished for a companion, and agreed.

I caught Mr Jesperson's eye as Lady Florence swept me away towards the door: he looked questioning and I merely smiled in response.

"I am looking forward to meeting Mr Chase," I said, seizing the conversational reins as we left the room.

"Oh! Yes, he is a very interesting gentleman. Rather unnerving, of course."

"Of course?" I frowned in perplexity.

"I mean, the idea that he is privy to one's thoughts. Disturbing to think one is an open book, don't you agree? I prefer to keep an aura of mystery, at least where gentlemen are concerned."

"He has read your mind? You have evidence?"

She stopped at the top of the stairs and met my gaze. "Just wait until you meet him."

She led me a short way down the hall to a little parlour, which had been turned into a sort of dressing room with two chairs and a chaise longue, and tables equipped with wash basins and jugs of hot water; a bowl of beautiful milled soaps, stacks of towels and face cloths, and bottles and jars of lotions and *eau de cologne* set out on a long table below a well-lit looking-glass.

"You are a dear to come with me," said Lady Florence, patting my hand. "I shan't be long; perhaps you'd like to . . . well, I won't suggest you need to do anything to your hair, or face, because you couldn't look lovelier; you may admire yourself in the glass until I return."

But when she'd gone from the powder room, never having been one to enjoy the sight of my own reflection, I crossed the room to look out of the window. The room was at the front, so the view before my eyes was of Belgrave Square. That lamp shining directly opposite was probably the very one that the sleepwalking Mr Creevey had paused beside as he stood before the house. What had he been waiting for? I wondered. A chance to break in? A signal from a confederate inside? What would have happened if that policeman hadn't happened to notice him? There was certainly much worth stealing within these walls. Although I could not believe that Mr Creevey was any sort of thief, the evidence suggested a villain who might be using him as a cat's paw.

I felt an unpleasant chill and moved away from the window. Quite suddenly I did not want to be alone. Where was Lady Florence?

Thinking I heard her approach, I went to the door and stepped into the hallway. But instead of the welcome figure of Lady Florence, a creature from nightmare was headed my way.

I saw an immensely tall, powerfully built man. He must have been seven foot tall, and proportionately large. His face was a broad, blank, hairless visage, the eyes set deep beneath a protruding brow. The hair on his head was pure white and as long as a woman's,

162

pulled back and bound into a club behind his neck. He wore a grey woollen tunic trimmed with black braid, and matching grey trousers tucked into high black boots.

I shrank back in fear as he approached, but he paid me no attention. As he passed by, I caught a whiff of a rank, unwashed male body and heard the faint creak of his leather boots: confirmation that this was no mere apparition.

My heart pounded like a trapped and desperate animal and I wanted to scream. Reason told me he was just a man — if an unusually large and ill-favoured specimen — but intellect was helpless before my fearful conviction that I had met him before, under the most terrifying of circumstances.

It was not the sight of a hideous stranger that paralysed me with fright, but rather that *recognition*. In a split second I had remembered seeing him before; I relived the moment when I opened my eyes to see that same horrible, pale blank face bent close to mine, and felt once again the powerful grip of his hands as he picked me up, utterly indifferent to my puny struggles to escape.

But no such thing had ever happened to me.

Yet, I remembered the terror in the night. I *knew* him from that fearful encounter.

The more intently I pursued the memory, desperate to recall when and why, the more it retreated. Surely I had never been abducted? It was hardly likely I could have forgotten such a terrifying event if it *had* happened. It must have been a nightmare. But this

163

reasoning did not solve my problem. For if that man was a stranger, unknown to me, why did the sight of him evoke such a powerful memory? If I had never seen him, how could he have featured in any nightmare? I'd experienced *déjà vu* before, of course, but never anything like this.

"Miss Lane? What's the matter? My dear, are you feeling unwell?"

I was so caught up in my mental struggle I had failed to notice the return of Lady Florence, who now stood before me, an expression of concern drawing faint lines on her smooth brow.

She took my wrist. "You look as if you have seen a ghost."

"I thought I had." With an effort, I regained control of myself and struggled to give her a smile that was not a pained grimace. "I'm sorry. So foolish of me . . . I have been frightened by the glimpse of a stranger. He was quite a terrifying creature: seven foot tall, with pale skin, sunken eyes and white hair."

"The Cossack." Slipping her arm around me, she drew me close. "My dear, I do sympathise. If I had encountered him for the first time alone in a dark hallway, I might have fainted dead away."

"Who — or what — is the Cossack?"

"He is one of Mr Chase's servants."

"He has servants?" I was startled by this unexpected information.

"Yes, indeed. A veritable retinue. Not only the very oddest of manservants, but he also travels with his own cook. That did not go down very well in the kitchen

164

here, as you may imagine." She gave an impersonation of an offended cook: "If Mr Chase needs his weggibles cooked a special way, he only need *aaask*." She went on to explain that, rather than discommode his host, he had rented a separate house for his staff.

"Really? It must be nearby."

"I suppose so. That Cossack must be going to and fro all the time; although I'm sure the servants *here* are all very relieved that none of *them* is obliged to share a room with him. But that's enough gossip about servants. Are you recovered enough to walk downstairs? Would you like to lean on me?"

I assured her I could walk unaided.

"Then we should go down — it wouldn't do to be late for Mr Chase."

As we made our way downstairs, I puzzled over her revelation about Mr Chase's servants. Although I had met some mediums who lived very well, it was always by the grace of their benefactors; they survived on gifts and the largesse of others. And what sort of man, if he could afford to hire his own servants, rented separate quarters for *them*, while living as a guest in another man's house?

It made no sense, but there was no time to quiz Lady Florence further, for as we re-entered the drawing room, it was to the chiming of a silver hand-bell, used by Lord Bennington to call for his guests' attention. When the noise of general conversation had died away, he cleared his throat and made an announcement.

"Welcome. I believe everyone has arrived. Some of you will have had the pleasure of meeting our special guest already, as he has been moving amongst us in his unassuming way. But now it is my very great privilege, and pleasure, to introduce you all to the man I consider the most impressive *physical and psychical* medium in the world. Ladies and gentlemen, I give you Mr Christopher Clement Chase." Turning to his side with a bow, Lord Bennington revealed this paragon to be a short, slightly built, sandy-haired man of no obvious distinction. His face was not unhandsome but, at least from my distance, it was pale and ordinary; clean-shaven apart from a small moustache, and too bland to arouse much interest. He was in evening dress, like all the other gentlemen present, and the only thing that might have made him stand out in any way was his diminutive stature. Although not a dwarf, he appeared to be shorter than even many of the women in the room. I found myself thinking how "the Cossack" would tower over him, and imagined the huge servant lifting his little master with one hand, then carrying him cradled like an infant in his mighty arms.

Mr Chase had not yet spoken when the butler appeared in the doorway, attracting the attention of Lord Bennington. The master of the house looked put out by this interruption and barked out a single, interrogatory "Yes?"

"I beg your pardon, my lord, but there are two late arrivals —"

"Well, show them in!"

The man hesitated before saying, cautiously, "Their names are not on the guest list, m'lord. However, one is a lady known to you, and she says she was given an invitation by another whose name *is* on the list. So I wondered —"

Lord Bennington gestured impatiently. "Never mind your wondering. If the lady is known to me I think we may dispense with the details. Show them in." He held up an admonishing hand. "But they are the last. No one else is to be admitted once the lights have gone down, do you understand? No one, and no further interruptions."

"Yes, my lord." With a bow the man backed out. Moments later he returned, announcing the latecomers.

"Miss Fox; Signora Gallo."

My old friend swept into the room, head high, a vision in her favourite purple gown, black lace gloves and black eyepatch to match the gleaming jet beads draped in two long strands about her neck. Bobbing in her wake, smiling broadly and gazing around with bright interest, the little Italian medium wore the same scarlet dress I had seen before.

There were murmurs, but if Lord Bennington was put out he covered it well. Gabrielle spotted me at once and was headed my way when Lord Bennington caught up to her. He took her hand and kissed it. "What a pleasant surprise! Miss Fox, I do hope you will forgive me for not sending you an invitation, but as busy with your own projects as I knew you to be, I did not dare hope you would have time to spare, and as Mr Chase was so particular about limiting the number of guests —"

"You disappoint me, sir. I should have expected you to realise I would always, *always* make an exception for a lady as *charming* and *beautiful* as Miss Fox."

Until he spoke, I had not noticed Mr Chase slipping up behind Lord Bennington. His soft, fluting voice was a surprise; and now that he was near, his face seemed less ordinary. He had a mischievous smile and narrow eyes of a faded blue.

Already Mr Chase's attention had shifted to Signora Gallo, and he'd barely finished mouthing the usual polite formula of making a new acquaintance before enquiring, "And your friend, Miss Fox? What are her gifts?"

Gabrielle stared. "How do you know she is gifted? Did Lord Bennington tell you?"

Mr Chase shrugged. "I should be a very poor sort of psychic if I could not sense at least that much . . ." He turned his gaze from Signora Gallo to Gabrielle. "You *call* her a medium. What talent does she claim?"

She responded with a cool smile. "It would be better for you to see for yourself."

Lord Bennington frowned uneasily. "Now, see here, Gab — Miss Fox. I know you feel very strongly about your friend. And perhaps I was a bit abrupt with you when last we spoke. I will reconsider and see what I can do to help. But not tonight. This evening is for C.C. You're here as part of his audience, and it wouldn't be right —"

Mr Chase interrupted subtly, with the slight pressure of a hand on his host's arm. "When I have finished, I

168

would have no objection to seeing a brief demonstration of the lady's talents — if everyone else agrees."

"That's most generous, old man, but you needn't —"

"You know I am always interested to meet others who claim supernatural abilities. And your guests may find it instructive to compare *my* talents with *her* performance." There was a slight mocking twist to his mouth, and I found something a touch sinister in his look, but my old friend thanked Mr Chase effusively, and beside her the Signora beamed, too, although she had little enough attention to spare for him, distracted as she was by the glitter of jewels and gleam of gold watch-chains and cufflinks adorning the well-dressed folk all around us.

Lord Bennington attempted to lead Mr Chase away — naturally impatient to resume the planned course of the evening — but just then the American's gaze fell on me. I had been staring at him too boldly. Foolishly, I had not expected him to notice, and certainly never imagined how he would respond.

But something in his first sight of me struck him with unexpected power. He looked unusually interested. I was not accustomed to being regarded in that way by anyone, and certainly not by a male stranger. His eyes darkened. He took a deep breath and his nostrils flared, almost as if he tried, like a hunting hound, to take my scent. I had to fight an urge to back away.

"We have not been introduced," he said, moving closer, his eyes fixed on mine. "Richard, you never told me you had invited *another* medium."

169

"Eh?" Lord Bennington stared in confusion from me to Signora Gallo. "But you heard — What d'you mean?"

Somehow, Mr Chase had taken possession of my hand and, I think, kissed it, although I felt only the brush of his moustache, not the lips beneath. When he looked at me again his eyes were level with mine and he was smiling in a weirdly conspiratorial way. "What is *your* special talent?"

Although unnerved, I told myself it was absurd to allow this little man to make me nervous and frowned at his impudence as I replied, "Rationality."

He looked taken aback for just a moment, and close behind him, Lord Bennington chortled. "Good heavens, man. Your psychic powers have let you down. Miss Lane is no medium. She's a — why, she's a *detective!*"

Mr Chase still stared at me, but it was a very different look from before, and I much preferred it. He looked quite confounded. Then he rallied, his lip curling, and turned to glare at his sponsor. "*This* is your detective? What about that young man? You said —"

Lord Bennington clapped him on the shoulder. "They are partners! Jesperson and Lane. Come, come, surely you won't insult them by suggesting a woman can't be just as clever and observant as a man? I first met Miss Lane through her work for the SPR. She was, at that time, the constant companion of our Miss Fox. But since then, well, they have followed different paths, as you see. But both Jesperson and Miss Lane take a keen interest in psychic phenomena; I expect they'll be every bit as impressed by you as I am. So let's not make them wait any longer, eh, what?"

CHAPTER
THIRTEEN

The Séance

Mediums generally work their wonders in a dark room on the grounds that light is inimical to spirits, and arguments that employ an analogy between the summoning of spirits and the development of a photographic plate have been made, but even if it were true that certain phenomena could flourish only in darkness, this situation had long made it difficult for scientific researchers, whilst it allowed all sorts of trickery to go undetected.

One of the most unusual and interesting things about Mr C. O. Chase was his willingness to perform his wonders in a well-lit room. His mediumistic powers were unaffected by such exterior elements as the light, location, weather, or the belief or disbelief of the audience. Yet even he held to one exception: if spirits were to make an appearance, he explained, it could only happen after the room had been darkened. But that would take place, if at all, only after he had convinced us of the reality of his own powers.

Mr Chase settled himself in a solid, comfortable-looking brown leather armchair that might have graced many a gentleman's club or library. Beside the chair was a small, round, spindle-legged table with nothing upon it and, immediately behind him, was a piece of furniture decidedly out of place in this elegant public room: a large, plain wooden cabinet with two doors, it resembled a cheaply made wardrobe.

We were invited to seat ourselves where we liked. The majority of chairs, couches, ottomans and padded stools had been arranged on three sides of Mr Chase's central position. Mr Chase informed us — his voice sounding soft and curiously high in contrast to the deep rumble of Lord Bennington — that he wanted us to feel comfortable and at liberty to move about, even to stand or change our seats if we wished.

"That is, unless I ask for the lights to be lowered. If we are to be blessed by any spirit manifestations, I beg you all to stay where you are and keep quite still. Do not attempt to approach — and certainly do not try to touch — any spiritual manifestation, for that might disrupt the flow, and it could be dangerous." He stopped to clear his throat and looked around. "Before I begin, are there any questions?"

"I have one." The speaker, on his feet, was a young man rather undernourished in appearance, with a thin, clever face, whom I guessed to be the journalist Lord Bennington had mentioned earlier. He went on, pointing with a quick, stabbing movement of his hand. "That cabinet, behind you, there — is that a spirit cabinet?"

"You are very observant," said Mr Chase. "Yes, that is my spirit cabinet."

"Will you be using it this evening?"

"I am not sure that I take your meaning."

I wondered why Mr Chase was being so coy. We all knew how a "spirit cabinet" was employed. Whether it was a large wooden box or simply an alcove curtained off from the rest of the room, it was a place of concealment used by mediums, allegedly to enable closer contact with the spirit world. It functioned in the same way as darkness, but more thoroughly, keeping the medium's movements a mystery.

The first to introduce the cabinet had been a pair of brothers called Davenport, who had shut themselves inside bound hand and foot. Voices and music had been heard, and materialisations had been seen issuing from an opening in the cabinet, yet when the door was eventually opened, the two mediums were still securely tied up with rope, which was taken as proof — at least by the credulous — that they could have had nothing to do with any of the "spirit" phenomena. Many others since had adopted a similar practice, claiming that the cabinet allowed for the collection and intensification of spiritual energy. If Mr Chase meant to hide himself away inside that portable closet, the lighting of the room was less significant.

The young man patiently expanded his question: "Do you intend to shut yourself inside it?"

Mr Chase gave him a look that seemed to say the very suggestion was in shockingly bad taste. "No. Not I. That is for the spirits — a place they may gather, coming near without encountering any harmful emanations, such as can be caused by disbelief or other

174

wrong thinking . . . they will be safe there, while also close enough for me to benefit from their kindly help."

The journalist persisted: "Are you going to let us examine it?"

"For what purpose?"

The other man shrugged. "Call it curiosity."

"They say it killed the cat."

The reply brought a broad grin. "You're telling me it would be *dangerous*?"

Mr Chase frowned. "It could be, if the spirits were disturbed. Mind, I don't say they would be . . . the cabinet is empty at the moment. There is nothing to see, no reason for you to inspect it. What could I possibly be hiding? I tell you, there is nothing to see."

At my side, Mr Jesperson murmured, "Methinks he doth protest too much."

The young journalist shrugged again, a movement that made it clear his jacket was too big for his slender frame. "If you say it's empty, it must be empty, of course. But I'd like to see for myself. I can't help it. Otherwise I'll have to tell my readers: 'The celebrated medium refused to open the large wooden cabinet that stood so close behind his chair . . .'"

At that, Mr Chase jumped to his feet, hurried around to the back of the chair and seized the handle of the cabinet. After a moment of jiggling as the catch seemed to stick, the door swung open.

Mr Jesperson, keenly interested, followed the journalist to inspect the interior of the cabinet, even though, from where we sat, it was obvious that it was empty.

"I hope you are satisfied," said Mr Chase sourly, as both men, not content merely with looking, put their hands in and tapped the wooden sides. "Now, *if* you don't mind, I should like to get on with the demonstration."

The journalist withdrew without another word and the medium shut the cabinet up again.

Mr Jesperson waited. "Thank you for being so patient," he said politely. "Once the question has been raised, you know, it is always best to respond . . . no matter how senseless it seems to you."

He did not appear appeased. "What did you expect to find, Mr *detective*?"

Mr Jesperson smiled. "Nothing," he said softly. "And I found exactly what I expected." With a little bow, he turned and walked back to seat himself beside me.

"Now, are there any other questions, or may I be allowed to begin?" Mr Chase raised his eyebrows and looked around in a challenging way.

Everyone remained still and silent, so he unbent and smiled. "Lord Bennington," he said. "Would you be so kind as to fetch the musical instruments?"

"Certainly." With a sigh of relief that the planned demonstration was back on track, our host walked to the drinks cabinet at the other end of the room. He opened it and withdrew a shining brass trumpet and a silver mouth organ. These objects he carried back to set down on the round table at Mr Chase's side.

"Now, if you would inspect them both," said the medium. "Hold them up so everyone can see and confirm that they are exactly what they appear to be, no more or less, without any wires or other hidden attachments."

Lord Bennington turned the trumpet over in his hands, and then gave a similar inspection to the smaller instrument before setting them down again. "One trumpet, one mouth organ. Do you want me to make a noise with them?"

Someone tittered.

"No, m'lord, I intend that the spirits should do that. But first —" He turned his head and looked directly at me. "Perhaps our *detective* should like to inspect them?"

I felt sure he meant me, but Mr Jesperson was on his feet before I could move, and the medium made no objection, saying only, "Do you see a tambourine?"

"Of course. On the wall, beside a painted fan."

I was glad, then, that my friend had gone, because I had not noticed those things and should have felt a fool needing to have them pointed out.

"Pray, bring them both to me."

Mr Jesperson brought the Spanish souvenirs to the table, inspected them and declared them to be just what they seemed to be.

"If you like, inspect the trumpet as well." Mr Chase cast a sideways glance at Lord Bennington, who was lingering uncertainly. "There is no point inviting a detective if you give him nothing to do, m'lord . . . Well, sir, are you satisfied?"

"The three objects appear ordinary enough."

"They are, of course. It is my own person you should be examining." Mr Chase rose and held out both arms as if inviting crucifixion. Mr Jesperson began to pat his arms and feel along his sleeves for any hidden objects. Watching, I was reminded of the way stage magicians and professional conjurers direct the attention to one thing precisely in order to distract it from another. But what might he be hiding, and where? Until we knew what he meant to do it was hard to guess what to look for. In any event, nothing was found. Finally, Mr Chase asked that the table be moved another six or eight inches away from his chair — making it quite clearly beyond his reach. He dismissed Mr Jesperson and Lord Bennington, telling them to "go and make yourselves comfortable", and then he resumed his seat and closed his eyes.

The atmosphere in the room changed; I felt it in the way one senses an approaching storm.

The trumpet began to move.

To gasps and murmurs from the watchers, the gleaming instrument rose slowly off the table and into the air, where it hovered uncertainly, dipping from one side to another, before stabilising about three feet above the table. It shifted about, as if in the hands of an invisible person who was readying himself to play, and then sounded a short blast.

Mr Chase was leaning back, apparently at ease in his chair; body relaxed, arms still, feet on the floor, eyes closed, and the faintest smile on his face.

The trumpet continued to sound, producing nothing approaching a tune. It was like listening to a child's attempts, and before long, even the fondest of parents would have taken the instrument away.

Mr Jesperson rose and approached the brass instrument that honked and brayed as it glittered in the gaslight. He reached out cautiously, and as soon as his fingertips touched it, it went silent and fell. He caught it easily before it could strike the table.

Small sounds — mingled relief and disappointment — passed like a breeze through the room. Mr Chase opened his eyes, saw Mr Jesperson with the trumpet in his hand and said coolly, "Is that your idea of a trumpet solo?"

"Hardly. That is why I thought to stop it."

The medium sat up, frowning. "You should not have interfered. Didn't I say it could be dangerous? Never approach a spirit!"

"I saw no spirits."

"But you heard them."

My friend carefully put the trumpet down on the table. "I heard a beastly racket that was getting on my nerves. I thought something ought to be done about it. You said we should feel free to stand up and move about if we wished."

The two of them stared at each other, tense and still. In some other setting, one might have thought a fight was about to break out, but in the elegant surrounds of Lord Bennington's salon, with this audience of well-dressed ladies and gentlemen, manners prevailed over the almost instinctive hostility felt by the two men for each other, and they both slowly relaxed.

Mr Chase replied in a voice that was soft yet carrying: "Yes, and you should feel free to *leave* if

179

anything else gets on your nerves, rather than disrupt the spiritual atmosphere again."

Turning away from the medium, Mr Jesperson bowed to the room. "My apologies. I did not mean to spoil your enjoyment. I promise I will not do so again."

He returned to sit beside me, and I knew by the way that he moved that he was not in the least downcast or apologetic — and, indeed, I am sure that most of the other guests were as grateful as I that he had stopped that blasted trumpet.

Mr Chase made us wait, probably to impress upon us that what he did was no small matter, but relied upon the favour of spirits. We were good — even Mr Jesperson and the journalist waited as patiently as lambs for the next wonder.

Eventually, inevitably, the tambourine had its turn to swoop and rattle and dip and spin in the air before making sounds that seemed to be the result of invisible fingers that slapped, tapped and drummed upon its tight surface. And, after the tambourine, the mouth organ — at least this instrument managed to play a tune, unlike the random bleats of the trumpet, which joined in after a few minutes to make up the most unlikely and discordant three-piece spirit band, all hanging in mid-air and played by invisible hands as the table below began a clumsy dance.

It was impressive in its way, but ultimately meaningless; an absurd and pointless show, that differed from any number of séances I had attended only in that it took place in a well-lit room, and that I

180

found it impossible to guess how Mr Chase achieved his effects.

It is my opinion — some may call me cynical — that the popularity of musical instruments in the spirit world was invented for the purposes of fraud. I have encountered mediums who play instruments with their toes, or use mechanical devices — various forms of player piano and clockwork — or have a confederate dressed all in black who cavorts about the room with a fiddle or a flute decorated with luminous paint, or use other tricks too numerous to relate. But nothing I had encountered before could explain what we all so clearly saw: objects that moved and twirled in the air of an ordinary and well-lit room, without any visible means of support or propulsion.

After its clumsy dance in the air, the table returned to the floor, and subsequently each musical instrument fell silent and landed to settle back into its natural immobility. Then it was the turn of the fan to flutter about the room like a lopsided butterfly, pausing to fan a select few — causing many gasps, exclamations and merriment — before it hung itself back on the wall from whence Mr Jesperson had removed it.

A burst of spontaneous applause resounded throughout the long room — even the servants had forgotten themselves enough to join in.

I was impressed — how could I not be? It was wonderful, and it seemed impossible that any trickery could be involved. I knew what I had seen. The events were trivial, yet remarkable. That it was evidence for the existence of spirits I could not say, yet surely there was no *material* explanation for the movement of those solid, ordinary objects — the table, the fan, the musical instruments that played by themselves. Mr Chase had powers, beyond doubt.

This, I thought, *this* is the evidence that the Society for Psychical Research has been seeking. The evidence of more than two dozen witnesses, with none of the complicating factors that usually leave room for doubt. Mr Chase was a true medium, and no mere trickster.

When the applause died away, Mr Chase opened his eyes, rose and bowed to us. "Thank you," he said in his soft voice. "I am delighted that I was able to please you with a little demonstration. I am sorry it could not be more musical. Alas, I am a mere instrument myself, upon which the spirits sometimes deign to play.

"The spirits have favoured me tonight. Or I should say, they have favoured *us* — for on my own I am so little, merely one small soul. In a group . . . massed together . . . with so many souls and so much life-energy, we call upon the spirits with a louder, more powerful voice to which they are more likely to attend.

"So I thank you all — and thank the spirits who are here with us tonight."

His voice had been gaining volume and power, and now he raised his arms high. "They are here in this room. So many! The spirits of your own, beloved dead. Do you feel them?"

As he turned his gaze to sweep the room I thought of a preacher trying to win souls, and like members of his flock, most of the guests were nodding — some shyly, others in vigorous agreement, some with tears in their eyes.

"Yes," he said softly, and it seemed to me he fixed someone in particular — although I could not tell who — with his look. "Of course you do! We believe they are here — we *know* they are here among us, all around us: the friends and relations we miss so much and continually mourn. But we should not mourn. They have not abandoned us. Their love for us, like our love for them, fills this room. *That* is what we feel: not their living, weak, human presence, but the best of their immortal souls: their love.

"Why can't we be happy instead of sad? Why don't we remember that we never truly lose the ones who have loved us?"

He paused, and in that moment you could have heard a pin drop. No one attempted to answer his rhetorical question. He let a few seconds pass in silence, then he nodded as if he had received the answer from an invisible spirit, inaudible to us.

"Of course," he whispered, nodding. His voice at normal level, he went on, "Of course, it is because we are *human* and *mortal*. Few people understand that we are also *spirits* — all of us. On this mortal plane, most of us want something more than memories of love, we desire more than spiritual knowledge. When we have loved someone, we wish to feel them near us, and to feel them physically. How we long for the touch of that beloved hand, a kiss, even an embrace . . ."

"Steady on," murmured Mr Jesperson, and I had to bite my lip to keep from laughing.

The slightest cloud passed over Mr Chase's bland face and I wondered if he had he heard. "Still, we are material creatures, and only a *material manifestation* will convince most of us."

He put his hands together in a prayerful gesture. "If you will allow me, I should like to give you what you crave — proof that your loved ones, although passed over, are not lost and love you still. Through the medium of my own fragile, physical, imperfect body, I will attempt to give you that which you most desire. I beg the spirits to allow me to become the conduit, the channel, between the two worlds."

He dropped his hands. "The spirit world has been called the night-side of nature. Darkness is necessary. Please, lower the lights."

By their rapid response it was clear the servants had been given their instructions earlier. "Leave the one that is nearest the door," said Mr Chase. "That will be useful in the event that anyone finds it necessary to leave. And please light that candle on the mantelpiece. A single candle, particularly when near a mirror, exerts an attraction upon the spirits."

As the gas jets were lowered, the long room filled with a deep, shadowy darkness. It was like a different place, and resembled the setting of a traditional séance much more. Details were obscured, and people and furniture alike became little more than a variety of dark shapes in the murk.

As the armchair enveloped him, Mr Chase seemed to disappear into its mass.

Then the chair rose slowly off the ground. There were gasps of awe and surprise. Distances were harder to judge in the darkness, but it must have been hovering at least four foot above the carpeted floor when it ceased to rise.

"Stay where you are and remain quite still." This instruction, in the medium's calm, high voice, was hardly necessary, for I am sure we were all too astonished to move.

"Do not be alarmed. I am quite safe, supported by the spirits, and will remain so as long as everyone in the room is calm and still. Whatever happens, remember this: We are all surrounded by love. The spirits are with us."

His face began to glow with an eerie, greenish light.

There were even more gasps and a few small cries, but his steady, monotonous voice repeating that we were not to be alarmed, that he was safe, that we must stay still and calm, worked as a sedative draught. Even I felt peculiarly calm — although it did not strike me as peculiar at the time. I felt clear-headed and observant, but also detached, almost removed from the scene.

"The spirits tell me that some of you have questions, and they are pleased to answer, using me. There is no need for anyone to speak or identify himself. The spirits know all. If you have a question you want to put to them you need only shape it in your mind. You may ask anything in perfect freedom, quite as if you were alone. I am merely the conduit. I do not know who asks the questions, or why. I will simply repeat the words of the spirits. You may recognise their significance to you, or you may not. But they will be true answers, so keep them close to your heart, and someday you may understand. Let us begin."

An even greater hush now fell over the darkened room, as all eyes fixed upon the eerily glowing moon-like orb scarcely recognisable as the ordinary face of Mr C. C. Chase.

When he next spoke, his voice, like his face, was changed. It was louder and lower in pitch, and his delivery was less fluent, somewhat hesitant and jerky, like that of a student who recites a lesson without understanding.

"First question. The answer. There is someone who has recently become very close to you. This person is not to be trusted. Take care. Be cautious, circumspect. Remember, old friends are the best. Do not entrust your secrets, no, nor any *material* treasures to someone you have known for scarcely a year."

He fell silent again for at least a full minute. I noticed how the glowing light extended in wisps and hair-like tendrils all around his face.

"Second question. The answer. You will find that which you have lost. It is in your house, but in an unexpected place. Do not despair. Keep looking. Seek and ye shall find."

The medium continued to spout similar platitudes and vague advice in response to another six questions. If people recognised their own mentally transmitted questions in these answers, I could not guess. Apart from an occasional gasp or subdued sob, the audience stayed as still and quiet as he had commanded. With the waiting silences in between each "answer", it must have taken about a quarter of an hour to get through all of the questions. It felt longer to me. Once the novelty of the floating, glowing medium wore off, I was not impressed. Although I could not imagine how he had made his chair lift off the ground, and must admire his swift and effective use of the luminous paint he must have had hidden in the chair, I found his "mediumship" to be no more original or imaginative than that of any run-of-the-mill medium on the present scene. Anyone might have cobbled together such answers — particularly after the chance to speak with members of the audience beforehand.

I leaned forward, straining my eyes against the darkness, wondering if I only imagined the change I was seeing. It seemed to me that the glow was fading from the medium's face and migrating to form another shape a few inches to the right of his head. Yes, I was right — a ball of glowing greenish-white light had appeared.

It looked like a head . . . for a moment, I thought I was mistaken and Chase had simply moved, but no, I could still make out his form in the chair, including his head, even as it ceased to glow. And now the other glowing object was quite clearly the head of a woman — a distinct personage with open eyes, undeniably real and alive. There was something familiar about the face, although I could not think how I knew it.

She blinked and turned from side to side, looking, searching for something — or someone. Emotion positively radiated from her features, a mixture of love

187

and sadness. Then her lips moved and we heard her speak in a voice that sounded nothing at all like that of C. C. Chase. It was a musical voice and undeniably womanly, thrillingly low and warm as she said, "My dear . . . where are you? Oh, my dear . . . why do you call me back?"

A shiver ran through me, and I'm sure the yearning emotion in her voice affected all who heard it, but no one as much as Lord Bennington, who gave a choked cry: "Lorna!"

I realised then why the disembodied head looked familiar to me. Lady Lorna was Lord Bennington's late wife, and although I had never met her in life, I had seen her portrait.

"Dearest, do not mourn," she said. "I have gone to a better place now, and we will someday be reunited — you, and I, and our children. Until then, think of me fondly, but do not grieve. Live your life, care for the children, do good and let me go."

"Lorna — Lorna — I miss you so." His voice cracked and broke. He stood up, a hulking figure in the shadows.

"I know, my dear," the gentle voice replied. "But I am closer than you know. Remember that — remember — but *let me go.*"

He swayed; then I realised he was moving forward, awkward amidst the seated guests in the dark, crowded room, pursuing the ghostly, floating head. "Wait — *wait* — please, let me touch you. I must know . . . if only I could feel . . . Oh, stay. Just one kiss?"

188

The woman's head bobbed, and then it was gliding through the air, flying towards Lord Bennington. They were on a collision course — they came together — the woman's head struck Lord Bennington's, halting him; and as soon as contact was made, the disembodied head collapsed; it became a ball of silvery smoke, then dissipated into a shower of bright fragments.

The room was in uproar; someone shrieked, I heard someone else weeping and a man reciting the Twenty-Third Psalm. In what faint light remained, I saw Lord Bennington put a hand to his mouth, feeling for the imprint of ghostly lips on his.

CHAPTER
FOURTEEN

Spirited Exchange

"Light. More light."

The words came out in a croak, but they were from Mr Chase and they reached the servants through the general uproar. When light was restored to the room, Lord Bennington could be seen slumped on a sofa, his head in his hands, Lady Florence standing over him, patting his back and murmuring endearments.

The medium was still in his chair — now once more on the floor — head thrown back, eyes shut, face very pale.

Light returned, shock subsided. Weeping, shrieking and prayer were all out of place at this fashionable London gathering, and after an awkward interval the low murmur of voices increased in volume as awe and fear were transformed into a heady excitement. Lady Lorna's ghost! Only a few of them had known her in life, but we had all seen her . . . there could be no doubt, no mistake about it — the spiritualists had it right. Death was not the end, there could be communication between our world and the realm beyond . . . Lord Bennington's wife had come back to tell us all.

Eventually, pale and subdued, our host recovered enough to stand up and offer formal thanks to Mr Chase, who opened his eyes but otherwise remained unmoving.

"As we can see, Mr Chase is, quite understandably, exhausted by his wonderful efforts on our behalf," said Lord Bennington, beginning to choke up again. "Wonderful . . . but let us not speak of it yet." He cleared his throat. "What I mean to say is — let us leave Mr Chase to recover from his exertions and repair to the dining room for a light supper."

In an instant, the medium was on his feet, confounding any impression of him as a spent force. He positively exuded vitality. His eyes were bright, his cheeks had a healthy flush, and he bounced a little on the balls of his feet as if the energy he contained would not let him be still. *He might have just come in from a gallop across open land*, I thought, the sort of exercise that might have left his horse lathered, but merely sharpened *his* appetite for an evening of dancing.

"Not so fast, your lordship," he cried. "The show's not over yet."

We all stared at him.

He laughed. "Oh, it is true that the spirits have done with me for now. But, I'm not the only talented person here. Didn't I promise to give the Signora a chance? I don't forget my promises. I'm sure no one will mind waiting a little longer for their supper."

Signora Gallo looked more than half-asleep, listing slightly in her chair. At her side, Gabrielle gave her arm a surreptitious pinch and smiled sweetly at Mr Chase.

"*Most* kind. I'm afraid Signora Gallo dozed off for a few moments . . . the darkness, you know . . . I almost nodded off myself."

His eyes flashed. "I hope you weren't *bored?*"

"No, no, certainly not," she replied with smiling malice. "It was all *most* interesting, I'm sure. Signora Gallo was quite *stunned* by the power of your imagination."

As accomplished as she at the use of innuendo, he replied, "I think perhaps some other type of *spirits* are to blame for the little lady's indisposition?"

She gave him a murderous look. "Someone else might take that as a libel. And she is awake now. Aren't you, dear? That's right — a wee bit drowsy, I know. It *has* been a long day, but you're going to show all these lovely people — and Mr Chase — how the *good* spirits have blessed you."

"Take my place," urged Mr Chase.

Gabrielle rose and hauled the little medium upright beside her. After a brief pause to make sure she really could stand on her own, she guided her to the chair recently vacated by Mr Chase, then spoke to the room:

"I hope you will allow me a few words of introduction. Fiorella Gallo comes to us from Italy. She has been learning English since her arrival on these shores, a matter of only a very few months, and although she is very intelligent, her fluency lags behind her understanding. Thus, I will act as her translator. Signora Gallo has a very remarkable talent. She is *psychometrist*. That is, she has the ability to read a person's history or emotional states and concerns from

192

almost any precious valuable object they possess. She is also able to exert a magnetic attraction to such objects, particularly to items made of precious metals."

She was still buying time for Fiorella to recover from her strange stupor, and, as I took in the drooping eyes and dullness of her usually lively face, I wondered if Mr Chase's insinuating comment had been right. But surely Gabrielle, so careful in her management, would never have allowed her charge to get drunk.

At last Gabrielle could string out her introduction no longer. It was time for Signora Gallo to perform — if she could. Seconds passed with agonising slowness, and still the little woman in the chair, the recipient of everyone's attentive gaze, did nothing more than shift her weight a little and moisten her lips. She looked bewildered. Then she closed her eyes and frowned, as if trying to remember some complicated formula.

There was a faint tinkling sound, as of a glass lightly struck, from the other side of the room, and then a small object passed overhead. Something like a necklace, glinting silver in the lamplight, flew straight towards Signora Gallo, then dropped, landing on her bosom.

She gave a start, her eyes popped open and she fumbled and took hold of the object and peered at it in a puzzled way. It was, I saw, one of the silver labels that are hung on the neck of decanters. Signora Gallo held up the chain and we could all see the large silver letters spelling SHERRY. Already the tinkling of glass from the top of the drinks cabinet warned of another just before the WHISKY label fell into her lap. This was followed

193

by PORT striking her shoulder and then sliding to the floor, and concluded as MADEIRA landed on her head, tilting like a tipsy crown. By that time the room was in an uproar, everyone laughing at the poor befuddled Fiorella.

Well, *nearly* everyone. I did not laugh, nor did Mr Jesperson, nor Mr Chase, although his lips were curved in a smile as he gazed intently. Gabrielle stood rigidly still and silent until all four decanters had been relieved of their labels. Then she gave her head a rebellious toss and glared until the audience calmed. She took a deep breath. "What an unpleasant joke. I wonder what these objects may have to tell us about it?" Turning towards the medium, she froze when she saw what the rest of us had already noticed.

Sound asleep, head fallen back, mouth open and snoring, bedecked with labels, the signora might have been a moral illustration warning against the evils of drink.

There were a few uneasy titters from the audience, but I believe almost everyone felt more discomfited than amused. Lady Florence rescued the situation with her usual grace by reminding us about supper and starting a movement towards the dining room, rounding up stray guests like an elegant sheepdog. She gave me a meaningful look, so I stayed behind with Mr Jesperson, Gabrielle and her sleeping charge.

A minute or two passed in silence apart from the occasional snore. Gabrielle's expression invited neither question nor comment. It was a relief when Lady

Florence returned and asked Mr Jesperson if he would see Gabrielle and Signora Gallo safely home.

"My pleasure."

"You'll take my carriage. Afterwards, I hope you will return and have supper."

"That is very kind, but I have a job to do."

"Of course! I suppose detectives cannot keep bankers' hours." Still smiling at him, she seized my hand. "But I hope you can spare Miss Lane for a little while."

"With difficulty," he said gravely.

I knew he would not need my help watching over Arthur Creevey, and assured Lady Florence that I was happy to stay. She gave me a more intimate smile and warmly pressed my hand.

In response to her conventional expressions of regret that she should have to leave so soon, Gabrielle gave a haughty stare and said bluntly, "Signora Gallo is not an inebriate."

"Miss Fox — I never imagined for a *moment* —"

"Nor is she a fraud, nor evil-minded — unlike Mr Chase. You think he's wonderful, but I see through him."

"Of course, of course," murmured Lady Florence with a pained smile, as one who puts off an unreasonable child. "We must speak again very soon, Miss Fox. I hope your friend feels better in the morning."

Mr Jesperson lifted the sleeping woman easily and carried her from the room. The butler was waiting in the hall and the carriage was already at the door.

After draping Fiorella's coat over her like a blanket, Gabrielle turned to me with a brooding look, her mouth tensed reproachfully. "Enjoy your supper."

I felt a pang, knowing she considered my staying an act of betrayal. "I am sorry . . . Goodnight, Gabrielle." Swiftly, I leaned forward to embrace her. This was not our usual practice and it took her by surprise. As I made to kiss her on the cheek I whispered, "We will speak tomorrow."

She looked happier when we drew apart. "Goodnight, my dear. Thank you ever so for the loan of your Mr Jesperson. Such a useful gentleman. And thank you for the carriage, Lady Florence. We'll send it back for Miss Lane."

"Not too soon, I hope," said Lady Florence, smiling and waving them goodbye before she steered me away to the dining room where the others waited.

I would not have presumed to think they waited for *me*, but as I entered, arm in arm with Lady Florence, Mr Chase made it clear he had been anticipating my arrival by the way he indicated the empty seat at his side.

"I am so glad that you were able to stay, Miss Lane. It is too bad about the foreign lady, but at least she has a friend to look after her. I believe *you* were at one time a very intimate friend of Miss Fox?"

There was nothing unacceptable in the words he used, and his delivery was bland enough, yet they put me on my guard. As neutrally as possible, I agreed that this was so.

"How did the friendship break? Some people have speculated that the reason you parted was your discovery of some sort of imposture or fraud in which *she* was complicit —"

"Mr Chase." I interrupted him deliberately, my voice and manner chilly. "Why do you imagine I should wish to hear unpleasant and unfounded gossip about someone you *know* to be my close friend?"

"So there was no break?"

I turned to the gentleman on my other side, but he was too deep in conversation with another lady to offer an escape. "I cannot fathom why such personal details should interest you."

He smiled, his pale blue eyes boring into mine. "Who can say why *one* particular person exerts a peculiarly strong fascination over another? I only know that it is so for me."

"Then you had better question Miss Fox, although after the events of this evening, she is unlikely to be sympathetic"

"It is not Miss Fox who fascinates me."

At that moment, one of the servants who had been moving around the table with a silver serving-dish reached my shoulder, allowing me to break eye contact. After slices of cold beef and chicken had been transferred to my plate, the man moved on without offering any to Mr Chase.

"You don't eat meat?"

"As the spiritual sense develops, the body is more refreshed by a diet restricted to healthful fruits, grains and vegetables."

197

I smiled down at my plate. "I've heard you travel with your own cook."

"So you *are* interested in me." He gave a delighted chuckle. "I was beginning to fear my feelings were doomed to be unrequited."

His words gave me an odd flutter inside, and feeling it would be unwise to meet his eyes again, I kept mine fixed firmly on my plate as I replied lightly, "*Everyone* is interested in you, Mr Chase. After you displayed such powers, how can you be surprised? But is it true that you travel with such a large retinue that they require a separate house?"

He made no reply as another servant arrived with a tray of raw vegetables — sticks of carrot and celery, finely shredded cabbage, radishes and hothouse tomatoes. I by no means despised any of those things, but an imp of perversity made me refuse. Mr Chase murmured under his breath, "Jack Sprat would eat no fat, his wife would eat no lean."

I took the bread roll that was offered next, and added pickles and chutney to my plate. The sound of crunching filled my ears as my neighbour thoroughly masticated the raw carrots and celery, and for a little while I was relieved of the need to make conversation, although I was aware that I'd had no answer to my question. If I raised it again, I feared he would revert to his own unanswered questions about my relationship with Miss Fox.

What did he know about my reasons for leaving the SPR? What did anyone know? Gabrielle had not mentioned it to me since our reunion, and I had heard nothing more about the investigation in Scotland beyond one vague reference in the SPR journal stating that a full report was "in preparation". Since I had never shared my reasons for leaving with anyone, there could be no breath of scandal attached to the name of my old friend, despite the insinuations of Mr Chase.

But why did I assume Mr Chase was reliant upon the usual sources of gossip for his information? The man had special powers. Perhaps he *could* read thoughts, as Lady Florence believed. What if it was my own lingering doubts about Gabrielle's honesty that had alerted him?

At the thought that the man beside me might be in secret conversation, quite unknown to me, with the depths of my own self, I lost my appetite.

"You are very quiet," he observed.

I stared down at the mess of half-eaten food on my plate and said nothing.

"I hope . . . dear Miss Lane, I hope I have not offended you?"

He sounded so anxious that years of social training took over and I had to turn to reassure him, and as soon as I met his gaze I was trapped again.

"I never answered your question," he said softly, looking deep into my eyes. "Are you angry?"

"How could I be? I apologise if my question was too personal."

His eyes, never leaving mine, narrowed a little as he smiled. "I don't mind personal questions . . . from *you*."

To drop my eyes now, I thought, would be to flirt and play a game of maidenly modesty — behaviour I despised, so I stared back boldly. "Yet you avoid giving me an answer."

"You think I have, or wish to have, secrets from you?"

I said sharply, "Mr Chase, I find your tone and your attitude towards me quite . . . quite *offensive*."

I did not intend to make a scene, nor did I raise my voice, but unfortunately my unease had spilled over into annoyance during one of those moments — everyone has experienced them — when a sudden lull fell upon the gathering. In that quiet moment my angry words were heard by everyone in the room.

"Forgive me," he said, speaking distinctly. "I had no wish to offend. English manners are different from what I was used to back home — and different, too, from those on the continent. I've put my foot in it, I see. Can you forgive me?"

Everyone heard *that*, too, of course. He knew they would; his apology was aimed at the audience, not me; and even though his eyes continued to bore into mine, as if to compel my compliance, I did not believe a word of it. But I had no wish to prolong the quarrel.

"Of course. If no offence was intended, it was my mistake."

"Then we are friends again. I am glad."

I gave him a false smile and said nothing more. By this time, the sound of conversation had risen very nearly to a roar as everyone else around the table vied with each other to prove they weren't listening to us.

Mr Chase said nothing more to me, nor I to him. I picked at my food and was grateful to the gentleman on my other side for initiating a conversation, however uninspired, until the meal ended. Then, even though it had not been a formal dinner, Lady Florence took on the role of her brother-in-law's hostess and invited the ladies to retire with her, leaving the gentlemen to their port and cigars.

At this, Mr Chase announced that, as he considered smoking an abominable habit, he would prefer to accompany us. In any case, he said, the company of ladies was always preferable to that of men alone, and he thought this old-fashioned habit of separation should be abolished. I think he meant to be charming, but Lady Florence did not appreciate his remarks.

Fixing him with a regal glare, she said, "You misunderstand the purpose of the custom. It is not for the benefit of the gentlemen, but to give *us* a rest from being always obliged to raise the tone in mixed company. If you don't fancy being wreathed in cigar smoke for the next half-hour — indeed, I do not envy it! — you may withdraw, of course . . . but not with *us*."

Although he kept his face bland and smiled as he shrugged it off, Mr Chase was surely surprised and displeased. I did not have to wait long to learn what had caused her sudden change towards him.

She led us upstairs to the ladies' restroom that I had seen before, and pointed out the location of the water closet, before we returned to the large reception room downstairs where tea was being served.

As soon as she had assured herself that everything was in hand, Lady Florence drew me aside for a private word.

"You are looking very well tonight, Miss Lane. Your dress is unusual, and uncommonly fetching."

"You are very kind. Why do I have the feeling you disapprove?"

She shook her head. "I'm sorry. But there is something you should know. I must tell you that Mr Chase has a wife."

I stared at her without speaking.

She put her hand on mine and squeezed. "I should have mentioned it earlier, but it never occurred to me that he . . . that he might . . ." She stopped.

"Find me attractive?" I finished for her, making a face. "Believe me, Lady Florence, I took no pleasure in his attentions. His marital status is a matter of indifference to me. But where is his wife? Back home in America, I suppose, with no idea —"

"She is here."

"Here?" Startled, I looked around the room, trying to recall any possibilities amongst the female guests.

"I mean, in the house. She is upstairs, in bed I suppose. She did not join us this evening as she was feeling indisposed. She is often unwell, I fear."

I imagined a pale, consumptive invalid. "Have you met her?"

"Of course. She is a sweet, shy, delicate little thing, and very young. Hardly more than a child, she seems. They met in Paris."

"She's French?"

"No, a Russian princess. You remember the Cossack?"

I shuddered. "I wish I could forget."

"He belongs to her family."

"A relative?"

She looked shocked. "How could you imagine . . . someone like that . . . I mean he is their property. A serf."

I reminded her that the serfs had long been emancipated, but she was impatient with my pedantry.

"Technically, perhaps, they are free, but you know old ways linger on. His parents were certainly born into the bondage of the land, and as such they are effectively slaves of the landowners. So it would not be surprising if —"

"Talking politics, Flo?" An older, dark-haired woman in a badly fitted blue gown joined us in our corner. She gave me a cordial nod. "Sounds suspiciously like socialism to me — property and slavery in this day and age. And that little speech you gave downstairs — are you planning to join the suffragettes?"

"Not at all, Agnes." Lady Florence gave a trill of laughter. "In fact, we were speaking of history. I prefer to leave politics, along with cigars, to the men. Have you met my friend Miss Lane?"

CHAPTER
FIFTEEN

Asking the Cards

I was eager to discuss the events of the evening with my partner, but he still had not returned to Gower Street the following morning when Gabrielle arrived with her protégée in tow. A good night's sleep had restored the medium's spirits and vitality, but not her memory. She recalled arriving at Belgrave Square, and the glittering room full of well-dressed strangers; she remembered sitting down beside Gabrielle and listening to "the big, handsome milord" saying something about the American medium, but of the demonstration she remembered little, only that she had felt so comfortable and relaxed that she had nodded off. Perhaps fortunately, she had no recollection of her public humiliation.

Concluding her brief explanation she said, "So, I am asleep, and den I wake up and find myself in my bed." She shook her head, perplexed. "How this ting happen, I not know. I very sorry for it."

"You needn't apologise, darling," said Gabrielle. "It was not your fault. Not one bit of it. *He* did it. I don't know how, but he made you fall asleep, and then he made those things fall on you, and now you're a laughing stock, and everyone who saw it must think Fiorella is a drunken sot."

Passionately she assured me that although the signora liked a glass of wine with her meals, on that day she'd had nothing more stimulating than strong black tea; and nothing had passed her lips whilst they were in the house in Belgrave Square. "Otherwise, I should feel sure that *he* must have drugged her."

"Do you mean Mr Chase?"

"Who else?" She glared at me indignantly. "You surely don't mean to suggest the *spirits* have turned against Fiorella?"

I remembered how Mr Chase had insisted the sleepy medium should be made to perform. It would not, perhaps, have been surprising if she had been unable, but what had happened was not a sign of failing powers, it was a deliberate mockery; and Mr Chase was, I guessed, the only person in that room capable of causing it.

"He's ruined our chances in London."

"But why? She posed no threat."

"I disagree. I think he *did* feel threatened, foolish though it may sound. For all his great powers, Mr Chase is a small, vain, greedy man. He can't bear to *share*. He wants it all — the attention, the praise and most of all the *money*."

Despite my distrust of the man, her description did not convince me. He had treated Signora Gallo very shabbily, and had a cruel sense of humour, but it seemed to me that his behaviour was not the result of fear or any lack of confidence. If anything he was

205

overconfident, and delighted in displaying his power over someone who could not fight back. But I did not say any of what I was thinking, choosing instead to pick up on her final point. "Money? His wife is a Russian princess, and I think she must be very rich."

"Oh, don't be so sure. Titles in Russia don't mean what they do here," she said, without so much as a flicker to suggest she was surprised to learn he had a wife. "And even if she has a fortune, you must have noticed that rich people never think they have *enough*."

"But how much can he need?" I told her what Lady Florence had said about the retinue of servants who required their own house. "I can't imagine that Lord Bennington is funding that. But if Mr Chase can afford to rent his own house, why doesn't he live there with his servants?"

This time I had managed to shift her attention from the harm done to Fiorella's reputation. She stared at me. "How very strange. It may be only a little mews house, of course, but it's certainly an odd way of proceeding. Married couples usually like to have their own home if they can afford it, and if they are paying servants they don't need whilst living off Lord Bennington, the wife must be rich as Croesus." An idea made her sit up very straight. "Perhaps they aren't really servants, but relations — rough yokels from the backwoods of America who would be an embarrassment in an English drawing room, but he must support them, so keeps them tucked away out of sight."

"More likely they are *her* embarrassing dependents," I said, and told her about the Cossack. The memory of my brief, unexpected encounter with that strange figure in the upstairs corridor of the house in Belgrave Square still had the power to chill my blood, but I went some way towards diluting my fear by turning the experience into an amusing anecdote.

After that we discussed our perceptions of Mr Chase and his powers — the conversation I had been longing to have with Mr Jesperson. Gabrielle was determined to believe that Chase was a fraud, but that was no more than prejudice; she wanted to believe psychic powers were bestowed upon deserving souls only.

"But how did he work his fraud?" I pointed out that Mr Jesperson, Lord Bennington and the journalist had all handled the instruments and found no wires or attachments that could have been responsible for their levitation and noise-making. Mr Chase had been seated too far away and in full view of all of us, making the usual methods of fakery impossible.

"I don't know," Gabrielle admitted. "He must be *very* clever — I can't deny that. But the way he treated Fiorella — would any honest medium ever try to discredit the genuine powers of another?"

"I don't say he's honest. But he must have powers above the ordinary. The things we saw him do in full light . . . clearly visible —"

She jumped in quickly. "He didn't do everything in the light. His own levitation and the manifestation of Lord Bennington's wife — that's what people were most struck by. That's what they will remember when they speak of the powerful medium Mr Chase; not that nonsense with the trumpet, but the idea that he made a dead woman return.

"Oh, it was very convincing — I've never seen an apparition done better — but a very effective ghost can be made using muslin, luminous paint and a photograph. It would not be difficult to get a photograph of Lady Lorna. What about that spirit cabinet? It must have been there for a reason. There may have been a person hidden inside, dressed up like Lady Lorna —"

I reminded her of the way the apparition had vanished, but she waved away my objections. "Come now, you are usually more sceptical than I. Surely you do not take Mr Chase at his own valuation? That man is crooked."

"I do not trust him any more than you do. But if he is using trickery, I don't see how."

"The spirit cabinet —"

"Yes, I find that suspicious. But we'll have to ask Mr Jesperson."

At that very moment the door opened and in he walked, a newspaper tucked under one arm and his pockets bulging with rolls and pastries. "What did you want to ask me?"

"Good morning!" I said, giving him a look.

Remembering his manners, he said good morning to us all, and enquired about Signora Gallo's health. Formalities concluded, he drew up a chair and snapped open his paper. "You may be interested in what the journalist had to say about last night's séance."

208

"Ah, the man who inspected the spirit cabinet with you," said Gabrielle. "We were wondering: what did you make of it?"

He smiled to himself. "I saw what I expected to see. I cannot speak for the journalist, of course — but let me read you his words aloud."

The report of "a successful séance in Belgrave Square" had the faintly mocking tone one had come to expect from the popular press, but on the whole, it was quite respectful. The author of the piece admitted that, on the witness of his own senses, and having been able to observe everything from such an unusually well-lighted perspective, he was convinced that no trickery had been involved, and suggested that Mr C. C. Chase might be the proof that researchers in the Society for Psychical Research had been hunting for these past two decades.

I noticed that he made no reference to the spirit cabinet.

"That is because he thinks it was not used. And because he thinks — having been allowed to look inside — that it was empty. He never asked himself for what purpose such a large, empty, useless piece of furniture should have been set up behind the medium's chair."

"But you also said it was empty."

He shook his head reprovingly. "I did not. I said that I found what I expected to find — nothing. We all saw an empty cabinet when Chase opened the door, but there are such things as false backs and false bottoms. As a boy, I had a box into which I would ask some unsuspecting soul to place a coin. I would close it, make magic passes, hand it back. Lo, the coin was gone. More magic passes, and when I opened it *the other way*, hey presto! the coin had returned."

I said, "So there could have been someone hidden inside —"

Gabrielle gave a triumphant wriggle. "What did I say? It would have been someone dressed in black and wearing a mask with the image of Lady Lorna."

Mr Jesperson refolded the newspaper. Signora Gallo looked bored and fidgeted in her chair, and I suddenly remembered the original purpose of their visit and went to fetch the deck of cards I had borrowed from Miss Jessop's room.

They were special cards, a pack of seventy-eight that were very different from our own familiar playing cards. When not in use, they were kept wrapped in a large purple silk scarf, which I had not disturbed.

Handing the silken package to Signora Gallo, I asked her gently if she felt up to the task, telling her that I did not wish to over-tax her powers.

She bounced a little in her chair. "*Si, si.* Yes. Is fine." She unwrapped the little bundle and ran her fingers over the cards. Her eyes closed and she sucked in a breath and then slowly exhaled.

"*Si, si.* She is there."

"Where?" Mr Jesperson leaned forward intently.

"She thinks often of these . . . they are her friends and she misses them. It not like she thought. The beautiful angel, the man who carried her away, he is gone. He not come back. He not take her to heaven but to a leetle room."

"Where?"

The medium's eyes popped open. She shook her head. "They no say. She no know."

"Can't you tell us anything more? Is she still in London?"

The medium shrugged.

"Think about the room," Mr Jesperson urged. "Is there a window? Can she see anything outside? Is she alone? If she's a prisoner, she must be fed. Someone must come . . . who is it? How often? Does he speak to her?"

Under this barrage of questions Signora Gallo began to look peevish and hesitated, until at last she burst out, "They no say, these cards. Only paper! *Cheap*. No good."

Mr Jesperson looked sour. "A gold ring would, I suppose, be more informative?"

"Much."

"Or a diamond-studded bracelet?"

Her eyes glittered. She smiled and kissed the tips of her fingers. "But you no geeve me anything like it. Only dat book and now *cards*."

"I did tell you," said Gabrielle with a reproachful look. "She has done the best she can with inferior materials." She leaned over and gave Fiorella a warm hug. "You've done very well, my dear. Very well indeed. I'm not sure Mr Jesperson appreciates how hard it is. Just fancy, all those questions, to a pack of cards. We know she is alive — that is very good, but how can we find her? Please, darling, will you try again? Ask the cards. For the sake of poor, dear Miss Jessop, who never could afford any jewellery. I know you want to help the poor lady. Just think, Fiorella, if it had been *you*."

The gentle, coaxing words stirred some sort of fellow-feeling. Fiorella's expression changed and she stood up, clutching the pack of cards to her bosom.

"Maybe another way. I try read cards like that poor lady. Maybe we learn more."

She made her way to the plain deal table at the far end of the room. This was used for dining and for work, and now it offered an uncluttered surface upon which the cards could be laid out.

Mr Jesperson fetched a cushion and adjusted her chair. Signora Gallo bent her head and brought the deck close to her lips as if praying to them before she began.

Riffling through quickly, she removed one card — "La Papessa" — which she put down first. This card showed a nun-like woman in a voluminous blue robe and headdress, her face veiled, seated on a throne. Next, Fiorella shuffled the cards and cut the deck three times in one direction, three more times the other way, then instructed Gabrielle to make three more cuts and draw three cards at random.

These cards showed, in order, a skull-faced character riding a white horse, a tower struck by lightning, and finally a man in a pointed red cap, wand in one hand and a disc in the other, standing behind a small table on which were displayed a variety of trinkets.

Looking up, Signora Gallo held out her hand. Mr Jesperson understood the gesture and took a small coin from his pocket. He used it to sketch a cross above the cards, then dropped it into her palm.

For a moment I thought she'd object — it was only a threepenny bit — but she closed her hand upon the small coin, accepting this token wage.

Stroking La Papessa with one finger, she informed us that it represented Hilda Jessop. The next card indicated her recent past, when she had been carried away out of her life. Hilda had not suffered an actual, bodily death as her friends feared — yet it was a profound change in her circumstances that might yet lead to death, for the tower struck by lightning was a perilous place, filled with flames, and if she could not escape she would most certainly perish. The third card represented the possibility of a future in this world. This was the Juggler, representing cleverness, skill and subtlety. These, rather than brute force, were the qualities that might set the prisoner free.

"And I sink," said Signora Gallo heavily, "she cannot free herself. One man put her in there, and another one must bring her out. I *sink* dis one —" she tapped her finger on the Juggler card — "I sink he is *you*." On the last word she looked up at Mr Jesperson.

He sketched an ironic bow. "I should feel more confident if I had some *clue* as to where this flaming tower actually *is*."

"You must find the clues," she replied swiftly. "You are a detective, no? Is what detectives do."

"The cards can't tell you the *name* of the skeletal chap on the horse who put her in that blasted tower, I suppose."

"The cards don't work like that," Gabrielle chided. "They tell a story, but we have to work out its meaning for ourselves."

"I could have made up a similar story without the aid of those garish little pictures. An unknown villain is behind the disappearance of Miss Jessop. If she is not dead, she must be confined. If she is not rescued, she must die. And as no one else is looking for her, there is no one but me to play the part of the juggling fool." His voice and manner were chilly.

Gabrielle tried to win him back. "You must not blame the cards, or their interpreter. We are all trying to find Hilda."

Signora Gallo abruptly pushed back her chair and stood up. "We go now."

"Oh —" Conflicting emotions did battle on Gabrielle's face. I knew very well that she was not ready to leave us, but neither did she want to risk a quarrel with her protégée. She could not afford to lose Signora Gallo to the dangers and temptations of London, so she must follow. "If we must . . . but you *will* let us know if there's anything more we can do?"

When they had gone, Mr Jesperson asked his mother to bring a fresh pot of tea to the front room, where he shared out the parcels of pastries and we enjoyed a second breakfast.

"Enjoy, for this will be the last," he said in doom-laden tones.

I looked up sharply. "Do not say that Cook thinks you are now quite fat enough?"

"To serve at a cannibal feast? Certainly not. I meant only that I shall be spending no more nights on guard duty to Mr C."

"Why not?"

He gave me a look of reproach. "Do you need to ask? Now that we know the significant factor is a *telephone* call, and since I have tested the possibility that Mr Creevey might walk again the next night if his attempt was foiled on the first — we must wait for the next telephone call. That there will be another is, I think, certain, and it will be soon.

"I was late returning this morning because I was making arrangements with Creevey's wife and his office boy that they are to let me know the very moment he receives another 'wrong number' via the telephone. When that happens I will be waiting outside the house, ready to follow."

Some time after this discussion the second post arrived with a letter addressed to me in an unknown hand. The letter was written in French and signed Nadezhda V. Chase.

She sent her apologies that her health had prevented her from making an appearance last night, and begged me to gratify her with my company at my earliest possible convenience. She was accustomed to receiving visitors at Lord Bennington's house, in the small drawing room, where we could be quite private, from half-past ten in the morning until one o'clock, and begged me to come very soon — tomorrow, or the next day.

"Not bad news, I hope?"

I looked up from the page to find Mr Jesperson gazing at me with some concern. "No, not at all," I said. "If I frowned, it was from the strain of reading a language not my own." I took a deep breath, trying to settle my nerves. "It is from the wife of Mr Chase. She has the curious desire to meet me — and as soon as possible."

"What is so curious about that?"

I looked down at the letter without seeing it. My cheeks felt unpleasantly warm. What had Mr Chase said to make his wife so anxious to meet me? She had wasted no time in sending this far-from-casual invitation. She must have written it late last night or early this morning and posted it immediately. I had not told Mr Jesperson about Mr Chase's unpleasantly intense interest in me at the dining table; indeed, I had not shared any of my personal, embarrassing feelings from the previous night, preferring to discuss the things we had seen together in a more intellectual and theoretical way, and I still felt disinclined to lower the tone. Mr Chase's interest was not something I had invited or wished to encourage, and even speaking about it to someone else might make it seem more important than it was. If he had mentioned me to his wife in a way that made her jealous . . . the idea that I could be the cause of a wife's jealousy or distress was as uncomfortable as it was unaccustomed; but if that should prove to be the case, I would deal with it; I would be able to make her understand that she had nothing to fear from me.

216

Mr Jesperson was still waiting for my reply. I looked back up at him and attempted a casual shrug. "Of course, she may wish to make more acquaintances in London; why not start with me? But there can be no urgency about our meeting. I simply cannot think why she should *summon* me like this."

"Perhaps she finds herself in need of a detective."

His words lifted my concern. All at once, I had a new way of interpreting her letter, and no longer dreading an uncomfortable encounter, I became eager to meet Mrs Chase.

CHAPTER
SIXTEEN

Tête-à-Tête in Belgrave Square

I set off the next morning more curious than nervous about my impending meeting with the Russian princess. It had been foolish of me to imagine that anything Mr Chase had said to her about me could have aroused any feelings of jealousy or suspicion in her breast. She might simply be curious to meet a female detective, but the emphasis on speed in her letter made me anticipate a mystery to be solved.

The fog had cleared away, and as it was neither raining nor snowing, I found the cold bracing and enjoyed my walk through the busy streets. It seemed no time at all before I was once again standing outside the house in Belgrave Square, then ringing the bell, and then admitted by the same superior butler.

"Good morning, Miss Lane," he murmured. "Mrs Chase is expecting you in the small drawing room. Please allow me . . ."

We went through corridors to a drawing room that could only be described as "small" by comparison with the very large one in which the séance had been held. It had a huge marble fireplace, thick Turkish carpets, large windows decked with heavy draperies, several sofas, numerous chairs and tables, bookcases and writing desks, floor vases with dried flowers and ostrich plumes, sculptures, and other ornaments and furniture in such an array it was quite bewildering. I would hardly have known where to look, or in which direction to turn, if not for the guidance of the voice that thanked the butler and welcomed me from a corner of the lavishly furnished room.

Mrs Chase — who I guessed the semi-recumbent figure must be — wore a yellowish-green gown that clashed slightly with the blue-green velvet of the chaise longue on which she reclined. She did not rise, only beckoned me to come nearer, and then, patting the cushion, to sit beside her.

She was a small woman, her skin pale and fine as porcelain, her golden hair in old-fashioned yet undeniably becoming ringlets, all of which combined to give her a doll-like appearance, but I did not understand how Lady Florence could call her "a child," for she looked to my eye nearer thirty than twenty. Of course, illness can be aging, but when I came closer, I found something sharp and suspicious in the way she watched me, something very far from childlike.

Although my spoken French was rusty, the old formulae of politesse flowed readily enough; I was able to assure her that meeting her was an even greater pleasure for me, to express my concern for her health and hope that she was better, and so on, and it was easy, too, to understand her equally formulaic replies.

It was only when that business was past and I had paused, waiting for her to raise the next topic of conversation, that I suddenly realised we were not alone in the room.

Mr Chase stood motionless near the window, his olive-green suit blending into the eau-de-nil curtains. When he saw that I had noticed him he stepped forward with a strange smile on his bland, round face.

"Good morning, Miss Lane. How nice to see you again. I am pleased you were able to answer my wife's invitation so swiftly. She appreciates your interest. It will be good for her to have a friend in London."

I found his gaze as disconcerting and as intimate as before, but this time it was easier to look away as I returned my attention to his wife.

"It will be my pleasure to call you my friend, but I'm sure you don't lack for company here. Although he is widowed, Lord Bennington entertains widely, and of course his sister-in-law Lady Florence — you've met her, I know — has —"

I stopped, guessing from her blank expression that she had not understood a word, and tried to say the same thing again in French. But I was flustered; I stumbled and groped for the right phrases while she gazed at me in silence.

"Relax," murmured Mr Chase, disturbingly close to my ear. "Relax, and trust me. I will not interrupt your tête-à-tête — I can make it possible for you to talk. Remember, I am a medium, a channel, a conduit. The spirits speak through me and so can you. My wife is happy to do so; you must agree. It will be much easier if you let me be your translator."

He moved to stand at the back of the chaise longue, placing himself between us as if he were a living telephone with magical abilities, and if I spoke into one ear in English, and Mrs Chase spoke into the other in French, our words would come out of his mouth in a way we both could understand.

I would have to trust him to translate accurately — and I did *not* trust him, and yet . . . it was somehow impossible to refuse. It would be an insult to him and his wife if I asked him to leave us alone together, but as long as he stood between us I might never know her *real* reason for summoning me. Perhaps she had a secret to confide, something only a *detective* might help her with?

Somehow, I would have to get through this awkward visit. At least my understanding of French was better than my ability to make conversation in it; if I noticed him taking liberties when he translated, I would call him on it at once; he might pretend to be offended, but he would have to explain himself.

In the meanwhile, I thought my best course of action was to accept his presence without allowing it to inhibit me; I would try to pretend he was no more than a mechanical translating machine — an object like a telephone — and I would speak to Mrs Chase about whatever I chose. What did I have to lose? *She* might tell me what *he* had not.

I began, prosaically enough, by asking her how she found London. She said she had scarcely seen anything of it; everyone had been extremely kind, but since their arrival more than six weeks ago, ill health had kept her largely confined to the house. This was not new; she had been born with a weak constitution.

This was my cue to enquire about her illness, causes, treatments, whatever, but after a brief expression of sympathy I stuck to my plan, regardless of how bizarre it might seem, and asked how their servants liked life in this city.

Our translator's gaze flickered with surprise, but he managed my question smoothly enough.

Widening her eyes, she murmured that she did not understand.

"It is not difficult," I responded. "You have a maid, I suppose?"

"Bien sûr."

"And your husband — a manservant?"

"*Oui, Pyotr, mais —*"

"They are Russian, *non?*"

"*Non,*" she said firmly. Then she shook her head, admitting that her husband's man, Pyotr, was certainly Russian, but her own maid was a sweet, intelligent girl from Normandy — and, she added, she was baffled by the interest I took in this matter.

I claimed that, in addition to my work as a detective, I also wrote articles for magazines, and said I was currently working on something about "the servant question" for that excellent journal *The Lady*. Before Mr Chase had time to translate this little fabrication, I added swiftly, "*D'ou vient votre cuisinier vivre?*"

Mr Chase forgot his rule of non-engagement long enough to stare at me and ask, "Did you really mean to say 'Where does your cook live'?"

I set my jaw stubbornly. "But of course."

Mrs Chase giggled. Then she said, her French so slow and distinct that I could not fail to understand: "We have no cook. Lord Bennington's cook is an Englishwoman and I suppose she lives somewhere upstairs, or perhaps in a room adjoining the kitchen — I do not know; I have not enquired. Why should I? Why do you think we have our own cook, when we are living here as the guests of Lord Bennington?"

I felt almost as big a fool as she must have thought me. "I do beg your pardon, Madame," I said softly. "I hope you did not find my question insolent. I admit, it sounds absurd, but . . . I am afraid I have been listening to gossip. I was led to believe that due to your husband's special dietary regime and your own illness, you travelled with your own retinue of servants, including a cook." At the last moment, I decided not to mention the part about the separate house required by these imaginary servants.

She laughed and, shaking her head, wondered where such an idea could have come from. She had a maid, as she had said, but so did most ladies, *n'est-ce-pas?* Her husband's manservant was in reality an old family retainer; he had no skills as a valet, but it had been an act of charity to take him on and give him a place to live. Had I not seen the Cossack for myself, I might have imagined she spoke of some doddering relic.

Eager to change the subject, I reverted to her health. Perhaps she would find a specialist in London who would be able to suggest a cure?

She sighed and shook her head. There could be no cure; it was not so much an illness that plagued her as a constitutional weakness. She had her good days — like today — and her bad ones. Her heart was not strong. She had been advised not to tax it, to rest, lead a quiet existence and not over-exert herself.

"But what sort of life is that?" she said. "I want to live — I *must* live until my heart gives out. Then I shall die. I would rather die young, doing what I want to do, with the man I love, knowing I am alive, than live like a solitary little mouse wrapped in cotton wool, afraid to run, afraid to squeak, only for the sake of a few more years, to die in that nest, worn out at the age of forty instead of burned out gloriously at thirty."

I was moved by her emotion, but it was strange and not very pleasant to hear her fluent, passionate French words turned into English by the flat American monotone clinging to her like an aural shadow. I found myself feeling more sympathetic now that I understood her situation. Perhaps we *could* be friends, after all.

But there were so many more interesting things to talk about, she went on; she did not wish to dwell on her physical health; sometimes it seemed that was all she ever talked about, and it was really so dull. She would rather hear about things that happened beyond her limited horizon — beyond the walls of this house, splendid though it was. Wouldn't I tell her something about my experiences as a lady detective? It must be so exciting! Was it dangerous? She could scarcely imagine. What case was I working on now?

"Oh, I'm sorry, but I really can't discuss any cases in progress," I said. "I'm sure you understand — when clients entrust their problems to us, it is not unlike visiting a physician. You would not expect your doctor to discuss your case for the amusement of others."

She pointed out, reasonably, that doctors did write about interesting cases, although that was more often for purposes of education than amusement. And the newspapers were full of crimes; baffling mysteries were all the rage, everyone wanted to hear how they were solved. She did not understand my reticence. Perhaps we only *hoped* to be detectives . . . or only solved uninteresting cases, apprehending boot boys who had stolen shoes? If privacy was my concern, I should use invented names — call my client Mr A and the villain Mr X, and so on.

I found it impossible to refuse, and decided there could be no harm in it. I would say nothing of our current investigations, but told her instead about the curious affair of the deodand — one of the first, and strangest, mysteries we had solved.

Unused as I was to being the centre of attention, I discovered there was something quite seductive in being listened to so attentively, with such obvious interest and respect, particularly as I was talking about an adventure in which I had played no small part.

Yet this experience was stranger by far than any ordinary conversation. I had never before spoken to someone else through an interpreter, and had not known how strange it could be to speak and then hear at my side another voice taking up my words and issuing them in different language. His voice in my ear was like a slow, corrupted echo; a soft, oddly-accented monotone.

The eyes of Mrs Chase, although rounder and wider, were the same faded blue as her husband's. They fixed upon mine and held my gaze. She seemed to hang on my every word and yet, at the same time, not to hear me at all, for she waited for her husband's voice, and so her understanding lagged behind.

The feeling of estrangement grew; it seemed I must listen to Mr Chase before I knew what I had said, and I began to lose my way in my own story. It was oddly dream-like. Mostly it was a pleasant dream, although at one point I became anxious that I had said the wrong thing, or voiced something that should have remained unsaid. I must have spoken my fear aloud, for Mr Chase said, and his wife chimed in her agreement, that I must not worry about anything, I had said only what was right and proper, and it had been most interesting.

When I left Belgrave Square an hour or two later, it was with warm feelings for both Mrs and Mr Chase. The unease he had inspired in me earlier was quite gone. I felt how unfair and irrational it had been of me to mistrust him in the slightest. And the idea that Mrs Chase could have been jealous of me or any other woman was patently absurd. Clearly he adored his wife, and she loved him; their love for each other was so strong, I almost felt a bit of it had rubbed off on me during our three-way tête-à-tête.

CHAPTER
SEVENTEEN

A Nightmare

When I got back to Gower Street in the early afternoon, I found Mr Jesperson getting ready to go out, but he paused long enough to enquire about my conversation with Mrs Chase.

"Oh, it went very well," I said, smiling, still buoyed by a pleasurable feeling I could not have explained. "She is a lovely young person, highly intelligent; we had a very nice gossip."

"Gossip?" he repeated with a disbelieving stare. "That doesn't sound like you, Miss Lane."

"Chat, then. Talk. Discussion," I said, a little flustered by his challenge. "What does it matter what word I use?"

"But what did you *gossip* or *chat* about?"

My mind was suddenly blank. "Nothing that would interest you," I said briskly, hoping to bring an end to this pointless interrogation.

"No mystery, then."

I frowned, puzzled, and shook my head. "No mystery at all."

"Too bad," he said, and it was only then that I remembered his idea, which I had taken up so enthusiastically, that Mrs Chase had invited me to call on her because she was in need of a detective.

"Never mind," he went on, making sure he had his pocket book and pencil safely stowed in a pocket. "It may be that our time will be more fruitfully occupied with this case. I am on the scent. I've just learned that a certain Colonel Evans *may* have seen Monsieur Ribaud getting into a cab on the evening he vanished. He has been installed at Carters' Hotel, with his wife, for the past two months."

When I looked blank, he explained: "Carters' is practically next door to the Albemarle. I am going to speak with him now. I've told Mother not to expect me for tea — but I will telegraph if I'll be very late. If there's any word regarding Creevey, leave a message at my club."

I had every intention of waiting up for him, but by ten o'clock I was yawning my head off and had no choice but to retire to my bed.

I must have fallen asleep as soon as my head hit the pillow, and slipped without effort into a deep, restful slumber — from which I woke suddenly, heart pounding in terror.

Even in darkness I knew I was in my own familiar bedroom. What had frightened me? The usual faint glow of the street lamp filtered through my curtains, but showed me nothing amiss. I strained my ears, trying to catch a hint of what had awakened me, but no footsteps echoed on the pavement, no wheels of traffic, no voice or any other human sound gave me a clue — I guessed it was very late. What made my skin crawl with dread?

Then I saw him.

A man stood motionless at the end of my bed, watching me. With the window at his back his face was shadowed, and I could make out nothing that might have allowed me to identify him. In fact, I could only see the outline and mass of his head and shoulders, but that was enough to reveal his large size and very great height.

I tried to scream, but it caught in my throat. For a horrible moment I was frozen, as in a nightmare, unable to make a sound or to move.

And then I broke free, thrashing about beneath the bedclothes until I managed to extricate myself, and rolled out of the bed on the side farthest from the intruder. Leaping blindly forward, arms outthrust, I managed to reach the door; my fingers connected with the knob; I flung the door open and all but fell into the corridor.

With a sob of fear, I scrambled towards the stairs.

Upstairs was in darkness, but downstairs a single light had been left burning in the hall for Mr Jesperson. From this I deduced — with the tiny bit of my mind that was not consumed by abject terror — that he had not returned, and so it was perhaps not as late as I had thought. But then, as I ran down the stairs so recklessly fast that only my fierce clutch of the banister kept me from tumbling head over heels, I saw his coat, scarf and hat hanging on the coat hook, beads of moisture still adhering to the fabric.

Isn't it a wonder how many thoughts can occupy the same space at the same time — and in what seems no time at all? In fear for my life, I was still able to absorb all these small details and understand that Mr Jesperson had just come in, and must be close at hand, most likely in the front room, stirring up the fire to warm himself, or seated at his desk, pen in hand, jotting down notes that he would share with me in the morning.

So why did I not run to him for help? As soon as I told him he would go upstairs and deal with the problem — with pistol, walking stick, or his own cleverness.

But even as one part of my mind considered this, I realised that I did not need his help. The problem was in my own mind. I had been frightened by a nightmare — startled half-awake by the sound of Mr Jesperson arriving home. There was no intruder. What would he think of me if I rushed in babbling about a big tall man who had scared me in my room?

I couldn't bear to have him see me as a weak and silly woman. I enjoyed our comradeship, with its ease and feeling of equality, too much. *Of course* I would not run to him with such a foolish fear.

All this *thinking* takes far longer to describe than it did to experience. At the same time as all that went through my mind, I was flying down the stairs, and still — despite my realisation that there was no actual living person in my room — driven by one powerful imperative: to get away.

It is impossible to give a reason for the urge I felt to go outside, because *reason* had nothing to do with it.

230

The force of my fear had impelled me out of the room and onwards; and made me feel I would not be safe anywhere in the house and that I must get outside. I was not aware of making a decision; I was driven by instinct.

Get out get out get out . . .

The distance from the foot of the stairs to the front door was not very great, and already as my feet came down on the hall carpeting, my arm was thrust out, hand ready to grasp and undo the bolt that would allow me to open the door, and I would have done just that and rushed outside if I had not seen the evidence of Mr Jesperson's recent arrival and if I had not paused to *think*.

I realised many of them were silly, random thoughts, driven by vanity, and now I saw how absurd it was to worry about shocking Mr Jesperson — the person I had come to think of as my best friend — with the sight of me in my nightgown, if I was willing to offer this same unedifying sight to any passing stranger.

It made no sense to run into the street. My safety was here, in this house.

Then I realised that, still acting without conscious intent — as if in a dream — I had attired myself in Mr Jesperson's coat and scarf, and my hand was on the door. But I had no shoes. I paused, confused. What was wrong with me?

Mr Jesperson came out into the hall. "I thought I heard —" His eyes widened. "Miss Lane. What's the matter?"

What a sight I must have made, draped in his coat with bare feet, his scarf pulled over my untidy hair, like someone forced to flee a burning building.

I tried to explain, well aware how feeble my explanation must sound. "I'm sorry — I had a nightmare." I began to back away.

He kept his eyes fixed on mine as if to keep me from fleeing. "*Only* a nightmare?"

I shrugged uneasily. "It must have been. I thought it was real, but . . . now I am awake —"

"Tell me." His tone brooked no argument.

I took a deep breath. "I woke, quite suddenly, and saw — *imagined* that I saw — a man standing at the foot of my bed. I was seized with terror; I could not scream, I could think of nothing but escape." I gestured at his garments now draped around me. "I must still have been half-asleep. I'm sorry to have disturbed you. I'll go back to bed now."

"Wait. I had better go with you — just in case. Don't move. I'll be right back." He returned in a matter of seconds armed with a lamp and his revolver.

He went up the stairs ahead of me.

There was no one in my room.

We both knew it at once. It is a question of atmosphere: an empty room feels different from one in which someone is hidden. Nevertheless, Mr Jesperson carried out a thorough inspection, making certain there was no one hiding beneath the bed or behind the curtains. The window was latched shut, and the pattern of condensation on the panes looked undisturbed.

I yawned and sat on the edge of the bed. My fear drained away, I was overwhelmed by tiredness.

"Tell me exactly what you saw, and where," he commanded,

"I *thought* I saw a man's head and upper torso — I would say in outline, but it was more solid, somehow. He stood with his back to the window, so I could not see his face; he was like a solid shadow." The fear came back, icy fingers prodding me. I shuddered. "He stood just *there*, about two feet from where you are standing, but he was much taller."

"*Much* taller?"

"At least a head higher. And more massive."

"Like Mr Creevey?"

"It was not Arthur Creevey," I said decidedly. "I shouldn't have felt so terrified if it was."

"Not even if he appeared uninvited in your bedroom? What strange power does that fellow possess? Not only the woman he married, but spinsters are equally susceptible to his charms."

There was something in his tone I did not like — or it may have been the word "spinster", warranted though it was — and it stiffened my spine. "I have told you, it was *not* Mr Creevey."

"How can you know that when you told me you could not see his face, or anything, really, but his size?"

"Because there was something sinister and terrifying about the figure, despite the fact that it was motionless; a dangerous, powerful menace that I simply do not associate with Mr Creevey." I sighed and shook my head. "We are discussing a dream, sir — a waking nightmare. Such things have their own logic, and it is pointless —"

"I'm not so sure. Do you customarily suffer from nightmares? Have you ever had one like this before?"

I sighed again, but this time the sigh turned into a yawn that brought tears to my eyes and made a reply impossible.

"I am sorry," he said. "I shouldn't badger you with questions — not now. You've had a dreadful fright and need to rest." He made his way to the door and then paused. "Shall I leave the lamp?"

I assured him I would not need it — my eyes would not stay open for much longer. As I heard the door shut quietly behind him I lay back on the bed, still wrapped in his coat, and fell fast asleep.

CHAPTER
EIGHTEEN

The Ghastly Head

The next morning I found Mr Jesperson in the kitchen making coffee, and deduced from the wildness of his curls and the faint shadows on his cheeks and chin that he had not yet faced the looking-glass. The kitchen was as neat as a pin except for a small area of the counter where Mr Jesperson had spilled ground coffee and splashed water.

"Your mother has already gone out?"

"Yes, some deucedly early meeting regarding charitable works, leaving us to fend for ourselves. I thought we'd breakfast on my extra-strong coffee and buttered bread — unless you'd care to take over cooking duties?" He gave me a hopeful look, but I shook my head.

"Coffee and bread suit me admirably. Your coffee is as good as any I've had elsewhere — if you will make it with heated milk."

With a martyred sigh, he reached for the milk pan.

I was glad he was treating me as always, and although I did not expect the subject of my nightmare to be ignored forever, I was relieved that he did not make it the first order of business.

Instead, when we were seated at the kitchen table with plates of bread and butter and cups of hot, strong, delicious *café au lait* before us, he told me about his own most recent investigations.

He had met with Colonel Evans and his lady, late of India, presently resident in Carters' Hotel. They told him how they had been walking in the direction of Piccadilly Circus on the evening of October 5th, when a hansom cab pulled up alongside, and the passenger called out "Ree-bow", which proved to be the name of the gentleman walking just ahead of them.

Although the man in the cab appeared to know *him*, Monsieur Ribaud seemed puzzled and approached with caution. But after a brief exchange — unfortunately inaudible to Mr and Mrs Evans — the Frenchman had climbed inside the cab and off it went.

None of this was likely to have taken us any farther, since there are approximately four thousand hansom cabs in London today — this figure courtesy of Mr Jesperson, who added that if you included "growlers" the number would rise to seven thousand — but it so happened that Colonel Evans had recognised the cab as the one he and his wife had taken from the theatre the night before.

This sounded far-fetched, but Mr Jesperson explained that the Colonel was a great connoisseur of horseflesh, and took notice of the animals wherever he encountered them. The horse pulling this cab was, according to him, "an unusually handsome grey", and he had fallen into conversation with the driver on such subjects as pedigrees and fetlocks. At any rate, he noticed the horse and exchanged a nod of recognition with the driver.

"I was able to find the cab driver based on the information I had from Colonel Evans, and although at first he positively laughed at me for imagining he should remember anything about a casual passenger he picked up a month ago, it turned out he remembered the horse-loving Colonel, and the coincidence of his passing by at the very moment that his 'queer fish' of a passenger called out to the Frenchman brought the memory back to him."

The driver had picked up this first passenger at Charing Cross. The man was, he thought, a northerner, or perhaps Irish, and had only recently arrived in London. He asked to be taken to the Albemarle Hotel, but then changed his mind and asked to be driven about for a bit, to see the sights. However, he soon demanded to be taken back to the Albemarle. He said he wanted to wait for a friend. Well, there was nothing wrong with that, as he was being paid just the same.

"Was he able to describe this passenger at all?"

"Unfortunately he hardly saw him. It was already dark and rather foggy when the cab was hailed, and there was nothing outlandish about the man's attire or manner, and nothing memorable about his face. Clean-shaven — he *thought* — but he couldn't be sure. And he wasn't very friendly."

"And Monsieur Ribaud?"

"He heard nothing of what his passenger said to him, only remembered that he took them to the Café Royal. So that's where *I* went next."

One of the waiters there recognised the portrait of Monsieur Ribaud, and although he could not be certain it was on the night of October 5th, he knew it was a few weeks ago and that there had been two gentlemen — two Frenchmen."

"*Both* of them?" I stared in dismay.

"They conversed in French. The waiter recognised the language. He said he might be able to recognise the other gentleman if I had *his* photograph, but as far as giving a description . . . 'Moustache but no beard, brownish hair, well-dressed but nothing special'."

"So we're no further along, really," I said sadly.

I got up and cleared away our breakfast things. When I began washing up, he joined me at the sink, a teatowel in hand. We worked together in silence for a few moments, and then he spoke.

"About your nightmare."

My heart beat a little faster. "Yes?"

"I know you have said you could not see the man in any detail. Even so, you felt quite certain who it was *not*. Not me and not Mr Creevey, although it was a man of a similar size. Did you instinctively feel that the man was a stranger? Or was it someone you might have recognised in the light?"

My skin prickled with horror as the answer came into my mind. I had not thought it before — perhaps had not let myself think it — but at his question, the huge, hulking figure and smooth, grey-white face of the Cossack appeared before my mind's eye.

I could not speak, but I managed to nod.

A little frown line appeared above Mr Jesperson's elegantly long nose. "Who was it?"

"It was . . . the Cossack."

"One of those Russian warrior chaps?"

"No . . . yes . . . it's what they call the man who works for Mr Chase. His servant. He must be seven-foot tall, and has the palest skin — he frightened the life out of me when I nearly ran into him in Lord Bennington's house. I — I may not have mentioned this before."

"No, you did not." From his tone, I could not tell if he considered my reticence natural, or to be apologised for.

But I suddenly felt much easier as I made this connection, and paced the kitchen thinking aloud. "Oh, well, he is a scary-looking fellow, but he can't help the way he was born. His real name is Pyotr — that's the Russian for Peter, I suppose. Makes a most unlikely valet, but he has worked for Mrs Chase's family for too many years for them to turn him out, so I suppose Mr Chase is stuck with him. Anyway . . . he gave me a fright and I put it out of my mind — I didn't want to think about it because my fear embarrassed me, it was disproportionate; I could not explain why a glimpse of a passing stranger — however large and weird in appearance — should have instilled such an extremity of terror in me, so it is hardly surprising that he should have haunted my dreams."

"Hmm," said Mr Jesperson. "Perhaps." His face was unreadable.

The front room was colder than the kitchen. The fire had gone out, or perhaps it had not yet been lit. In a house without servants, it is never possible to take such simple comforts for granted. Mr Jesperson spent some time creating a crackling blaze in the hearth, but although it looked comforting, it made little difference to the chill in the air.

"Now," he said when he had done what he could with the fire. "There was no time, when I saw you yesterday, for you to tell me what you gleaned from your 'gossip' with Mrs Chase."

My skin prickled again. I remembered using that word and how he had taken me up on it. "You will be disappointed."

"How so?"

"I'm afraid that they learned far more about me than I about them."

"They?"

"Mr Chase did not leave us alone for a minute."

"Ah! Interesting." He frowned at the flames and stroked his chin. "For what reason, do you think?"

I thought of the looks they had exchanged, and how Mrs Chase had gazed at her husband. She did not exhibit that cowed, submissive aspect that you see in women who go in fear of their masters. She loved him, and would never betray him.

"It could be that he was afraid she might say something that would reveal a secret, either deliberately or inadvertently," I said slowly. "After all, I went there believing she might be ready to confide in me, to ask us to investigate something that worried her."

"But you no longer think that."

It was not a question, but a different question lay behind that assertion. I nodded, but could not bring myself to share my uncomfortable feeling that, despite the display of marital harmony I had witnessed, there was something excessive and *wrong* about Mr Chase's interest in me. To put it into words would give it even more weight. I hoped I was over-sensitive, or had misinterpreted his manner.

Mr Jesperson had fixed me with that unnervingly penetrating gaze that made me feel transparent. "If he had no reason to fear what his wife might say to you, why not leave you alone with her? Did he have nothing better to do? Is he so fascinated by female gossip that he would stay where he was not wanted?"

Put on the defensive, I said that Madame Chase did not speak English, and as my French had let me down, he'd volunteered to serve as translator. "Besides, I think she was happy to have him there."

"All the more reason to separate them: divide and conquer. Invite her to visit you. You must speak to her privately, find out what it is he does not wish her to tell us. I am sure your French will do well enough . . . and she may have more English than you suppose."

"She will not come. She is not strong. She scarcely leaves the house."

"You seem very certain. Will you not try?"

"Of course I will try."

I spent some time swotting over an old French grammar, determined to improve my vocabulary and conversational skills before my next encounter with

Mrs Chase. I also had another lesson in unarmed combat, and learned more of the theory behind this oriental art. Sometimes it was necessary to stay in place, standing firm as a rock; at others, to yield, to bend and flow like water. The decision must be made in response to the attack, without pause for thought.

"But how is that possible?" I asked, frustrated once again by the way both of them made it look so easy. "I *have* to think to work out the best way to respond —"

"But then it is too late," he said. "You must not think — not in the head. Let the body think for you. Don't look like that; I know you don't understand, but with practice it will come. You already know how — you just don't know you know."

"That's nonsense."

"No. We are taught to think, to observe and learn in a certain way, but there are other ways not dependent on the slow process of rational thought."

"Instinct?"

"The knowledge of the body. When you sense someone coming towards you before you can see them — and know if they mean you harm. What is it that lets you know, within moments of meeting someone, that you want to know them better — or would rather not? You may *feel* someone is dishonest, not to be trusted, yet the world says he is a model of rectitude, a pillar of the Church . . . who do you believe? I say you should trust your own feelings. We say sometimes that someone has a 'sixth sense', but I think we *all* have that sixth sense . . . and maybe a seventh and an eighth. Only we haven't learned how to develop those senses properly."

I'd had similar discussions with others in the SPR, but never with anyone who had been able to demonstrate what they meant. Mr Jesperson had actually learned another way, developing a sort of hyper-alertness in himself, a connection between his conscious and unconscious thought processes.

He did not claim to have developed any *psychic* talents, and yet I couldn't help suspecting there might be a very close link between what others labelled "clairvoyance" or "telepathy" and this nameless knowledge of the body, this ability to be in tune with the world around you.

When I went to bed that night, I confess I felt a pang of unease, remembering my vivid nightmare. What if my room was haunted? I scoffed at the notion, but made sure to look under the bed and behind the curtains; tested the window latch, and then locked the door and put the key under my pillow. I made sure there was a candle and a box of matches on the bedside table, close to hand, before I put out the lamp. My bed was warm and comfortable, and, convinced I was safe and determined to have only good dreams, I soon drifted off to sleep.

But it happened again.

I woke with a start, certain there was an intruder in my bedroom.

I thought of Mr Jesperson's words earlier in the day, about the knowledge we have through extra senses, and although I also remembered that last night's fearful certainty had proved false, the pounding of my heart and my screaming nerves insisted I was in danger.

I held my breath and strained to hear any sound that might alert me to the position of an intruder — a creaking floorboard, movement, breathing. Last night, my nocturnal visitor had seemed to stand at the foot of my bed, but I was looking in that direction now, and I could see the lighter space within the darkness that was the window; there was nothing in front of it.

I turned my head — and saw a ghastly pale face, like a moon floating in the dark. The head was so close beside the bed that I knew the Cossack must be leaning down to grab me.

I screamed — at least, I tried. My mouth was open, and I strained in terror, but there was no sound.

It's a dream. But reason had no effect on my terror. Every nerve in my body implored: *get out get out get out!*

I rolled away, scrambled off the bed, rushed to the door — and jiggled the knob uselessly. The door would not open.

This is a nightmare. How could I be locked in?

Then I remembered: I had locked the door myself and put the key beneath my pillow.

It meant I had to go back to the bed to get it. Through my panic, a voice was telling me that I *must* get out of the room — and out of the house. It told me that I would not be safe from the creature who menaced me until I was away.

But I did not trust that voice. It was not instinct, but panic. Panic was not to be trusted. I knew I must stay, confront my demon and deal with it now.

244

So, although I moved back towards my bed, when I reached the little table I located the box of matches and managed, with shaking fingers, to strike one and light the candle.

Light will banish him. I held it out and saw the flame trembling like my nerves.

But I was wrong: I was wide awake and the nightmare was still there.

A man's head, bodiless, floated in the air like a miniature moon, four or five feet above my bed. It was ghastly pale and the eyes were closed — it did not look alive, but reminded me of a death mask, one of those horrid souvenirs taken from a hanged criminal. It bore some resemblance to the Cossack's grim countenance.

It was a hideous, unnatural thing, but how could a mask, or a disembodied head, harm me? Knowing I was not menaced by a living intruder, I felt my curiosity engaged, and it was easier to ignore the part of my mind exhorting me to run away.

I was thinking more clearly now, and I had slept in this very room too many nights to believe it was haunted. This was no ghost, like the apparition in Wilkie Collins' *The Haunted Hotel*, but must be some trick or illusion, and I was determined to get to the bottom of it.

Taking a deep breath, I went very slowly around and behind the bed to approach the ghastly thing, candle in my hand. As I went, although I tried to keep my eyes fixed on it, I was also scanning everywhere — the floor, ceiling and air around me — for hidden wires or anything else that didn't belong. That was one reason for moving slowly; the other was that I still did not know what I would do when I reached it. Did I dare to touch it?

My progress was interrupted by a sudden, sharp rapping. I cried out, so startled by this unexpected noise that I could only associate it with spirit communications.

"Miss Lane? Are you all right?"

Mr Jesperson's voice was followed by the vigorous rattling of the doorknob.

"Yes! Wait and I will let you in."

I hurried to fetch the key from its hiding place and unlocked the door. There stood Mr Jesperson in his dressing gown, his red curls wild, a lamp in his hand.

"I hope I haven't disturbed you, but I thought I heard —"

"Come in — you *have* to see this." I stepped back to allow him entry.

"See what?"

I turned and gasped with dismay at the sight of — nothing. The head was gone. "It was there, on the other side of the bed — an apparition — a head, hanging in mid-air."

"You should have called me at once."

Already he had crossed the room and was now crouched down, looking at something on the floor. I hurried to join him and saw what appeared to be a crumpled bit of linen, just as Mr Jesperson touched it.

His finger sank into it and the stuff dissolved. It shrank rapidly, like a pile of soft snow melting away to nothing. In a matter of moments there was nothing left but a smear on the carpet that glinted in the lamplight, and then that too was gone.

"What was it?" I asked in a whisper.

"Some call it spirit matter. A gentleman in France — Doctor Richet — has proposed the term *ectoplasm*. The stuff from which genuine materialisations are formed. Theory has it that this mysterious matter, something between gas, fluid and solid, is produced and extruded from the bodies of a certain class of medium for the temporary use of visiting spirits. After all, spirits, being naturally insubstantial, must get the material for their occasional appearances from *somewhere*. I've read about it, but never actually encountered it before — have you?" He rose to his feet, gazing at me with bright-eyed fascination.

The horror had come back. I had a great internal struggle to speak normally. "Yes. At least, I think so. Only once. I saw a medium produce the stuff. I confess, I suspected her of fraud, but it was difficult to prove. The very manner of its production from her person, and the unpleasant nature of it, made one disinclined to probe . . ."

As I spoke, I turned and went to light my own lamp and extinguished the candle, which was dripping inconveniently. Then it struck me how improper it would undoubtedly appear to any outside observer for me to be entertaining a young man in my bedroom, and I hastily wrapped myself in my dressing gown.

"I wish I could have seen it," he said wistfully. "I do think you might have called for me . . . if you had only screamed —"

"Believe me, I should have liked nothing better. I tried with all my might to scream, but as in a dreadful nightmare I made not a sound. Which naturally made me wonder if I was truly awake. If I had not locked the door and hidden the key last night, I should have run away, like before. I don't understand why . . . of course I was frightened to see such a thing in my own bedroom, and yet . . . haven't I made a career out of investigating such things? My curiosity, and the chance to prove the existence or not of such physical manifestations of spirits should have made me eager to investigate, yet every nerve in my body screamed at me to run away, and I nearly did."

He gazed at me intently, then suddenly caught his breath and exclaimed, "Of course! He *meant* you to run away. He wanted to frighten you into running *outside*."

"Who?"

But with a muttered oath he ran from the room, and I heard him galloping down the stairs to the front door.

I went into the hall, where I met Edith, candle in hand, wearing an unusually fierce expression on her face below a nightcap. "What on earth is going on?"

I gave a small shrug. "Mr Jesperson had an idea."

"He couldn't wait until a decent hour to discuss it with you?"

"I'm sorry if we disturbed you, Edith," I said apologetically. "But I was frightened by another apparition in my room — this time I could see it was no real, solid person — but then, after we'd talked about it, your son thought —"

248

"I see: he is 'your son' when you disapprove, but 'my partner' when he has done some clever bit of detecting."

I saw from the softening of her features that she was joking and smiled back at her. "It may be that he's done another clever bit of detecting — I don't know; I'm still in the dark about it."

"As we both are — *and* in the cold," she said. "Come into my room dear; we shoud wait somewhere more comfortable than this draughty hallway for Jasper to come back and enlighten us."

We were sitting up snugly in his mother's bed and I had described my encounter with the ghastly head, when we heard Jasper come back into the house; Edith called out to him when he reached the top of the stairs.

"No luck," he said glumly as he entered. "I was too late. He has gone."

"Too late for what? Who?"

He looked at me. "Have you not worked it out? Who is the most powerful medium in London? Also the one most given to malicious displays of power?"

I scowled. "Leaving aside the question of *how* for the moment — *why*?"

"Why did he play that nasty trick on Signora Gallo?" he shot back. "Yes, Miss Fox says it was to discredit her, but that is no real answer. With his abilities compared to hers, surely there was no need to make her appear a hopeless inebriate? As for you . . ." He stopped looking at me and stared down at his feet, letting his shoulders slump. "I'm sorry, you will not like to hear this, I know, but it is true: Mr Chase has taken a very great interest in you from the very first moment he saw you. One might even call it something worse. You have done nothing to encourage it — no one could imagine that! — but it could be a dangerous fascination for *you*."

I took a deep breath against the anger that rose in my breast. I knew I had no cause to be angry with Mr Jesperson, even if I disagreed with him. And I did not disagree — not entirely. Yet it was a very great leap between knowing I exercised a strange fascination over Mr Chase and thinking that he was haunting me in this fashion.

"I am aware of his interest and I do not like it," I said quietly. "But that manifestation . . . if Mr Chase was responsible for it, what was its purpose? Might it not have been unintentional? If he dreamed of me and reached out in some immaterial way . . . You must agree, as everyone does, that the control *any* medium has over the spirits they channel —"

"It's nothing to do with spirits!" Mr Jesperson looked angrier than I felt. "Please do not take refuge in dogma you do not believe. He did it on purpose to frighten you — to scare you into running right out of the house and into his waiting arms. If you refuse to see that —"

Edith suddenly entered the argument, and just as well, for otherwise I might have responded most intemperately. "But, dear, he was not waiting," she said gently. "As you discovered — no one was — with open arms or otherwise."

"No, Mother. He had gone by the time I went outside — of course he had," he said impatiently. "He was watching the house. He would have realised when he saw my lamp or my shadow against the curtain that he had failed in his aim for a second time."

"He was not there because he was *never* there," I said crisply. "Your theory fails. Who would expect me to run *outside* for help? In my nightdress? While there were other people in the house? It makes no sense."

"It makes no sense," Mr Jesperson repeated, giving me a curious look. "You are right — and you never behave irrationally. Until last night. You would have rushed out into the street in your bare feet if I had not stopped you in time. And perhaps again tonight, if you had not had the foresight to remove the key from your locked door before you went to bed. You know that is so. Can you explain why we both had to stop you from behaving in such an irrational manner?"

I shook my head. I was a puzzle to myself. "People do foolish things when they are frightened. But it could not have been predicted."

"*He* could predict your behaviour because he had suggested it."

"Suggested?" I suddenly understood the connotation of the word in connection with previous discussions on the topic. Mr Creevey's somnambulatory destination had been the result of "suggestion". I exclaimed, "You have hypnotism on the brain. What a ridiculous idea."

"Perhaps. But why does my ridiculous idea make you so angry?"

I realised then that it was not anger that I felt but fear — and disgust — at the idea of being secretly controlled by a stranger. If someone could make me

251

behave so irrationally as to run away from the person I most trusted to help me, what other unwanted and harmful "suggestions" might be waiting like traps to be set off? I said none of that aloud, but only declared, as if saying it could make it true, "I have not been hypnotised."

"There is no shame in it — anyone may be hypnotised. Well, almost anyone. And Chase is so cunning and sly . . . You know, it had occurred to me that one way he might work his psychic tricks is through hypnosis. Of course, mass hypnosis is another thing — but Chase had a chance to speak to everyone in the room before his demonstration. If he had an accomplice to help him — perhaps secreted in the cabinet — and we were all prepared in advance to ignore this helper when he appeared, he would be invisible, and the things he lifted or played would seem to move on their own. I have seen hypnotists do something like that — of course, they are able to choose their subjects, whereas Chase —"

With what dignity I could muster, I rose, wrapped my dressing gown more tightly about myself and declared the discussion at an end. "I'm going to bed. We can talk more about this tomorrow, when I hope we may all be thinking more clearly."

CHAPTER
NINETEEN

Sunday in Gower Street

The next morning, Edith went to church after breakfast as usual, leaving us reading quietly by the fire in the front room.

There was no mention of the events of the previous night, and I felt sure Mr Jesperson had decided, in his gentlemanly way, to leave it to me to decide when I felt ready to talk.

Of course, I could think of nothing else.

While my partner sat reading yesterday's newspapers, I skimmed through *Phantasms of the Living*, searching in vain for a reference to any medium who might have demonstrated the ability to cause a spirit form to appear in another room or at a distance from himself. I wondered if I had been too hasty in discarding the idea that the room itself was haunted. Or was it possible that somewhere in the world an aged, forgotten relative, lying on his deathbed, was thinking about me? No, that was the least likely explanation of all. Although I was desperate to find some alternative to Mr Jesperson's idea that I was under the hypnotic control of Mr Chase, there were limits to what I might believe instead.

"Aha!"

I looked up to see Mr Jesperson peering at an article in his paper. "Another jewel theft. But there is something else mentioned . . . Is it different, I wonder, or is this the thread that links them all? But if so, why has it not been mentioned before?"

"Are you only speaking to yourself?"

"Oh! I beg your pardon." He cleared his throat before describing what he had just read. "Mrs Davenport, widow, of St John's Wood, discovered her diamond necklace missing on Friday morning. A very valuable item, not only in monetary but also in sentimental terms, for it had been an engagement present from her late husband. She did not wear it often, for since the death of her husband she seldom went out in public, and least of all to the sorts of events calling for the display of such a necklace.

"She knew it was safe when she went to bed on Thursday, for her maid helped her undo the clasp, and then she put it into its box, and the box into the drawer of her dressing table. As always, Mrs Davenport locked the drawer then put the key beneath the clock on her mantelpiece."

"Where any thief might look."

"The hiding place was known to her maid, and also to the 'tweeny' responsible for dusting said mantelpiece and cleaning the grate and setting the fires."

"The police think it was an inside job?" Suspicion had fallen upon the servants in the other houses where jewellery had been stolen, but nothing was proved.

He nodded. "There was no sign of a break-in, and the thief can only have come during the night while she slept, or on Friday morning. She discovered it was gone at about eleven o'clock."

"Did she usually inspect her jewellery in the mornings after wearing it?"

He smiled and shook his head. "A sudden whim to hold the necklace in her hands."

"That sounds unlikely."

"Not when you know her reason for having the diamonds on her person on Thursday evening . . . an evening when she did not go out."

"The anniversary of her engagement to her late husband. She wore them in his honour." I thought that was a clever deduction, but he shook his head.

"No. She took them out for a visitor who came to her house that afternoon. Described as a foreign woman who had the power of channelling the spirits of the departed through precious stones, who was able, by merely holding the diamond necklace, to transmit a most touching and welcome message from the late Mr Davenport to his still-grieving widow."

I felt a queasy, sinking sensation.

"After that," Mr Jesperson went on, "Mrs Davenport could not bear to put the diamonds away, but wore them for the rest of the day, feeling that as they touched her neck they continued to keep her close to her late husband. The next morning she had the desire to touch them again, but . . ." He raised empty hands.

"Do the police suspect Signora Gallo?"

"Mrs Davenport was quite clear that she'd had the diamonds in her own possession for many hours after the medium left."

"But *you* think she did it."

He shook his head again. "If she returned to the house later that day, or the next morning, she would not have needed the key. We have seen for ourselves that material barriers are no obstacle to her talent: the brooch that was pinned to your jacket beneath your coat, the watch or cigarette case hidden in an inner pocket . . . they would seem to de-materialise and then materialise again in her hands. What are her limits? Could she draw a necklace to her through the solid walls of a house?"

"Oh, what are we to do?" I said.

He looked at me, surprised, and scratched his head. "Why . . . nothing. No one has asked us to find the missing diamonds. It's not our case."

"But she must give them back. And stop her thieving. I think she has no more moral sense than a magpie. I'm sure you noticed . . . she would have been happy to keep a few things she picked up during her performance if Gabrielle hadn't stopped her."

"Then I think you should speak to her — to Miss Fox I mean. She is best placed to discover if there is any truth to our suspicion. For it *is* only a suspicion."

"I will speak with Miss Fox," I said. Yet a worm of doubt crept in. Gabrielle was no thief, but her morality was built on shifting sands, enabling her to justify deceit for a good cause — and her own well-being was the best cause she knew. Might she turn a blind eye to

256

her protégée's crime? To have diamonds in her possession, believing no one suspected, might be a temptation too great to resist.

Shortly after dinner — ham and leek pie served with cabbage and a carrot and onion chutney, with apple tart for afters — there was a knock on the door. It was a young lad from Lord Bennington's house with a letter for me from Mrs Chase.

"I'm to wait for a reply," he told me.

Holding the envelope, still unopened, I bit my lip at the thought of the time it would take me to compose a suitable response in French and, as if my thoughts were written on my face for him to read, the boy added quickly, "You don't have to write nothing. He said you could just tell me a time and if it's today or tomorrow."

He said? I looked again at the front of the envelope where my name was written; I thought it was *her* handwriting . . . Was it a slip of the tongue, or a reminder — as if I needed it — that anything this woman wrote or said to me was likely to be at her husband's behest?

"I still have to read it and consider my answer," I told him. "Won't you come in out of the cold to wait?"

Hearing our voices in the hall, Edith emerged and invited the boy into the kitchen. "You can get warm by the stove," she told him. "Have a cup of tea . . . and I think there's a nice bit of apple tart for you."

I went back into the front room, explained the letter to Mr Jesperson, and then read it. In response to my invitation to her to call on me in Gower Street,

257

Nadezhda Chase regretted to inform me that as her husband would not be available to accompany her, it would not be possible for her to go anywhere all week. Mr Chase was entirely occupied with the preparations for his debut on the London stage. The Alhambra had been engaged for a single performance, now less than a week away, and he must supervise every aspect, down to the smallest detail of the stage sets.

The Alhambra. I paused as the image of that enormous theatre, dominating Leicester Square, filled my mind's eye. It cast Fiorella Gallo's London debut into the deepest shade.

Yet I did not doubt that the large hall would be filled to capacity, for Mr Chase's plan, aided by Lord Bennington, of demonstrating his powers to a select few in advance of his *one night only* public performance had been as shrewd as his selection of guests. Word had spread rapidly; already the American medium was the talk of the town. Not only had there been notices in the newspapers, and excited gossip from everyone who knew anyone who had been at the séance, there were also the advertisements on the sides of omnibuses, and on hoardings in public places . . . By comparison, how pathetic were the few limp handbills to promote Signora Gallo.

Mrs Chase beseeched me to take pity on her lonely, solitary state. She had felt a bond of sympathy between us, and felt sure we would manage perfectly well without a translator — she even ventured to suggest that in the absence of her husband our friendship would have more room to flourish. There were some things — she was sure I would agree — that could only be said from one woman to another . . . things she did not wish her husband to hear . . . something she dared not write, but *must* speak to me about.

How soon could I call upon her? Was it too presumptuous to hope it might be this very afternoon? She found the hours so difficult to fill when her husband was away. She understood I had many claims upon my time. Tomorrow? A carriage could be sent for me. Reaching the end of the letter, I could not resist a shudder.

"She sounds quite desperate," I said.

"*He* is the desperate one, and no wonder," he answered promptly. "He thought he would have caught you before now, but his plan failed. He wants another chance, so he has set Mrs C as a lure . . . or a Judas goat."

I thought of my vision of her as a beautiful little marionette whose limbs twitched and mouth moved accordingly as her husband pulled the strings. Had he set her to write this letter? Sensing my distrust, he wanted me to think he was spending all his time backstage at the Alhambra so I should feel it safe to visit his wife in Belgrave Square.

And yet . . . what if she really *did* have a secret to confess? What if she needed my help?

I proposed to Mr Jesperson that we should go there together, straight away, but he was unwilling. Turning to the window he indicated the icy rain. "I'd rather wait for better weather. Besides, you don't imagine you could hide me about your person?"

His comical look made me laugh. "No, but if we turn up together they can hardly refuse to let you in. If Mr Chase really is not there, you can go away on some excuse."

"Tomorrow, perhaps."

I went back to the kitchen where the boy was licking sugar from his fingers, looking much happier than when he had arrived. He jumped to his feet when he saw me. I told him to tell Mrs Chase that I would try to call on her tomorrow morning. "Say that I am sorry not to be able to give a definite time, but I'm sure she'll understand that, in my business, things sometimes come up . . . Tell her I will do my best. If I cannot make it on Monday, I'll surely call on Tuesday. Do you want me to write it down?"

He shook his head. "I'll remember. I'll tell him all that."

I frowned. "The message is for *Mrs* Chase, not her husband."

"I know, Miss, but she don't speak our language. She wouldn't understand, unless I tell *him* and he tells her — see?"

I saw too well — and again I wondered if it would be better to give him a letter to be put directly into her hands — but it was too late; the boy was already in the hall, eager to be on his way.

CHAPTER
TWENTY

A Telephone Call

The only disturbances to my sleep that night were caused by my own anxiety. I woke several times with a pounding heart, fearful that my unwanted visitor had returned, but never saw anything amiss.

The next morning, over an unexpectedly lavish breakfast of eggs scrambled with butter, onions and cheese — one of Edith's friends from church had made her a gift of freshly laid eggs and a parcel of butter from a country farm — Mr Jesperson and I fell to arguing over our plans for the day. I thought we should go to Belgrave Square; he was keen to dissuade me, and said my time would be better spent reading a recent study of hypnotism.

"Or if you like, I could hypnotise you . . . no? Perhaps I might be able to put some defences in place? Well, suit yourself. Depend upon it: Chase has hypnotised you once, and since it did not allow him to achieve his aim, he will want to try again. You should avoid him at all costs; that you are so eager to rush back there suggests that he still has some hold on you."

I scowled at him as he calmly buttered another slice of toast. "It is not *Mr* Chase I want to see, but his wife.

After all, if he is such a threat, shouldn't we find out if she needs our help? She did say she had something important to tell me —"

"In a letter written to his dictation? You told me yourself what an adoring, loving couple they were."

I decided to ignore that. "*You* will be with me. Surely, even if Mr Chase is waiting there for me like a big spider in his web, I will be safe with you at my side."

"Your faith in me is touching," he said with a smile. "I should do my best, of course, but ... it's not enough, though naturally I never like to admit to any gaps in my ability. You should read more about hypnosis, so that you may understand. Having once been hypnotised, a subject is more vulnerable to the hypnotist — although it may have taken him quite some time and effort to entrance you in the first instance, upon a second meeting he may need nothing more than to say a particular word to have you again under his spell."

I looked down at my plate. Although there were a few morsels left, I found I had lost my appetite. I hated the thought of being under the influence of Mr Chase — or indeed of anyone.

"I'm only proposing that we put off this visit a little longer — to arm ourselves as best we can," he said gently. "More tea?"

Perhaps an hour later, as I was ploughing my way through the stodgy prose of an essay titled "An

Experiment in Hypnotic Suggestion", a telegram arrived.

It had been sent by Mr Creevey's office boy, informing us that his employer had been in receipt of a brief, mysterious telephone call barely ten minutes ago.

"At last!" Mr Jesperson seized his coat and hat, then turned to me with an impatient look. "Come along, come along. There's no time to waste. Or will you stay here?"

I looked at him stupidly. "Where are we going?"

"To the telephone exchange!" With that, he was out of the door. Still not understanding, I snatched my coat and trotted after him.

"I don't understand . . . do you mean to speak to Mrs Creevey?" I panted out my question as soon as I caught up to him.

"Why should I do that? We want the Lime Street exchange. There — that 'bus . . ." He seized my arm and pulled me along with him, running for the approaching omnibus.

Once we'd managed to board he said, "This may be a fool's errand, but if we can get there quickly enough, I hope one of the telephonists may remember directing a recent call to Creevey's Careful Removals — and where the call came from."

After the rush of excitement that had propelled me with him thus far, I felt let down. "Think of all the call-offices available in this city; if the villain — whoever he may be — has telephoned from a major railway station, or a tea shop, how will that help us?"

"Don't always expect the worst," he said, smiling down at me. "You never know where a clue may lead. We know *when* the call was made, and if we discover where from, we'll have a chance to find a witness. Someone may have noticed and be able to describe him."

He was clutching at straws. I thought of the A.B.C. cafes with their brand spanking new call offices, and how busy they were likely to be at this time of day. The girls who worked there would never notice a man who slipped in and then quickly out again after making his call, and as for a witness at any of the tables — they would be long dispersed. We would never find our man this way. It was pointless — not so much a fool's errand, as he had said, but an excuse he'd seized upon to get out of the house. He would rather gallop around London all day and play at detecting than be bored at home.

"I know it seems — indeed it *is* — a very long shot, but that doesn't mean it will be a waste of time," he said, the ease with which he followed my thoughts once again disconcerting. "We've had so few clues in this case that we cannot afford to pass up a single scrap without picking it up, examining it beneath a magnifying glass, and *squeezing* it for any tiny droplets of information that might emerge."

His miming of these actions made me smile, and I agreed, wondering if he had another motive for this excursion. For so long as he kept me busy, I should be unable to take up Mrs Chase's invitation to visit her in Belgrave Square.

264

★ ★ ★

The telephone exchange was immediately obvious from some distance away due to the imposing network of wires that crowned its roof, like some vast geometrical spiderweb. For all his rush, Mr Jesperson's fascination with modern technology brought him to an awed halt, and he put his head back to gaze in wonder for a few moments before we entered the building.

It was a good thing he'd had the foresight to get a letter from Arthur Creevey stating that Mr Jesperson and Miss Lane were acting under his orders, and requesting cooperation, because without it, I am quite certain we would not have been allowed past the front door.

Even with the letter from a United Telephone Company subscriber, after it had been frowningly read and re-read by the manager, a pale and fretful man called Mr Bliss, we seemed unlikely to get very far.

Removing his pince-nez, he handed the document back to Mr Jesperson with a pained look.

"I will not have my young ladies disturbed or interrogated," he said. "Members of the public — you are not subscribers yourself? — often have the most peculiar ideas about telephony and the activities of telephonists. All my good young ladies do is to *connect* and — when the time is right — *disconnect* the call. They never, ever listen in —"

"Heaven forbid," murmured Mr Jesperson. "I assure you, Mr Bliss, I would not *dream* of quizzing your telephonists about the *content* of any conversation. We only wish to know — that is, *Mr Creevey* is most

265

anxious to learn — from which telephone the call was made."

Our eyes went as if magnetically drawn to the face of the large, railway-style clock on the back wall of Mr Bliss' office. The two hands had just met in prayer over the twelve — one hour had passed since the call.

"I realise your telephonists are very busy, far too busy to retain the memory of just one connection out of many, but as it was only an hour ago, and because it is so important — for reasons I am not at liberty to share — I beg you to give me the chance to ask them if they can help."

Sighing, Mr Bliss gave a short, grudging nod. "Under other circumstances I could not allow such a disruption, but as it happens, the morning shift has just ended. All the operators on duty will shortly be coming out to go for their lunch. I will question them in the first instance. If anyone remembers this peculiarly important call, and *if* she is agreeable to giving up some part of her lunch break to speak with you — you may ask her what you like."

He was still speaking when a set of double doors swung open and a crowd of young women emerged in twos and threes, skirts flouncing, amidst laughter and a buzz of voices. All noise and movement ceased as they caught sight of their manager with two strangers lying in wait.

"Ladies," he said, voice squeaking slightly as he raised it. "Ladies, there is no cause for alarm, and I shall endeavour not to delay you unduly, but I must have a word with each one of you before you go. One at a time, please; the rest wait quietly."

They didn't look too pleased — I imagined it would be a rush to get a bite to eat before hurrying back to work, even without this unexpected delay — but no one objected. They shot us curious glances, some bold, others shy.

While Mr Jesperson gazed in an interested way at the crowd of young females — some of whom looked back with equal interest — I kept my eyes on Mr Bliss as he spoke to the women, but his voice remained too low to carry, and alas, Mr Jesperson had not yet managed to teach me even the rudiments of lip reading. But it was easy enough to understand as each one in turn shook her head — one with a positively Gallic shrug. That is, until the fifth young lady. She alone did not shake her head, but turned it to look at me with intelligent, interested eyes.

"The rest of you may go," said Mr Bliss, raising his voice again, and causing a gentle, giggling stampede.

"This is Miss Fowler," he said to us. "I should call her one of our best telephonists if there were no danger of you presuming that *any* of our employees are any *less* than the best. Miss Fowler, this is Mr Jesperson and, err . . . As they are acting on behalf of one of our subscribers, please answer their questions to the best of your ability."

"Miss Lane," said I, and shook her gloved hand.

Her manager gave a slight, huffing cough. "Please remember Miss Fowler is on her lunch break. Our young ladies work hard and need to keep up their strength with regular meals. If you are not back at work on time, Miss Fowler, your pay will be docked."

Then he retreated into his office, closing the door and leaving us standing in the chilly, high-ceilinged entrance hall.

Mr Jesperson got straight down to business. "You remember putting a call through to Creevey's Careful Removals this morning, about an hour ago?"

"Yes."

"And do you remember the caller?"

She was clearly about to agree when she checked herself, replying primly, "You must not think that telephonists ever listen in to calls."

"No, of course not. I only thought you might remember which one of your subscribers was telephoning to another — unless, I suppose, the call came from a public call office . . . it would be too much to expect you to remember *which*."

She could not repress a small, satisfied smile. "Oh, it was not from a public telephone. Creevey's is a small concern, and while it may be very successful for all I know, they don't get many 'phone calls — their customers usually aren't subscribers. So for one of our other subscribers, and I may say one of our most *distinguished* subscribers, to enter into negotiations with Creevey's must be a great boost for their business. And quite naturally, I was struck by how unusual this was." She stopped and frowned. "But I do not understand. Why should Mr Creevey need to ask? I put the call through and he answered —"

"The connection was broken. Not your fault," Mr Jesperson improvised swiftly. "The office boy . . . but never mind all that. Suffice to say, Mr Creevey is naturally most anxious to learn who telephoned to him this morning at eleven o'clock, so that he might return the call. If you would be so kind as to tell me the name of this distinguished subscriber . . .?"

She gazed at him doubtfully. "Usually, if a subscriber has a complaint or a question they speak to one of us here at the exchange, directly." Her eyes moved to the letter of authorisation Mr Jesperson still clutched, and evidently she found it reassuring, for she decided to trust us with the information.

"The call was placed from Lord Bennington's house in Belgrave Square."

CHAPTER
TWENTY-ONE

Tracking the Spider

"Chase is behind it all; *he* is the spider at the centre of this web."

I hurried to keep up with my friend's long strides after leaving the exchange. We were of one mind on this; it was unthinkable to imagine Lord Bennington, his children, or any member of his household staff as the master hypnotist controlling Arthur Creevey, and that left only one possible suspect. But I felt I must ask Mr Jesperson what he meant by "all".

"Your hauntings, Creevey's somnambulism, the missing mediums — also, perhaps, the stolen jewels — but leave that until we know more. It was Chase in the cab that picked up Ribaud. And remember that the De Beauvoir sisters were introduced to Chase the same evening they met Ribaud? It was *Chase* who subsequently seduced or abducted them."

"And Miss Jessop?"

Noticing I was having a struggle to keep up with him, Mr Jesperson slowed his steps and offered me his arm. "You remember her vision of being carried off by an angel?"

"I remember."

"She saw herself in the arms of a tall, strong, handsome man. Being too sensible to imagine she was soon to encounter a passionate human lover, she thought her beautiful, sweet-spirited abductor could only be an angel, bearing her off to Heaven."

"Whereas in reality it was Arthur Creevey under the control of C. C. Chase?"

"Exactly."

"But why?"

"It would appear that Chase is making a collection of psychic mediums."

The word "collection" recalled my introduction, as a child, to the delights of butterfly collecting. I had enjoyed the chasing, the capturing with nets, the sight and even the handling of the tiny, fluttering creatures, but when I had learned what happened to them — their little lives snuffed out in the killing jar so that their beauty could be preserved, pinned in rows on a tray, placed behind glass to be admired by other collectors — I lost all pleasure in it. Since then, to me, the notion of "collecting" has borne a deadly aspect, and from his grim expression I guessed Mr Jesperson had some similar thought.

But he only said, "We must hope that Mr Creevey will lead us to the answer tonight."

"We" he had said, and "us". So simply, without need for discussion or argument, it was agreed: I would be by Mr Jesperson's side, an equal partner as we followed the somnambulist and — with a bit of luck — foiled not only this latest planned kidnapping, but the whole dastardly plot.

Back in Gower Street, while Mrs Jesperson was busy elsewhere, Mr Jesperson paced up and down and I sat feeding bits of wood and coal to the smoky, fretful fire, trying to coax it into giving off more heat as we worked out a plan of action.

Ultimately, we were forced to admit that we knew too little to make planning feasible. We had no idea of the identity of the possible victim, or Creevey's destination. Mr Jesperson thought it likely that the somnambulist would go again to Belgrave Square, where Mr Chase would be waiting to give him further instructions, their previous meeting having been foxed by the patrolling policeman.

Ideally, we should like to observe *everything*, allowing the planned kidnap to take place in order to discover where the abducted mediums were being held. If, that is, they were all still alive. But we did not dwell upon the grim possibility of murder, preferring to take heart from Signora Gallo's reading of the cards, with their message that Miss Jessop still lived, a prisoner in a room, though we knew not where.

The thought of Miss Jessop thus imprisoned reminded me of something. Now that we knew Chase was the villain, Lady Florence's bit of gossip about his having rented a house to accommodate his retinue of servants became significant.

Mr Jesperson stared at me, wide-eyed. "Why did you never tell me this before?"

"Because it was obviously untrue: Mrs Chase laughed off the ridiculous notion of a horde of servants.

272

She has a maid, of course, and there's the Cossack, but no others."

"You believe Chase's wife is more to be trusted than your old friend Lady Florence?"

I felt my cheeks heating. It was unfair; I had done my best to investigate this unlikely claim. Surely he did not expect me to share *every* scrap of gossip that came my way? I told him, rather stiffly, "Lady Florence loves to gossip, and she is happy to pass on any story, with embellishments, rather than keep silent. You must admit, it is most unlikely — why, if they had servants and also the funds to rent a house in London, would a married couple choose to stay as guests in another household?"

"Of course. But I wonder . . . you know her. Does the Lady Florence tend to *invent*, or only pass on bits of gossip she's heard? If her maid told her a story she had from the under-butler, who had it from Cook, who had been told by her brother . . . What I mean is — where did this idea of the other house originate?"

I took his point. "I don't think she does make things up, not like that. She might come up with an explanation for an oddity, for example, if someone told her that Mr Chase had rented a house she might assume he had a retinue of servants that need accommodation."

Inspired, I put down the poker and moved away from the fire, towards the desk. "I will write to her at once and ask where she had this story from."

But he stopped me. "Not now. It may be unnecessary after tonight. If not, well, writing it down leaves a trail of evidence that could rebound on us. Better you speak privately with Lady Florence. We certainly don't want Chase to know we are interested."

We discussed a few more details, but soon agreed we could only try to be prepared and be ready to improvise on the spot.

"That's life, isn't it?" said he. "A constant improvisation. Still, we will take precautions. I'll have my revolver and my stick. You should wear garments that won't impede you — I have some old clothes that may fit. Not only will you find it easier to run, but you'll be less noticeable — no one looks twice at a boy out at night."

From the boxes stored beneath the stairs Edith found me a pair of trousers that were a reasonable fit, a well-mended shirt that must have been her son's in his boyhood and even a pair of boots. They were sturdy brown lace-ups with thick soles that looked as if they'd scarcely been worn — a fact she confirmed.

"He must have had another growth-spurt the day I bought these. Two weeks later, he could hardly squeeze into them. I'm not sure why I kept them all these years — feet never do grow smaller — but I'm glad you'll get some use out of them."

Worn over two pairs of socks, the boots were comfortable. A baggy grey fisherman's sweater, an ancient tweed jacket several sizes too large for me, and a soft cap capacious enough to hide my piled-up hair completed my outfit. It was simply impossible to be ladylike in these clothes, and I enjoyed the feeling of

274

freedom. Laughing at the ragamuffin figure in the mirror, I had to agree that no one would look twice at such a creature.

"Although a policeman might wonder what mischief I was up to." I inspected myself more critically. "My skin is much too clean." I paid a visit to the ash pail, and after a few moments as Edith watched in dismay — Mr Jesperson smiling — I was as grubby an urchin as any who won his dirt the hard way.

It was a cold, damp night, and although there was no fog to be seen outside the Creeveys' house, I sensed its lurking presence in the still and clammy air. We had a long, boring wait, and heard the bells at midnight before our somnambulist at last emerged, walking out of his front door and down the path as smoothly as though his eyes were open.

Excitement coursed through my blood, warming me. I exchanged a glance with my partner, he gave a nod and we were off.

Our sleepwalker never once looked back and gave no sign of worrying about being followed — just as Mr Jesperson had said. For the most part the streets we walked through were quiet and empty, and clear of traffic, the buildings shut and dark. Once a cab came by and slowed, but as Mr Creevey did not pause or show any sign of interest, the driver flicked the reins and the cab jolted forward as the horse resumed a faster pace.

We had suspected Mr Creevey's destination from the start, and after crossing Sloane Street knew it for a certainty. When he reached the far corner of Belgrave

Square — the farthest from Lord Bennington's mansion — Mr Jesperson and I came to a halt. We knew we must keep out of sight; we could not risk being noticed by Mr Chase, if he came out.

We watched as Mr Creevey approached Lord Bennington's house. He mounted the steps to the front door and then he vanished. It was impossible to tell from our position whether the door had been opened to him by someone, or if he had opened it himself.

Although we were prepared for a wait, he was not inside for long. Barely five minutes had passed before we saw him coming out again, burdened with something in his arms. When he passed beneath a street lamp we saw the sleepwalker was carrying a man who looked no more than a child in his arms. With his head lolling back, eyes closed and the utter relaxation of his limbs — still clothed in bed-wear — he was evidently a sleeper snatched from his bed. There was a cloth over his nose and mouth, but although it half-obscured his face, I recognised Mr Chase.

Far from being the evil genius who controlled the somnambulist, Mr Chase, limply unconscious in the big man's powerful grasp, appeared to be his latest victim.

I expected the alarm to be raised momentarily. Surely his wife would scream, or his manservant come running after — but house and square alike remained silent and still, while Mr Creevey walked past us, Mr Chase like a baby in his arms.

We fell in together behind the somnambulist, feeling no reason to hang back. If we encountered a policeman

— I half dreaded, half wished for such a meeting — would he be able to help us?

Whether luck was with or against us I could not say, but we did not encounter another soul as we walked on. The elegant streets and squares of Belgravia might have been in a city of the dead. As we moved southwards, the fog appeared in snaky fronds and clumps, rising from the ground and slithering around corners, clinging to the outer edges at first, but then growing bolder and snatching with long, stinking yellow fingers at our clothes.

Somewhere past Sloane Square we heard a man singing, then catcalls and laughter made him break off, but we could not see anyone, and it was impossible to tell how near or far away they were. The fog confused me; I lost my bearings as it thickened. But then I recognised we were passing Chelsea Barracks. On the other side of the road, shrouded in heavy, smoky curtains, would be the Royal Hospital and Ranelagh Gardens. We were headed for the river.

Dread clutched my heart. Until that moment I had been carried along by excitement and curiosity, eager to know the end of this story, but like the reader of a novel, never truly alarmed by the events. Now I knew this was no story. This was real.

Mr Creevey was carrying Mr Chase to the river. Unless a boat waited, he could have but one intention. Bodies were fished out of the Thames nearly every day, some never identified. Who could say for certain how they came there? Accident, suicide — or murder?

277

As the fog became darker, thicker, more insinuating and more determined to come between us, my fear grew.

"We have to stop him," I murmured urgently.

"Let us wait and see."

"See? But we can't see." I stared at Mr Creevey's back, close at first, then suddenly more distant as the fog took him away. I darted forward, no longer worried about colliding with him, and was just in time to see something fall. I caught it up — a piece of cloth — the reek of ether made me pull my head back.

We had reached the embankment. The river, invisible in the fog, was directly below us. Mr Creevey had stopped walking and I wondered what he was waiting for. Perhaps his master's voice?

Mr Jesperson moved closer to the somnambulist and put his hand on his arm. "Creevey," he said firmly. "Arthur Creevey, wake up."

There was no response from the somnambulist, but the man in his arms moaned faintly and gave a weak cough.

"Listen to me," said Mr Jesperson in a loud, stern voice. "Wake up and turn around. Turn your back on the river. Come away."

Whether the sleepwalker had heard his voice or not, it was impossible to say, but it got through to the man in his arms, who coughed again and said in a weak voice: "What? Who's there? Where am I? Oh!"

As he realised his position, Mr Chase began to struggle, crying out in his high voice: "Put me down. How dare you? Help! Please, somebody, help me!"

278

Mr Creevey's grip tightened and he pulled his captive closer to his broad chest. Mr Jesperson laid a hand on Mr Chase and urged him to be calm. "I'm trying to help, but this man is asleep — he's been hypnotised — I'm afraid he may not respond unless we hit upon the right phrase."

I had been thinking about that very problem. The word or phrase to compel the somnambulist's obedience could be anything — even a made-up word — in which case we might go through the dictionary and never strike it. Twice, at least, the somnambulist had made his way to Belgrave Square after receiving a brief telephone call. Despite the standard protestation that telephonists never, ever listened in to conversations, everyone suspected that they did. An unusual word or a nonsensical, meaningless phrase might attract unwanted attention. But if someone were to say, for example —

"You're wanted in Belgrave Square."

I spoke clearly, and attracted the surprised attention of both Mr Jesperson and Mr Chase, but my voice had no effect on the somnambulist.

"Where are we?" Mr Chase asked.

Mr Jesperson replied. "Chelsea Embankment."

"He means to throw me in the river." Mr Chase spoke flatly. "Jesperson, isn't it?"

"That's right."

"How do *you* come to be here? Who *is* this man?"

"You don't know him?"

"I never saw him before in my life! But you do, I think!"

"He suffers from somnambulism. We have been following him —"

"You saw him take me — you followed him *here* from Belgrave Square and never stopped him?" His voice went up and nearly squeaked.

"He's under the command of someone else. I can't —"

Mr Chase trembled — perhaps with anger or fear, but it may simply have been the cold, for he was very lightly dressed and the night was raw. "You let him continue! Why didn't you get the police? Have you a revolver? A pistol at least?"

Mr Jesperson frowned. "Threats are no use; he's not aware —"

"I don't expect you to threaten him — shoot, damn you! Just shoot him! You have a weapon — you *must* — you'd never be such a fool as to go out unarmed."

"I won't shoot an innocent man."

"Innocent? This creature means to kill me!"

But did he? As time passed, a faint sliver of suspicion had grown larger. How long had we stood here, with the somnambulist as unmoving as a piece of furniture? If he'd carried Mr Chase to the riverside with the intention of throwing him in, what was stopping him? What was he waiting for?

"This man is an innocent pawn in someone else's game. I won't kill him."

"My life means less to you than his?" Chase was red in the face. "If you won't shoot him, give *me* the gun! Help me! Help!" He renewed his struggles, flailing and punching, but Creevey held him too close; his punches

280

lacked strength, and his kicking legs scarcely connected.

Mr Jesperson, meanwhile, had gone still, in a way I had seen a few times before. He was possessed by a strange calm. I knew he was preparing to fight, using the techniques he had told me were meant for defence. That meant he must stop seeing our client as someone he was bound to protect, and instead look upon his body as an object to be moved — moved in a way that would not harm his prisoner.

When he began, Mr Jesperson appeared more a dancer than a fighter. He took a long step back, then pivoted to one side and kicked straight with his left leg, striking at the back of Mr Creevey's right leg. Another step, another kick — this time with his right foot, striking the back of the left leg.

The big man wobbled. He swayed. Mr Jesperson readied himself to kick again.

Mr Chase chose that moment to scream at his captor: "*Monster!* Let me go, you *monster!*"

Arthur Creevey wobbled, his knees buckling under the force of the kicks, but at the same time he raised his arms — lifting Mr Chase to shoulder-height — and then flung him away suddenly, throwing him hard in the direction of the river.

The fog that shrouded everything and wrapped us in our own private world made it impossible to see how far or near we were from the edge of the paved embankment. I held my breath and waited helplessly to learn if Mr Chase would strike the railings, or fall on solid ground, or go over into the water where, even if he could swim, he might be lost forever.

I watched Mr Chase flying backwards through the air, struck by how slowly he was moving. He seemed to float. The expression on his face changed from wide-eyed surprise to a frown of concentration. And then — the shock of it was like a blow to my chest — he stopped. He hung in the air, in the fog, bare feet dangling down, unsupported, as if held up by giant, invisible hands.

He smiled then, and there was something crafty and gloating about that smile, and his eyes sought out mine — as if, I thought dizzily, it was for *my* benefit that he displayed his power.

How long did he hang there in the air? Probably no more than a second. Yet that second extended itself in a curious, timeless fashion, a frozen moment. Or perhaps that was only a fantasy of my reeling brain, for I felt close to falling myself.

Then he came forward and sank slowly, gently to the ground, landing softly on the paving stones, so near to me that if I'd taken even two steps forward I would have collided with him.

But I did not take a step forward. I tried to step back, but my head was spinning.

Mr Jesperson caught me before I could hit the ground. Dressed as a boy, I fainted like a silly girl.

CHAPTER
TWENTY-TWO

In the Web

I came round to Mr Jesperson chafing my wrists.

In the faint, yellowish glow of the streetlamps that filtered through the dank, shifting curtains of fog, I saw Arthur Creevey stretched out on the ground, chest rising and falling gently in time with the faint, whistling snores issuing from his nose. Strutting around him like a victorious bantam cock was Mr Christopher Clement Chase, declaiming his victory.

"You see, I am not so easily destroyed. You attack a small, weak man, but though my body is small, my soul holds mighty powers thanks to my spirit friends."

I struggled to rise. "What happened?"

"You fainted," Mr Jesperson informed me.

I had feared as much, but protested it was impossible, I never fainted, and especially not without reason . . .

"You had quite a shock, seeing what happened."

I wanted to object that *he* had witnessed the same thing without fainting dead away, but having no desire to dwell on my weakness, asked instead about Arthur Creevey.

"It sounds as if he's fallen into a natural sleep. If you don't need me . . .?"

"I'm perfectly well." To prove it, I rose to my feet unaided, but the effort made my head spin and I had to close my eyes for a moment. Once up, I must remain standing, much as I wished to sit down.

Mr Chase imperiously commanded us to fetch the police.

"That is unnecessary."

Eyes bulging slightly, Mr Chase protested: "The creature who tried to kill me must be arrested. I won't be able to sleep in peace so long as that man is free."

"You need not fear him. Your enemy is someone else, who has been controlling him by hypnotic command."

He snorted. "A likely story! I don't suppose you can *name* this mysterious master of hypnotism — this person who hates me so much and would benefit from my death?" The little man stamped his foot. His eyes glittered with rage. "Well, can you? Who is it?" It struck me that Mr Chase was enjoying himself.

Mr Jesperson watched him in an interested way. "Only *you* can answer that question."

From his startled expression, Mr Chase had not expected such a reply. "What do you mean?"

"It is someone close to you. Consider those you live amongst. The person who controls the somnambulist has ready access to the telephone in Lord Bennington's house."

Mr Chase shuddered and wrapped his arms around himself. "I'm perishing."

"I'm sorry — take my coat." Mr Jesperson stepped forward, unbuttoning his topcoat, but the medium waved him off peevishly.

"No, no, that's no use, it's far too long, I'd hardly be able to walk." Abruptly he turned to me. "This boy. He's nearer my size and well bundled up — surely he can spare a garment?" Despite the fog and the darkness, he had recognised me — I was certain of it. But I said nothing, only shrugged out of the heavy jacket and handed it over.

He took it without a word of thanks. "And boots. I can't walk far in bare feet, on a night like this, but a healthy young lad like you —"

"That's enough." Mr Jesperson moved between me and Mr Chase. "Ask those spirits you're so friendly with to carry you home. You boast of your powers and are keen to show them off, but they don't seem to be very *useful*."

Mr Chase gave a noisy, contemptuous sniff. "Oh, you know all about psychic powers, do you? The spirits saved my *life* — have you forgotten that already? I won't ask them to fly me home as well — although they *could*, of course. But I'm not greedy or ungrateful . . ."

I slipped away; Mr Jesperson's reference to Mr Chase being carried home had given me an idea. As I made my way to Mr Creevey — still stretched out on the cold, hard ground — I heard Mr Chase continuing his argument.

"If you'll think of this using more material concepts, perhaps you will understand. There is an economy to everything, in our world and the other. Coal shovelled into a furnace will provide heat only until it all burns away — then, for your furnace to work, more coal must be added. If a strong man digs and carries coal all day, but isn't allowed to rest, finally he will collapse. Would you call him *weak* because he can work full-out for ten hours, but not for twenty-five?"

I crouched down beside Mr Creevey who slept as peacefully as a child. It seemed almost a pity to wake him, but how else could he get home? Jogging his shoulder gently, I said his name.

His eyes had been moving beneath their lids, but now stilled. His breathing altered. His eyes opened. Seeing me, he blinked. A look of confusion passed across his face as he sat up. ". . . I've been sleepwalking."

"Yes."

He looked around, trying to get his bearings, but the fog made it impossible. "Where am I?"

"On Chelsea Embankment. Mr Jesperson is here, and — another man." I decided not to name the man whose voice still carried to us, expounding on theories of energy, curious to see if Mr Creevey would recognise him.

Seeing Mr Creevey approach, Mr Chase reeled back, putting up his hands in a melodramatic gesture of fear. "No! Get away! Don't let him touch me!"

"You are perfectly safe," I said coolly. "Now that he is recovered from his trance, our friend will not hurt you."

"He will make amends by carrying you safely home again," Mr Jesperson said, barely repressing a smile. "Is that not the ideal solution?"

Mr Chase only shot an evil look at him before turning and walking away.

"We had better follow to see he doesn't get into trouble," said Mr Jesperson.

I had scarcely walked ten steps before I had to stop. I felt so weak and lightheaded that I feared I might be about to faint again.

Mr Jesperson noticed. "I say, Creevey, would you mind awfully? Miss Lane could do with a lift."

Before I could object, I was lifted off my feet to be cradled like a baby in Arthur Creevey's large and powerful arms.

"There's a good fellow. Now, Miss Lane, be reasonable and don't make a fuss. It's no good you telling me to go on without you — I wouldn't leave anyone in this horrid fog — and I know you agree we must keep Chase in view — and Creevey doesn't mind, do you, my good man?"

I felt my bearer shake his head. "You're as light as a child, Miss."

"Enjoy the experience," Mr Jesperson suggested. "Pretend you're one of those ancient kings who were so respected their feet were never allowed to touch the earth."

But I, too, had read *The Golden Bough*. "As I recall, those blessed monarchs were killed after their year of being worshipped."

"I promise, you are not for sacrifice, Miss Lane."

The experience of being carried gently and safely about by a larger, stronger person is so intrinsically linked with infancy that I suppose it is no wonder I responded like a child rocked in its father's arms and fell fast asleep.

No apparitions or nightmares disturbed me that night. I roused just enough, after we reached Gower Street, to get up from the chaise longue where Mr Creevey gently deposited me, and make my own way upstairs to bed.

The next thing I knew it was morning; the weak, stained, muffled light of a foggy London day in November filled my room, but it was not that which had awakened me. Although the house was silent now, I sensed the after-echo of a door slam, and voices from downstairs.

I got up, washed and dressed quickly, and went down to discover that I was indeed alone in the house. A note, quickly scrawled on a torn piece of paper, had been left for me:

Police have taken J for questioning.
Creevey under arrest. J says YOU MUST
HAVE NOTHING TO DO WITH CHASE!!
Wait here — Edith

Clutching the note to my breast, I went back to the kitchen to make tea and toast. Bread, butter, plates and cutlery had not been cleared from the table, which gave an indication of how abrupt Edith's depature had been.

I had no doubt that it was Chase who had set the police on Mr Jesperson, and was responsible for the arrest of Arthur Creevey. I wondered how, or if, my partner would manage to convince the police that Mr Creevey was an innocent pawn of the villain they *should* be looking for?

But who *was* that villain?

As I put the kettle on, I pondered who could have used the telephone in Lord Bennington's house. The Lord himself I ruled out — it was not merely that I could not imagine him in the role of such a conniving villain, but there were surely easier ways at his disposal if he wished to get rid of his guest. Likewise, I could not seriously consider any of his long-serving staff.

Which left only four possibilities.

The Cossack; that frightening figure might have been top of my list, for he seemed a dangerous man, but the type of threat he represented was very different from that of the hypnotist, who used mental powers rather than physical violence. I found it hard to envision the Cossack making a telephone call and whispering his commands down the line. And if the servant wished to kill his master, why summon another man to do it? The method would not even deflect suspicion from him, for if Mr Chase had been found dead in the river, dressed in his night-clothes, who but his powerfully-built manservant would have the best opportunity to commit the act?

Mrs Chase was physically weak, but might be spiritually and intellectually strong, and certainly if she was feigning love and illness, she must be a very cold-hearted villain. But for what motive?

Which left only Mrs Chase's French maid, a person I had not met — still, it seemed most unlikely that she was a hypnotist in disguise, biding her time, with a most complicated, slow plan of conquest.

I stopped spooning tea into the warmed teapot, nagged by the feeling that I was missing something obvious, and went through the facts again.

The hypnotist had telephoned from Lord Bennington's house.

The hypnotist, apparently a man, was in Paris two years earlier, and prepared Mr Creevey for his future service.

At the hypnotist's command, Mr Creevey abducted Miss Jessop. If Signora Gallo's reading was to be trusted, Miss Jessop was not killed, but kept imprisoned.

Also at the hypnotist's command, Mr Creevey abducted Mr Chase and carried him to the river and tried to throw him in. If not for the intervention of the spirits — or Chase's own psychic powers — the medium would have died.

That was the contradiction that nagged at me. If the other mediums were murdered, where were their bodies? If they were being held captive for some purpose, why should Mr Chase be the exception?

A great conundrum relating to hypnotism is whether, or how far, the hypnotised subject may be forced to act against his will. There was a sensational recent case in France in which a woman admitted she had helped her lover commit murder, claiming she had been hypnotised into doing so. Expert testimony was given to the effect that any sufficiently impressionable subject is no more than the unthinking extension of the hypnotist, without choice or free will.

She had been found guilty, nevertheless, but given a lighter sentence than her controlling paramour.

I thought of how Mr Creevey had waited on the Embankment. Had his conscience been putting up a fight against the hypnotic command to throw Mr Chase into the river? Or was he waiting for another command, a password from his hypnotist?

I remembered exactly what Mr Chase had said before Mr Creevey hurled him away. I recalled the particular emphasis he had laid on the first word, as he demanded his release: *monster*. It was not a word he had used before, and he had cried it out at the last possible moment — if he had waited even a few more seconds, he might have been out of danger.

That is, if he had ever truly been in danger.

I stared unseeing at the teapot and remembered my feeling that Mr Chase was acting a part, speaking lines in a script he had prepared ... until Mr Jesperson surprised him. He knew Mr Jesperson would be following Mr Creevey — he probably learned that from me — but he could not have imagined, because it never occurred to *me*, that it would be possible to locate the very telephone from which Mr Creevey was given his orders.

I had been right not to trust Mr Chase. He was not a victim. Mr Jesperson had already suspected his hypnotic powers and I had felt them myself. Now I guessed that he had used those powers to orchestrate his own "kidnapping". And why else but to throw us off the scent?

Mr Jesperson was right. The man was a hypnotist of incredible ability, and might have made us only imagine we were witnessing a display of astonishing psychic powers. Although what we had seen in the fog beside the river could not be explained away so easily. Chase had risked death in order to make us believe that *someone* *else* was behind the disappearance of the missing mediums, and also to make us believe the others had been done away with. But why? If he truly had the power to hover in mid-air, supported by nothing but invisible "spirit hands", why should he bother with hypnotism? And what possible motive could he have for organising the abduction of the other mediums? Even if he was determined to eliminate the competition, surely only Monsieur Ribaud, of all the missing mediums, was in any way a significant threat to Chase's crown as the most powerful medium of the age. He surely had nothing to fear from poor Miss Jessop, or those two little girls.

No, I could not understand it. I continued to brood while I ate my breakfast, but I was still very much in the dark.

When the post arrived it brought me two letters. One was the much-anticipated reply from the theatre manager in Paris; my fingers shook as I tore it open, and I held my breath as I read, but, alas, the author regretted very much to disappoint me. The hypnotist I referred to had been a last-minute replacement for another act, and he could find no record of the man's details; but, in any case, he understood that the *artiste* in question had gone abroad — most likely back to his own country, the United States of America.

It was not proof, but that line was enough to convince me that Mr Chase had been the hypnotist the Creeveys had seen on stage during their honeymoon;

the villain who had exploited Mr Creevey's vulner-
ability for his own wicked ends. I wondered if Arthur
Creevey was his only victim. There might be others
waiting for his signal — were the mediums he'd had
kidnapped only part of some much greater criminal
scheme?

My mind reeled with fantastic possibilities, and I
wished for Mr Jesperson to come home so that we
could have a proper discussion.

The other letter was from Mrs Chase. It, too, was in
French. Again, she begged for my company, hinted at
secrets she longed to share with me and offered to send
a carriage if I would only agree to come. I could not tell
if her letter was a genuine cry for help, or merely a lure
set by her husband, but tempted though I was, I
remembered the warning I'd been given and I did
nothing.

Edith returned in the afternoon, alone. Her son had
not been arrested, she told me, but he was helping the
police with their investigation — which was, of course,
already in part *our* investigation. Mr Creevey, alas,
remained in gaol. Jasper had done his best to convince
the police to let him go, insisting that the best way to
find the missing mediums was to release their prisoner
and keep a close watch on where he went by night.

"Does that mean the police now admit that mediums
are being abducted?" We were in the kitchen and I was
helping her chop vegetables for soup while we spoke.

She sighed. "Yes and no. They have been made aware
that the two Miss De Beauvoirs are missing, and after
what happened to Mr Chase — publicly proclaimed as

the most talented medium in London — well, Inspector Spokes is inclined to consider the strong likelihood that *all* mediums may be under threat. Which is why he believes it is too dangerous to release Mr Creevey at present. The man himself cannot be blamed for what he has been forced to do whilst unconscious, but until they know *who* the villain is, they won't risk it. There are not enough policemen in London to protect every potential victim, and Jasper's plan of following the somnambulist could fail — just imagine if they lost him in the fog."

"Poor Mr Creevey," I said sadly, and handed her my board of chopped onions, which she swept into the pot along with mounds of chopped cabbage, carrots and potatoes.

"Jasper has an idea that may help him and the police as well. If he can hypnotise Mr Creevey, he may learn where he took Miss Jessop. Unfortunately, Mr Creevey is violently opposed to any suggestion of hypnosis — the strength of his resistance makes Jasper think it must have been instilled by the person who first entranced him." She gave the pot a good stir.

"Mr Chase."

"I beg your pardon?"

"Mr Chase was the person who hypnotised Mr Creevey," I said.

She looked startled. "Oh no, you can't mean Mr *Chase* — he was, well, he was almost one of his victims."

I explained the process of my reasoning to her and, by the time the soup was simmering merrily, Edith had understood and accepted the conclusion, which she thought her son must share. "That explains a remark of Jasper's," she said.

"What did he say?" I asked eagerly, but she shook her head vaguely and protested that she could not recall exactly; but it was in the context of a conversation with the police about the lack of any obvious suspects.

"Something about . . . not wishing to be sued for slander. Of course, it was Mr Chase who swore out the complaint against Mr Creevey, and the police undoubtedly see him as a victim. It will not be easy to get them to accept that Mr Chase orchestrated his own abduction and attempted murder."

Edith and I dined alone that evening on soup and bread and cheese, as Mr Jesperson did not return. I was not worried — he had warned his mother he might be very late — but I felt frustrated to be unable to discuss our theories and make plans together, and I felt a twinge of jealousy, too, that he should be helping the police and carrying the investigation ahead, whilst I was stuck at home with nothing to do.

Wearied by the stressful events of the morning, Edith retired early. I did not feel sleepy, but having no appetite for sitting up alone trying to keep the smoky fire ablaze, I soon went to bed myself. Despite my certainty that I should do nothing but lie awake and fret, I must have fallen asleep as soon as my head hit the pillow, for I knew nothing more, and had no notion of how much time had passed when I was startled awake.

The room was dark and still, but my heart was pounding. Once again, I was gripped by the sick, frightened certainty that I was not alone.

Oh, not again.

Despite the physical fear that gripped me, I managed to be annoyed by this familiar intrusion into my sleep. I saw nothing out of the ordinary as I blinked into the darkness, but this time I noticed an odd smell.

I turned the other way, groping for the box of matches, and as I turned I saw him.

Not just a head and not a shadowy shape at the foot of my bed, but the large, solid, unmistakable form of a man I had seen for the first time in a corridor in Lord Bennington's house. Then, I had been frightened by an impossible memory of a previous encounter, of that pale, sinister face looming over me as I lay helpless in my bed.

Now, the Cossack loomed over me, and with a thrill of horror, I realised my vision had come true.

I opened my mouth to scream, but as I sucked in a breath, a cloth came down over my nose and mouth, pressed down with his huge hand. The cloth was the source of the smell I had noticed; the pungent, sickly-sweet, oblivion-bearing scent of ether was the last thing I knew.

From the personal notebook of
J. J. Jesperson, Esq.

She is gone! Taken! In his evil clutches — and I am to blame.

How could I be such a blundering, idiotic, cloth-headed donkey? I *knew CC* wanted her — knew, moreover, AC was not his only servant. AL herself warned me of the Cossack & her (she thought irrational) fear of him. I had all the information necessary, yet it did not prompt me to be more careful, to never leave her unprotected. I should have spent the night couching at her door.

Were this only a battle of wits between CC and myself I should have to bow my head, admit defeat, but with AL's life at stake I can never give up. I must rescue her immediately.

Finding the house where CC keeps her & the other prisoners will not be difficult; am confident I'll have the address within 24 hours. But what might happen to her in that time? The odds, I think, are that she will be kept safe — perhaps not comfortable, but unharmed — with the missing mediums. Yet, what if I am wrong?

What connection between AL & mediums? Most likely none; only having successfully abducted four people for one purpose, CC used same method for a different purpose.

What purpose?

1st poss.: The basest. I cannot bear to think — surely he is not so low? After all, he is civilised (n.b.: American), married — wife resides with him — and with sufficient personal charm, cash and cachet to win the favours of any number of women, without resorting to abduction. Yet I must not flinch from this possibility. I know there are men (or animals who look like men) who take pleasure in a woman's pain and fear.

2nd poss.: Mistaken identity. At first meeting, CC thought AL a medium. Taken aback when Lord B laughed. Could it be he still believes AL has psychic powers? How fixed is this idea in him? What wd he do when forced to accept she does not? (Return to first problem: why is he collecting mediums?)

3rd poss: Hostage. He takes her as a move against me. Feeling under threat, he wants me to know that unless I leave him alone to carry out his plans unhampered, she will suffer.

CHAPTER
TWENTY-THREE

In the Dark

I woke with a throbbing headache in a cold, dark room. It was as black as a tomb, but I could feel that I was lying on a bed with a blanket over me.

I sat up carefully and concentrated on not being sick. My mouth was dry, and there was a foul taste — probably, like the headache, an after-effect of the ether. I had no idea where I was, or how long I had been unconscious.

"Hello?" My voice creaked rustily, but the sound reassured me I was not entombed. "Is anyone there?"

I swung my legs over the edge of the bed and put my bare feet down on carpet. It was rough and felt gritty, and was obviously not often swept. This, with the dusty, damp, faintly mousey reek in the air made me wonder how long this room had been unoccupied. I felt a chilly draught against my ankles, which I guessed came from the gap beneath a door, and as I tried to work out the direction of it, I heard something.

Footsteps. Coming closer.

They stopped.

I got back onto the bed, tucked my chilly feet beneath me and held my breath.

There was the sound of metal against metal, a key turning in a lock, then the door swung open.

There stood Mr Chase, the lamp in his hand lighting him against the darkness. He smiled at me as if the situation was perfectly normal and said, "I do hope you have not been awake for too long. It can be rather disconcerting, waking in a strange place in darkness. There is a lamp and matches over there — but you weren't to know."

He came in, closing the door behind him, and went to a table set against the wall. He lit the large lamp there, and for the first time I saw my prison.

It was a large room — larger than my bedroom in Gower Street — but bare and unwelcoming, furnished only with two beds and a long plain wooden table such as you might find in a farmhouse kitchen. The window in the wall to my left was boarded up.

"What would you like for breakfast?" Mr Chase enquired. "I can offer you porridge, eggs, toast . . . or perhaps you'd fancy a kipper?"

His inappropriate hospitality was almost as horrible as the Cossack's intrusion. "I won't stay for breakfast," I said, keeping my voice level. "I'd like to go home."

He smiled. "Oh, Miss Lane. This is your home now. But don't be downcast. It is rather primitive, I know, but we will be moving on before long, and I hope we may find better accommodation. Boiled eggs, fried, or scrambled? Bacon?"

"Where is this place?"

"That need not concern you."

"You can't keep me here."

His smile grew wider. "I think you will find that I can."

"But why?" Wrapping the blanket about myself, clenching my teeth against their inclination to chatter, I struggled to understand. "Why kidnap *me*? What do you want?"

His smile grew wider. His eyes gleamed. "Come now, surely you are not still in ignorance?"

"I'm not pretending. I have no idea what you want with me."

He stared at me. "You don't know. You really don't know." Then he laughed. "Ha! Well, well. The great lady detective. You have been investigating the curious affair of the missing mediums — as one might call it — but still you don't know a thing."

I frowned. "We worked out that *you* were behind the disappearances, using Mr Creevey as your tool. But that's no reason to kidnap *me*."

"Is it not?"

I was at a loss. "Surely you don't think that will stop my partner? You've given him an even greater incentive to foil you . . . and he will report it to the police."

Mr Chase put his hand to his mouth, pretending to stifle a yawn.

"You won't get away with this," I said angrily. "He will find me, and then —"

He looked bored. "Forget Jesperson. You belong to me now."

"I don't belong to anyone!" I sat up very straight, backbone stiffened by his offensive remark. "No one owns me — no one owns anyone; in this country, in this day and age, not even in *your* country — why, it's thirty years since slavery was outlawed by your President Lincoln. I won't —"

"Stop." He held up his hand. "This is nothing to do with slavery, you silly girl. The relations between us —"

Relations. The word struck me like a blow. "You're a married man."

"Just so. I love my wife." He gave me a long, dark look. "I love her very much. And she loves me. We are devoted to each other. But my Nadezhda is not strong. And for that reason I would spare her, you see. And I can, with your help."

He had not moved, but the way he stared at me made it seem he was coming closer, until I felt his face looming over mine like the relentless, impassive countenance of his servant last night. The Cossack had come to carry me away — to give me to this man who now said he owned me.

"Why do you look so frightened? It won't hurt. I will not hurt you. It can be good for you, too. You're so much stronger than Nadezhda. When you trust me — trust me. Relax. Put your faith in me. Relax. There's nothing to be afraid of. You are safe. Safe and relaxed."

He spoke in the monotonous yet compelling drone I recognised as a tool of the hypnotist, and I knew I must look away and resist, but although I strained to turn my head and escape his gaze, I could not move. His eyes bored into mine; he would not let me go.

Determined to fend him off, I managed to choke out a few words:

"What . . . what do you want? What are you going to do? You mustn't! It's wrong — I don't want — I don't love you."

My final protestation sparked a response — bemusement and then anger, and with that his hold upon me slackened. His eyes widened. "Love? You little fool. How could you imagine . . . think for one moment that I . . . that you . . . Stupid girl. Your ignorance disgusts me. Go to sleep. Sleep . . . sleep . . . sleep."

The connection between us broken, his command had no force. Yet he seemed not to realise this, and as I had no desire to alert him to the fact, I pretended to be overwhelmed. Letting my eyelids flutter, I performed the actions he expected and fell back on the bed, pretending to sleep. But I was as alert as I could be. I might be innocent, and as ignorant of some things as he thought me, but I did know one area where men differed physically from women, and that was their weakness, and I was prepared to act quickly and decisively. If he dared attempt an outrage on my seemingly unconscious body, I would seize the moment — seize his prized emblem of masculinity — and *squeeze* without mercy.

At last he sighed, and as I concentrated on keeping my breathing even I sensed him backing away. "You will sleep now for another hour, and when you wake you will feel refreshed and relaxed. You will not fear me; you have no reason to fear me." He went on more quickly, "Although you must *respect* me, and do whatever I command. Nothing I ask of you will be wrong or immoral. You want me to be happy. Then you will be happy, too. No harm will come to you, so long as you please me. You want to please me. You will forget your foolish notions about . . ." he stumbled, hesitating, "about me."

There was a long silence then, but I was certain he was watching me closely. I struggled to continue breathing regularly and keep my body relaxed, afraid that he had become suspicious. But he was probably trying to work out the contradictions of what he wished to say to me — that he was both my friend and my master, that he was an honourable man who had taken a woman prisoner, that he would not force me against my will, yet I must do whatever he commanded . . .

Finally, he left me. I heard him lock me in and waited until I heard his footsteps going down the stairs before I opened my eyes.

Then, I must confess, a few tears leaked from my eyes, and my chest heaved with quiet sobs as I indulged in a bout of nervous self-pity.

But not for long. Despite what I had said to Mr Chase, despite the very great trust I had in my partner, I frankly lack the patience that is required of kidnapped maidens in old-fashioned tales, and the prospect of waiting quietly until the police came to batter down the door, or submitting to my fate if they did not, was never on the cards.

Besides, don't they say that God helps those who help themselves?

Aided by lamplight, I took stock of my situation.

On the table with the lamp and matches there were also two jugs of water — one was cold, the other warmish. There was a wash basin and a sweet-smelling block of soap, and several hand-towels. There were two glasses. I filled one with the cold water and drank it down thirstily before exploring the rest of the room.

I found a chamber pot in the corner beyond the second bed, and there was also a wooden chest. Inside it were more sheets and blankets. I added the blankets to my bed and gave some thought to ripping up one of the sheets to wrap around my feet. They were like two cold bricks now. I couldn't bear it any longer, and retreated to the relative warmth of my bed, where, huddled in the blankets, I sat and shivered and chafed my feet to warm them.

There was a fireplace in the room, but it was cold and bare with nothing more than the whiff of cold soot to suggest it could be used to provide heat. The only potential fuel in the room was the small wooden chest and some of the bedding. But that wouldn't last long, and for all I knew the chimney might have been blocked up like the window. I could see nothing that might be turned into any sort of useful tool. I wished my conversation with Mr Chase had gone in a different way and that I could have ordered breakfast. If offered another chance I'd go for kippers — not because I fancied fish for breakfast, but because a fish knife could be useful, and possibly even the bones.

I mourned my clothes. If only I had been abducted when fully dressed. No shoes, no hooks or buttons, no belt or brooch, no coat with any useful items tucked away in a pocket . . . only my flannel nightgown. I had seen Mr Jesperson open locks using one of my hair pins, and I was sure that given enough time and determination I could do the same. But, alas, I'd let my hair down and braided it before I went to bed, so instead of the pins that usually kept my hair in place, I had only a scrap of ribbon.

After a while, when my feet were a bit warmer, I wrapped them in one of the blankets, draped another one around me like a shawl, and shuffled over to inspect the boarded-up window. The job had been well and thoroughly done, so I could not escape through the window, nor push my head out to scream for help, nor get any idea of where I was. I stood there for some time quietly listening, and was rewarded by the occasional sounds of traffic — wheels and horses' hooves clattering, shouts and distant calls as people went by. I guessed that I was at the back of a house on a quiet street somewhere in London, or one of its nearer suburbs.

Perhaps even not that far from Belgrave Square.

My heart beat a little faster as I thought of Lady Florence's remark about the house Mr Chase had been obliged to rent for his servants. Was this it? Were the mediums he had kidnapped imprisoned in other rooms?

Hurrying to the door, I crouched down and peered through the keyhole. The view was not very inspiring — a dim and dusty corridor — but I could see another closed door on the wall opposite. I listened as hard as I could, and eventually heard creakings and a soft whispering sound — skirts, perhaps? Or was it a human voice?

306

It might, of course, be Mr Chase and his wife . . . but hope flared as I thought of other possibilities. Without pausing to worry about it, I gave four sharp determined raps on my own door.

The soft sounds stopped at once; I imagined startled glances. I gave two more raps and then I called out: "Can you hear me? Who is there?"

"Oh, yes!" It was a young female voice. "We hear you."

"I am Miss Lane," I cried. "I have been kidnapped."

"So have we." Two young voices chimed together.

I sighed and smiled, feeling oddly relieved. "The Misses De Beauvoir, I presume?"

They introduced themselves — Amelia and Bedelia — and told me they shared their room with Miss Hilda Jessop.

Tears started to my eyes. "Thank goodness!" I said, and choked up. "Thank goodness you are alive. We have been looking for you — are you all right? Are you well enough?"

Well enough, they assured me, but awfully bored. It was dreadful never being allowed to go out. Although — one of them giggled — Mr Chase had been a perfect gentleman, really quite charming, and he assured them it need not always be this way. He had promised to take them to America, where they would have a very different and entirely pleasant life . . .

I had been so caught up in our shouted conversation that I had not heard the footsteps on the stairs; it was only when a huge fist pounded against my door —

ONE, TWO — that I knew — we all knew — without a doubt that it was over.

I reeled back from the door at the first blow. The key rattled in the lock, the door was flung upon and the ghastly, gigantic creature called the Cossack loomed over me once again. I retreated, but in a single stride he was on me; one big hand closed upon my arm as I gave a shriek of pure terror.

Anger flared in his eyes and he shook his head. He raised a finger to his lips, indicating that I should be silent. I nodded rapidly, desperately eager to comply, but I suppose it was not enough, for he gave no sign of being appeased. Swiftly he pulled my arms together behind my back — I was powerless to resist — and he bound my wrists together with some sort of cord. Then he pulled a cloth from his pocket. I remembered the ether-soaked cloth that had sent me into an oblivious sleep, and I could not repress a frightened bleat. "No — please don't — I'll be quiet —"

He used the cloth to gag me, stuffing part of it in my mouth and tying it behind my head.

I shook my head desperately, to no avail. He had already turned his back on me and was on his way out of the room. A moment later the door swung shut, and then I heard the key turn in the lock and I was alone.

From the personal notebook of
J. J. Jesperson, Esq.

I have found the house.

But it is the Cossack, Pyotr Ivanovitch, who has rented it, and he guards it day and night. If I should tell the police of my suspicions, all the prisoners could be free today and the Cossack under arrest, but CC would still be at large.

The loss of his mediums might incommode him, as would the loss of his usefully large and powerful servant, but it would be no more than a temporary hitch. After all, there are plenty of thugs for the hiring and more mediums for the taking, and he clearly feels no inhibitions about using his hypnotic powers for illegal gain.

Miss Lane, forgive me! I long to see you safe and free, but am sure you would agree it is better to hang fire until we have proof against CC — proof the police must accept. I fear he will have somehow ensured that none of his prisoners will be able to give convincing evidence against him — I know all too well what confusion a cunning hypnotist may sow. It would be horrible for his prisoners to be forced to bear false witness. And I cannot allow his servants to bear the blame, especially not poor, unwitting Arthur Creevey.

CC must not escape. I have discovered his crimes, and now must build the case against him. Find undeniable evidence of his villainy.

Jewel thefts — all have taken place since CC has been in London. Significant? Find out: do any/all households have telephone? Family or staff in Paris in last year?

The theatre — has been reported in the theatrical columns that CC rented the Alhambra for more than a week, tho' will use it for one night only. He paid handsomely for unusual proviso that theatre is to be "dark" until his performance. No other shows and no one allowed inside — explained that his set would take some time to assemble and he could not risk having it disturbed; nor to have the "surprise" ruined by advance description in newspapers, etc. Cd be mere publicity — every time CC is mentioned in papers, public interest grows — but my curiosity is piqued. And even if he hides no great secrets there, it could be useful to get inside.

CHAPTER
TWENTY-FOUR

A Worse Imprisonment

I felt the weak, childish urge to cry, but if I gave way to tears my nose would be blocked, and it would be very difficult, if not impossible, to breathe. Besides, I was determined not to give in to my captors if I could help it. The Cossack had made it impossible for me to talk to my fellow prisoners for the moment, but I would not accept him as the final authority. Rather than sit helplessly, waiting for Mr Chase to come back and free me — as I had no doubt he would take some pleasure in doing — I would do my best to free myself.

The way he had tied my hands made it difficult, but not impossible. I was still relatively young and lithe — not so young and lithe as when my boy cousins had been playing Red Indians and made me their captive — but I knew how to escape and eventually, although it was a sore struggle, I managed. Once my hands were free I was able to get rid of the gag.

Then I drank the rest of the water in one jug and used the other — now as cold as the first — to wash myself.

I stared at the door, wishing I dared resume the conversation with my fellow prisoners, who might have more useful information, but it would be too unwise. Next time, the Cossack might tie me hand *and* foot, or bind me to the bed. No, I would pick my battles carefully.

Without a clock or any view of the outside world I could not tell the time, but by my stomach — which was beginning to feel the lack of breakfast very strongly — I guessed it to be early afternoon when Mr Chase came calling, bearing a platter of cold meats, pickles, bread and cheese, a glass of milk and a cup of tea.

If he was surprised to find me unbound he gave no sign. Perhaps he had no idea of what had happened in his absence and would have been deeply shocked — if not amused — to find me bound and gagged. I wondered again about communication between the brute and his master — undoubtedly Mr Chase was able to give the Cossack simple instructions, but I was less certain about the Russian servant's ability to report back to his master. I guessed that the Cossack had been instructed not to allow the prisoners to make any noise — and how he did so was up to him.

I began eating at once and Mr Chase leaned back against the door, arms folded across his chest as he watched me, amused by my greedy haste. "Now you're sorry you didn't have breakfast."

I shot him a frowning look, but otherwise made no reply.

"Pyotr will bring you your supper. I shall be busy this evening — Lord Bennington is giving a very select party in my honour."

312

Again I did not respond, although I was scarcely able to repress a shudder when he named the Cossack.

"He'll bring you fresh water and . . . is there anything else you need?"

I raised my eyebrows and paused deliberately in my eating as if giving the matter careful thought. "Only one thing."

"Yes?"

"My freedom."

He smiled and shook his head. "Freedom comes from within. I meant anything *material* that would make your stay here more comfortable."

"Clothes," I said at once.

"You won't need them while you're here. When we leave, then I'll make sure you have the proper clothes to travel in."

"Is it really so much to ask?" I glared at him angrily. "You try sitting in here all day in just a flannel gown. If I can't have a fire —"

"I'm afraid you can't. I'm sorry. Perhaps a dressing gown and slippers would make you more comfortable?"

I grudgingly agreed. With the edge off my hunger, I could think of other things. I carefully cut a slice of beef into small pieces, wondering if I could use this rather blunt table knife in any way that would aid my escape if — as seemed unlikely — he left it behind.

"Anything else? I do want you to be as comfortable as possible, Miss Lane."

I patted my hair. "A comb, a brush and a mirror would be nice. I'd like to be able to do my hair."

He gave me a knowing smile. "Vanity, thy name is woman. You may have the brush, but your hair must stay down. No hair pins or anything else that might serve to pick a lock. Really, it is for your own safety, my dear. If you managed to get downstairs you would find the exit guarded by a dog much fiercer and far less concerned with your comfort than I."

His mockery stung. I put down my knife and fork and pushed the plate aside. "How long do you imagine you can keep me locked up?"

"Long enough. Are you finished?"

"You won't get away with it. Mr Jesperson will find me."

"Well, and if he does?" He shrugged, a half-smile playing about his lips.

I felt a pang of anxiety. What if this was not about me at all? What if I had been taken only to provide the bait in a trap set for my partner?

"He won't come alone — he'll bring the police to arrest you."

His eyes bored into mine. "All the better. Your friend will be made to look a fool, and the police will certainly *not* arrest me when you beg them to go away as you swear you are with me by your own free will."

Although I tried, I could not break eye contact. "What do you mean?"

"I see a demonstration is required. Should your Mr Jesperson be foolish enough to attempt to take you by force, this is what will happen."

Without conscious intent, I found I was off the bed and on my feet, and then, as Mr Chase gave a casual turn of his hand, I sank to my knees before him, clasping my hands in supplication. I was still struggling to come to terms with the fact that I appeared to have become a puppet moved by the will of another when something even worse occurred. I heard a voice — *my own voice* — saying, in the most abject, pleading tone:

"Don't let them take me. Please, I beg you, let me stay with him. Mr Chase is the greatest man I have ever known. My only wish is to follow and serve him."

I was looking up at him the whole time, and he wore a look of serene concentration. Much as I should have liked to accuse him of ventriloquism, I knew the voice was my own; I could feel the lying, impossible words emerging from my own mouth. Tears stung my eyes; the sense of helpless horror only increased as I felt one roll down my cheek.

"What a touching picture it is," murmured Mr Chase as, leaning down, he caught my tear on his fingertip. "A man would have to have a heart of stone to deny your simple wish. And my wife is *so* fond of you . . . you may travel with us as her nurse. You'll be like a member of the family." Taking out his handkerchief, he wiped his hands.

"Get up, my child. No more tears. Of course you can stay. No one will force you to leave. Now go back to your bed and rest. Relax and rest easy. Sleep, and when you wake, know that you are where you belong. Sleep now. Sleep."

From the personal notebook of
J. J. Jesperson, Esq.

The Alhambra is owned and managed by a consortium who maintain an office in the West End. Upon this office, Señorita Garcia y Velasquez — an excessively tall but proportionately buxom Spanish dancer — paid a call to enquire about taking the theatre for a three-week term in February. But before she would agree to sign a contract, she wanted to see the premises for herself, to be certain it was appropriate; for in addition to her own dancing, the stage was to accommodate the needs of a high-wire act, several acrobats and a magician who specialised in sudden appearance and disappearances.

The manager in residence that day was eager to assure her of its suitability, fetching out detailed architectural plans, drawings, even photographs, but she insisted on a personal visit. She would be in London for one day only, and did not plan to return before February. If the management of the Alhambra would not gratify her, perhaps she would receive a warmer welcome at the Palace or the Empire . . .

He decided it could do no harm: a short visit, to get a feel for the place.

There were men (hired by CC) guarding both front and back entrances, but of course, they had no authority to forbid the property owner, the man with his own key, from carrying out his necessary duties, and as for the female person who accompanied him . . . knowing looks were exchanged, and I have no doubt this information will be passed on to CC in due course, but while the unwarranted intrusion may annoy him, I hope it will not alarm him, or rouse any suspicion of my involvement.

Our tour was as brief and superficial as expected; he pointed out a few things, e.g. the traps and flying wires I had enquired about, but I was not allowed to step onto the stage — the set that occupied it was, of course, property of Mr C, and he hoped I would respect the fact that he was taking a great risk, for it was technically a breach of contract for anyone not in Mr C's employ even to *glimpse* it.

That glimpse was most illuminating. Glorious Aphrodite! I now have an idea — mad though it would sound to the police — of the use he means to make of his stolen mediums. And I suspect that he means to abduct one more before the night of his performance.

Our tour had to be cut short, as my guide, feeling he should be rewarded, proved himself no gentleman. Of course the Señorita was well equipped to discourage him, and I think he may be more respectful — or at least more cautious — when next he is alone with a lady who carries a fan. (N.B. fan more damaged than he was; M not best pleased.)

The guard at the door burst out laughing at the sight of Management in futile pursuit of the amazingly swift, tall Spanish lady, storming off in high dudgeon, oblivious to his pathetic wailing: "But the contract? Forgive me? You haven't signed . . . Won't you come back to my office and sign?"

Who will be his next victim? Can — or should — I foil this attempt?

I know that CC has been introduced to at least 20 people who claim psychic or spiritualistic gifts. He has already captured four (plus AL), leaving 16. Of those I may perhaps disregard the 3 not presently in London, leaving a list of 13, of whom 8 are female. Until now it had not struck me how women predominate over men in this field. CC would seem to have a preference for females, but does that reflect the natural division, or his choice to go for smaller, physically weaker victims?

My strong suspicion is that he will try to take Sra. Gallo next, and that he will make the attempt very soon. I could foil him in this, and it would give me great pleasure to do so, but I must hold back, for the same reason that I've refrained from rescuing Miss L and her fellow prisoners. It is not enough to deprive him of his servants if CC remains able to get clear away. He already plans to leave London after the show, to go on to conquer New York and the rest of his native land. That must not be allowed to happen.

I will inform all 13 potential victims to take extra precautions for their safety over the few nights remaining. If they manage to foil him, all to the good, but it will make no real difference if he has 6 captives hidden away, or only 5.

The end result will be the same. I must defeat him once and for all, in public, before a large audience, on the very stage where he imagines himself to be in control. I will make him helpless — steal his secret weapons — and reveal him for the charlatan and parasitical thief that he is.

But I need help with the preparations. Particularly, I need someone backstage. What a time to be deprived of my partner!

CHAPTER
TWENTY-FIVE

Another Prisoner

At his command, I had retreated to the bed, put my head on the pillow and closed my eyes, but sleep was impossible; the feelings of horror and terror his little "demonstration" had aroused in me were not conducive to relaxation. I felt lightheaded and breathless, and my heart was beating like a wild bird in a net.

He had made me say those words, but he could not make me *mean* them.

Although that distinction mattered to me, it was not helpful. Mr Chase had just shown me — through hypnotism or sorcery — that I was his puppet. If he made me perform like that before the police, they would certainly believe I had made my own choice and was not in need of rescue. And Mr Jesperson? What would *he* think?

Oh, if only I could write him a letter!

But there was nothing in this bare room with which to write; no pen, ink or paper, and even supposing Mr Chase should be so "kind" as to allow me a sketchpad and pencil, or a book to read, there would still be the much greater problem of how to smuggle it out of the house and how to ensure it reached the intended recipient.

So I went on thinking, going over and over the details of my situation, searching for a way out for the next several hours, until finally I heard the footsteps I recognised as belonging to the Cossack — an astonishingly light tread for such a large man — and sat up, tensed and ready for anything by the time he opened the door.

But this time he had come to bring me the items Mr Chase had promised: a thick, warm dressing gown and two pairs of heavy socks. He put them down on the end of my bed and took away the two empty jugs.

As soon as he was gone I examined my new garments. The dressing gown had a label inside and was new. I wondered who had purchased it. The Cossack would surely attract too much unwanted attention if he bought a woman's dressing gown in Oxford Street — perhaps Mr Chase had ordered it to be delivered, although I had not heard knocking, or any of the minor commotion that usually accompanies deliveries. Of course, I didn't know how big this house was, or if there was more than one staircase. It was possible that Mrs Chase's maid was in on the secret and served as a messenger and delivery girl, for if the Cossack really was the only manservant, it was unlikely that Mr Chase would wish him to leave our prison unguarded, even for an hour.

I thought of the excessive caution Mr Chase displayed in his refusal to allow me clothing I could wear out of doors, or hair pins. Yet I had encountered the Cossack in Belgrave Square on the night of the séance — who then had guarded the house? Had Mr Chase felt easier when he knew no one suspected the various disappearances were connected? Or was it me — did he think his other prisoners lacked the courage and strength to escape?

I felt a bit more hopeful then. If Mr Chase thought there was a way, I must find it.

I wished I could speak with the others. Together, we might have been able to concoct a plan of escape. The Cossack surely slept sometimes, and with both eyes closed like any other man. And if he left the house we must take advantage of his absence. I would have to listen even more carefully and notice every sound, every change of atmosphere.

When the Cossack returned I was sitting on the edge of the bed wearing my new dressing gown and socks. He brought a bowl of beef stew, and as I settled down to eat it he retreated, leaving his lamp behind and taking mine.

I tasted a piece of meat cautiously. It was flavoured in an unusual way, the red sauce peppery and spiked with dill and caraway seeds. Was it a Russian dish? The Cossack was probably cook as well as guard, and he might not hear what was happening upstairs when he was occupied in the kitchen.

When he returned for my tray, I said that I did not find it comfortable to eat all my meals in bed, and asked if a chair could be brought to my room so that I could sit at the table. He stared at me with his usual stolid expression and made no reply.

So it went on for another day, the Cossack my only visitor. I was not sorry to be left alone by Mr Chase, but I found my solitary confinement deeply boring. There was nothing to do but think, and without outside stimulus, thinking itself became a trap, my thoughts as limited in scope as the room around me.

Then everything changed.

I was asleep until the clatter of the key in the lock woke me, and as the door opened I saw the enormous figure of the Cossack clutching a bundle of blankets close to his chest.

As was his custom, he said nothing, merely entered and dropped his burden upon the spare bed before making a swift retreat. He shut the door, plunging the room once more into darkness.

I would have liked to call a curse down on his head for disturbing my sleep, but was too much of a coward to do more than mutter under my breath.

On the other bed the bundle moved and called upon *Jesu e Santa Maria la Madonna* for protection.

I sat bolt upright. "Signora Gallo?" I exclaimed. "Let me get a light . . ." I was glad now that I had moved the lamp and box of matches to the floor beside my bed, and it was only a matter of seconds before I had it lit. I scarcely had time to put it down safely before the excitable little woman had her arms wrapped around me, weeping and exclaiming.

"Hush, hush," I whispered urgently, and gave her a warning shake. "Quietly! If he hears us, that beast will come back and bind and gag us both."

She quieted at once. We stood there in the lamplight, tense and alert, holding hands and listening. When I felt sure the Cossack was not coming back, I said, "Come and sit with me in my bed — we'll be warmer that way, and you can tell me everything."

"Ah, Miss Lane! Miss Lane . . . so happy to see you, and not be here all alone. Also, I am so, so glad you are not murdered as I fear."

After she had hugged and kissed me again several times in the overflowing of her emotional nature, we snuggled beneath the blankets to keep warm, as I assured her that I was indeed unharmed, safe and well. I also informed her that there were three other kidnapped mediums in the room across the hall, who had also been well treated. "Whatever Mr Chase has planned for us, I do not think it involves death or injury. Although I am still at a loss to know why he keeps us imprisoned; he feeds his prisoners well, and even supplied a dressing gown and socks when I complained of the cold. Now, tell me what has happened to you — how did it come about that you were snatched from your bed?" Her nightdress, as well as the lateness of the hour, told me that was how it must have been.

She confirmed my suspicion, explaining in a low, hesitant voice how she had been fast asleep in her bed, in the room she shared with Gabrielle, when something — she knew not what — caused her to swim up out of sleep and open her eyes upon the terrifying sight of the pale, white face of a strange man looming over her in the darkness. When she opened her mouth to scream for help, a thick cloth, smelling pungently of ether, was

324

pressed firmly against her face; she could not help but breathe in the fumes, and so she passed into unconsciousness.

Listening to this description of her dreadful experience gave me gooseflesh as it triggered memories I would rather have forgotten, but there was something even worse than that, for the very fact that her abduction had been carried out so easily showed something else — Mr Jesperson was failing in his task.

One might argue that London was full of psychic mediums, many of whom Mr Chase must have had occasion to encounter, and therefore no one could have predicted which he would have made his next target. Yet I could not help feeling that Mr Jesperson *should* have known, *should* have deduced from a dozen small signs that no one else would have noticed, and having made this deduction, he should have made arrangements that would have foiled the attempt, landed the Cossack in police custody and led to a swift resolution and freedom for all Chase's prisoners.

Perhaps I was too easily impressed and too much inclined to take Mr Jesperson at his own valuation.

I thought of how often during the nearly five months of our association it had occurred to me that this undeniably talented man had something childish in his nature. He had grown up nourished by his doting mother's belief that her son could do and be anything he wished. Now it seemed I was the childish one, having placed my trust in him, believing he could solve any mystery to which he set his mind, believing he could triumph over the villainous Mr Chase with ease and rescue me — rescue us all — from danger.

What a fool I was, to trust in anyone but myself. How often must I be disappointed before I would learn that obvious lesson?

I dragged my attention back to Signora Gallo. "So, your experience replicates mine. I suppose you knew nothing more until you regained consciousness, lying on that bed —"

"No, no, no!" She shook her head so hard in denial that a shudder rocked the bed. "I wake up inna coach . . . cloth fall off, I think, and I inna coach where bad man put me."

"Alone?" A sudden hope seized me. "Could you look out of the window? How long was the journey? Did you see where you went?"

"I not alone, no. *He* there, too — Case, Meester Case."

"Chase," I corrected her without thinking. "You spoke with him?"

"No." She reared up indignantly, and even though her face was in shadow I saw the indignant sparkle in her eyes. "I not talk — I pretend I still . . ." she made a snoring noise. "I not want him put that cloth back on face. So, keep eyes shut, not say nothing, not see nothing. About . . . ten minutes? Coach stop and . . . *monster* . . . come down, and Meester Case he push me toward him, and monster pick me up and carry me like sack of clothes, you know?"

She told me she had continued to pretend she was unconscious, although it clearly had been a great effort not to struggle and scream for help, and as she was borne away, helpless, into the house, she'd heard the clatter of horses' hooves and the wheels of the carriage as it rolled away.

I gave her a hug. "You poor thing. I know just what you have been through, but I am glad to hear your story, for it confirms that Mr Chase has no one to help him now that Mr Creevey is in jail, except his servant, the man you call 'monster' and others know as the Cossack. He's the one who snatched you, and he would have been driving the carriage when Mr Chase was inside with you, and then Chase will have driven back to Belgrave Square, leaving him here to guard us overnight. If only I had known that he'd left us here unguarded. Perhaps it was for no more than half an hour, but it could have been a chance."

I sighed, thinking that it was not enough of a chance unless I had some means by which to pick the lock, and then I peered more closely at Signora Gallo. Like mine, her hair had been tied back in a long, loose braid, with no hair pin in sight. It seemed unlikely that her heavy grey flannel gown had pockets filled with hidden treasures, but there was no harm in asking.

"If I only had a hair pin, or something similarly small and flexible, I think I might be able to pick the lock on that door," I told her. "Do you have anything? A piece of jewellery, or anything at all?"

With a sly, triumphant smile she opened her hand to reveal a diamond tie pin. I had seen it before, adorning Mr Chase's elegant shirt front.

"You clever girl," I said, admiringly. The diamond was ostentatiously large, but the pin itself was rather short, and as it was gold it might be too soft for a useful lockpick, but I was happy to see it for another reason: Signora Gallo's special talent might make it useful to us in another way.

"Dear Signora Gallo, can you read something about Mr Chase in that gem? Can it tell you what he means to do with us? Why he kidnapped you and the other mediums? Why he wants *me*?"

Then I clamped my lips together, knowing it was not good to overwhelm her with too many questions all at once.

She nodded and concentrated her attention on the diamond in her palm. A rapt, contemplative expression appeared at first, but soon her face darkened in a scowl.

"Bad man," she muttered. Her chin came up and her eyes blazed. "He is a *thief*!"

"Oh? Well, we'll get to that in a moment — do you know why he's kidnapped so many mediums?"

"Because he is *thief*," she repeated impatiently. "He want what we have. Not like ordinary thief, who steal money and jewels — but he do that too. Mr Chase kidnap us because he wants us *power*."

She saw that I did not understand and expanded: "Mr Chase is *psychic* thief. He *feel* when somebody is like me — when we have power. He know, like I know from diamond."

I stared at her in astonishment. I suddenly understood what Mr Chase's singular power was. In addition to the hypnotic abilities he had trained himself to use, he had been born with an additional sense: the ability to sniff out psychic talents in others.

328

And then, having discovered them, he stole them. That was the meaning of her phrase "psychic thief".

"But how?" I asked, bewildered. "How can anyone steal something so . . . so intangible?"

She shrugged and shook her head with a dark, glowering expression. "You see what he do to me at Belgrave Square."

"Ah, yes," I said slowly. It began to make sense. "He used your talent against you. Maybe he deflected it in some way, or —"

"He *steal* it," she said emphatically, and waved the little pin so that the diamond head sent out flashes of brilliance as it caught the light. "Not like I steal from him, but . . . he take it from me, and take and take and take until . . ." she mimed collapse.

"Like pumping water from a well," I guessed. "At first there's plenty, a steady stream, but gradually it dies away to a trickle. It is not exhausted, though, not forever, because it restores itself, and after a few hours there is more."

"Not like water," she corrected me solemnly. "Like *blood*. Case like a flea who drink blood. Take a little bit, not so bad." She shook her hand from the wrist. "Flea only little, can't drink too much. But *him* . . ." She let her hand flop.

"When I feel it first, I not know what he do to me. I not know *why* I so tired, why I can't do what I try. Now, I understand. Now, *he* tell me." She waved the diamond pin.

The diamond had told her its owner's story, and thanks to Signora Gallo's talent, now I understood, too.

Chase was a fake, a liar, and a parasite. He had no "spirit helpers" and no great gift of his own. Signora Gallo did not know when or how he had discovered he had the ability to sense psychic talents in others; she thought he must have been born with it, but he had made his living as a conjurer and a hypnotist until he met the lovely young Russian princess who had fallen head over heels in love with him.

It was she who gave him the diamond tie pin, and she who had given him access to her own powers — consciously, gladly; a gift of love.

"She a silly little girl, afraid of her own powers," said Signora Gallo, clutching the tie pin and frowning with concentration. "She think God put her on earth to serve one man — she give herself to him, she give him *everything*."

"Why couldn't he be content with her sacrifice? Why wasn't that enough for him?" I asked bitterly. "Greedy, I suppose."

She shook her head slowly. "No, not that. Remember what I say about flea? A few bites from a flea, no great matter. But if something much bigger than a flea should drink — and drink and drink and drink, for hours at a time, night after night —"

"You mean, he's killing her?" I recalled how Chase had spoken to me of "sparing" his wife, and I felt the heat of a blush rise again at the memory of how I had misunderstood his meaning. "But . . . it's not blood that he's taking from her — or from you —"

"Not blood, but is life, even so. Is life," she repeated solemnly.

330

Any effort, any exertion took something from one, I reflected. It was natural, and people recovered their powers after resting, eating, replenishing the body and mind. But if forced to go beyond their natural limits . . . pushed to destruction . . . Probably Chase had not realised at first what he was doing to his spouse, for I believed he loved her; and she adored him too much to complain when his demands made her ill. In the heady delight of exploiting his new-found abilities, Chase had severely and permanently damaged Nadezhda's health.

He would not consider giving up his promising career. If the task was too great for his wife, he must find other sources of power. And thus he had evolved his plan of kidnapping mediums.

"He must have started preparing for this in Paris, when he hypnotised Mr Creevey," I said.

"And the others."

"Others — you mean his horrible Russian servant?"

"No, not him. There are more, more peoples he meet in Paris, that now are living in London, not knowing that they do his bidding.

"I say he is thief, and he is; he thieves jewels, too." She told me that in addition to Creevey — chosen for his size and strength as well as his susceptibility to hypnosis — Chase had also hypnotised several young ladies, all now serving as maids in London households — and there was even one respectable London matron who was responsible for robbing herself. Individually, and completely unconscious of their criminal activities, they had stolen diamond rings and necklaces from half a dozen houses and passed them on to Chase's manservant.

Creevey had aided Chase in the kidnappings of Miss Jessop — who took him for an angel — and the De Beauvoir girls. Chase had used his own hypnotic powers to spirit Monsieur Ribaud away, and employed the Cossack to abduct Signora Gallo and me. This brought me up short.

"Why did he want me?"

The medium looked surprised. Abruptly she began to laugh, shaking the whole bed with her merriment. "You no know?"

I frowned at her. "No, I do not know. Does the diamond? Please tell me."

She stopped laughing and wiped a tear from her eye with the back of one hand. "The reason is, you are like his wife."

A chill went through me at her words and I had a dreadful memory of being on my knees before him, acting the part of his love-struck puppet. It was a moment before I could speak. "How? How like her?"

"She not use her power — not know she has it, until she meet him. You are the same."

I did not want to believe her. How was it possible that I could have a power and yet remain unaware of it? I, who had been studying these matters for years? And yet I could not deny my experience, or the truth of what I now knew about Mr Chase.

Mr Chase had sensed my latent power, like a mosquito or a flea scenting warm blood. He knew it was there because he could use it.

332

"What is my talent? What can I do?" I demanded. Signora Gallo could only shrug helplessly. How would she know? She had always — well, nearly always — been aware of her talent. Even as a small child. Although, such was the poverty of her upbringing, she rarely had the opportunity to handle valuable objects; still, she could hardly remember a time when gold, silver and precious stones did not call out to her, eager to tell her their stories.

I remembered again how Mr Chase had put words in my mouth. If that was hypnosis, how did I *know* what he wanted me to say? If he had used psychic powers against me, whose powers had he used?

I thought of the martial arts Mr Jesperson had studied that relied on invisible forces, lines of energy — *chi* — and the important principle of utilising your enemy's own strength against him. Was that what Mr Chase had been doing to me?

I heard footsteps on the stairs — they were not the catlike tread of the Cossack.

The door flew open and there was Mr Chase, face pale except for two high spots of colour in his cheeks.

"Where is it?" he demanded, his voice rising to an unimpressive squeak. He stepped into the room and for once did not pause to shut the door behind him. His eyes, narrowed, were fixed upon Signora Gallo. "*You* have stolen it; give it back to me, at once!"

She stared back at him, her jaw set stubbornly. Any struggle between them took place in silence without any outward sign, until, abruptly, he turned to me.

"I think I should like it better if *you* returned my diamond pin to me, Miss Lane. You appear on terms of some intimacy with this guttersnipe you have allowed into your bed. Did you know her to be a thief? Surely *you* do not approve of her thieving ways? She has stolen my property. If she will not give it back of her own volition, *you* must take it from her. Go on. Now. Take it from her."

Reaching the end of his speech, Mr Chase made a movement with his hand that I felt quite as if he had taken hold of my wrist and pulled my arm.

I tried to resist, but my attempt to pull away only added force to the movement he wished me to make, and my arm shot out, beyond my control, and I found that I had seized hold of Signora Gallo's hand. She gave a yelp of dismay, but my fingers, as if they belonged to someone else, clawed at hers, indifferent to any harm they might do, and determinedly prised open her fist.

The diamond pin now revealed, Mr Chase darted forward and snatched it himself.

He snarled: "If you ever do such a thing again — dare to steal from me — expect a much worse punishment than *this*."

At this word my hand flew up, and slapped Signora Gallo across the face, twice.

She cried out and so did I; our shock, if not our pain, was equal.

"Oh, Signora, I'm so sorry!" I cried.

"Let that be a lesson to you both," said Mr Chase, and slammed the door behind him.

From the personal notebook of
J. J. Jesperson, Esq.

Obliged to take Miss F into my confidence. She lacks many of the qualities that make AL such a good companion, but F has a reasonable understanding and is surprisingly stout-hearted, even bold — a woman of strong constitution. Her flirtatious manner is a nuisance, but I may learn to overlook that.

She would not have been my first choice of assistant, but has taken the role upon herself. Instead of gratefully accepting my advance warning re: CC (for I felt it better to confide in her, rather than terrify Sra G), she pursued me, insisted I shd & cd & must do more. She proposed I hide nearby, keep watch on the building where they lodged, and follow him — offered to cover cost of carriage rental.

She did not ask me to foil the kidnapping, but to follow and discover where CC kept his prisoners. (Did she think I have done nothing since AL's abduction?) Obliged to explain this unnecessary: location of prison house no mystery. To her credit, she understood why I have not yet informed police; her own loathing for CC burns too fiercely to permit him any possibility of escape, so . . . how are "we" to catch him?

So — "we" it is. On the night of the show, we shall rescue the prisoners. My helpers (must enlist at least one other) will whisk them away from under his very nose, whilst I keep him occupied on stage. Once they've given their statements to the police, we may count on arrest being made swiftly, but before that happens, I mean to humiliate him before his audience, reveal what a fraud this great "medium" really is; bring him low before he's led off in chains.

Like her namesake animal, F is clever and bold. Convinced her protégée (and roommate) would be the next victim, she catnapped by day and kept watch at night, so when it happened she was alert, only feigning sleep. Thro' slitted eyes she watched the Cossack creep into the room and seize poor Sra G & bear her away.

As soon as they were gone, F was up and at the window; saw the coach waiting in the street below, saw the arms of Lord B on the door, and recognised CC as the driver who sprang down quickly to exchange places with the Cossack, taking charge of the kidnapped medium inside the coach. F noted every detail she could, and looks forward to testifying against these "demons" in court.

She had developed a vague but lurid idea involving blood sacrifice as the reason behind his kidnapping. To settle her nerves, I explained my theory.

The Chinese call it *chi* — the energy or life force that is in us, in nature, and runs throughout the entire universe. They have developed not only a philosophy, but a science that utilises this, and have ways of feeling and tracking and using *chi* often very effectively (e.g. in their medicine), although this entire aspect of life remains hidden and incomprehensible to most in the West.

I remember my first trip abroad — I cannot have been more than 8. Papa was still alive, but poorly, and we were in search of a healthier climate for him, and settled for the winter in some unfashionable watering spot in Italy, where my attention was caught by a newly-wed couple staying at the same *pensione*. We never spoke with them — they were Hungarian, I think — but I watched them secretly, intrigued by the stark difference between the two. Although they were a close and loving couple, rarely apart, they could hardly have been more different in appearance: she, young and fresh and beautiful, he — although in reality probably only a few years older than his bride — thin, balding and prematurely aged. As the days and weeks passed, the difference became ever more pronounced. She bloomed and grew, thriving on the food and fresh air, whilst he dwindled and aged. She was *enceinte* — a fact that became increasingly obvious as her belly swelled — and he was clearly dying of some wasting disease, but my childish ignorance, allied with a penchant for ghoulish tales, created a more fanciful and frightening explanation. She was feeding upon him, I imagined, growing fatter as she sucked the life out of him night after night. The only question was why he let her do it. Had she gained control over him by some dark art? Or was it possible he remained in ignorance even as he was dying, besotted with love, unaware of the fatal bargain he had made in his marriage, never realising how his wife battened upon him, like a tick on a dog's head? I even plotted how I might rescue him and expose the wife for the monster that she was. Fortunately for me, he died before I could humiliate myself. Yet even now, although I know better, the memory of that fat, fair wife, her rosy cheeks glistening with tears and her great belly straining at her ill-suited widow's weeds, just days away from giving birth when her husband was buried, makes me shudder.

I had not finished my explanation of *chi* and how it might help to explain what CC was up to before F was ahead of me, exclaiming, "Why, the man is a vampire! A psychic vampire. Instead of blood, he feeds upon their souls. Or, as you would have it — their *chi*. He drains their energy, then uses it against them or for his own purposes. As we saw for ourselves in Belgrave Square: poor Fiorella, almost too exhausted to speak whilst he danced around like a demented flea."

Question: CC feeds upon the power of mediums — for that reason, he kidnapped a selection. But why include AL?

F felt sure of the answer. Her eye gleamed like a cabochon.

In vain did I repeat that *chi* exists in all of nature, is found in everyone. Mediums are not special in that respect, although CC might believe the life force possessed by mediums to be superior, or perhaps he had found it easier to tap into them. F cut me off. "Di

338

is a medium. I always said she was sensitive, but — imagine."

She was keen for me to agree, but although what I witnessed in AL's room was highly suggestive of mediumistic powers I said nothing of it. I could only think how unpleasant Miss L would find this conversation, our speculation upon her supposed supernatural powers — I must hope, therefore, that her power, if she has it, does not extend to clairaudience or bilocation, or any other of those convenient attributes which allow one to spy upon one's friends — and I responded repressively to F's excited suggestions, pointing out that it would be a much better use of our time to concentrate on the plans for defeating CC and rescuing his prisoners. When we have set our friend free, then she may choose to enlighten us.

CHAPTER
TWENTY-SIX

Lessons Learned

I had sometimes been told by people thinking to flatter, that I was spiritually "sensitive" or "intuitive", but I had never made such claims for myself, and preferred to attribute any successes that I had achieved to close observation and the exercise of rational thought. No one, so far as I was aware, had ever suggested I might possess any sort of psychic talent, and I had never experienced any powers in myself that might be at all mediumistic. Like most people, I sometimes "knew" what another person was about to say, or anticipated the arrival of an unexpected visitor or letter, but these small acts of precognition, even if they cannot be explained by science, are so common that they hardly singled me out.

Yet Mr Chase had added me to his collection of mediums. Signora Gallo's explanation supplied the reason he had tauntingly withheld.

Later, as I lay there in the dark, the sound of gentle snoring coming from the other bed providing an unexpected source of comfort in my formerly lonely prison, it occurred to me that if I had not encountered Mr Chase, my psychic talents would have remained entirely unsuspected. I thought of the many studies that had been made of hypnotised subjects who demonstrated remarkable mental powers — the ability to read thoughts, see events happening at a distance, and more. It went back to the early days of "animal magnetism" and mesmerism, and although under the name of hypnotism in modern times the induction of a trance state had become more scientifically respectable, its connection with clairvoyance and telepathy was not so often discussed. Still, the evidence was there.

Now it occurred to me that Mr Chase was able to *induce* psychic abilities in me and thus draw upon my power for himself, by the act of placing me under his hypnotic control. If I could avoid being hypnotised, I would be of no use to him.

Alas, even if that were true, I did not see how it would help me as long as I was his prisoner. Clearly, he did not require my consent to work his power.

Would I be better able to resist him if I learned how to use it myself?

Consider the case of Signora Gallo. I had seen for myself how she had been victimised — her own power turned against her — at the séance in Belgrave Square. And yet, earlier this evening, *after* she had been made aware of what he was, she had managed to resist his command. True, she had kept the tie pin for only a few seconds, but he'd had to use *me* to take it from her. I wondered if, rather than risk defeat by continuing his battle of wills with her, he had reasserted his control over me instead.

It was my ignorance and lack of practice that made me his ideal weapon. But now I knew that resistance need not be futile.

I could not wait a moment longer to find out how she'd managed it. I got up and lit the lamp, then went over and gently shook her awake.

She was startled and confused and it took me some little while to make her understand. When she did, at last, comprehend, she denied that she had *done* anything. Signora Gallo, I realised, was an instinctual creature with little or no intellectual grasp of her own actions. She did not plan; she responded. When I continued to press, she credited the diamond, claiming that it "liked" her and did not wish to leave her possession to return to that nasty man. Her little fairy tale invested the treasures she loved so much with volition and consciousness.

This was her way. Although she knew she possessed a gift given to few, she did not perceive it as being under her own control. Rather, she had the childish notion that the precious objects she craved were equally drawn to her. They had stories they wanted to tell, and she was one of the few people in the world who could hear them. This was the purpose of her talent. She could explain no more about it. She yawned and burrowed into her pillow.

I extinguished the lamp and returned to my own bed, although with so much to occupy my mind, sleep was not a likely visitor.

In the morning, the Cossack brought our breakfasts: porridge, toast, a pot of jam, milk, sugar and a pot of tea. I was bold enough to ask: "Will Mr Chase be coming later?" but received no reply.

Signora Gallo was of the opinion that the Cossack could not speak — or at least, not in English. I had no idea how master and man communicated, but imagined much could be conveyed in mime.

While we ate — the signora turned up her nose at the porridge, but was enthusiastic about the jam — I asked if she could teach me how to use my psychic gift. She laughed merrily at the very idea and said that nobody had ever taught her — it was an ability you were born with, like sight, or hearing. Had anyone ever taught me to *hear?*

"No," I said, "But one can be taught to *listen* — to pick out particular sounds, or to listen with appreciation to music."

She shrugged and pointed out that I was not asking her to help me sharpen or refine a particular sense, as would be the case of teaching someone to listen more attentively. Could I teach a deaf person how to hear?

I saw her point.

The standard opinion, amongst those who did not dismiss it as a load of nonsense, was that certain people were born with a particular gift — whether it was the "second sight" or an ability to commune with spirits. The spiritualist line on extraordinary powers, such as telekinesis, levitation, or materialisations, was that they were produced by spirits of the dead and enabled by the medium. Why the dead should wish to communicate with the living in such a bizarre and roundabout way — materialising flowers, playing trumpets, rapping on tables — rather than sending straightforward messages through their mediums, was a question no true believer would ask.

Serious researchers had been trying for decades to establish the truth about psychic phenomena, but the more rigorously scientific they attempted to make an investigation, the more likely it was to fail. Science is based on the replication of results, and I had yet to encounter a single medium whose psychic gifts were as reliable as the laws of nature that science explained. Sometimes the spirits were unhelpful, or there were disturbances in the atmosphere, or energy levels were low. The "crisis apparition" was well known, as were the phenomena of premonitions and many other occasional small acts of telepathy or precognition that could not be reproduced in a laboratory.

Indeed, it could not always be produced to order anywhere, which led to the downfall of those like Miss Jessop, when they turned to deception rather than disappoint their audience when their gifts failed. If their talents were more reliable — or if they knew better how to use them — Mr Chase would never be able to keep his abductions secret. He could lock up his prisoners, could even have them bound and gagged, but there was no such obvious way to bind psychic gifts. Monsieur Ribaud was famous for his materialisations, I knew, so why did he not send a message to one of his friends? Why weren't sitters at séances all over the city being warned every evening that Mr Chase was a dangerous and evil man who kept half a dozen prisoners in a secret location?

I might not doubt the existence of psychic powers, but I did question their usefulness.

Mr Chase did not come at all that day, which was disappointing. I longed for another opportunity to observe his use of my power, and by that, perhaps, to gain some understanding of how I might exert it myself.

Eager to avoid another brutal and punitive visit from the Cossack, I spent much of the morning by the door, straining my ears for any sound, peering through the keyhole from time to time and irritably shushing Signora Gallo when she attempted to strike up a conversation. At last, the clatter of what could be cooking utensils and the faint smell of frying onions encouraged me to hope we would not be overheard, and I made my attempt.

I caught the attention of the women in the room across the hall with a short series of raps — my sequence of raps was repeated back to me in a manner so reminiscent of primitive spirit communications that it made me smile. But spelling out messages to each other by knocking out the alphabet — or even one for yes, two for no — would take far too long, and might be as risky as shouting. Undoubtedly, too many knocking sounds from upstairs would attract unwanted attention as readily as our raised voices.

So, I called out to them, my lips near the keyhole, and told them that I must be quick, but I had information to share. Then, as clearly but as economically as I could, I explained that I had discovered the reason for our captivity.

I could feel their combined surprise in a sort of disturbance of the air, then Miss Jessop's voice: "You do not mean that he has no power of his own? But how can that be? Why, the things we have seen him do!"

"He did those things by drawing on *your* power," I replied. "Bear that in mind. *You* — we — are the ones with the power. *His* only power is to sense it in others — and steal it. He has tricked you into thinking that he is more powerful than you, when in fact —"

"But that cannot be." It was one of the De Beauvoir girls who objected in her clear, high voice. "Mr Chase is very powerful — quite terrifyingly so. And as a mesmerist —"

I interrupted her. "He has some skill as a hypnotist, I don't deny it. But a hypnotist is only as powerful as *you* allow him to be. I want you all to know this so you can guard against it. You *can* resist him — we all have the ability to resist. Think of this: he covets your power. And because *your* power is greater than his, you will be able to refuse him."

One of the young ladies would have objected, but I cut her off. "There is no time to argue. *Think* about it, please. Don't be negative . . . don't be too ready to give in to him. And it may be that all together we will be more than his match. Now, tell me quickly. What has become of Monsieur Ribaud?"

Miss Jessop had not heard of him, and it took the sisters a few seconds to recall the name of the young French medium they had once met. I had not really expected that they would know . . . Even if he had not adopted the divide and conquer system, Mr Chase

346

would hardly have lodged a young man in the same room with three ladies.

Probably he was somewhere else in the house, perhaps held under greater restraint — chained to a wall, or bound and gagged. I prayed his confinement was not so dreadful, but at this reminder of my own experience at the hands of the Cosssack, I made haste to end our risky conversation, urging them all to remember what I had said and not to give up hope.

"You're not helpless. Remember that."

Yet even as I tried to sound encouraging, in truth, I felt far from hopeful.

Where was Mr Jesperson? I had put all my faith in him and yet, after three days he had still not managed to rescue us.

I was not very good company for Signora Gallo that day, spending most of my time locked within my own mind. I tried to send myself, in thought, to the house in Gower Street. The rooms were so familiar to me already — so well loved — that I could easily conjure them up in imagination.

But I could not convince myself that what I saw was anything more than my imagining. And even if I did somehow appear, like a ghost, before the astonished eyes of my partner or his mother, what good would that do? They knew I had been abducted, and Mr Jesperson could easily guess by whom. Because I did not know *where* I was imprisoned, I could not give them the address.

By now he should have found me. If free, I was sure *I* could have done it, tracing the trail of gossip from

Lady Florence to a letting agent and to the front door. Or he might have followed Chase, or questioned Mrs Chase — I still wondered if she had meant to warn me. And there was Arthur Creevey; Mr Jesperson might have hypnotised him and found the knowledge buried in the mind of the somnambulist.

Had my friend truly failed on every score? Why was I still a prisoner?

The conclusion I came to was grim.

Unable to believe he had not managed to discover where Chase had stashed his prisoners, I could only presume my friend was unable to act upon his knowledge, either because he had been taken prisoner himself, or because some even worse fate had befallen him.

A wave of hopelessness washed over me.

CHAPTER
TWENTY-SEVEN

The Stage is Set

Late the next day, as Fiorella and I sat playing another round of scissors, paper, stone in an attempt to while away the hours, I was distantly aware of a carriage stopping outside, and said, "Perhaps Mr Chase has finally deigned to call upon us."

She grinned and winked at me. "Oh, *now* you have the clairvoyance."

Although I had spoken more in hope than expectation, there soon came sounds from elsewhere in the house that indicated an arrival. When they were followed by the unmistakeable creaking of the stairs, I knew my casual remark had been proved true.

He stood in the doorway for a moment, as if inviting our admiration, his arms piled with boxes. Then, fixing his eyes upon mine, he said, "Miss Lane, I have brought you new clothes. Please be so good as to prepare yourself to go out, and do so as swiftly as you are able. I shall return for you in a quarter of an hour."

Depositing the boxes at the foot of my bed, he backed out of the room and locked us in again.

"None for me?" Signora Gallo was quicker than I to approach the boxes, and I hurried to join her as she began to open them and pull out everything packed so carefully in tissue paper inside.

They were all — undergarments, stockings, dress, coat, shoes — of the finest quality, and could have been made to measure for me. Mr Chase must have had a good eye for the female form — unless he had simply plucked my measurements from my thoughts. Although I shivered uneasily at his presumption and hated the power he held over me, I will confess I also took a certain pleasure in these new clothes. It was a relief to get out of my well-worn nightgown, and a positive delight to exchange it for such fashionable and well-made attire.

Fiorella helped me with the fastenings, all the while grumbling under her breath because *she* had been overlooked. I felt a flash of fear then: after the dullness of captivity I was excited by the prospect of change, but the fact that I was being taken and my companion left behind made me apprehensive.

I had just finished lacing up the soft kid-leather shoes when I heard the sound of the key in the lock, and then Mr Chase appeared carrying a hat box. This he gave me along with a paper of hair pins.

"Ten minutes will, I hope, be sufficient for you to arrange your coiffure?"

What a relief it was to be able to put up my hair again. Then, finally, I stopped feeling like an invalid. The hat was modish, except for an exceptionally long and heavy veil. I was still struggling to fold it back — an impossible task with no extra hat pins at my disposal — when Mr Chase returned.

350

Fiorella immediately demanded to know what was happening — where was he taking Miss Lane? Why must she stay behind? Where were the nice new clothes for *her*?

He ignored her, his attention focussed on me as he made a sound of disapproval.

"You must wear the veil *down*," he said. "Arrange it better than that. Your face must not be seen." As he spoke, I felt the faintest brush of his will against mine, and I hastened to obey rather than have him force me.

He gave a smile of satisfaction. "That's right. Now we may go."

"You take me too!" cried Fiorella, and she rushed towards the door.

His smile disappeared, his face went blank, and I saw poor little Fiorella lifted off her feet before she was pushed by an invisible force across the room.

"Oh!" I cried out in horror, and turned — *tried* to turn — but all my muscles seized up and I could not move.

I could only move my eyes. I looked at Mr Chase. His gaze in return was dark and penetrating, and I had the horrible fancy that he sent some tiny sliver of himself sliding along the path of our shared gaze, directly into my soul, from where he would now and forever control my every move. I tried to resist, but the harder I fought the more firmly I was held. I felt his wordless, profound pleasure as he forced me to turn away from him and walk down the stairs without looking back.

Fiorella, I cried within myself. *I am sorry!*

I heard him pause to lock the door while I continued to descend. He took his time following me, satisfied that he had nothing to worry about, no fear that I could do anything that was not his will.

I could not break free. I could only do what he wanted me to do. It was impossible to run. My body was bound to him so tightly it might have been another limb. Inside, I was screaming, but I am quite sure that even if anyone could have seen my face beneath the heavy veil, none of my distress would have been visible.

A carriage was waiting outside the door, but because Mr Chase bowed my head, and kept my gaze fixed on my feet in their pretty new shoes as he helped me climb inside, I saw little of it.

"There you are, my dear," he murmured. "Quite comfortable, I hope?"

From this I guessed he meant for the coachman to believe I was his wife, which suggested the driver knew him; probably he was in the employ of Lord Bennington. A little hope flared up in me at the thought that I need only do something unexpected to catch the man's attention and make him suspicious — if I could make a noise, jerk my chin up, flail about . . . anything at all to surprise him, give him something to gossip about, and allow it to reach receptive ears . . .

But it was worse than useless. The more I struggled to do something — anything! — the more tightly I felt the vice-like grip of his will; by the time I was settled on the seat inside, well out of the driver's sight, I felt as if there were bands of iron around my chest. I could only draw breath by giving up the fight.

Seated beside me as the carriage rattled off, Mr Chase said not a word, but I could feel his self-satisfaction as strongly as if he'd bellowed his triumph to the skies. He had made his point. I could not hope to prevail against his will, for his strength was greater than mine.

But — it was not *his* power Mr Chase was exerting; it was mine. He was making me fight against myself.

I suddenly remembered a little souvenir Mr Jesperson had brought back from China. I had noticed it lying on a bookshelf, a primitive tube woven from dried rushes.

"It's a finger trap," he'd said. "Put one finger in each end. Now try to pull it off."

When you pulled, the woven bands tightened. The harder one pulled, the more tightly the fingers were trapped.

"They're also known as Chinese handcuffs," he had said.

It would have to be a very ignorant, or wildly terrified captive who was unable to work out how to escape, I'd thought. Obviously, if pulling tightened, then the opposite action would relax the bands. Instead of pulling and tensing, one must relax, pushing the fingers into the tube until it loosened.

Sometimes, in order to win one must surrender, was the morsel of wisdom represented by this simple toy, and the reason my friend kept it in view.

Every instinct in me warred against the idea of giving in and submitting to Mr Chase. To *pretend* to submit was one thing; actually to give up all resistance was anathema.

But pretending to relax had not released me from the finger trap. Edith Jesperson had not pretended to give in when her son — or I — attacked. She had done something else: she had used my own force against me by deflecting it, by stepping aside while I charged ahead expecting resistance that was not there.

And just as Edith had used my own force against me, so did Mr Chase. I imagined I was fighting against him, but I was fighting against myself. Just as when I struggled in the bonds of the Chinese handcuffs, my own actions trapped me.

The carriage stopped. Looking out of the window, I saw we were in a narrow alleyway, where there was a door and a lighted sign with the words "Stage Door" above it.

Of course. Despite counting the days of my imprisonment, I had forgotten that this was the night when the celebrated physical medium Christopher Clement Chase was to appear on the stage of the Alhambra. Now I knew he intended to use me to ensure his success.

He opened the door and got out, then turned back to me, his hand extended to take mine. I could feel his will working; he had exerted himself to take control, too cautious to entrust me with even the small amount of autonomy involved in getting out of the carriage without any fuss.

I moved as he wished me to; took his hand and allowed him to assist me as I climbed down from the carriage. I did not exert myself with any futile struggle, but nor was I his puppet. *I climbed down.* Yes, I did his bidding, but it was my choice to do so. He did not force my limbs to move. I knew what he wished me to do and I did it myself. A fine distinction, you may think, as the result was the same, but *I* felt the difference — whereas I think he did not. He was used to meeting my resistance and drawing power from it — the power by which he made me dance to his tune. That was not happening now, yet I think he was unaware of any change. He only knew that what he wanted to happen was happening.

Later, when I had more time to think about it, I concluded that he was more concerned with outcome than process, and that his understanding of his own powers might be scarcely more sophisticated than Signora Gallo's. He had a suspicious nature, but as long as he got the results he expected, he could be fooled.

So I went on pretending to be his slave and hoped I was not only fooling myself.

A powerfully-built young man had been lounging against the wall beside the stage door, but he straightened up and touched his cap respectfully as we approached.

"Afternoon, Mr Chase, sir."

"Good afternoon, Rolly. Everything all right?"

"Oh, yes, sir."

"Anyone been sniffing around, asking questions, trying to get in?"

"No, sir, nobody. But I'd 'ave sent 'em off with a flea in their ear if they 'ad! I've got me orders, and I don't let nobody in, 'cept if they're with you."

"Excellent. Good work. I have brought my wife" — he squeezed my arm, a familiarity I was compelled to accept — "to have a look at the set. We'll probably leave by the front . . . I hope Dave has been as good a guard there as you have back here."

Although he professed himself gratified, Mr Chase did not seem entirely pleased to hear that no one had come by asking questions, although it may be that I was attributing my own emotions to him, so closely bound were we. I *did* feel a flash of disappointment so strong it was close to despair, wondering again what had happened to Mr Jesperson.

"You are disconcertingly silent," said Mr Chase, after we had entered the building.

"Did you wish me to speak?"

He gave a soft snort, then directed me with a slight touch to my elbow to turn along a narrow corridor. "When did a man's *wishes* count when it came to women's conversation?"

"Good conversation is inspired by congenial company."

"Oh, ho! You're not so submissive as you'd like to appear."

I stopped in the chilly, dimly lit space and faced him. "You seem to wish to have me *appear* to be your wife." Struggling a bit to fold back the veil, I gave up and pulled off the hat entirely.

He chuckled. "A bit of misdirection, just in case. In future, you may travel with me openly."

I shuddered. "No thank you."

His smile curdled. "I can make you beg."

I dropped my eyes and bowed my head, hoping to disarm him with a show of submission. "I know."

It was enough. I felt his mood lift at this proof of my defeat. "Come along," he said, more kindly. "Let me show you our stage set."

We proceeded through the nether regions of the theatre, and then he led me onto the great stage of the Alhambra. I had been inside, in the audience, only once or twice before; I remembered a seat far back in the stalls where I had once sat with my sister and our parents watching a ballet.

"Look upon my works," Mr Chase declaimed. Then, in a more conversational tone: "Look upon these painted gods — you won't have another chance to see them as the audience will, and they are worth the price of admission."

I followed the grand sweep of his arm with my gaze. The stage setting was presumably meant to represent an ancient Greek temple: a sequence of classical pillars painted brilliant white, with a backdrop suggestive of dark blue sky, rocks and a hillside above the sea had been set up. But the most striking thing about the whole ensemble were the six towering statues of ancient gods and goddesses, brightly painted, each one probably twenty feet high: Artemis, Apollo, Athena, Aphrodite, Hermes and Zeus.

"My helpers," he said with a sly smile, fixing me again with his gaze, and I understood: the wood and plaster statues were hollow and would provide the necessary hiding place for the kidnapped mediums. *That* must have been the purpose of the spirit cabinet in the drawing room. His wife would have been hidden inside, near enough for him to feed upon her power.

It took no imaginative leap to recognise which among the Olympian crowd was mine; as my gaze swept across their garishly painted faces, I guessed that the twins, Artemis and Apollo, would be allotted to Amelia and Bedelia De Beauvoir; wise Athena would hold Miss Jessop; Hermes, that quicksilver trickster, was for Signora Gallo, and bearded Zeus — the only one of the figures that was unambiguously masculine — must be meant for Monsieur Ribaud.

"The audience will be encouraged to imagine that these ancient gods are working through me, giving me their powers."

"The spirits of the dead not impressive enough?"

"Don't be catty, Miss Lane. We shall have spirits, too. But this is a bit *different*, which is appropriate, as I am different from the average run of psychic mediums. I am sorry you won't be able to watch my show . . . but you'll have your part to play behind the scenes; your very important contribution to make." He paused to fish his watch from its pocket, and after he had consulted it, snapped it shut. "Charming though I always find your company, we must part for a little while. I must finish my preparations. And you must take your place, Aphrodite."

358

Pinning me with his gaze, he made a showman's sweeping gesture at the towering figure of the goddess I had been named after, and as he gestured, it moved. I flinched, thinking it was about to topple over onto us, but then felt foolish, for it was not falling, but opening.

The statue was hinged like a cabinet. The hollow inside was lined with dark satin, the same colour as my clothes. I thought of a coffin, and then I thought of a telephone cabinet.

If he had instructed me, I would have obeyed, but he said nothing. I felt the now unpleasantly familiar mental pressure urging me forward and — would I never learn? — at once stiffened, resisting. My resistance was turned against me; the force now irresistible, I all but *flew* across the stage and into the satiny embrace of the hollow statue, where a cushioned seat awaited me.

"I hope you are comfortable?" His smile was of the most unbearable smugness: once again, I was complicit in my own defeat. When I did not reply, he continued. "I understand you may find it a bore to be in darkness, so closely confined, but you will be alone for only a few hours. Then you will have your part to play. For now, I suggest you rest. Go to sleep. Rest . . . close your eyes . . . relax . . ."

I thought he meant to put me into a trance by hypnosis, but perhaps he felt my unwillingness, and with little time to spare decided to hurry matters along. I became aware of his sixth sense seeking out mine. It's hard to describe this feeling. If I had to draw a picture, I might sketch a snake . . . or, no, some sort of fragile, frond-like pseudopod sprouting from his head to poke blindly into mine where it quested for something immaterial — the psychic version of a scent. Once on the scent it would follow it, find me, and our wills would merge. My only chance was to keep it from touching me, to evade and slip away again and again. Through a variety of mental or psychical wriggles I managed to avoid his touch, but the chase could not go on forever. He had already entered my soul — it was as if we were trapped together in a small room and eventually, inevitably, he would have me.

It was only a matter of time, but for once, time was on my side. He was in a hurry, impatient to leave, and although he must have known I could not avoid him for long, he would not spend the minutes that might be necessary. Without saying another word, as if our silent battle had never happened and this had been his intention all along, he took hold of the front of the statue and swung it shut on me.

At once I was plunged into darkness. I heard the sound of a bolt sliding home, and knew that I was locked in.

But I did not feel trapped. Instead, for the first time in days, I felt freedom was almost within my grasp. Yes, I was still his prisoner, but no longer his slave. Listening to the sharp, angry sounds of his boot-heels retreating, I knew I had just proved to both of us that I was not as helpless, nor he as thoroughly in control, as it had seemed.

From the personal notebook of
J .J. Jesperson, Esq.

CC set a guard on the front door and the stage door but never thought of the door in the roof. I have been able to come and go as I please.

Sims on board — stout fellow — and he was good enough to lend me the services of his handyman: a carpenter who does very neat work. Even if CC gives his set another inspection before the show he is unlikely to notice how the statues have been altered.

With a few borrowed books about magic & stagecraft & a good imagination, I have been able to set up some nice illusions. Have been practising my flying — wish I'd had equipment like this when I was with the travelling show in India, they would have worshipped me as a god.

CC won't know what's hit him.

Roll on show time.

CHAPTER
TWENTY-EIGHT

A View from the Gods

At first the darkness of my prison was absolute, but within a minute or two my eyes had adjusted and I noticed two spots of light, right at my eye level. When I touched that area I found a scrap of cloth glued along the top edge. Lifting it, I was startled by the glare and had to blink and wait for my eyes to adjust. When I could see again, I discovered that two eyeholes had been carefully cut out of the wood, offering me a good view of the stage.

I was pleased by this discovery, which made my confinement easier to bear, but I was surprised, remembering Mr Chase's comments earlier: had he not implied that I should be unable to watch the show? But I knew how he liked to mislead and hold back information.

Some time went by — an hour or two — and then I was alerted to the arrival of others backstage by a sudden burst of sound. I heard footsteps coming nearer and then they were on the stage. I peeped out and saw two pretty, slender young girls of identical appearance in yellow dresses, walking slowly hand in hand. Immediately behind them I recognised a thin, faded spinster in a blue dress, Miss Jessop, and then — the sight made me flinch back, heart pounding — the Cossack.

I took a steadying breath and leaned forward to look out again. Just as I began to wonder about little Fiorella Gallo, I realised that the Cossack was carrying her close to his chest; she wore a dark red dress the same colour as his jacket. Although she was very still, she was not unconscious. Her eyes were closed, but from the rigidity of her body and the fixed line of her mouth, I could see that she was completely aware of her situation and hated it. I wondered if she had tried to make a run for it, and her reward for that act of rebellion was to be carried like a sack of laundry, imprisoned in the Russian's powerful arms. Was she the example that made the other three females walk so meekly, I wondered, or had they been hypnotised?

I recognised the confident ring of approaching boot-heels, but the next figure who appeared on the stage was a stranger — a sad figure who stumbled and lurched, a limping young man in dishevelled clothes. The sight of his anguished face, bruised and bleeding as it was, made me catch my breath in sympathetic horror. Scarcely recognisable from his photograph was the missing French medium, Monsieur Ribaud. It was evident at once how hard he had fought and continued to fight against his captor, and it tore my heart to think he might continue struggling to his death without ever understanding that his resistance only increased Chase's power over him.

Mr Chase stepped forward onto the stage in full evening dress, the diamond pin that twinkled in his tie no more brilliant than his eyes. I could see how he enjoyed himself, drawing power from his prisoner and taking extra pleasure in inflicting pain as he did so.

Monsieur Ribaud shook with the effort, the useless, painful effort of attempting to resist the invisible pressure that forced his every footstep forward. Mr Chase made a sweeping, theatrical gesture and called out in a booming voice, "You see the gods? Even *they* respond to my will when I command them to *open*."

One by one, each of the towering wooden statues fell open to display their hollow, satin-lined interiors. All but mine, that is. I felt a quiver run through the wood of the door in front of me and the bolt rattled, but held it firmly shut.

No one questioned why one statue should ignore his command — I suspect his prisoners were all too confused by their situation to wonder at such a detail — but the vanity of Mr Chase would not risk the possibility that anyone might think his power was less than complete, so he said suavely, "Only Aphrodite I have given leave to keep her secret for now. But as you see, the gods await you. Miss Amelia, if you would be so obliging as to step inside the statue of Apollo? And Miss Bedelia, you will find a comfortable seat within his twin sister, Artemis."

The satin lining of each cabinet matched the colour of the dress of its intended occupant. I watched as the two young ladies obediently climbed inside. Nor did Miss Jessop make a fuss when she was directed to take

364

her place inside Athena. Signora Gallo was not given an opportunity to disobey; when Mr Chase indicated the crimson lining of the open figure of Hermes, the Cossack carried her across and deposited her within as his master said with malicious glee, "Hermes, god of luck and travellers, also the god of thieves, Signora."

Now, only the unhappy, black-suited figure of Monsieur Ribaud remained on stage, and only the black interior of Zeus remained empty.

"I have saved the most powerful for last. Zeus, king of the gods, shall provide a temporary resting place for you, *mon ami*. Won't you step inside?"

I watched anxiously, willing Monsieur Ribaud to accede for once. Surely he must realise there was no point in continuing to resist? What could he possibly hope to gain? Had he learned nothing? I would have been willing to bet that never once in all his struggles had the young Frenchman managed to best his captor. And every time he tried he would have been punished — as his poor, battered face showed. Yet still his stubborn pride insisted; he would never give in.

The young man stood still except for the quivering of his muscles.

Mr Chase gave the dramatic sigh of the put-upon, yet I thought he looked not angry, but pleased to have another chance to show off.

"You only hurt yourself, you know," he remarked, and Monsieur Ribaud's right hand flew up to slap himself across his own face: first one side, then the other.

"Will you do as I ask?"

The slapping had opened a cut; a small trickle of blood ran down the side of his mouth. But the stubborn set of his jaw never relaxed as Monsieur Ribaud shook his head.

"Do you think you will wear me out by making me exert myself unduly before the show — my most important engagement in London? If so, you are mistaken. I have great reserves of power. More than enough to deal with you." His voice lowered and his expression darkened, becoming more sinister. "I tell you one last time: *go in*."

He looked frightened, but the young man was no coward. I pitied his foolish pride, but could not help admiring his courage and determination, no matter how misguided. He declared, "I am not your slave."

Chase smiled. "Oh, but you are. You are my slave for as long as it pleases me. And if you make too much trouble and it no longer pleases me, then you will be my *dead* slave." He raised his arm, hand open like a claw, and made a short throwing gesture. "*Go!*"

A powerful, invisible force knocked the young Frenchman back on his heels, then lifted him off his feet and propelled him into the open statue. His head hit the satin-lined but solid wooden back wall of the cabinet with a crack that made me wince, and elicited gasps from the other ladies. His eyes rolled up in his head until only the whites were visible. His eyelids fluttered, then closed, and he slumped down and sideways in his seat.

I saw a brief but powerful flash of anger twist the usually bland features of Mr Chase, and knew he was annoyed with himself. He had used too much force; an unconscious medium was of no use to him, or so I surmised.

But Mr Chase regained his self-control in the next moment, and with a wave of his hand caused the front of the cabinet to close so that the mighty, bearded figure of Zeus frowned down upon the house. Then, one by one, the other god boxes all shut, hiding away the mediums who would provide the power for whatever wonders he had planned.

Yet perhaps it would not be as easy as Mr Chase supposed. Although of course I did not wish any permanent harm to Monsieur Ribaud, it might be that he would remain unconscious at least through the early part of the performance. And I guessed that Fiorella had her defences in place. It would not do to be overconfident, but my earlier encounters with Chase had taught me that I could resist him. Not forever, but it might be enough simply to put obstacles in his way, to slow him down and make him less certain of his own abilities. And if that served to make his powers appear less impressive, if the audience was not convinced that he was the greatest of living mediums, then he might delay his trip to America, and the longer he remained in London, the greater the chance of our escape and his arrest.

I saw Mr Chase turn in my direction, hastily let the cloth fall over the eye holes and sat back — I would give him no chance to catch my gaze. It had occurred to me that this must be why he had drilled the holes. He did not *need* to look into my eyes to gain control over me, but it would make it easier for him to hypnotise me.

Now standing outside my statue, he lowered his voice to speak to me alone. "I am sorry you were unable to see what just happened, Miss Lane. You have missed the instructive example of what befalls those who try to thwart me."

Why was he pretending I had no way of seeing beyond the walls that imprisoned me? Did he think I had not uncovered the secret? Or — was it possible he did not know? That *someone else* had made the spyholes?

The thought made me breathless with hope.

"Miss Lane?"

Was that the sharpness of worry in his voice? I held my breath and said nothing. After a moment I sensed something like that tendril I described before *feeling* for my presence. I could compare the experience to a game of hide and seek in a dark house, with Mr Chase the seeker. He believes I am near, and so walks in boldly with his arms outstretched, expecting to encounter me at once. But I keep still, and take my cue from the sound of his movements to slip to one side whenever he comes too near . . .

In a game, the seeker would know this, and take equal care to listen for my movements, to catch me out — but Mr Chase had no idea. He thought he had only to reach out and he'd find me. He was alarmed by my inexplicable absence.

The bolt slid back and the door of my prison swung wide, the sudden flood of light making me screw up my eyes.

"Miss Lane. Why did you not answer me?"

I blinked and essayed a yawn.

"Were you asleep?"

I peered at him with a slight frown, trying to look innocently puzzled. "Why . . . yes. I think so. You *told* me to sleep."

"Ah. So I did." I could not tell if he was reassured, or if he found something suspect in my manner. "Very well, but for the next few hours you must remain awake and alert, and also quiet." Fixing my gaze with his — too late to escape — he leaned in and placed his finger gently against my lips as he said softly, "Not a word."

As soon as he had withdrawn I opened my mouth to ask a question — I had in mind a query about whether I was to be called onto the stage during his show, to further establish my naïveté, but not a sound could I utter.

He shook his head with a mocking smile. "Remember what I said? Not another word from you — not until it's over."

CHAPTER
TWENTY-NINE

The Show Begins

I sat in the dark and silence, and waited.

Outside my box, away from the stage, the theatre was slowly coming to life. At first there were only occasional, random noises: distant voices, a shout, laughter, footsteps, the sounds of things being moved around.

The orchestra arrived; I listened to them settling into their places in the pit and tuning their instruments. Soon afterwards came the audience, at first a trickle, then a steady stream, and finally a torrent; the muffled, murmuring roar of life beyond the curtain.

There were occasional footsteps on the stage, and although I did not recognise the confident click of Chase's boot-heels among them, still I did not quite dare to lift the fabric that masked my peepholes and look out, for fear that he might be prowling, on the alert for anything different. The thought that I might peek out and catch his eyes looking back sent a chill down my spine. I had rather leave that chance for after the show had started, and the eyes of hundreds were fixed upon the stage; then, I thought, if I surprised him, his surprise might work against him.

Someone, a stranger, was speaking, telling someone else that the house was full and people wanting tickets were being turned away. He was so close I thought about trying to attract his attention and opened my mouth to yell. It was no good; my vocal cords were still locked by my captor's command. True, I could knock, but if I could not explain to the stagehand who'd let me out why I was in there, I'd get no help. Chase was bound to be near at hand, and he would come up with some story about the "nerves" of his "assistant" before locking me up again. My fists uncurled.

"He's the talk of the town," said another voice. "They say he's the real thing, no conjurer but a miracle worker, and he does it all with the aid of the spirits."

"Spirits, is it?" said the first man. "Is that what he calls them? Pagan gods, *they* are. And if they're not Christian, my old mam would call them demons."

"C of E don't have the monopoly on God. You know Chase is an American —"

"That don't mean he ain't a Christian."

"Maybe not, but I've heard that when he's done here tonight, he's going back to America to start his own religion."

My eyes widened in the darkness. The other man chuckled. "You don't say? Well, then, if he succeeds, tonight should go down in history."

They went away. The orchestra began to play "The Ghost Melody" from *The Corsican Brothers*, and when it ended, the curtain rose. I lifted the flap that had covered the eye holes and looked out to see Christopher Clement Chase standing in a single spotlight that left the rest of the stage shrouded in darkness.

"Ladies and gentlemen," he said. "Welcome. It is my privilege to appear before you tonight, as it will be your privilege to witness wonders — things that many would say are impossible. Yet they will truly happen just as they appear on this stage, before your very eyes. No matter how incredible, there is no trickery involved. I am no mere conjurer or stage magician. Indeed, I would never call myself a magician. The powers I intend to display tonight are not my own, but rather a gift from the spirit world — for reasons I do not claim to understand, the spirits have chosen *me* as their conduit to the material world. I —"

A great, rolling crash of thunder interrupted his speech — it was stage thunder, produced in the rafters, and from the shocked expression on the speaker's face it came as an unpleasant surprise.

Before he had recovered enough to say anything more, a second light glowed upon the stage behind him. A pale, ghostly figure appeared, hovering several feet behind Chase and to his left. The audience stirred, emitting little ripples of surprise and amusement. It was funny because Chase appeared oblivious — a moment so redolent of pantomime that I expected a chorus of "It's behind you!" to ring out.

But the next sound came, like the thunder, from above: a booming, magnified voice that roared "Foolish little man! Fake! Mountebank! The spirits reject you and your claims of power."

372

It was Mr Jesperson. Distorted though it was, I recognised his voice, and my heart soared with joy. In a flash I understood: he was here now, as he must have been earlier, making his careful preparations to disrupt Chase's plans; drilling holes in this statue for me, and setting up the apparatus to make a "ghost" appear on stage. I knew that there were several ways to produce this impression, but the most usual involved a large sheet of clear glass and careful positioning of lights and the calculation of sightlines.

Mr Chase must have come to the same rapid understanding of the situation. After the first moment of stunned shock had passed, as he turned and saw the spectral, semi-transparent figure behind him, he knew exactly where the sheet of glass must be, and he responded with one of his own tricks.

A metal cymbal flew up out of the orchestra pit, went whizzing through the air and struck the glass with sufficient force to shatter it, sending shards across the stage — some of them struck the row of statues, sounding like a short, sharp rain of hail.

"Mountebank?" Chase howled after the destruction of the glass had vanquished the ghost. "You are the only fraud, sir, with your cheap theatrical tricks."

"I admit, I use stage magic. I make no pretence. Whereas *you* claim to have spiritual powers, which is a lie. The only powers you use are stolen from others." The ghost was gone, but the voice still boomed out sternly, its source impossible to guess at. I watched Mr Chase, whose eyes darted about the stage until his gaze found some biddable backstage boy whom he directed with a jerk of his head to deal with the intruder.

To the audience, of course, this was all part of the show. They imagined the conflict to be a dramatic invention under the direction and control of Mr Chase.

"Show yourself!" Chase shouted. "Do you dare accuse me to my face?"

There was a dramatic pause and then a man flew down from above, to swoop across the stage. He was dressed entirely in black, even his hair beneath a knitted cap, the better to stay hidden in the shadows. As he flew past Mr Chase, the challenger slapped him smartly across the face with a black leather glove and shouted, "*J'accuse!* You are a thief, a fraud, and a craven pretender."

The audience gasped and moaned, happily thrilled by this development. From their perspective, the flying-wire was invisible.

Chase stared, mouth hanging open, after his attacker. He was out of my range of sight by then, so I did not understand the gasps, chuckles and whistles of appreciation from the audience until Mr Jesperson flew back into view, approaching Chase with a fencing foil in each hand.

"Will you fight, sir?"

Moving quickly, Chase managed to catch the weapon by the pommel, but then he frowned and made a show of throwing it down in disgust. "*You* insulted me," he shouted. "Therefore, choice of weapons is *mine*."

"As you wish." With a quick flick of his wrist, the flyer made his own foil vanish, and won a smattering of applause. "What is your choice?"

His lips curved in a sinister smile, Chase paused deliberately before saying, "Psychic powers."

Compelled as I was by the drama unfolding before my eyes on stage, I had been only vaguely aware of a series of scratching and creaking sounds from behind me, until I felt a cool draught and heard an urgent whisper: "Miss Lane, I'm here to rescue you. Stand and lean forward, please, so you don't fall when I lift the back panel."

I did as the male voice said, and in a few seconds found myself being gently pulled backwards out of my prison. The back of the hollow statue had been cut away, but the front was still facing the stage and the audience beyond. To them and to Chase it would not appear that anything had changed; I was still hidden by Aphrodite.

The statue that hid me also blocked my view of the stage, so I had no idea why the audience was applauding. Finally able to see my rescuer, I was startled to recognise Mr Sims, the agent from whom the Jespersons rented the house in Gower Street, and the brother of Mrs Creevey.

He put a finger to his lips and gestured to me to follow him off the stage.

I came to a halt in the wings, unwilling to go further, concerned about my fellow prisoners. I struggled to find my voice, to tell him —

Mr Sims patted my arm and whispered, "It's all right. The others are safely away. You are the last. Don't worry, Miss Lane, it is over."

I felt a burden lifted from me at his words and knew I would now be able to speak. But it was *not* over.

As the applause died away, Mr Chase said, "You have managed to please my audience with your conjuring tricks, but I did not challenge you to a display of trickery, Jesperson. You proposed a duel and I say we must use *psychic* powers as our weapons — those powers you have insulted me by saying I only pretend to possess. But I know that *you* are the only pretender here and I will prove it to you in combat. Come down, sir, and face your master."

Laughter rang out, and although Mr Sims was tugging at my arm, urging me to come away, I could not resist turning back to see what was going on. My friend was standing in mid-air, balancing easily on nothingness, arms folded, grinning down at Chase like an impudent elf. "But why should I come down? I have heard that your famous powers include levitation. Why don't you come up here, Chase? A duel in mid-air would be a proper show for all these good people who have paid for the privilege of seeing you perform."

Mr Chase grimaced; sweat stood out on his forehead; he was clearly uncomfortable. "*Your* flight is by artificial trickery. You have no psychic powers."

"Nor have you, Chase. You're a fraud, whereas I —"

"Whereas *you* are above yourself, Jesperson!"

His voice had changed; it had become venomous and gloating; he was once more sure of himself, and with that change came one in me — I felt that sense of oppression I had come to know during my days in captivity and knew I had made a terrible mistake.

376

"I will bring you down to earth," said Mr Chase, just before I heard the whip-crack of wire snapping. There was a loud gasp from the audience as the man in black fell out of the air and hit the stage floor.

Chase laughed. And as he gloated over his fallen foe, his mental grip on me was loosened just enough that — although I felt too weak to move on my own — when Mr Sims pulled me, almost lifting me off my feet in his determination to get me away, I was able to go with him.

"I don't call that fair," Mr Jesperson remarked, sounding as cool and unruffled as if he'd just stepped off a train, rather than fallen from the air. "By *code duello*, one man chooses the weapons, and the other names the *place*."

What a relief to me it was to hear his familiar voice behind me, to know I had not greatly harmed my friend with my stupid insistence on staying to watch the show.

Applause from the audience covered our retreat, and as we fled through the backstage regions, Mr Sims assured me all was well. "He landed on his feet. He's a proper acrobat, that young gentleman. And he has a great many tricks up his sleeve, as I'm sure you must know, Miss."

All the while in our progress to the stage door, I expected to feel again the debilitating grip of that evil man's will upon my own, and to be pulled back — would Mr Sims have strength enough to prevent my return — to be used as his weapon against my dearest friend.

Bursting, almost tumbling out of the door into the narrow street behind the theatre, I was grabbed by Gabrielle Fox, who clutched me to her bosom as she cried, "Oh, my dear, at last. We've been so worried!"

In the light from the stage door lamp I looked into her one visible eye and asked urgently, "Is it safe? Are we far enough away?"

She nodded vigorously. "As long as you are outside the building — I *think*. Fiorella says that while he doesn't need to be able to see you, he needs to know *where* you are — and it must be very close by. In the same room, almost certainly. But never mind now." She pulled me away from the door, linking arms.

"We'll join the others."

"Where are they?"

Leaving Mr Sims behind, she took me along the deserted back street and towards the corner that opened on to Leicester Square. "At the police station, with Edith. They're swearing out complaints and they're waiting for you."

We had come to the front of the Alhambra, where quite a few people were still hanging about. These were mostly the sorts you will always see in public places in London, at any time of day or night — an old woman selling flowers, a young girl peddling sweets and cigars, a few ragged urchins, a variety of men idling about or conversing with each other — but there were also a few respectable-looking, well-dressed couples loitering uncertainly, as if, having failed to gain admission to the theatre, they could not make up their minds how else to spend their evening.

378

I stopped and looked up at the front doors. "But *he's* still inside," I murmured, unable to shake off my anxiety. It was very hard to feel that my place was beside him, but to know that it was my presence that presented the greatest danger to Mr Jesperson at this moment.

Gabrielle squeezed my arm. "He'll deal with that creature, don't you worry. He's perfectly safe now that all the *real* mediums are away. The star of the show has lost his secret weapons, but Mr Jesperson still has plenty of tricks up his sleeve — and under the stage." She giggled. "He's got the trapdoor rigged. If it all goes to plan, Zeus will pronounce judgement and send Mr Chase down to Hades. Then the police will take the visiting American conjurer into custody charged with the abduction and false imprisonment of six people."

She gave me a little tug. "Come along, do. It's not far. After you give your statement we'll come back here with the officers and see the fun." She paused after offering me that inducement and wrinkled her nose. "Or perhaps we better not. Your Mr J says under no circumstances are we to let Mr Chase set eyes on you or any of the others. He's not to be given the chance, or he might play some final trick on the police and get clean away."

Still I resisted, frowning as I gazed up at the impressive front of the Alhambra. "What if there are mediums in the audience? There surely will be — some because they hope to pick up a new trick to use themselves, but there will be some with genuine powers, whether they know it or not, and *he* — "

"Oh, that's all right. If they're people he doesn't *know* he won't be able to sense their power at such a distance, no more than you or I would recognise the voice or the face of a passing stranger in a crowd. He sensed *your* power and Fiorella's when he met you both at Lord B's."

"Sensed a power I never knew I had," I murmured and shook my head. "I *still* don't know what it might be — and how can someone else use it when I cannot myself?"

"Psychic energy," she said promptly. "Now you know you've got it, you can work out how to use it. I'm so jealous, Di. I'd always thought that of the two of us, I'd be more likely to develop a sixth sense."

"So Mr Jesperson worked it all out." I was impressed. Even though it had been happening to me, I had needed someone else to explain it.

"He said it was most unlikely . . . and he resisted the idea . . . but finally it was the only theory that made sense. He told me all sorts of things about the Chinese system. It's nothing to do with spirits, apparently, or not the way our mediums explain it; instead, it's something called *chi* — a sort of invisible life force that's everywhere . . . oh, I don't understand it, but when he told me it made sense. You'll have to ask him. He's very clever, Mr J. But come, we can talk about this as we walk." She gave me a little pull, and this time I did not resist.

Mr Jesperson had worked it all out. He was in charge now, he was very clever, he understood more than I, and I must obey his instructions. The anxious feeling

380

that still plagued me, that urged me to turn back as we walked away from Leicester Square, was equivalent to doubt, and he did not deserve to be doubted.

But what if, for all his cleverness, he had overlooked something that could put him in danger?

The feeling nagged at me. What was I forgetting?

"Di, are you listening to me?"

"Of course."

"You were miles away, admit it."

"Not miles," I objected. "Only back inside the Alhambra. I wish I could see what Mr Jesperson is doing."

"I am sure he would wish that," she said warmly. "Under different circumstances. You *ought* to be there, you deserve to witness his triumph. But it is too dangerous. Mr J was very clear that you and all the others who were kidnapped must stay away from the theatre. He is safe only so long as Mr Chase has no one else to give him strength."

As she spoke, I had a sudden, vivid mental image of the pretty, doll-like face of Mrs Chase, gazing with adoring eyes at her husband as she lent him her strength and witnessed his triumph on the stage below — the triumph *she* would ensure.

"We must go back."

Gabrielle blinked at me, bewildered by being halted so abruptly. "Weren't you listening? I said —"

"That Mr Jesperson is safe only so long as there is no one else for Mr Chase to feed upon," I said. "What about *Mrs* Chase?"

"Oh, we need not worry about *her*. I hear she does not go out at all."

But I knew that she would not want to miss her husband's triumphant appearance tonight. Whatever my friends had been led to believe, and however weakened her system, I was certain that Nadezhda Chase was in the audience. Even at this moment she might be lending her powers to enable her husband to defeat his opponent.

I turned around and walked as fast as I could towards the Alhambra.

Gabrielle caught up with me. "Wait! You can't go back!"

"I must. We both must — to get *her* out."

"But even if she is here, her husband would not dare . . . Mr J said that is why she is so ill, because of how he has used her . . . that if he continued, it would mean her death. So he abducted —"

"Yes, and now that he has lost *us*, he will go back to using her; depend upon it!"

"Even knowing it might kill her?"

We had reached the grand entrance. "He won't stop to think," I said, pushing open the door. "By the time he does, it will be too late. We have two people's lives to save, Gaby. I know it is a risk, but as long as Mr Chase does not catch sight of me he need never know I am near, and I shall be careful — there is no time to waste. Hurry!"

CHAPTER
THIRTY

The Fall of the Gods

The foyer looked quite deserted as we entered, and I guessed that the staff — all the attendants, ushers and ticket takers — had taken the first opportunity to slip inside in order to see the celebrated psychic medium perform.

But just as I had allowed myself a feeling of relief that no one would try to turn us away, a young lad in an usher's uniform appeared, looking anxious but determined as he informed us that the house was sold out and the performance already in progress.

In view of his youth, I turned upon him my most severely governess-like face and declared, "There is an emergency at Lord Bennington's home. We must speak to him at once."

The boy took me at my word, offering to deliver a message to his Lordship.

"No, it is better if I — if we — speak to him personally," I said. I gestured at the large and empty foyer. "Besides . . . you appear to be on your own here. If you go, who will watch the door?"

He agreed that he could not desert his post — but it would take him only a moment to fetch another —

"You are wasting our time," I scolded him. "Lord Bennington would not be pleased with you for delaying us. Just tell me where to find him."

Gabrielle put her beautifully gloved hand on mine. "I know the box," she said. "I was one of a theatre party there not long ago." She turned her smile on the boy, who gaped, looking quite stupefied, as we hurried away.

Mounting the stairs, I said urgently, "If Mrs Chase is there, we *must* get her out. What shall we say to convince Lord Bennington? She will no doubt protest."

"I will manage him," she said, and I could only hope her confidence was not misplaced.

The theatre may have been sold out, but Lord Bennington's private box had spare capacity, occupied as it was by only the lord himself, his eldest daughter and three other ladies, one of whom was, as I had feared, the Russian princess.

No one looked around at our entry; all eyes were compelled by the drama unfolding on the stage below. The orchestra, struggling with the complete collapse of the planned programme, had gone for another reprise of "The Ghost Melody".

Within the semi-circle of huge, garishly-painted ancient gods the two antagonists were spot-lit: Mr Jesperson was on his knees, head bowed before Mr Chase who stood unsupported in the air a few feet above him, his arms folded across his chest, smiling with a loathsome smugness.

"Now you acknowledge me as your master. But that's not much fun for our audience, is it? We must give them a proper show. Get up, sir. We must fight!

You are the one who called this duel. Or will you forfeit and be labelled a coward?"

Mr Jesperson remained where he was for a few more moments in absolute stillness, then rose in one graceful movement to his feet and lifted his head to look up at his challenger. How much that movement cost him, whether it was the end of a battle with an invisible force, or whether Chase had forced or allowed him to stand, I had no idea.

Chase levitated higher until his feet were at the level of Mr Jesperson's head.

"Rise, I said — *rise* — won't you face me?"

His voice steady, Mr Jesperson replied, "I can go no higher. You appear to have the better of me."

"Yes!" A gleeful smile. "Yes, I should say I do." Chase pulled back his foot, and with casual, deliberate brutality, kicked his victim in the head.

There were gasps of shock from the audience, a few girlish shrieks and mutters of disapproval. I heard a man in the next box say, "That's not cricket!" Another: "There are ladies present."

Although he staggered, Mr Jesperson did not fall. He had made no attempt to avoid the kick, and now did not move away or try to retaliate. I was well acquainted with the rapidity of his reflexes, so I knew — even if the rest of the audience did not — that he was being kept prisoner: Chase was using his stolen power to hold him there.

I looked anxiously at Gabrielle, whispering into Lord Bennington's ear and then at Nadezhda Chase, a small figure dressed in cream-coloured silk, seated at the very front of the box, alone, leaning forward, all her attention fixed on the stage. To anyone else it must have seemed she was gazing adoringly at her husband, but I guessed at the power contained in that gaze, and it made me want to scream at Gabrielle to hurry. But the last thing I wanted was to alert Mr Chase to my presence, and so I hung back, remaining still and silent.

But Chase had misjudged the mood of the audience, whose affection he risked alienating. The music had changed to something more darkly sinister, and only a fool could have imagined that Mr Jesperson was the villain in this scene.

"Beg pardon, old man." Chase exclaimed with false bonhomie, as he began a gradual descent. "I expected you to block that kick, or at least step aside. You are a little off your game tonight, aren't you? But I'm sure your head is hard enough to take a few knocks." By the time he got to the end of this wheedling, conciliatory speech, Chase was again standing on solid ground, directly confronting his enemy — and exaggerating the effort required of him to look up at the taller man.

"Now, sir, your head is higher than mine, but I don't complain. We are as equally matched as *nature* allows, and our only weapons will be those we have by birth or training, and whatever powers God or spirits or unknown forces grant us . . . agreed?"

"Stop your buzzing," Lord Bennington exclaimed irritably, pulling away from Gabrielle. "We are trying to watch the show. Either sit down and be quiet, or get out."

She fluttered about him anxiously, insisting on the importance of her errand, but annoyed him more with every word. "I fear I must ask you to leave, Miss Fox."

My greatest fear was that Mr Chase would become aware of my presence and once again use me as a weapon against my partner. If *Mrs* Chase saw me, and if I was right in thinking that she would be able to transmit her own perceptions to her husband instantly, it would be just as bad . . . But it was a risk I had to take, or I might as well have stayed away. So I stepped out of the shadows and interrupted the angry tête-à-tête. Lord Bennington nearly jumped from his seat at the sight of me. "Miss Lane. I thought — but where have you been? What —"

"There is no time to explain. You must trust me," I said hastily. "It is truly a matter of life and death. Mrs Chase must leave this building at once."

A puff of white smoke appeared centre stage and rapidly thickened and formed into a face as white and still as a death mask. The audience gasped and murmured with pleasure — *this* was more the sort of thing they had bought their tickets to see.

Below the face was more smoke, and it formed into two quite solid-looking hands. They flew like predatory birds towards Mr Jesperson's throat.

Lord Bennington looked distrustfully from me to Miss Fox and back again. "Can you can explain this extraordinary demand?"

As my partner glided and turned on the stage, evading the threatening hands with a grace and economy reminiscent of the stylised movements of a

Spanish toreador, I managed to summon something of his powers of invention. "I have been sent to you by Mr Chase, who fears for the life of his wife. He has learned that there are certain vapours in the air of this theatre — quite harmless to us, but to one suffering a congenital condition of the heart, like Mrs Chase, they could provoke a crisis — and kill her. He warned her, but the brave, foolish, stubborn girl was determined to witness his triumph on the stage. He has begged me, and he begs you, to save her life by taking her outside."

Had it been anyone else spouting such nonsense he might have argued and refused to believe, but my reputation for unadorned, unimaginative honesty worked in my favour. Casting an uneasy glance at the stage he muttered, "That smoke . . . it will not harm my daughter?"

"Certainly not. Everyone else is safe. It is a weakness peculiar to her."

"Very well. Since her husband wishes it . . . you must have a word with her."

My heart sank just a little. Lord Bennington was large and strong enough to be easily capable of picking up the little Russian princess and carrying her away at speed, even if she put up a struggle, but it was clear from his posture and his manner of speaking that he would do no such thing. Perhaps he had his doubts about my story. With an inclination of his head, he indicated that he would not interfere.

"Why don't you *engage*, sir? Are you a coward?" Mr Chase's petulant demand rang through the theatre.

A balletic leap from Mr Jesperson won him a little burst of applause. He laughed. "If you call it cowardice to avoid strangulation."

"I do, sir. You must engage. Here are my hands. Now put up yours."

The spirit hands had ceased their pursuit and now curled into fists, pugilist style. At Chase's demand, Mr Jesperson displayed his own fists.

Gabrielle and I looked at each other and agreed without words that there was no time to be wasted. Our only hope was to drag Mrs Chase away by brute force.

The small, slender figure trembled but made no resistance as I seized her by one arm and my friend grabbed the other. Her attention remained fixed upon the stage as we pulled her out of her chair. Although she did not struggle, neither did she help, and it was not an easy task to get her to her feet.

Her breathing was laboured, and I was aware of a film of perspiration over her pale face with its fixed, staring eyes. Briefly, I followed her gaze. That one glimpse was enough to show me how far Mr Jesperson's strength had been sapped while the smirking Chase stood observing the fight waged by the spirit-fists.

The impossibility of ever winning against an invisible, bodiless opponent was obvious. With no head or body to be hit, there was no target for Mr Jesperson's blows except the smoky white hands. Fighting them was like punching clouds: it did no damage. Yet, although they seemed to be without substance, they possessed enough force to wound. Eventually they must wear him down. And although it seemed most unlikely to me that Chase would dare kill anyone — even by spirit-hands — in such a public manner before so many witnesses, I was equally sure that he was determined to inflict a painful, lasting punishment on my friend.

With a rough jerk I pulled the princess closer to my side and clutched her hard. I led the way, and with Gabrielle helping to lift her we managed to haul her unresisting yet unwieldy weight into the aisle and up the two steps inside the box, towards its exit.

Disturbed by this unexpected activity, the other ladies in the box buzzed and clucked, but I had no attention to spare for them, or whatever explanation Lord Bennington was giving, for I had more urgent matters on my mind.

Suddenly I felt a change: a crawling sensation that warned me of Chase's psychic presence. Had he sensed mine? We had almost reached the door — in just a moment we might pass through the curtained alcove and reach the corridor beyond the box, where no one would see us. An inner sense of urgency directed me to continue, not to pause and certainly not to look back — but, as foolish as Lot's wife — that is what I did.

I did not think he could have seen me; I knew how unlikely it was that anyone on the stage below would even notice, let alone be able to recognise the three figures in the shadows at the back of the box, but he might well have missed his wife, for I had noticed him occasionally casting a glance up at her, where she leaned over the rail and gazed back. If he saw she was gone, he would be on the alert.

390

One swift look at the stage told me what I needed to know. Chase looked up, not at Lord Bennington's box, but rather at Aphrodite's column. He had sensed my presence — perhaps my proximity to his wife had made that inevitable — but he did not know where I was. For a time, my energy had been beyond his reach, but he sensed it now, and he had assumed I was where he had put me: inside the hollow statue of Aphrodite.

He moved away from the boxing match at centre stage, stepping further back and sidling closer to the statue.

Any moment now I knew he would relinquish the connection with his wife and seize control of me. He had the wrong idea of where I was, but I was not beyond his reach. The thought spurred me on; as I moved towards the exit, I heard Mrs Chase give a great wheezing moan.

Abruptly, I found myself in darkness.

I froze and put out my free hand to feel for the heavy velvet draperies I knew hung across the doorway. My knuckles grazed bare boards. I tried to step back, but there was nowhere to go; my back pressed against satin that had first appeared to me like the lining of a coffin.

I was back inside the Aphrodite, trapped once more in the piece of stage scenery Chase had had built to hold me. Through its thin walls I could hear the muted roar of the audience, whose bloodlust had been roused.

Nearer to me, I could hear the light, bounding footsteps of Mr Jesperson as he dodged and parried and desperately tried to avoid punches thrown by the spirit hands. There was a meaty smack of fist against flesh and the audience roared. I ran my fingertips over the front of the narrow enclosure, trying to find a different texture, seeking the piece of cloth that covered the two eye holes.

It was not there. The holes were not there.

This was not *my* Aphrodite, altered as it had been by my friend to give me a view of the stage. I knew then that this was a psychic trap; my physical body was still above the stage in Lord Bennington's box, and only my *mind* was held captive inside an imaginary wooden statue.

I felt him coming for me. As before, we were near each other in a small space, blind yet aware of each other. He sought me and I evaded him, moving to one side then wriggling to the other. I thought of Mr Jesperson dancing lightly on the stage. I remembered how I had seen Mr Chase edging closer to the statue, and I knew almost exactly where his physical self would be at that moment.

All this in less time than it takes to write.

I felt him coming for me and I kept still, as if unaware of my danger, until at the last possible moment I moved, flinging myself hard against the front of the cabinet, just to the side of where I expected his attack. I heard a crack and felt myself falling.

I opened my eyes to find myself above the stage, looking down, watching as the tall, wood and plaster hollow statue of Aphrodite rocked forward, unbalanced, and came crashing down on top of Christopher Clement Chase.

As he vanished from view, the pale white hands froze for a moment, then turned to misty swirls, glittering in the footlights.

CHAPTER
THIRTY-ONE

Afterwards

My senses rushed back. There was confusion and noise everywhere, but close at hand there were quieter voices, the sharp odour of sal volatile and the uncomfortable sensation of having my wrists chafed by Gabrielle, who repeated, "Are you unwell?"

I pulled away from her. "I hate smelling salts."

She looked at me sadly. "Well, they brought you 'round, at least. Poor Mrs Chase — God rest her soul — is beyond our help."

"Oh."

I saw the small, crumpled form of Nadezhda Chase in her cream and ivory gown through the figures of Lord Bennington and one of his lady guests who crouched over her on the floor, searching in vain for signs of life.

Gabrielle helped me to my feet and I pulled away from her, eager to see the stage. Mr Jesperson stood beneath a spotlight, wiping blood from his lips with his sleeve. Not far away, a couple of stagehands were extricating Mr Chase from the wreckage of the fallen Aphrodite. He was covered in plaster dust and looked shaken but unharmed.

Four uniformed policemen thundered onto the stage like inexperienced extras who had missed their cue, and their commanding officer, more attuned to the drama of the situation, strolled on after them. In a loud and carrying voice, he announced that he was arresting Mr Christopher Clement Chase on six charges of abduction, six charges of false imprisonment, and other charges including coercion, fraud and receiving stolen property.

The orchestra and the audience had fallen silent as they witnessed this curious departure from the show they had expected.

Mr Chase did not protest nor try to make his escape; he only asked if he might say goodbye to his wife before he was taken into custody. He spoke politely, and criminal though he was, received the response due a gentleman:

"And where is your wife, sir?"

I shrank back, out of sight, as he turned to indicate our box. "She is a guest of Lord Bennington."

Hearing his name, Lord Bennington came forward and looked down with a long, mournful face. "I'm afraid she is no longer with us. She ... I am most dreadfully sorry, old chap."

Chase did not flinch; I think he had already known it was too late. More than that, I believe he had felt it the very moment she ceased to exist, and that it was the painful, sharp, sudden awareness that he had lost her that had fuelled his last, desperate attempt to capture me.

Looking up at Lord Bennington, his sponsor and host in London, Chase said, "You will arrange for . . . whatever needs to be done, if I cannot?"

"Of course, of course. Don't give it a second thought. But I'm sure this . . . misunderstanding will soon be cleared up and you'll be back in Belgrave Square shortly," said that trusting, innocent man. "My solicitor is at your disposal. Do ask for anything you might need."

"Thank you." Nodding vaguely, Chase turned aside and held out his hands to be cuffed. "You may take me now."

I watched the police lead him away and wondered rather resentfully what had taken them so long. Had they been quicker off the mark, Mr Jesperson would have been spared a beating and perhaps Mrs Chase need not have died.

Back in Gower Street, much later that night, Mr Jesperson told me not to be so hard on the police. Once the prisoners had been released and their statements were taken, the police had more than enough evidence to make an arrest and had gone to the Alhambra to take Mr Chase into custody. They were inclined to break up the show the moment they arrived, but Mr Jesperson had left instructions at the stage door, asking them to wait until the end. He'd had a somewhat different conclusion in mind, which would have seen Mr Chase dropped through the trap door to the accompaniment of demonic laughter and the distant screams of the damned, while special lighting effects would have made it appear that he was falling into the fiery pits of Hell.

"I thought, as I had deprived Chase of the power to give it to them, I owed his audience a memorable conclusion," he said, ruefully admitting he had been overconfident in his belief that he had rendered his opponent helpless.

He had certainly been punished for making that mistake; the swellings and cuts on his poor, battered face bore testimony. He leaned back in his chair, cradling a medicinal brandy, the bottle of which had been a gift from the police surgeon who had patched him up while I was giving my statement. "No one else is to blame for the death of Mrs Chase, and certainly not the police. She had a weak heart. She knew it and her husband knew that he was putting an intolerable strain on her constitution — yet he continued, and she allowed him to. One is forever being told not to speak ill of the dead, but she was his willing accomplice."

"When did you first suspect her?"

He gulped down his brandy and reached for the bottle to pour another measure into his glass. "I was quite certain that it must have been *she* who was inside the spirit cabinet. The cabinet had been constructed with a false back; only quite a small and flexible person would be able to squeeze inside the hidden compartment — not the Cossack, whom I should otherwise have been inclined to suspect as his invisible assistant, but only Mrs Chase.

"Of course, at that point my theory was that Chase accomplished his wonders by means of hypnotism and

397

an accomplice. I dismissed the idea that spiritualistic powers had anything to do with the matter — I had decided he was a complete fraud.

"But how to account for the kidnappings? It was clear from the start that the only thing that linked the sudden disappearances of the Misses De Beauvoir, Monsieur Ribaud and Miss Jessop was that they all possessed some genuine psychic talent. If Chase had been bent on eliminating the competition he would not have chosen those particular females; Miss Jessop had retired from public view since being exposed as a cheat, and the young ladies were as yet unknown to a wider public — unlike at least half a dozen others who attract audiences he might have envied. No, if he was kidnapping mediums — and after the drama he staged for our benefit there could be no doubt who was behind the abductions — it could only be because he needed them for what they were."

"And did you reach this conclusion *before* I was kidnapped? Why did you not share it with me?" Perhaps it was ungrateful of me, but I felt rather hurt, thinking his silence on the matter indicated a lack of trust. "Aren't we *partners* in this business?"

He sighed and took another careful sip from his glass. "Please . . . it was hardly a conclusion at that point, more a hare-brained idea. If I shared every thought that passes through my head while I'm trying to work something out, you would think me a complete idiot."

"I doubt that. I am very impressed that you managed to figure out how Chase operated. Even after I was his prisoner I still had no idea — not until Signora Gallo told me — and our good thief had the story from his diamond tie pin."

Mr Jesperson laughed, then flinched and touched his lip. "It's nothing," he said quickly, when he saw me looking. "I am lucky to have suffered no broken bones, nothing but bruising and a few minor cuts. It looks worse than it is."

"Are you sure of that?"

He gave me a look. "The police surgeon said I'll be as good as new after a good night's sleep. Anyway, as I said before, it was my own fault for not making certain of Mrs Chase. I had already concluded that his only possible conspirator and aid in fraud was his wife . . . and if it was not fraud but genuine psychic power, then *she* must be a genuine medium and he the poser who took credit for her abilities, keeping her close at hand but out of sight of the audience." He sighed and looked sheepish. "I was a fool. When everyone said how ill she was — too ill to go out in public, even to travel to Gower Street at your invitation — I thought this meant she would not make it to the performance. I even checked with Lady Florence, who told me that Mrs Chase would *not* be attending and that she herself had agreed to forgo the theatre to keep the poor invalid company. It should have occurred to me that a loving wife would surely never miss her husband's debut upon the London stage . . . and that I should not have been so quick to trust in Lady Florence."

"Lady Florence wasn't there," I said, recalling that she was one of the people I had expected to see in Lord Bennington's party.

"She had a sick headache that came on very suddenly. And Mrs Chase was feeling so much better . . . of course, she *could* have stayed with Lady Florence, but that sort of headache doesn't like company and only responds to darkness and silence. How dull for Mrs Chase. How she would adore seeing her husband's greatest public performance. This all resulted in a change of plan at the last minute, and Mrs Chase decided to attend after all . . . what a blithering idiot I can be."

"Of course you are not — how can you say that?"

"I should have been less trusting. If I had played my cards closer to my chest, it would have been better. I cannot say I was not warned. You told me how Lady Florence likes to gossip. I would have done better to ask nothing of her at all, because of course Mrs Chase learned through Lady Florence that I had enquired about her health and her plans for the evening. And why, when I had never met her? It was very suspicious, and her natural impulse was to protect her husband — be on hand in the event that she was needed. I don't know, of course, but perhaps, as a small act of revenge, she even gave Lady Florence a sick headache."

He picked up the brandy bottle. "Are you sure you won't have a glass? It helps wonderfully with the pain."

"No, thank you. No one has been punching *me* . . . I am not feeling any pain, and I find I enjoy the experience of a clear head."

The sheepish look was back. "You must think me awfully selfish, leaving you and the others captive so long . . . but really, it *wasn't* because I wanted the glory

400

of unmasking Chase so dramatically and defeating him before a cheering audience."

I bit my lip. "*That* had never occurred to me."

"You see, I knew that if I could get you all safely away from his influence, and you were able to give statements to the police, it would then be impossible for Chase to deflect the blame onto anyone else."

"Yes, yes, I understand. But . . ." It was hard to ask, but I must face it. "You managed to deduce the reason why Mr Chase wanted mediums. How did *my* abduction fit into your theory?"

He swirled the brandy in his glass and watched it glinting darkly. "That gave me pause, I admit, but only at first. You remember, I am sure, that Chase took you for a medium at first meeting?"

I nodded.

"So, one possibility: that Chase had kidnapped you under this delusion. Second possibility: you are, in fact, a medium."

My heart gave a curious little flutter. "You really considered that?"

His eyes met mine across the desktop. He raised his glass to me. "Sure you won't have one?"

When I shook my head he drank off the rest, put the glass down and sat up straight. "I not only considered it, but came to the conclusion that it was correct."

I am not sure how to define the feeling that mounted in my breast. It was a mixture, I think, of fear and excitement. "Why? What did you have to go on apart from Mr Chase's delusion? I have never, ever —"

"Never?" He gave me an intent, searching look. "What about the materialisation in your bedroom?"

"A hypnotic suggestion implanted by Chase."

He raised an eyebrow. "You would suggest that Chase somehow managed to implant the suggestion in *me?*"

"But you did not see it!"

"I saw the residue of the spirit matter ... the ectoplasm," he reminded me.

The thought that the ghastly head had been something produced by *me* — not my imagination, but physically exuded from my own body — brought on a shudder I could not repress. "Oh, but that ... that might have been anything!"

"Anything that can take different forms, hang in the air, and then disappear into nothing," he said calmly. "Can you name me two things, other than ectoplasm, which that rapidly vanishing matter on the carpet might have been?"

Of course I could not.

He went on. "And there was another instance: you will recall how Creevey flung Mr Chase towards the river — in response to his pre-arranged command, of course — and then we saw him hang suspended by nothing in mid-air? How he did not fall, but seemed held up by invisible spirit hands? It was the same trick he performed in the drawing room in Belgrave Square — only more dramatic.

"But in Belgrave Square he had his wife's power to support him, or he may have stolen the energy from Signora Gallo. On the embankment that night, unless he had powers of his own, or unless the whole thing was a hypnotically induced hallucination, he must have stolen the psychic power he required from one of the three of us. And I am sure you have not forgotten how utterly exhausted you were afterwards. You fainted. You could barely walk. You fell asleep in Creevey's arms as he carried you home. That was not your normal reaction — you remarked upon it yourself at the time; you could not understand why you should have fainted. But if you see it as a natural response of a body suddenly depleted of spiritual energy — *chi* as the Chinese refer to it — then it all makes sense.

"Oh, Miss Lane," his voice was warm and coaxing. I met his eyes again and saw in them the lively interest and intelligent curiosity to which I had always been drawn. "This is remarkable! You have a rare talent, one that is little understood and given to only a few — surely you wish to learn more about it?"

Hadn't I spent years of my life investigating the very question that now yawned like a terrifying chasm before my feet? He was right, of course. The fact that I was frightened and, even now, somewhat disbelieving, was no reason to flinch from exploration.

He continued: "You accused me earlier of not playing fair, and not treating you as a full partner, because I did not share every half-formed idea I had about who was controlling the somnambulist. Now it is my turn to ask why *you* are holding back. Are you ashamed? Is it because you simply gave up while you were his prisoner and became his passive slave? Is that what you fear to tell me?"

Stung, I leaned forward, fists clenching in my lap. "Of course not! How can you think —" Then I saw that he had *meant* to provoke and I relaxed, shaking my head reprovingly. "I'm not afraid to tell you anything — it's only that it's all so vague and difficult to explain."

I took a deep breath and began. "I could not understand how, if I had powers that Mr Chase could steal, I could not use them myself. Signora Gallo was not helpful; she said it would be like teaching a deaf person to hear. It was as if I had been deaf since infancy, and now must try to puzzle out what it meant to hear before I could do it.

"Since she was no help, there was only Mr Chase to be my teacher. I began to suspect that he was happier to keep me in ignorance, in the same way that he kept me locked in a room without shoes or hair pins — I was his prisoner and yet he did not think I was helpless. That encouraged me to try to resist."

I paused and recalled the sensations, so impossible to describe. "I soon found that the harder I struggled, the more powerful he became. And I remembered that little toy of yours" — I gestured vaguely at the bookshelves, unable to see in the shadows cast by firelight where it was — "the one you called Chinese handcuffs —"

He understood at once; I saw by the subtle shift of his expression and I nodded.

"Since I must not resist, I could only try to evade him. Oh, I can't explain how; it was all inside my head."

"Not only in yours — in his, too," said Mr Jesperson. "There must have been some sort of thought transference . . . perhaps *that* is your power?"

"Did you receive any of the many, many thought messages I sent you?" I asked dryly.

"Perhaps they were misdirected."

"Or lacked sufficient postage — and for postage, read psychic strength. No, it's no good — I do not have the power to read thoughts or send mental messages, useful as that would be. I was able to utilise some sort of sixth sense in my encounters with Mr Chase, but those were very special circumstances. Apart from that, I could do nothing with my supposed power."

He gave me a hard, challenging stare. "You call the fall of Aphrodite *nothing*?"

Since it had happened, it had come to seem more and more like a dream — a desperate fantasy, born of fear. I evaded his question.

"Not *nothing*. It was very fortunate," I said. "But . . . it was an accident, surely, caused by the activity on stage shaking the boards — even, perhaps, the arrival of the police in such a mob backstage."

"Hmmm. True, those gods were all heavier at the front than at the back; even more so after I had that carpentry work done to provide a secret exit. But I am more inclined to believe in unfortunate accidents than in *fortunate* ones. My first thought was that Sims had come back — or even my mother — and pushed it over to help me. But, of course, no one came back except you and Miss Fox. And neither of you were near enough to touch it. So it can only have been you using the power of your mind." He looked at me curiously. "Am I wrong?"

I sighed, suddenly aware of how tired I was and what a very long, strenuous night it had been. "Perhaps it *was* me. I wanted something like that to happen. I was trying to save myself and save you by using Mr Chase's own energy against him, the way you and your mother have been trying to teach me."

I stopped. "It seemed real enough at the time, but now . . . now I think there must be another, better explanation. When did merely *wishing* for something make it happen? How could I — or even Mr Chase and I together — have made that enormous thing fall, with just the power of the mind?"

He stood up, eyes alight. "That's a very good question. Shall we try to answer it?"

Uncertainly, I watched him scan the bookshelves on the wall behind the desk, searching for something amongst the variety of small trinkets, toys and souvenirs displayed before the ranks of books. "How?"

"Oh, any reproducible model will do. Rather than risk breaking the furniture, we'd best start with something small. Let's start with this." He picked up something about the size and shape of a cricket ball, made of some very light wood and painted to resemble a globe of the Earth. He handed this to me, then moved the brandy glass and bottle before clearing the piles of paper and books away.

"What am I to do with it?"

"Feel its weight and size, then put it down on the desk. You are going to try to make it move without physically touching it, only imagining that you are pushing it."

406

Rather self-consciously, I rolled it in the palm of my hand. It was even lighter than I had expected, and the painted continents were badly misshapen. It would never pass muster in any geography lesson. I set it down carefully on the flat wooden surface.

"Give it a push with your hand, first, to see how it rolls."

I gave it a gentle tap and it rolled in a wobbly way, stopping well short of the edge. I picked it up and returned it to the original spot.

He sat back in his chair, hands in his lap, not touching the desk at any point, and I copied his posture.

"In your own time," he said softly.

I looked at the ball. I thought of nothing. Then I thought of how it had looked when it rolled, and imagined it rolling in the same way as before, remembered the wobble and the sound it made. Nothing happened.

I sighed. "This is silly."

"How did you make the statue fall? Can you think about the ball in the same way?"

I shut my eyes, imagining myself back inside Aphrodite, remembering how it had been . . . I opened my eyes again.

"Mr Chase was there, after me, as though in a game of hide-and-seek, but deadly serious. If he caught me . . . if I couldn't keep away from him . . . I *had* to do something, and pushing the statue over seemed the best thing. I didn't even push it myself, but made *him* do it. All in deadly earnest. This is too different."

"You're saying that it only works when you're frightened?"

"Don't you dare!" I spoke sharply, moving back in my chair.

"Miss Lane." His look of wide-eyed, wounded innocence was overdone, but I apologised all the same for my expression of distrust.

He shrugged, then admitted that it had crossed his mind to give me a scare, but "I could not think of any way in which pushing a ball across this desk would ease your anxiety, or free you from any imaginable danger. Although, if I could irritate you enough to make you hurl it at my head —"

"If I was that annoyed I'd pick it up and throw it," I retorted.

"Yes, that did occur to me. Go on, you're not concentrating."

I stared at the ball again, as if I might push it through the strength of my eye beams — as the poets would have it — but nothing happened. I stopped before I induced a headache. It was easier with my eyes shut to imagine I could make the ball move — prodding it with an imaginary finger, or thinking about jogging the desk with my feet, the way some mediums rocked and lifted tables.

I opened my eyes. The ball was still in the same place. I looked at my friend who gazed back expectantly. "How long?" I asked.

"It's only been three minutes."

The thought of doubling or tripling the time made me weary. "Nothing will happen in ten minutes, or two hundred," I said. "Not even if it would save my life." All of a sudden I was certain of it. "It wasn't *my* mental force that toppled the statue — it was *his*. I told you, I deflected *his* force — that's all."

"That's *all*?" he smiled, gently mocking. "I call that quite a lot — and it was enough."

"Enough," I agreed, and stood up. "Well, I am glad I was able to do it, whatever it was I did when the need was there. But it has been a long day."

He quickly rose to his feet. "You're right. We'll try this another time, when you're well rested."

I waited as he made sure the fire was safely banked, and then together we turned towards the door.

At that moment, I heard a familiar sound. Looking at the desk, I saw the ball was rolling. It moved slowly at first, then with gathering speed until it reached the edge of the desk and dropped, landing softly on the thick Turkish carpet.

We looked at each other, startled. I began to laugh.

CHAPTER
THIRTY-TWO

Another Problem

I was still smiling as I stepped into the hall ahead of Mr Jesperson and began to mount the stairs, when a sudden sharp volley of knocks sounded on the front door.

I stopped, fingers gripping the banister, and turned back. My eyes met those of Mr Jesperson and I saw he had no more idea than I did as to who might be calling at such a late hour.

Perhaps it was the police, I thought, with yet more questions? Although, with Mr Chase safely in their custody, surely they might wait until morning?

I waited, curious, and watched as my partner went to unlock the door.

As soon as the door was open a man stumbled in, almost throwing himself into the hall without waiting to be invited. In those first seconds I saw a stranger: a youngish man, perhaps in his late twenties, with brown hair and a neatly-trimmed beard, well-dressed in top hat and evening clothes beneath his black overcoat. The most striking thing about him was his expression of absolute terror. Just to witness it made my skin prickle with apprehension. Beads of sweat stood out on his face, even on this cold night, and his eyes were wide and the pupils so greatly dilated that they appeared almost entirely black.

"I say," said Mr Jesperson assertively, quickly moving to stand between the intruder and the stairs where I stood. "May I help you, sir?"

"Help me," the man repeated, turning his frightened gaze on Mr Jesperson. His teeth were chattering so hard that he could scarcely spit out the words. "Please . . . Or I am dead!"

"Whom do you fear?"

But the man, now panting heavily, scarcely seemed to hear the question. He turned his head quickly from side to side in an agitated search. "Is it safe? Can you help? Will I be safe here?"

"Of course. You are safe now." Mr Jesperson put a steadying hand on the man's arm. "Let us help you. Tell me, who is after you? What do you fear?"

"Witchcraft!" As he spoke, his head jerked up and he noticed me, standing slightly above him, looking down. The sight of me made him more anxious. He raised his hands, one seeming to ward me off, the other pointing accusingly. "She is a witch!"

"No, no, that is Miss Lane — my partner. You need have no fear of her. Come, let us sit down — perhaps you'd like a glass of brandy? And you can tell us how we may help."

"Witch!" he repeated, still staring at me, ignoring, or perhaps simply not hearing what Mr Jesperson had said. Locked in his own fearful imaginings, he was unaware of anything else. "I am cursed . . . it's too late . . . no one can help me now . . . too late . . ."

His eyes rolled, his knees buckled, and before my friend could manage to catch him, our mysterious visitor had collapsed to the floor, eyes wide and unseeing, his body unnaturally still.

A line from Shakespeare's Scottish play ran through my head: "Macbeth hath murdered sleep." It required no special gift of clairvoyance to recognise that we were unlikely to get any sleep that night. Not with a new mystery to solve.

Other titles published by Ulverscroft:

A MEDITATION ON MURDER

Robert Thorogood

Aslan Kennedy has an idyllic life as leader of a spiritual retreat for wealthy holidaymakers on the Caribbean island of Saint-Marie. Until he's murdered, that is. The case seems open and shut: when Aslan was killed, he was inside a locked room with only five other people, one of whom has already confessed to the crime. Detective Inspector Richard Poole is fed up with talking to witnesses who'd rather discuss his "aura" than their whereabouts at the time of the murder. But he also knows that the facts of the case don't quite stack up. He's convinced that the person who's just confessed is the one person who couldn't have done it. Determined to track down the real killer, DI Poole is soon on the trail, and no stone will be left unturned.

BLOTTO, TWINKS AND THE STARS OF THE SILVER SCREEN

Simon Brett

The Dowager Duchess of Tawcester knows America is full of wealthy young men, all of whom will fall in love with her daughter, the supremely gifted Twinks — and marriage to a Texan millionaire would solve the Tawcester financial problems once and for all. So, along with trusty chauffeur Corky Froggett, the intrepid Twinks accompanies her brother Blotto on his Californian cricket tour. On arrival in Hollywood, they are invited to a glitzy party where they are introduced to a firmament of Hollywood stars, directors and gossip columnists; but the mood of the party suddenly curdles with the breaking news that beautiful starlet Mimsy La Pim — the (former) love of Blotto's life — has been kidnapped. And Blotto is determined to make it his personal mission to rescue her . . .